TURN FOUR

Also by Tom Morrisey

Yucatan Deep

TURN FOUR

A Novel of the Superspeedways

TOM MORRISEY

ZONDERVAN™

GRAND RAPIDS, MICHIGAN 49530 USA

ZONDERVAN™

Turn Four

Requests for information should be addressed to:

Zondervan, *Grand Rapids, Michigan 49530*

Library of Congress Cataloging-in-Publication Data

Morrisy, Tom, 1952–
Turn four : a novel of the superspeedways / Tom Morrisey.
p. cm.
ISBN 0-310-23969-9
1. Racetracks (Automobile racing)—Fiction. 2. Automobile racing drivers—Fiction. 3. Automobile racing—Fiction. I. Title.
PS3613.O776 T87 2003
813'.54—dc22

2003023255

All Scripture quotations, unless otherwise indicated, are taken from the King James Version.

Interior design by Michelle Espinoza

Printed in the United States of America

04 05 06 07 08 09 10 /❖ DC/ 10 9 8 7 6 5 4 3 2 1

For Adam Petty

TURN FOUR

Wherefore seeing we also are
compassed about with
so great a cloud of witnesses,
. . . let us run with patience
the race that is set before us.
—Hebrews 12:1, KJV

PROLOGUE

Ross County, Ohio—Spring,
Twenty Years Ago

The farm was old, but the late afternoon sun was kind to it, painting the barn a deeper, richer red, and etching relief into the scalloped eaves of the porch-surrounded, two-story white house. The door of a metal toolshed stood open, affording a shadowed glimpse of a ten-year-old John Deere tractor, green and yellow and idle, and the worn gravel turnout beside it held a red Ford pickup, its fenders powdered lightly with the dust of country roads.

On soft hills above the farmyard, a broad swath of black oaks and hickory stood dressed in the emerald of newly opened leaves. The bottomland below was brown with the loam of freshly planted soil, all except for a single broad field of winter wheat, already dense and tan in the low, slanting light.

The section between was pasture, but a pasture in name only, the horses and cattle all sent off to auction in an earlier generation's recession. Yet the coarse grass and thistle had been bushwhacked back to ankle height and then rolled to a semblance of flatness.

On the two acres nearest the house, a narrow dirt track had been scribed like an elongated "O" in the turf, its corners scrubbed broad and fringed by rain-silvered hay bales, the straightaways narrow as an old country lane. And on it was the only thing moving in this landscape: a black and yellow go-kart raising dust clouds in the low, gold sun, the padded roll cage enclosing a driver who appeared to be mostly helmet.

Beside the track stood a man in a faded brown Carhartt chore jacket, scuffed Redwing boots, and jeans. He was in his late thirties, his moustache and hair halfway along their journey from jet-black to gunmetal gray. He took his feed cap off to drag his sleeve against his brow, and the whiteness of his unsunned forehead was startling. The man replaced the cap and scrutinized the nickel-plated stopwatch in his hand, his eyes pale blue behind steel-framed glasses. Pinching a half-burned Marlboro in his lips, the smoke of it making him squint, he clicked the watch hands dead.

He looked up, held out a thumb.

The engine note dropped as the kart scrubbed off speed. It stopped at the man's feet, the race-cammed engine popping erratically at idle.

Bubble goggles came off and a nine-year-old grin beamed skyward.

"How'd I do?" the boy asked.

"You did good," the man told him, not wanting to say the time. "Real good. But remember, there's gonna be lots of other karts up there at the fairgrounds. You keep goin' wide like that, you're gonna be hittin' guys, and it won't go fast no more if it's bent. You know?"

The boy nodded soberly.

"So what you want to do now," the man continued, "is drive skinny. Like you're threadin' it right through the eye of a needle. Go just as fast, but brake a little deeper in the turns, and bring it down toward the corner, like I showed you. It'll still want to slide up, but don't you push it up. Okay?"

The red helmet nodded again. Small hands in deerskin chore gloves pulled the goggles back into place. Engine whining, the kart shot back onto the track, dust curling up in brown wisps behind it.

The man let the boy run two laps and then timed the third. Another quarter of a second down, and the boy wasn't driving wildly now. He traced the same line each time, as if the go-kart were riding on rails.

The man waved him in again and the boy, hot now, pulled off the helmet, exposing an unruly shock of sandy gold hair.

"Good job," the man told him. "You found the groove. It won't be the same all the way through the race—it'll move. But if you listen to the kart, feel it, it'll tell you where to go. Okay, let's—"

The distant clanging of a bell interrupted him.

"Nate! Chance!" A woman's voice came drifting up from the shadows of the porch. "It's time!"

"Time to eat and get ready for church, Chance." The man tucked the watch into his shirt pocket. "Better put the kart up."

"Aw, Dad." The boy scowled. "Do we have to? We already went to church once this morning."

"And the doors'll be open again tonight," his father told him. "It's Sunday. God's day. So you tell me. What's more important? Racing or God?"

The boy tightened his lips, thinking.

Thinking.

"God," he finally said.

"There you go." His father nodded. One nod. "Let's get cleaned up."

"One more lap?"

"Okay." His dad smiled. "One more. Then we gotta go."

Nodding, the boy tightened his seat harness. He bowed his head, lifting the well-scuffed helmet.

TURN ONE

CHAPTER 1

Michigan International Speedway—Brooklyn, Michigan
June, One Year Ago

Chance Reynolds tugged the racing harness tight, dipping his shoulders left, then right, pressing himself more deeply into the seat until no further movement was possible. He ducked his head forward to clear the roll cage and pulled the full-faced helmet on.

The helmet smelled new, which it was; his sponsorship agreement with the maker called for a fresh one, custom-fitted and finished in his team's colors, every race.

Four hundred miles from now, that helmet would stink of sweat, spit, burned oil, and greasy rubber—the grim, primal smell of the work he did. But he liked the feel of it now, the tricot lining clean and smooth against his face.

It would warm up soon enough because the helmet was padded with better than an inch of high-density foam. But right now it was comfortable, cool against his head. Chance set his driving gloves on top of the dash, routed the flexible tube from a sports bottle up and over the polymer chin of the helmet, and took a sip of Gatorade.

A roar swept the air over the Michigan infield; 200,000 spectators leaped to their feet in a single, spontaneous cheer. Chance peered up through the open window just in time to see a diamond formation of F-16s streaking overhead, hurtling south over the infield on afterburners, the leader peeling off and bolting straight up into the clear blue, late-spring sky.

The jet shrank to a pinpoint, nearly imperceptible even to Chance, with his exceptional racecar driver's vision. He followed it as far as his helmet would allow.

A photographer aimed a long lens at the open window, and Chance smiled as the strobe flashed, knowing that his eyes would convey the warmth even though the helmet covered his mouth. Then the photographer turned away, and a familiar face moved into view.

Andy Hofert, crew chief for Robert Vintner Racing, leaned in through the window, smelling of mint toothpaste and Aqua Velva, not a hair out of place under his headset. His E-World Broadband team uniform, like Chance's, red, white, blue, and spotless. Pressed and dressed; that was Andy at the beginning of a race. But by lap 200, he'd be ready for someone to turn a hose on him.

"How you doin', Hoss?" Chance asked as Andy double-checked the closures—helmet and harness both—plugged in the leads to both radios, and put the steering wheel in place on its hub, pulling the release out twice to make certain it was locked on and that the safety cable was out of the way. He snapped the lanyards to the head restraint onto Chance's helmet, and secured the radio wires to the chin bar with a little piece of duct tape so they wouldn't pull loose during the race.

"I'm doin' good, Boomer."

For what seemed like the thousandth time, Chance wondered why it was that everybody on a race team had a nickname. He'd always assumed that it was some county fairgrounds thing until he got to Cup and discovered that nobody there got called by the right name either—at least, not in the garage area. Even the owners and drivers, many of them millionaires several times over, got referred to as "The Captain," or "Smoke," or "Happy." There was one driver who was just called "Herman," but his real name was Kenny.

Go figure.

"Radio check," Andy said. This time, his voice came not through the muffling foam of the helmet, but through Chance's custom-molded earpieces, a slight burst of static sounding as the microphone cut out.

"Ten by ten," Chance said.

"Gotcha, guys," came the call from his spotter, high atop the center grandstand.

"Got you, Pooch," Chance replied.

"You need anything?" Andy accepted the squeeze bottle and handed Chance his gloves.

"Thanks, Hoss. No. I'm good to go."

Chance made every effort to sound casual, and he did this for Andy's sake every bit as much as he did it for his own. Medical studies showed that a crew chief's pulse rate just before the start of a race was actually about 20 percent higher than the typical driver's. You had to respect that; it wouldn't do to have a thirty-two-year-old guy dropping over on pit road from a heart attack just before the start of a race.

"Only seventy-two points out," Andy said.

"Just for now. We'll close that up today."

"There you go."

There were volumes of implications in that brief exchange. Chance was in second place in the Nextel Cup championship points race. And for the first time this season, the margin between Chance and first place had shrunk to double digits.

Chance looked up, through the windshield.

"Give us a second, will you, Hoss? Brett's coming."

Brett Winslow, chief Nextel Cup chaplain with Speedway Christian Ministries, straightened up from the window of the car ahead and came walking back, shaking hands as he moved. In his sunglasses, red SCM polo shirt, khaki slacks, and Topsiders, dark brown hair ruffled by a light breeze out of Turn Four, Brett looked more like a golf pro than the ordained doctor of theology that he was. He got to Chance's Taurus, smiled, and leaned in over the broad blue sill-plate.

"Chance, can I have a word of prayer with you?"

"Absolutely, Preacher."

The two men closed their eyes as Brett spoke.

"Oh, gracious heavenly Father, we ask that you guard your child, Chance, as he does his job here today. We ask you to calm and comfort Cindy with the knowledge that Chance is under your constant care, and we beg a heavenly hedge of protection around this racecar and every car on the track here today, on the drivers, the crews, the officials, and the fans. Please allow the work done today to be excellent and worthy, and we ask that the outcome glorify your name. And all this we ask in the name of your precious Son, Jesus Christ."

"Amen," they said together.

"What'd Cindy give you?" Brett asked.

"Psalm 37, verses five and six," Chance read from the handwritten label stuck above his oil pressure gauge.

Brett nodded. "'Commit your way to the LORD; trust in him and he will do this: He will make your righteousness shine like the dawn, the justice of your cause like the noonday sun.' She does know how to pick 'em, doesn't she?"

"That she does."

"She's a good lady."

"That she is." Even the thick foam of the helmet could not muffle the fondness in Chance's voice as he spoke of his wife.

"Race safe, Chance," Brett said. The SCM chaplain never said anything that showed favoritism, and he never wished an individual driver luck. He couldn't. Of the forty-three drivers on the starting grid, more than half had attended Brett's chapel service, held in the tech-inspection garage just after the race-day drivers' meeting. So he never played favorites. Safety and strength of character: that was what he asked for them all, instead.

The two men shook hands and Chance pulled on his driving gloves as Brett walked on to the next car in line.

That done, a rare thirty seconds of inactivity passed. Then somebody—at this race it was the chairman of the race sponsor, a national chain of outdoors shops—called, "Gentlemen, start your engines" over the public-address system. While Chance couldn't hear this, Andy did, saying, "Engine start" over the radio as Nextel Cup officials up and down pit road mixmastered their fingers in the air. Chance reached for the long switch on the left side of his instrument panel, flipped it up, and lifted the spring-loaded toggle next to it.

The big Ford V-8 engine—larger by two cylinders and 650 horsepower than anything in the Tauruses at the local dealership—shook itself to life with a bone-numbing roar. Two crewmen bent to the rear bumper, unhooking the hose-like umbilical that had been feeding warm oil through the crankcase.

Andy lifted his thumb, and the nearest Cup official did the same, telling those who needed to know that the engine had fired. Then the crew chief was back at the window to "button up" the racecar—securing the window net that would keep Chance's head and arms inside the car in the event of a rollover.

Chance saw Andy straining, and helped him from the inside, lifting until he felt the releases click at the net's upper edge. Like most crew chiefs, Andy labored under the illusion that a window net was more aerodynamic if it was tighter than the proverbial banjo string. Two more strips of duct tape—the most indispensable material in racing—were wrapped around the releases to keep them from popping. Then there was the familiar double-thump as Andy patted the roof of the car, and Chance was alone, the racecar trembling around him.

A human tide receded back to the pits, the race crews, photographers, and well-wishers leaving the tarmac. In the pit boxes, crew members were exchanging high fives, getting pumped for the work to come. All that remained on the pit road itself were the racecars, the officials, and a single television camera crew that had obviously signed a mountain of liability releases for the privilege of serving as a human traffic island.

On a signal from the chief steward, a camera car and pace car rolled slowly out into Turn One, followed by the entire field of forty-three NASCAR Nextel Cup racecars, their brilliantly painted hoods, decks, and fenders tattooed with sponsors' decals.

Chance breathed a little easier as he let the clutch pedal out. The clutch on a racecar is a relatively delicate thing, deceptively easy to break in the simple act of going from sitting still to moving. Without so much as touching the clutch pedal a second time, Chance upshifted to second, trying to keep the water temperature down until he could get air running through the partially taped-off grille.

The first lap was driven purely for the function of forming the field, running in third gear at low RPMs so the one or two teams that hadn't started on the first try could catch up. Then came the parade lap, driving in close formation as the corner workers, mostly emergency crews now that lights had replaced the secondary flagmen, came out for the traditional salute. This one was run at precisely 55 miles per hour, the pit road speed at this track, and Chance pressed his radio button and called out, "Second gear, twenty-nine hundred"—letting his spotter know the tach reading since his car, like every racecar in the field, was not equipped with a speedometer.

The second time they came up on pit road, the camera car and the second pace car, leading the rear half of the field, pulled off, and everyone went to third gear. The fire crews went back behind their barricades, and the field was back to business.

Chance had qualified seventh: inside of the fourth row. It was a good, but not outstanding, place in which to start a race, not high enough to get a prime pit box, but close enough to the front to see when the pace car pulled off, which was good just in case the radio broke and nobody told you when to begin racing.

Chance sawed the wheel back and forth, weaving tightly, heating up the tires to build grip. They passed the start-finish line and the pace car doused its strobe lights and picked up speed, fourth gear finally and accelerating steadily. The weaving stopped, and Chance experienced, as he always did at this point, something that the sports psychologists called "perceptual narrowing." The crowd in the stands, the hundreds of flag-festooned RVs in the infield, the television boom cameras mounted on dollies along the infield fence, the blimp and helicopters orbiting overhead, the rainbow of crew uniforms along pit road, and the JumboTron TV monitors facing the grandstands . . . all of these faded to a muted and unimportant haze as Chance concentrated on feeling what his car had to say. The tach needle crept higher as he accelerated steadily into the turn, the pace car bringing the field up to speed.

Back straight, and the car was starting to feel like a racecar now, which is to say that it rode like a cross between a speedboat and a Magic Fingers motel bed. The broad asphalt track, seamlessly smooth from the fans' perspective, had dips and rises that were more than perceptible at speed. And the harshly stiff racecar suspension transmitted every bump, seam, joint, and ripple up into Chance's thinly padded aluminum driver's seat, bolted directly to the Taurus's flat steel floor. The big steering wheel thrummed in time with the race-cammed engine, buzzing his hands and forearms.

As they entered the third turn, Chance could see the compact outline of the pace car dropping down to the inside, ready to head for the pits if NASCAR's chief steward said the field was in shape. Chance pulled closer to the car ahead of him, tucking into its slipstream. The noise level dropped dramatically, and the nose of the Taurus quieted down as the air smoothed out around it. A glance at the long, panoramic rearview mirror showed that the rest of the field had also tightened up in anticipation of the start.

He cleared Turn Three. The lead car dropped off the track.

"Pace car's pitting." Pooch's voice crackled in Chance's earpieces.

"Get ready . . . green flag," Pooch said rapidly, as if saying it faster would somehow make the radio work more quickly. "Green! Green! Green! Green! Green!"

Even before the first syllable was out, Chance had his right foot all the way to the floor.

Like a huge cat uncoiling in one great, powerful leap, the forty-three-car field sprang out of Turn Four, accelerating down for the straight, V-8

May you find the reading of this book a real enjoyment and blessing.

Daniel Webster said, "If religious books are not widely circulated, I do not know what is going to become of us as a nation."

The Circuit Rider is the name I use as I fulfill the commitment to bring inspirational products to the general market place. I am grateful to the many store managers who make space available for these products. You may wish to thank them also.

Please contact me, or someone in the store office, if you want to acquire a specific title; several copies of a title; study group materials; or a book table for an event.

The Circuit Rider
16102 Hand Road
Huntertown, IN 46748
260-637-5447
plcn@wmconnect.com

engines roaring wide open now, rapidly gaining momentum. The pack streaked under the starter's box, where the governor of the state—honorary starter for the event—danced the green flag up and down. Chance kept closing until he was riding just inches behind the Chevrolet Monte Carlo in front of him, the "Dupont Automotive Finishes" script under its rear spoiler moving up and down and side to side in his windshield, like a rail commuter's view of the next car. They entered the first turn and the centrifugal force pressed him heavily against the right side of the seat, like being dropped into a gargantuan carnival ride.

The wall was a blur off to his right, and the engine noise had risen to a high, raw rumble, loud even through the helmet and the earplugs. The Taurus was shuddering, twitching from side to side as if shaken by a giant hand. Chance corrected with the wheel constantly, holding his line as the turbulence fought back. In his mind, it was as if the minute hand had just clicked twelve on a time clock.

It was time to go to work.

Racing was the only job Chance Reynolds had ever known. He had never flipped a burger at the local McDonald's, never had a paper route, never cut any lawn except his family's own, back home on the farm in Chillicothe.

Still, the racing had started out being something Chance did just for fun—flinging go-karts around county fairground tracks on Saturday afternoons back in Ohio, or charging around a hay-baled course up and down the town square during the annual Harvest Days celebration. He was a farmer's kid, and he raced other farmers' kids in competitions that were outwardly social, but inwardly as hard fought as if money had been riding on the outcome. And for Chance, that had eventually turned out to be true.

Nate Reynolds hadn't possessed half the resources that some of the other kids' dads had at their disposal. He'd built Chance's kart engines up himself rather than ordering them from the race shop over in Columbus, and he tried to keep Chance competing at dirt tracks as much as possible. Tires run on dirt could be stretched through a month of race weekends, while asphalt attacked tires like sandpaper, and concrete ovals could wear them out in a single heat.

For a couple of seasons, the family had actually hauled a carnival popcorn machine along in the trailer, and Chance and his mom had taken turns selling popcorn between races, bringing in enough money to help keep him on the track.

But even though Chance's equipment and financing had been a step or two below that of his competition, his competitive edge and driving skills had eventually placed him in a league of his own. If the engine kept running and the tires stayed up, Chance won, pure and simple. He rarely made mistakes and showed an uncanny ability to capitalize on it every time his opponents made one. While most kids his age fought constantly for the lead, every lap, all through the race, Chance had learned to lag back in fifth or sixth place, let the leaders use up their karts, and then move steadily up and make the winning pass somewhere in the last three laps—showing a level of maturity that was rarely seen, even among the adults in that caliber of racing.

He'd graduated from go-karts into midgets and had stayed there only half a season before turning his first lap in a sprint car.

Chance had been thirteen the summer he'd begun to race sprints professionally. That made him nearly four years junior to his youngest competition, and as much as five decades younger than some of the series regulars. Not every track had let him drive at that age; a lot of his racing had taken place in Indiana, where the liability climate and the insurance industry looked more favorably upon racecar drivers young enough to play Little League.

Sprints had been a very serious step up for the budding driver. Chance's go-kart engine, nominally rated at five horsepower—about the same as the average lawn mower—had been tuned, tweaked, and massaged by Nate Reynolds until it had produced more than six times that amount. And his first midget racer had generated 215 horsepower, more powerful than the family's station wagon. But the sprint car's race-tuned engine had produced almost 700 horsepower—nearly three times as potent as the big, brawny pickup that his father used to haul the race trailer.

And all of this horsepower had been put in the hands of a kid—a kid who would have to wait thirty-six months until the state of Ohio would deem him mature enough to drive the family car on a country road.

One lap into the race, and Chance had already picked up a place, although that had been more of a gift than a prize. The pole-sitter, the rookie member of a heavily funded two-car Dodge team, had so zealously guarded his inside racing line that he had actually gotten too low in Turn Two. This allowed the outside pole-sitter, a fourteen-season veteran, to switch to the high line, brake late, and go barreling around for the land despite the fact that the high groove had been washed away by the previous night's rain. It had been an awesome display of horsepower and driving skills, feasible only on first-lap-fresh tires. But when the next car back tried to perform the same feat, his setup wouldn't allow it, and so this unfortunate soul got slowed by the wall of air before him, and the entire front end of the pack—eleven cars in all—had freight-trained right on past.

Chance powered on down the front straight with the rest of the pack. He'd noticed something: the Chevy ahead of him was not following the same line around the racetrack as Chance and the other four lead cars. Instead, he tended to drift nearly—but not quite—a full car width higher on the track, powering back down to the inside lane as he exited Turn Four. When they'd gotten back onto the front stretch, a gap of more than twenty yards had opened between the Chevy and the four cars ahead.

Chance had seen the same condition so many times that he didn't even have to think about it. The car ahead of him was loose—its rear wheels dancing to the outside in the turns. So the only way the Chevy's driver could come square out of a turn was to let the car drift up out of the groove. That used up more racing surface. And that slowed him down.

Chance knew how to take advantage of a competitor's loose car. Braking later in the first turn, he let himself drift up to within a few inches of the Chevy's rear bumper and stayed low, with just the left front fender of the Taurus hanging out in the wind. This deflected the air running over the Chevy's spoiler, stealing the downforce.

The red racecar skated abruptly to the right.

Keeping his foot down, Chance shot past him on the inside and took fourth.

"Outside." Pooch's voice was crystal clear this time on the radio. "Outside. Stay low. . . . Clear. You the man. Good pass."

Chance went hot into the third turn, using up his tires a little, wearing a millimeter off his brake pads, but closing on the three-car lead group. He tucked in on the Turn Four exit and felt it: the calmer air of the draft, that invisible, suction-like tube being punched through the air by the cars ahead of him.

"One-ninety-eight to go," Pooch advised him. "Doin' great. Might want ta' just turn laps for now. We can race 'em later."

"How's she feel, Boom?" Andy asked him.

"Good going into One, neutral in the middle, just a little loose coming out of Two," Chance replied, keying his microphone button as he set up for the turn at the end of the straight. "Not much at all, though. And we're neutral all the way through Three and Four. Temperature's perfect—don't touch the tape."

"That looseness in Two—track bar?"

"I don't think so." Chance grunted at the G-forces as he swept through both turns, his arms growing heavy, making him cling to the wheel with both hands. He keyed the mike again as he powered back onto the straight. "Let's wait and see. Might just be fuel load."

"Outside," Pooch interrupted from the spotter's perch.

Chance glanced to his right and saw the nose of the Cheerios Dodge draw even with his window and then fall back as they entered the third turn.

"Clear," Pooch told him. "He's fadin'."

"Tires are right on," Chance said, quickly cueing his radio. "Car's perfect, Hoss. Let's not touch it."

"You got 'er," the crew chief replied. "Cindy wants to know if you can see her waving."

Chance allowed himself the briefest possible glance at the pits as he swept down the front stretch. He got a fleeting image of blonde hair and an upraised right hand from the timing-and-scoring seat next to the crew chief's, high atop the team's big red-white-and-blue toolbox.

"Tell her that I see her and I like the new nail color."

"You just drive the racecar, Romeo. You just drive the car."

CHAPTER 2

"Cindy? Cindy!"

The tap on her ankle finally got the attention of Cindy Reynolds. Sitting high atop the pit cart—the $100,000 toolbox that every team brought to every race—it was easy to block out one's surroundings and focus on the race. Pulling off her radio headset, she saw who'd tapped her, and smiled to hide her sigh.

Looking up from the narrow lane between the pit wall and the pit cart was Vivian Frankel—"Perky" to the regulars on the crew.

How Vivian had gotten her nickname was no mystery. Petite and bubbly, she walked with such a bounce in her step that her bobbed red hair seemed to have a life of its own. Once, after Chance's jet had been delayed by thunderstorms on a flight into Sonoma, Cindy had called Vivian's hotel room at three in the morning to let the team's public affairs liaison know that Cindy and Chance would have to scrub an early-morning talk-radio appearance. And even then Vivian had sounded upbeat and sweet. It was positively spooky.

"It's time?" Cindy asked, knowing the answer.

Vivian nodded.

Sighing openly this time, Cindy tapped Andy Hofert on the arm and pointed at Vivian. Andy nodded, accepted Cindy's clipboard, and then held his headset more closely to his ears, listening to his spotter as Cindy climbed down from the cart.

Away from the track, Andy, who had been born and raised in the South, would have shot to his feet the moment Cindy got to hers. And he normally would not so much as entertain the thought of allowing a lady, particularly a married lady, to navigate unassisted down the steep six-rung ladder.

But this was different. The race had started, the green flag was out, the pits were hot, and Andy would not have risen to his feet or glanced up from his notes had the queen of England strolled into his pit.

The entire field was roaring down the front straight when Cindy got to the ground, the sound of forty-three unmuffled exhausts so thunderous that she could actually feel it in her chest and shoulders. So Cindy left her radio headphones on as she followed Vivian down the crowded walkway behind the pits. Showing the red-vested security person their passes, the two women walked through into the garage area, where the tarmac was nearly deserted. The sound level dropped dramatically as soon as they left pit road. Cindy slipped the headset down, pulled her ash-blonde hair out from under it, and let the head set around the collar of her bright blue Robert Vintner Racing polo shirt. Turning a knob on the radio at her belt, she squelched the chatter coming from the headset.

"I hate to pull you out of the pits like this," Vivian said. She didn't sound as if she hated it. "But we put this poor lady off twice already, once yesterday after Happy Hour, and once this morning after the drivers' meeting."

"No need to apologize," Cindy told her. "I'm tracking fuel, so they won't really need me until after Chance pits. And I should have told you that we were going to that kids' hospital in Ann Arbor yesterday."

She didn't add that scheduling an interview after the drivers' meeting had been Vivian's error because that's when Brett Winslow held SCM's regular weekly chapel service. Chance and Cindy never missed the service; it was the only church they had available to them on weekends.

Vivian should have known this. Scheduling something on top of chapel was a mistake. But, having made it, Vivian wouldn't make the same mistake again, and Cindy understood this. To bring it up again risked friction, and in the small, close-knit family of a race team, friction was something you avoided like the plague.

"Who's this lady with again?" Cindy asked instead.

"*Vista* magazine," Vivian said, checking her clipboard. "It's the Sunday supplement for Squire-Watkins Newspapers, a chain of dailies around the Midwest."

"Not a regular then, huh?"

"No. I think she said yesterday that this was her first NASCAR race."

They turned the corner at the big Nextel Cup trailer, and Cindy could see the reporter standing under the big porch-like lift at the back of the number 53 team trailer. A middle-aged woman, slightly paunchy, she had close-cropped, graying hair and one of those long white reporter's notebooks in her hand.

Not for the first time, Cindy wondered why it was that so many journalists dressed as if they were about to embark on safari. This one was decked out in green cargo pants, work boots, and—over an MIS T-shirt—one of those tan mesh vests with pockets everywhere. Pinned to the bottom of her vest was a clear plastic credentials holder the size of a junk-mail envelope.

"Cindy," Vivian said as soon as they got within hand-shaking distance of the woman, "this is . . ."

The reporter's name was drowned out by a tremendous roar from the stands.

A lead change, Cindy decided—it was the noise of an excited crowd, not the long, sinking "Ooohhhh" that accompanied a wreck.

"I'm happy to meet you," Cindy told the reporter, shaking the woman's hand and smiling warmly. She glanced at the roof of the transporter. "Would you like to go up top so we can watch the race while we talk?"

The three women climbed an angled, railed ladder to the top of the big transporter semi-trailer, where an aluminum observation deck afforded a panoramic view of the racetrack. Simple seats were built into the corners of the railing, but Cindy didn't invite the reporter to take one; she knew that interviews tended to go faster when done standing.

The reporter wasn't looking for a seat. She was turning a slow circle, taking it all in. To the west, north, and south were the grandstands, a mountainous, rainbow-hued wall of waving, roaring humanity. To the east, in the infield, thousands of sunburned race fans were standing on their own observation decks atop flag- and banner-festooned motorhomes, many of which were actually home-converted school buses. Several of the infield fans recognized Cindy, even from a hundred yards away, and they waved and whooped in greeting. Settling a pair of Oakleys onto her face, Cindy waved back, triggering a fresh chorus of whoops and whistles. The forty-three cars roaring down the backstretch at more than 200 miles an hour seemed almost an afterthought.

The journalist blinked behind her tinted bifocals, apparently remembering what she was there for. Blushing, she took a ballpoint out of one of her several pockets and touched the pen to the top of her notebook.

"I must say, Mrs. Reynolds," she began, "you're even prettier in person than you are on those iced tea commercials."

"I doubt that." Cindy laughed. "It took three people to get me made up and ready for those commercials. And please, it's 'Cindy.'"

"Why, thank you—Cindy." The writer studied her notebook and then looked up. "You met Chance in victory lane, didn't you?"

Cindy smiled. She liked reporters who got to the point.

"Yes and no," Cindy said. "I worked for Pennzoil, the sprint series' sponsor, and one of my jobs was to stand there in a Pennzoil jumpsuit and hold the big check during the victory lane ceremonies. But Chance and I actually first met during a sponsor's breakfast at DuQuion, in southern Illinois. Still, it was only after I'd appeared with him after he won a feature at Eldora . . . that's in Ohio, Rossburg, Ohio . . . that he mustered up the courage to ask me out."

"And you accepted right away?"

"No!" Cindy laughed. "I couldn't! The sponsor wouldn't allow me to date drivers in their series. And I don't think I would have, anyhow. Chance was nineteen years old the season that he won the USAC championship, but I just assumed he was older, and I was eighteen—fresh out of high school. But I liked him enough to give him my phone number, back home in Pratts Fork, and later that fall, when he moved up to ARCA—"

"Arka?"

"Automobile Racing Club of America—their ReMax Series," Vivian explained to the writer. "It's sort of the farm league for national-level stock car racing."

"Anyhow, Chance called my folks' house and asked my father for permission to see me."

"He asked permission?"

"Sure," Cindy nodded, smiling. "We may both be Buckeyes, but we're southern Buckeyes—from the Ohio River Valley—and things tend to follow certain proprieties down there, you know? So Daddy talked with him and found out that he was really not all that much older than me, and from a good family, and that he was a believer—"

"A believer?"

"A Christian." Cindy did the explaining this time. "Neither Chance's family nor mine believed in dating for dating's sake. We both thought that when a guy asks a girl out, it should be so the two can evaluate what they have in common, and whether they would make good marriage partners for one another. In fact, I'd only gone out with two boys before Chance, and Chance had never been out with a girl before me . . ."

"Never? Not even for homecoming or a prom?"

"He hadn't had the time." Cindy shrugged. "All through high school, to hear Chance tell it, when he wasn't actually on a racetrack, he was home with his head stuck in a carburetor, getting his car ready for the next race. That and keeping up his studies. So it wasn't until he got really successful that he and his daddy could afford to hire a crew to work back at their garage. I don't know, I've always thought that Jesus has somebody all picked out for every believer from the time they are born. I was just fortunate that mine found me right away."

The reporter blinked rapidly behind her tinted bifocals as she composed her next question. "Any children?"

"Not yet," Cindy said, adding with a twinkle, "but it's not for lack of trying! I'm sure God will bless us in his time."

"And you live in North Carolina now?"

"On a private lake about a half hour out of Charlotte," Cindy said, deliberately not naming the lake. "Lots of the drivers live near Charlotte. In fact several live on the same lake as us. Robert Vintner Racing put Chance under contract about a month before we got married, and even though he spent three years doing the A-B-Cs—"

"The A-B-Cs?"

"ARCA, Busch Series, Cup," Vivian explained. "It's become the accepted way to bring a promising young driver into Nextel Cup, particularly one who came up in open-wheel racing, like Chance. The stock cars are similar in all three series, so you move up from one to the other, and the last year, before coming to Nextel Cup full time, you drive three or four Cup races to get accustomed to the change."

"And Vivian tells me that you fly to a different racetrack just about every weekend." The reporter tapped her notebook. "Isn't that hectic?"

"I knew what I was getting into," Cindy told her. "Chance and I talked about this—how it would go if he was successful at racing. I knew I was marrying a driver."

"What about if he hadn't been successful?"

"I never really gave that a lot of thought. Not after I'd seen Chance drive and saw how naturally gifted and competitive he was. I just knew this was what he was cut out for. I never even considered the possibility that he might wind up going back into farming or something like that."

"But isn't this a dangerous way to make a living? How do you feel about having a husband who's involved in something so dangerous?"

"I pray for his protection," Cindy told her frankly. "And I also understand that nothing's truly safe. Look at Payne Stewart—the PGA Tour player that was in that terrible airplane wreck. The one where the plane flew all across the country before it ran out of fuel and crashed. I remember watching that on TV and just feeling so sorry for his poor wife. But he was a golfer. How safe should that be? Yet he died during travel that was a routine part of his job."

The reporter nodded.

"So I'd have to say," Cindy continued, "that my answer is this: when you do the math, the probability of getting seriously injured or killed in Nextel Cup actually comes out pretty low, but in the end, probability doesn't really matter. Nationwide, the death rate, as my old pastor used to say, is still the same: one per person. And in light of that, it doesn't matter what you're doing for a living. All that matters is what you've chosen. And in Chance's case, I know he's chosen Jesus. So sure, I worry about him all the time. But I also have great confidence in him."

And then, almost as if it had been timed that way, a cloud of gray tire-smoke erupted from the beginning of the back straight, accompanied by the screech of tortured tires, and a sound like a gunnysack full of quarters being dropped onto a sheet of plate glass.

Cindy gripped the aluminum rail with both hands, dizzied by a cold wave of fear. Without saying a word, she switched on her radio and held one side of the headset to her ear.

She looked up, color beginning to creep back into her ashen face.

"Uhm . . . excuse me," she told the reporter and Vivian. "The yellow's out. I'm sorry . . . I have to get back to the pits."

CHAPTER 3

Chance had been coming out of Turn Two when he saw it: a quick puff of smoke from the right rear tire of the red Monte Carlo leading the race. He blinked, thinking that perhaps he'd mistaken a wisp of steam from the cooling-system overflow, whipped into the slipstream of the racecar.

But no. In seeming slow motion, the red car began to yaw, its nose aimed at the lower edge of the distant Turn Three, its tail seeming to search the upper wall for a clue. Without even thinking about it, Chance switched both hands to the bottom of his steering wheel and held on.

It was the best way to brace for a crash.

The red Chevy had cut down a tire. That had been the smoke. A cut-down tire was survivable on the straights—you'd get more thrills than you ever wanted, but with careful, controlled movements, you could slow the racecar down enough to collect it on a straightaway.

But here? The turns at Michigan were canted up, 18 degrees from the horizontal, but the back straight was almost flat: just enough banking to shed rain. Going from the one to the other was dramatic enough; you went from the additional downforce of the turn—all that centrifugal force squatting the racecar down on its suspension, distorting its tires—to the sudden release of the straightaway, where only aerodynamics and inertia kept the car stuck to the track.

And that was on four fully inflated tires. The Chevy didn't have four. Its right rear wheel was riding on the inner liner now, like switching to a marshmallow for a rear tire. It couldn't keep the car on a straight line.

And it didn't. As Chance watched, the Monte Carlo came unstuck and began to slide sideways, its nose angled down at the infield, smoke boiling from all four tires.

"Inside," Pooch's voice hissed urgently in Chance's ears, and Chance kept his eyes glued to the track ahead. There was a car to his left; ducking that way was out of the question.

The red Chevy seemed to recover for a moment, then it swung the other way around, only this time it didn't stop. It spun all the way around until it was going backwards, its roof flaps popping open from the airflow, killing the lift and keeping the car grounded to the track. The tires were smoking like a house afire now, great billowing clouds of blue-gray smoke erupting from all four corners, and the car disappeared in the middle of it all, gone who-knew-where.

"Spin at Two," Pooch said. "Lost him. Nothin' but smoke."

The last time Chance had seen the car, it had been directly in his path. Keeping his hands low on the wheel, he mashed the gas pedal all the way to the floor and kept it there as he barreled directly into the gray wall of smoke.

It had been Chance's second midget race, a decade and a half earlier, when he'd learned the lesson the hard way. He'd been running on the dirt oval up at Flat Rock, Michigan, a little county "bull pen" north of Toledo. In his second heat of the night, the car directly ahead of him had ridden up too high on the cushion—that curb-like ridge of dirt packed up by the racecars' wheels—jumped it, gone up on two wheels, and come down in a spin. He couldn't have ended up more in Chance's way if he'd planned it.

Panicking, the twelve-year-old Chance had hit the brakes hard and headed for the outside wall . . . and then drilled the spinning car as it jumped high as well. Stunned, rattled like the clapper in a bell despite the five-point harness and the helmet, Chance had then gotten hit two more times in the pile-up that followed. He hadn't been hurt—not even a bruise—but his shiny black racecar, product of a winter's worth of his father's work, had been reduced to a mangled and scarred mess.

Chance remembered the long ride home afterward—an all-night drive down Int. 75 to Chillicothe after they'd pulled his racecar up onto the hauler with a come-along. The midget racer's wheels had been so splayed that they'd had to improvise on the tie-downs.

"So what're you thinking?" Nate Reynolds had asked as they passed Bowling Green State University.

"Oh . . . nothin'," Chance had told him. He'd peered out the window at the darkened university stadium.

"Hmm. I bet it's more than nothin'." Chance's father had paused then, lighting a Marlboro with his beat-up chrome Zippo, the light of the flame creating a reflection of his face on the passenger's side window. "I'll bet you're thinkin' about how you wrecked your racecar, when you mighta won that race, if only you'd pulled the other way. Am I right?"

Chance had nodded.

"Well, wreckin' is part of racin', Chance," his father had told him. "And there's no gettin' round that fact. Sure, you banged up a car tonight . . . worse than you ever have before. But it's not so banged that we can't fix it, just as good as and just as quick as ever. And even if you'd busted it so bad that it couldn't a been fixed, we would have just gone ahead and built another car. Rate you're goin', getting better and winning races, we're gonna want to keep a backup car ready and on the trailer pretty soon, anyhow. You start worryin' about bendin' that racecar, you'll slow down, and slow don't win races. Y' know?"

Chance had nodded, feeling better.

"So the only question is, what did you learn tonight?" Chance's father had glanced sideways at him as he'd asked that. "Because a good wreck's worth it if it taught you something."

Chance had thought about that in silence for nearly a minute.

"Well," he'd finally said, "I know that dodging high didn't work—he just skidded up high too, and I nailed him."

"You sure did. So what's your alternative? Dodge low?"

"That's the part I can't figure," Chance had said, looking at his father. "It seems to me, lookin' back on it, that there was just as much chance that his car would have shot low on the track."

"You're exactly right," his father had told him, nodding, the red coal at the end of the cigarette bobbing up and down in the darkened truck cab. "When a guy's loose like that, he's spinnin' only until his tires get grip again. And as soon as they do, he's gonna shoot off whatever way they're pointed—high, low, or in-between."

"So if I can't go high and I can't go low, which way do I go?"

"You tell me."

Thinking for a moment, Chance had finally asked, "At him?"

"That's right."

"But . . . that's crazy!"

"Is it?" Nate had glanced his way. "Just think about it. Something like 90 percent of the time, that racecar is going to shoot low or high out of a spin—by the time you get to where it was, it's gonna be someplace else. The other 10 percent of the time, well, he might stay on the same line, but at least he'll still be movin' on down the track, so it won't be like you was hittin' him standin' still. I mean, you need to drive it the way you see it, Chance. But it seems to me that it just might be safer all around if you keep your foot in it."

So, all these years later, Chance kept his foot in it—the quivering hood of his racecar aimed directly at the point where he had last seen the spinning Chevrolet. Acrid smoke enveloped Chance's car, rushing in through the open window netting.

"Lost you," Pooch radioed tersely. "Looking . . . looking . . ."

And then, just as quickly, Chance was clear, emerging full-throttle from the dense gray wall. For the briefest of all possible moments, Chance had a glimpse of flashing red sheet metal through the tire smoke, off to his right, up against the outside wall of the track. Glancing up to his racecar's panoramic rearview mirror, Chance glimpsed the Monte Carlo again, terribly close—scant inches from his Taurus's red spoiler this time. The Chevy was heavily crumpled, the sleek, polished lines of the car reduced to a shredded, jagged mess from the rear window on back.

The wreck receded in the mirror, and then jumped uptrack again as it was struck by following traffic.

"Inside," Pooch told Chance in his earpieces, reminding him of the car below him, to his left. "Wreck behind you in Two. Three cars. Four. Five. More. Big wreck. Lotsa cars. Still inside."

And then, half a second later, "Inside. Yella's out. Race back to the line. Inside."

Close, Chance thought. Then another thought nagged at him. He keyed the black transmit button on his steering wheel.

"Where's LD?"

"He's who's inside," Pooch told him.

Chance glanced to his left. There was the familiar midnight blue Ford, no stripes, no flames, no design of any kind under the patchwork of sponsor decals, the primary-sponsor logo on the hood, and the familiar, slanted, pearl-white "35" on the rooftop and doors. Through the Plexiglas of the car's right-side window, Chance caught the familiar form of the driver—a rough-hewn, mustached, and goateed figure in a blue open-faced helmet, his steel-gray eyes visible even through the clear bubble goggles that he wore. As Chance glanced a second time, the other driver motioned for Chance to pull wide and fall in behind.

Chance shook his head minutely, as far as the helmet's restraining straps would allow. "LD" was Lyle Danford, a twenty-year Cup veteran, a three-time champion, and the driver of the number 35 Perkins Tools Taurus in Robert Vintner Racing's two-car stable. He'd begun driving for Vintner while Chance was still in high school.

He was also the guy Chance was trailing in the points race.

But that, Chance knew, was not why Danford was making the hand signals, trying to boss him around.

Danford pulled that stuff with everyone. The joke was that everybody else in NASCAR used their eighteen-wheel transporters to haul their cars, while Lyle Danford needed his to carry his ego. He was gruff, outspoken, and given to telling reporters that their questions were stupid. When the green flag dropped, he drove as if every other car was appearing in a supporting role to his performance. He crowed when he won, stomped off to his motorhome when he lost, and half the fans in NASCAR hated his guts.

The other half worshiped the very earth on which he walked.

And this season, for the first time in six years, Danford was carrying the points lead as the middle of the season approached. It wasn't the sort of advantage that he was likely to give up willingly.

Chance moved up the track until a bare fraction of an inch separated his car from the concrete wall whizzing by at 200 miles an hour. Then, as he approached Turn Three, rather than dropping in obediently behind his teammate, he stayed off the brakes until the very last moment, following the middle racing groove to creep a bumper's length ahead of Danford's dark blue car.

War had been declared.

The two cars couldn't stay as they were, side by side, all the way through the corner. To keep his speed up, Danford would have to let his racecar slide, drifting up the banking, using the entire bottom half of the track. But Chance was already in the lane that Danford would have to drift into.

"Inside," Pooch reminded him.

In the back of his head, Chance could hear his high school science teacher: Two objects cannot occupy the same space at the same time. Which law of physics was that? Newton's third? His fourth? Chance hadn't paid enough attention to remember.

Besides, the only laws that mattered here were the NASCAR regulations. Chance had the racing line, and Chance was ahead—however minutely—and therefore he had the right-of-way. If LD moved up into him, he'd be fouling him.

LD displayed his customary disregard for the NASCAR rulebook. He drifted steadily up the banking. As Chance glanced his way, the older driver signaled again, telling him to make room.

Chance held his line.

Another hand gesture popped up in the midnight-blue racecar—not a racing direction this time.

The blue car drew closer. Chance's car shuddered, and there was a sound like the world's largest belt-sander being run right next to his shoulder.

The cockpit filled with the smell of burnt rubber. Danford had run his front wheel all the way up against Chance's car, the rapidly spinning tire printing a blackened "doughnut" into the door-panel numbers.

Chance held his line. A cushion of air appeared between the two cars—three inches . . . six . . . twelve. Then, without the side-bite to hold him low on the track at speed, Danford's car began to creep back.

"Inside," Pooch said, just to let Chance know he wasn't clear yet.

Chance was about to relax a bit when the back end of his car jumped two full feet to the right. Heart doing flip-flops, he wrenched the wheel the same direction, putting his shoulders into it, keeping the front wheels rolling, not sliding. A blue blur flashed by, and Chance corrected the other way as his Ford fishtailed back and forth, high into Turn Four. By the time Chance had his car and his breathing back under control, Danford was five car lengths ahead of him, already on the front straight.

"Field's six seconds back," Pooch told him, letting him know that he didn't have to worry about being overtaken by anybody else.

Nerfed.

That's what they called it. He'd been nerfed. This wasn't what he'd done to the Chevy earlier in the race, taking the air off a guy's spoiler. No, Lyle Danford had simply drifted back until his front valance was behind Chance's rear wheels, and then punched the accelerator, swerved right, and hit him.

It wasn't a hard hit. It wouldn't even get Danford a rough-driving penalty from NASCAR as long as Chance didn't wreck, and Chance's reaction times were quick enough to keep him out of the wall. But the distraction certainly allowed enough time for Danford to make his pass.

Above Chance, all along the outside wall, a steeply angled mass of humanity had leaped to its collective feet—a mass of dot-like heads and faces and hands, all moving, most waving hats. Danford's car passed under the starter's box with its dancing yellow flag, and yellow flames spat out the left-side exhaust box as the race leader lifted off the gas and downshifted. As for Chance, he was still five hundred feet short of the start-finish line when Pooch called, "Pace car's out. Fall in behind the 35."

Chance was still pumped. Every fiber of his being wanted to go flying up the remainder of the front straight and knock Lyle Danford and his menacing blue car into the next county. He drew several deep breaths, willing the adrenaline out of his system, and settled for closing in on Danford's back bumper and giving him the most subtle of taps, letting the other driver know that he was there.

Tellingly, the radio stayed silent. Neither Pooch nor Andy wanted to say anything that might reignite the situation. Slowed to a sedate 45 miles an hour, parading single file behind the pace car, the field threaded its way back through the accident scene.

Two cars were hard against the upper wall, fluid leaking down the banking from beneath them. Five more were strewn at various angles along the grass between the inside wall and the racing surface. All had their window nets down to signal to the safety crews that the drivers were okay. The last car, halfway down the back straight, had apparently ruptured a fuel cell in the crash—the entire rear end was engulfed in flames, black smoke rising in a slanting column above it. Its driver, still wearing his helmet, was out of the car and back a safe distance, watching with his arms folded as two safety workers shot powdery white fire retardant into the curling orange tongues of flame.

Far down the straight, two of the rolling wounded had gotten refired and were making their way into the turn, trying to stay ahead of the pace car so they wouldn't lose a lap.

Chance's earpieces crackled with static as somebody keyed a "talk" button.

"Hey, Boomer." It was Andy. "Pit road should open this time around. Robert wants you and LD to pit together."

Robert wants you . . . Robert Vintner—the team owner—was calling the shot. Why? Danford had qualified in the top four, high enough to get a pit behind one of the breaks in the wall. He didn't have to worry about getting trapped behind another car in his pit. On the other hand, the oldest trick in the book was to stop short in your pit box. That way you could hold up whoever it was that was pitted behind you.

And Chance's pit was behind LD's.

Chance keyed his mike.

"Say again?"

"I said Robert wants you and LD to pit together."

"Is that what you want, Hoss?"

There was a pause. Then Andy came back on the radio.

"Robert wants you and LD to pit together," he said. "Copy?"

Now it was Chance's turn to pause.

"Copy that," he finally said.

Danford's car moved over to the left as they came out of Turn Three. Chance did the same, driving down next to the apron. Then they got within sight of the pit road entrance, and the entire front half of the field pulled off onto the apron, actually accelerating a few hundred RPMs to get up to the pit road's 55-mile-per-hour speed limit, as—yellow flag or not—the object on pit road was to get into one's pit box and get back out onto the track just as quickly as regulations would allow. Pitting under the yellow generally allowed enough time to get tires and fuel without losing a lap, but you could still lose track position—both to the cars that beat you off pit road and those that stayed out on the track and did not pit.

"Pit road's open," called Pooch.

"Roger that," Chance said. The pace car continued past the entrance with its caution lights strobing. Danford's midnight-blue racecar moved even lower on the apron, inside the white lane markers designating the pit road entrance. Chance followed him.

Then, at the last possible moment, Chance darted back up onto the track, rear tires spinning, rear spoiler missing the pit wall's water-filled Fitch barrier by mere inches.

His tires caught, and Chance accelerated down the front stretch, catching up to the pace car.

"Whoo-ee!" Pooch chortled. "Looks like the 35's spotter is getting hisself an earful!"

Chance caught up to the pace car and tucked in several yards behind it. They crossed the line under the starter's box.

The radio crackled again.

"Hey, Chance." The voice was Robert Vintner's, one that Chance rarely heard on the radio during a race. "What're you up to, guy?"

"Looks like I'm leading the race, boss."

Unspoken, but understood, was the fact that Chance had also just picked up five bonus points.

The Cup wasn't won on the basis of race wins alone. NASCAR's points system was designed to award consistency, so there were also points for things such as winning a pole position and leading the most laps in a race. And NASCAR also awarded five points to a driver for the first lap he led in each race. Lyle Danford had gotten his five points in the race back to the yellow flag. And Chance had just gotten his by staying out, rather than pitting.

Going into this 500-mile race at Michigan, only seventy-two points had separated the two drivers. And by staying out on the track, Chance had ensured that it was still seventy-two points, and not seventy-seven, that separated them at this stage in the race.

Chance's earpieces crackled again as Vintner rekeyed his radio.

"Didn't Andy tell you I wanted you to pit?"

There were all kinds of outs here. Chance could say that someone had stepped on the radio transmission, that he'd misunderstood Hoss, that he'd turned aside because he thought he was coming in too hot for the pit road limit. But Chance had never lied to his team owner, and he never would.

"Sure did, boss," he said instead.

"Well, son, what do we have to do to get you to pit? Ask NASCAR to black-flag you?"

Vintner's voice didn't sound all that upset. He even seemed mildly amused. Then again, he could have been faking that—something like ten thousand of the fans around the track, plus nearly all of the working media, had scanners to monitor the race team radio traffic, and the majority of those were tuned to the leading teams' frequencies. The crew on the Fox TV broadcast also liked to pick up the interesting bits and repeat them, as long as the language didn't get too colorful.

Still, Vintner owned both the first- and second-place teams in the points chase, so no matter who was ahead, he was in the catbird seat. In that case, he might actually have been genuinely amused at his organization's intra-team rivalry. Either way, Chance didn't want to say anything that might further aggravate the situation. And he already had his five points.

He keyed the talk button clamped to his steering wheel.

"You ready for me next time around, Hoss?"

"You bet," Andy replied. "Four tires?"

"Four tires," Chance agreed. "No pressure change; we'll have time to warm 'em up before this goes green. Water's one-ninety-five, so you can tape a little more grille if you want. Everything else is good. We're hooked up. Best car we've had all year."

Considerable progress had been made at the wreck site. Both of the cars up against the wall were about to be loaded onto ramp-backed recovery vehicles, wreckers were getting hooked up to three of the cars in the grass, and safety crews were busy putting tan granulated oil-dry onto the track. The fire had been put out, although the car still sat there, coated in the flat white fire retardant, the grass around it charred black, while the safety workers conferred with one another, waiting for the wreck to cool. Two ambulances were leaving the scene, but that was standard operating procedure—if you wrecked too hard to continue, NASCAR's rules required a check-up in the infield care center.

Chance followed the pace car into the turn, and Pooch called out, "In Three." That was for Andy's benefit, to let the crew chief know when to put his people on the wall.

Through Three, into Four, and Chance dropped to the apron for real this time. He turned into the pit road entrance.

"Twenty-nine hundred, second gear—twenty-nine," Pooch called out, reminding Chance of the tachometer reading—2,900 RPM—that he needed to hit in order to stay right at the 55-mile-per-hour pit road speed limit.

His pit sign—a yellow "53" on a navy blue oval—danced up and down on the end of a fifteen-foot aluminum pole at the far end of his pit box, a quarter of the way down pit road. Chance kept his revs at 2,900 until the last possible moment, rolling smartly through the empty pit box before his, covering the ground to his stall just as rapidly as regulations would allow, and then sliding to a stop with the nose of his car kissing the sign. Seven helmeted men, two wearing kneepads and two in silver heat-resistant aprons, swarmed over the wall and surrounded his car.

"Pace car's in One," Pooch told everyone, and Chance silently urged his crew to work faster.

CHAPTER 4

The walkway behind pit road at Michigan was more than six feet wide, but even so, Cindy found herself walking sideways and squeezing through as she made her way back to the RVR pits. Up and down the sidewalk, stony-faced crewmen were hustling through, pulling wagons loaded with tall, long-necked fuel cans. Photographers trotted from pit box to pit box, padded camera cases hanging heavily from their hips. Firemen stood in their coveralls next to stacks of tires, taking it all in. Down the walk, the tall, giraffe-like amble of a boom microphone announced the presence of a TV crew on the move. And behind them all were spectators who'd come down from the corporate suites, standing three deep in places, craning their necks to see the pit stop action taking place on the other side of the big metal pit carts.

What Cindy saw when she finally got back troubled her: Lyle Danford's crew was scraping and gauging tires, and their gas man had his helmet and head sock off—all signs that LD had already pitted. But Chance's crew was still standing at the wall with tires at the ready, so he hadn't come in yet.

Cindy's heart dropped all over again. Pooch had radioed that Chance had cleared the wreck. But maybe Pooch had been wrong. Then Cindy glanced up at the big scoreboard atop the grandstand, and saw Chance's car number in lights under the first-place placard.

A smile lit her face. She edged past a pair of photographers, climbed to the top of the pit cart, took up her clipboard, and resettled her headset. She had just taken her seat when Chance's red-white-and-blue Taurus came growling through the shallow turn at the entrance to pit road.

Cindy sat up.

Over four years of marriage, Cindy had witnessed hundreds of Chance's pit stops. She could witness hundreds more, and it wouldn't diminish the thrill.

Part of it was the sheer athletic precision of the crew—seven men who trained all week for these fleeting, quarter-minute events. They swarmed over the wall carrying tires, air wrenches, a gas can, and a jack, zipping off lug nuts and dumping in fuel in one seamless, choreographed instant.

But mostly it was the fact that, during these few, fleeting seconds, her husband was right there, so close that Cindy could see his hazel eyes through the webbing-hatched window as he lifted his visor to take a drink. He was close enough to blow a kiss to, nearly close enough to touch. He was there, he was near her, and he was safe—off the track and away from its two-hundred-mile-per-hour clamor. They were short, these stops; added all together, they made up less than two minutes of a race. But corny as it sounded, Cindy loved the nearness of them, and she would not miss a one.

Thirteen seconds, fourteen seconds, fifteen, and then the stop was over, the racecar's engine roaring, its rear wheels spinning even as the jack was coming down. Twin wisps of smoke curled from the tires as the racecar leaped onto pit road.

"Outstanding, guys," Chance's voice sounded amazingly clear in Cindy's headset. "Great stop."

His car was out of sight already, gone around the sweeping exit lane, headed back onto the track.

"Backstretch," came Pooch's voice, letting Chance know where the back of the field was so he wouldn't overtake them under caution.

There was another tap at Cindy's ankle, and a crewman handed up a clipboard. On it was scrawled a list of numbers: "22—17.1," "36—18.0," and so on.

These had come from the team's transporter driver, who also served as their team cook and pump-watcher. This last job was the easiest: you hung out at the Union 76 filling station in the garage area and jotted down the pump readings as the other teams refilled their gas cans.

A laptop at Cindy's elbow scrolled through data from NASCAR's timing-and-scoring computer, showing the lap on which each team had made its stop. Armed with that and her pump-watcher's list, Cindy could calculate what sort of fuel mileage each team was getting at this point in the race.

Tapping the buttons on her clipboard's built-in calculator, Cindy found herself wondering why NASCAR didn't just figure each car's gas mileage itself and then make those figures available to everyone. It was one of those unanswerable questions, such as why fuel gauges weren't allowed on Cup cars. If you pondered all the stuff like that, though, you'd go crazy. You just had to accept it as part of the romance of the sport.

And secretly, Cindy enjoyed having a reason to be in the pits and help her husband in his work. She'd tried other things—some wives crossed over to the grandstands through the tunnel before the parade lap and watched the race from there. Some kept busy by taking turns watching kids in the infield playground.

But Cindy preferred to work with the team. It made her feel useful. It made her feel closer to Chance.

The Nextel Cup official in the team's pit box turned and held up one finger.

Andy nodded and moved the boom mike closer to his mouth.

"NASCAR says that we're going green next time around," he announced. "Got that, Boomer?"

"Got it," Chance's voice came crackling back.

"You copy that, Pooch?"

"Copy," the spotter reported from his perch. "Green in one."

The field had re-formed into two lines—cars still on the first lap, in the lead, were running now on the outside of the track, while cars a lap or more down were on the inside—poised to fight their way back around the track and possibly get a lap back.

"Stay high for the restart," Cindy heard Pooch advise Chance. "We got us a couple a walkin' wounded in the lapped cars."

Chance had been running in first place when he'd headed into the pits. After coming back out, he'd had to line up behind the cars that hadn't pitted, and those that had come in a lap ahead of him. That put him in the twenty-first position.

It sounded awful, but it wasn't. Not really.

Of the twenty cars ahead of Chance, the first five were drivers who hadn't pitted at all. Some were probably banking on the likelihood of another caution within a few laps. The one in front might have stayed out to pick up his five leader's points. And some might have stayed out just for the two or three minutes of fame—and TV time—that might turn the tables in their search for a sponsor, or a contract renewal, or the sale of an underfunded team to a more deeply pocketed owner. But what they all had in common was that they were running on worn tires, with light fuel loads that would cause the tails of their cars to ride higher, exposing more of the spoilers to the wind. Those two things would slow them, and Chance was pretty sure he could overtake all five cars within two laps.

That left fifteen entries ahead of him, but of those, four had chosen to take only right-side tires, again gambling on the possibility of a second yellow in which to change the other two. Taking two tires cut as much as seven seconds off of a pit stop, but on a moderately banked track such as Michigan, a car with four fresh tires would inevitably run down and pass cars that had only taken two.

And then, of the eleven cars that had taken four tires, two or three were battling setup problems that they'd been unable to rectify in the fifteen-second window of a pit stop.

So the first car that Chance really had to worry about would be running only a little over two hundred feet ahead of him at the restart, and some of the cars between that one and Chance's would be dropping back swiftly.

Two hundred feet was less than three-quarters of a second at race speed. And Chance knew that, in this caliber of racing, any number of things could happen in three-quarters of a second.

He entered Turn Three.

"Pace car's pitting," Pooch called to him.

Chance tightened up, running scant inches behind a Dodge advertising "CAT DIESEL POWER" on its rear valance.

"Green flag," Pooch called.

This time it wasn't the same shot-from-a-cannon feeling that one got at the start of a race. NASCAR put an orange highway cone on the outside wall, and the rules said that the race leader was to go to race speed "in the immediate vicinity" of that cone.

But "in the immediate vicinity" was a pretty inexact phrase, and racers loved rules with inexact phrases.

In this case, it meant that the leader of the race could keep his speed low until he was just a couple of hundred feet shy of the start-finish line, and he did. Low speeds bunched the pack up, and in a bunched pack, nobody got to lay back and create a gap in which he could get a jump on the car ahead of him.

It would only delay the inevitable. There was no way that a racecar with worn tires was going to remain in the lead. But it did create enough difficulties to keep the lead car—an unsponsored Chevy with a conspicuously blank hood—out in front and on several million television screens nearly all the way into the first turn.

That made the view from Chance's perspective something like rush hour on an L.A. freeway . . . only much faster.

Cars were breaking both left and right, trying to find racing room. Those that tried to dive all the way inside were being held up by the slower cars in the lapped car file. But when they tried to move back up the track, they were getting mixed up with cars trying to drive the second groove.

A few desperate souls had shot high, right up near the wall, trying to pass on the outside. They couldn't stay there. Tiny bits and pieces of tire rubber had collected in the upper lanes of the turns—and drivers called these "the marbles" with good reason. The few cars up high were now trying to dart back down again, but they couldn't—the field was too tightly packed.

It was three-wide racing, thrilling for the fans, but only the center file was making progress.

"Inside . . . got one looking high . . . hold your line, driver," Pooch urged.

Chance saw no reason to argue. He followed the Dodge ahead of him, and the most damaged of the lapped cars—its crumpled rear deck riding half a foot higher than normal—receded on his left like it was going backward. He continued this game of follow-the-leader through all four turns, then did the same for another lap, staying glued to the yellow-and-black car ahead of him. Only then did the field open up enough for him to maneuver.

"Outside—clear low," Pooch radioed, even as Chance was glancing to his left. "Running ninth."

Ninth place.

Not bad, Chance thought. He'd picked up a dozen positions in two laps, just by not doing anything stupid.

With a spot open in the bottom groove, Chance dropped low and kept his foot flat, running the engine all the way up to 9000 RPM. He lifted off the gas and entered the turn a bit too close to the apron for the groove, but on fresh tires the car had the side-bite to stay there. Before he'd even exited the second turn, he was back on the throttle and had picked up another spot.

"How's she feel?" Andy asked.

"Great," Chance radioed back. "I can go anywhere I want."

"One looking high," said Pooch, all business.

Cindy completed her first-stop fuel calculations and pursed her lips. In the crew chief's seat next to her, Andy Hofert turned and lifted one side of his headset away from his ear. She did the same.

"How're we doing?" Andy asked.

A straggler swept by on the track, its flattened exhaust note advertising the fact that it was firing on just seven cylinders.

"Good," Cindy told him. "All the cars with better mileage are slower than we are. And in the top ten, there's only one that can match us."

"Who's that?"

"The 35," she said. "Lyle Danford."

CHAPTER 5

Lyle Danford, Chance recalled, had never raced anything but stock cars. Not even modifieds: just late-models, the kind of racecar that looks a lot like what most folks drive every day.

Chance, on the other hand, had spent five of his teenage years driving sprints. And that, he told himself, gave him an advantage. Because, after 180 laps around Michigan International Speedway, that was what this 400-mile race was boiling down to: a twenty-lap duel—a sprint race.

"Point five eight," Pooch called, giving Chance the interval between himself and Danford, the race leader.

It had been six-tenths of a second one lap earlier, and seven-tenths the lap before that.

Keying the radio, Chance asked, "What'd Lyle take on the last stop?"

Fifteen seconds later, Andy replied, "Four tires. Same as us. Think he's going away?"

Chance watched the dark blue car, just a bit over fifty yards ahead, as it barreled down the back straight, scant inches from the outside wall, and then made the transition into the entry of the third turn. There was no hesitance, no bobble, and the car rode exactly in the center of the blackened pavement of the upper groove. And when LD came out of Turn Four, he did so perfectly square—no wiggle, no hesitance in getting back on the gas.

"No," Chance finally radioed back. "He's laying back—saving his tires."

Chance began lifting off the gas earlier as he went into turns, modifying his pace until the intervals stayed steady and he had matched Danford's pace. With twelve laps to go, less than half a second separated the two cars as they threaded their way through lapped traffic.

Chance tried swallowing. No good; his mouth was dry. He checked his oil-pressure and temperature gauges, then listened to his engine. Everything looked and sounded strong: water temperature staying put, no fluttering oil needle, the exhaust note strong and steady.

Through the rear window of the blue Ford ahead of him, Chance could see Danford motioning to the drivers of the lapped cars, moving them over. But LD didn't do that with the last two—he nipped around them entering a turn, using them as obstacles between his car and Chance's, making Chance use up his tires a bit to get past them.

"Open track ahead of the 35," Pooch told Chance. "Third place is the 22. He's seven seconds back."

It was a two-car race.

The radio went silent and stayed that way until Danford's car crossed the line; then Pooch came back on again.

"Ten to go," he called.

Chance drove through the first two turns exactly as before, following the high groove, shadowing Danford's every move.

Then, as they neared the end of the backstretch, Chance feinted high before dropping low, going for the bottom groove. Danford darted down to block him. It was the only thing to do, but it was murderous to the leader's tires, putting several laps' worth of wear on them in a split second, and leaving them warmer, with less grip.

Danford moved higher, running halfway between the two racing grooves. This line was marginally slower than what he'd been running, but the race was no longer about speed. With a comfortable cushion between the two Robert Vintner Racing cars and the rest of the field, the leader's object now was to make the track too narrow for a pass.

Chance ran just three feet behind Danford, making sure he filled the leader's mirror. With most drivers, this would rattle them, get them to make a mistake, but he harbored no illusions it would do that with Lyle Danford—the man had practically invented the tactic.

After two laps of this, Chance braked early for the first turn, letting a small gap open between him and the leader, and then used the interval to make a run at him, dropping to the inside. Danford went low, trying to squeeze him off, and the two cars came side-by-side out of the second turn, their tires kissing and sending up twin puffs of smoke. Chance fell back and tucked in behind Danford again, unable to keep up the speed in the inside lane.

"Five to go," Pooch radioed as the two cars raced down the front stretch.

Danford was running the high groove again, so Chance faked another low pass, making the leader abuse his tires to block him.

That did it. There was no question about who was faster now. Chance knew that Danford's tires were just about spent.

With almost any other driver, Chance would be on the radio with Pooch, asking his spotter to make a deal. Danford had led the most laps in this race—he'd get valuable championship points for that. True, Chance would get more for the win, but Danford would still hold the Series lead. The logical thing for Danford to do would be to let the faster car win, and let them both build a nice cushion of points between themselves and everyone else.

But Chance didn't even bother keying the mike. Lyle Danford would never willingly give up a race—not while he had breath in him. For him, the championship was just a by-product. He raced for wins.

And that was what Chance would have to do as well.

"Three to go," Pooch called.

Chance faked low, got Danford to move down for the block again, heating up his tires even further, and then darted up, to the outside.

Danford mirrored the move, and Chance dove low again.

The thing for Danford to do was to "shut the door"—to move low and block Chance again—but he couldn't. Danford's tires were virtually exhausted.

The two cars were side-by-side now and stayed that way down the backstretch. Chance kept the throttle wide open, forcing the motor to rev well past the 9000-RPM mark on his tachometer, knowing that Danford would be doing exactly the same.

In the grandstands across from the pits, nearly 200,000 people shot simultaneously to their feet. Cindy didn't even have to turn and glance at a JumboTron to know that Chance was making a move.

Cindy glanced over at Danford's pit box, where Robert Vintner was standing, his radio headset clamped under his trademark porkpie hat. Both of his cars were in the lead for this race, but he wasn't smiling. Both, Cindy knew, were also in position to take one another out of the race.

As Cindy watched, Vintner turned and looked at the Turn Four exit. His gold mirror sunglasses hid his eyes, but not the grim set of his mouth.

The two cars, one midnight blue and the other red, white, and blue, came around the turn side-by-side, with not an inch of room between them.

Chance got on the throttle as early as he could risk it, and the inertia crept his Taurus higher on the track, squeezing the available racing lane, forcing Danford up, ever closer to the marbles.

It worked. Chance saw the nose of Danford's car drop slightly as he lifted off the gas, and Chance held his racing line as the blue car receded.

"Clear," Pooch said. "Great driving, Boomer. Outstanding. White flag—one to go."

In his peripheral vision, Chance was aware of a swarming, milling motion—the crowd, on its feet, cheering him on. He couldn't hear them—the engine was too loud. But just seeing them upped his adrenaline level a notch further, and he drove deep into the first turn and took the high line through the second, wringing every available bit of handling out of the racecar, using it up.

He couldn't see a bit of track in the rearview mirror now. It was all Lyle Danford. As they completed the backstretch, Chance's car shuddered, and he didn't have to look to know that it was LD, hitting him from behind for a bump-and-run.

Chance didn't lose control, but the momentary lapse in traction made him enter Turn Three high, leaving the bottom groove open.

"Inside," Pooch told him.

"That's nuts," Chance radioed back. "He can't hold this."

At least three people—Pooch, Andy, and Vintner—were listening to his frequency. Chance knew that. But nobody replied.

The two cars swept through the turns, Danford's creeping ahead. But you had to have some space to drift up into with a move like that, and Danford didn't have the space. Chance already had that line. He didn't lift.

Neither did Danford, and the older driver almost made the pass, but the last ten inches of his car did not. With a bump that Chance barely felt, the right rear quarter panel of Danford's car clipped Chance's front fender.

There was a rare, magic-act moment as Danford's car seemed to float, keeping pace with Chance's Taurus even as it turned sideways on the track ahead, its nose panning the outside wall. Then the blue Ford came rushing back, the hood of Chance's car buckled, obscuring his windshield, and the whole car swiftly rotated, the high-banked turns that he'd just completed swinging swiftly back into view.

Chance braced himself against the seat back, and an electric jolt of pain slapped him, head to toes, as the car slammed heavily into the outside wall.

CHAPTER 6

Tire smoke, thick and acrid, filled the cockpit of Chance's car as he ground backwards along the wall, sliding down the front stretch, shredding bits and pieces of racecar at more than 120 miles an hour. Through the gray fog of smoke, he could see a faint trail of orange flames following him.

Oil line, he decided dimly. He'd ruptured an oil line in the impact.

The car canted and slammed hard against the wall one more time, bringing stars to his eyes. He was going slower now, with something on the undercarriage dragging heavily against the asphalt. Then the whole, twisted hulk swung and came to a rest, nose pointing drunkenly toward the infield.

Chance shook his ringing head, dully annoyed that the straps of the HANS device were restricting him. He could see the NASCAR timing-and-scoring stand in pit lane, over on the far side of the racetrack, and it seemed to be slightly to the left of him. That meant something—something significant—but he couldn't quite remember what.

"Stay put," Pooch commanded—there wasn't a hint of suggestion in his voice. "Hold the brake. Leave the net up. You got cars racing for position below you."

Chance shook his head again, trying to clear the cobwebs. Blinking, he reached back to unclip the tether straps. The stars before his eyes began to recede.

"Boomer! Boomer?"

It took a moment for him to register that Andy was calling him. Chance knew he should talk back, but it just seemed like too great an effort. He took a deep breath and his vision finally brightened.

Fumbling, he found the mike button on his wheel and keyed it as a Technicolored posse of 800-horsepower racecars flashed by just a foot beneath his car.

"Where's Lyle?" Chance asked.

"You okay, guy?" Andy radioed back.

"Yeah, I'm fine. Where's Lyle?"

"In the grass off Four. He's got the net down. We can see him moving around inside."

"Well, who won?"

The radio erupted with Pooch's laughter.

"You," he said. "You the man!"

Chance's first thought was to refire the engine and try to limp to Victory Lane. Then he remembered the oil trail, decided that the engine would be toast, and reached instead to the center of the dash, turning the switch to the battery leads off, cutting off all electrical power to his car. That killed the radio as well, but it didn't matter. The race was over.

He'd won.

Chance sat still for a moment, letting the fact soak in.

The last few stragglers swept by beneath him. Down the track, at the pit road exit, a wrecker sat, yellow lights flashing, waiting for the all-clear signal from NASCAR before coming out to get him.

Chance was just reaching for the window netting when he saw it: a movement in the broad expanse of grass that ran the length of the front stretch. It was something blue.

A car, he realized, peering through the gap in front of the netting. Heavily damaged, its front end crumpled, one tire shredded, and with steam jetting from the ruins of its radiator. But it was a car and it was moving.

Danford.

As Chance watched, incredulous, the wreck of Danford's Taurus wobbled up out of the grass, onto the front stretch, and accelerated to perhaps 20 miles an hour, a shredded tire flailing mercilessly at the ruin of its right front fender.

He's finishing the race, Chance thought dully, wondering why the older driver would bother. Chance supposed that it would give him credit for the full distance of the race, although he couldn't immediately recall if that would do him any good in terms of points.

Then, as Danford's car got nearer, it dawned on Chance that its front end was not pointed straight down the track at the far turn. It was canted uptrack.

Pointed directly at him.

Crossing his arms tightly and inching as far to the right as the harness would let him, Chance braced himself. There was a loud crunch, and his entire car lurched and slid another five feet down the track as the blue car ran into him.

That did it.

Shaking a fresh set of stars away, Chance stripped off his harness and HANS collar, and dropped his window net.

A hiss of hot steam greeted him—Danford's radiator.

Seething now with anger, Chance popped the release on the steering wheel and threw it onto the dash. Reaching through the jungle-gym of roll-cage tubing, he pulled the cables that released the right-side window and tossed the Plexiglas sheet and its cooling tubes behind him, back atop the ticking oil reservoir.

Bumping his helmet, hitting his shoulder against the radio and getting even angrier as he did that, Chance squirmed halfway out the right-side window, got caught, realized that his radio lead was still plugged in, backed up, unplugged it, then got the rest of the way out of the car. He tore off his heel protectors as he swung his feet out. Then he ripped off the gauntlet-like driving gloves and threw them back into the car.

He was storming around the front of his wrecked racecar, unbuckling his helmet, when he saw Danford climbing out of his with his pit cap on.

For some reason, the fact that Danford had actually taken the time to remove his helmet and put on a pit cap pushed Chance right over the edge.

Tearing off his helmet, Chance took it by the chin bar and threw it at Danford, who darted to his left and ducked.

The red-white-and-blue helmet hit Danford's car at the top of the windshield and bounced up, almost touching the upper curve of the catch-fence. It dropped to the pavement and rolled, like a patriotic coconut, down the track and into the crowd of uniformed crewmembers and NASCAR officials storming up from the pits.

The crowd roared its approval as the two drivers trotted toward one another, loosening their firesuit collars.

Chance blinked.

Danford was smiling. Not just smiling—he was grinning ear to ear.

No way, Chance thought. His heart pounded in his ears. *He's actually getting a kick out of this!*

And then, while six feet still separated the two drivers, the crowd from the pit surged in and Chance and Danford both were grabbed and held by their respective gas men—big, ex-football players chosen for their speed, their size, and, most of all, their strength.

"Chill out." Abe Benteen, Chance's crewman hissed it up close, right in his ear. "Get hold of yourself, man. You on TV."

Chance stopped and took a breath, shaking the big man's arms off of him, staring daggers at the still-grinning Danford. A helmeted Nextel Cup official stepped between the two of them.

"That's it," he commanded sternly.

"You," he pointed at Danford, "are needed in the media center.

"And as for you," he turned to Chance, looked back at the ruins of Chance's car, dipped his head to make a call on the radio, listened, and then nodded. "Well, I guess we'll be doing Victory Lane out here today, just as soon as the 35 gets towed away. And gentlemen?"

Both Chance and Danford turned back to the Nextel Cup official.

"Jake Crockett needs you in the NASCAR hauler just as soon as the winner's press conference and sponsor greet are over," he told them. "Drivers and crew chiefs, both."

CHAPTER 7

He apologized? Are you kidding me?"

"I kid you not."

Still in his driving suit, Chance leaned back in the swivel chair at the motorhome's small dining table and continued, "After I talked to the reporters in the media center, Perky took me upstairs to say hello to the Ford folks, and when I came out of there, Lyle was waiting, and he was like, 'Hey, I didn't realize how much I moved up on that last pass; I thought you were moving down on me. But I saw it on video in the hauler, and now I know you drove me clean. So I was way out of line, hitting you like that.'"

"Did he say that in front of Jake?" Cindy asked.

"LD?" Chance laughed and shook his head.

"That's probably asking a bit much," Nate Reynolds rumbled.

"Well," Marilyn Reynolds said from the kitchenette, where she was pouring iced tea, "that sounds like nothing more than half an apology to me."

"Maybe," Chance told his mother. "Still, that's half an apology beyond what anyone else has ever gotten out of him. But wait—there's more."

"Tell us," his father said, leaning forward on the motorhome couch.

"Well," Chance continued, "LD asks me what the deal was with me throwing the helmet, and I told him that I was sorry I did that and glad I didn't actually hit him, and he says, 'No, it's not that—I'm just surprised you threw it at all, you being such a Christian. I thought you guys had to turn the other cheek or something.' And I told him no, that was Jesus advising his disciples on how to handle persecution by authorities, and there's nothing in the Bible that says a Christian has to be a punching bag. And old LD thinks about that for a second and says, 'Well, I guess I got a lot to learn.' Next thing I know, he's asking Cindy and me over to his place tomorrow for a cookout."

"Tomorrow?" Cindy's eyebrows shot up. "What am I supposed to bring?"

"Nothing," Chance replied. "He just said to come."

Cindy sighed. "I'll call Dottie in the morning."

"Going to his place," Nate Reynolds said. He let out a long, low whistle and touched his shirt pocket. It was an old habit: his wife and son had finally talked him into quitting cigarettes eight years earlier.

"I don't see why you think that's so special," his wife told him as she closed the refrigerator door. "Chance is a Cup driver, just like Lyle Danford. Even better. He beat him today, didn't he?"

"Mom . . .," Chance began.

"Now, Marilyn, you know what I'm talking about," Nate said. "They don't call Lyle Danford 'The Wolf' for nothing. The man's a loner. He almost never has folks over to his place. If he and Dottie are asking these two over, that's really something."

Marilyn Reynolds harrumphed and handed out the tea.

"Why don't you come with?" Chance asked, taking his glass.

"What?"

"LD hears me talk about the two of you all the time, and he sees you at the track most weekends. I'm sure he wouldn't mind, but I can call first and make sure."

"No way." Nate shook his head. "We ain't butting in. Besides, I got the motorhome to take care of."

"The crew's still here, waiting for the car to finish inspection," Chance pointed out. "I can have one of them drive the motorhome back, and you two can fly to Charlotte with Cindy and me."

"The motorhome's not going back," his mother told him. "Your daddy and I are playing hooky in the morning."

She turned to Cindy. "We're going up to Frankenmuth. You know, the town with the big Christmas store and the cuckoo clocks and all? And I hear they have a restaurant that makes chicken dinners that are just to die for."

"Ohhhh . . ." Cindy set her tea down. "Can you pick me out a cuckoo clock?"

Marilyn nodded.

"And after that," Nate Reynolds added, "we're driving back to Chillicothe to check on the house and do laundry, before we head up to Pocono. So it sort of looks like our week is all planned out, you know?"

Chance nodded. Asking his parents to drive his motorhome from race to race was something he had done his first year in Cup so they could come to the races. It had turned out to be a great idea. Not only did Nate and Marilyn feel they were being useful, they got to sightsee around the country ten months out of the year, and they got paid handsomely for it, to boot. They drove the motorhome to the drivers' paddock the morning before Chance was due to arrive at the track, and then they unhooked their little Ford Focus from its trailer, checked into a motel, and went antiquing.

Marilyn stocked the refrigerator with Chance and Cindy's favorite foods, put fresh-cut flowers on the nightstand for Cindy, and kept the home on wheels spotless. Everybody won, especially Chance, who cherished having his folks along, just as it had been when he'd first started racing.

"Well, okay," he told his father. "Sounds like you've got a full schedule."

"Get back to the story," Nate urged him. "What happened at the hauler? What'd Jake Crockett say?"

Chance's face reddened. Jake Crockett was president of NASCAR; reporting a conversation with him felt suspiciously like reporting a conversation with his high school principal.

"Well, he said that we were both far enough along in this sport that we ought to know better than to behave like a couple of fairgrounds rednecks," Chance confessed. "And then he reminded us that Fox had its cameras on us, and that they replayed Lyle hitting me five times, and me throwing the helmet at Lyle three times. And he told Lyle that he could have seriously hurt me if I'd been climbing out when he hit—"

"What'd Lyle say to that?"

"He said he knew I was still strapped in, and that I didn't even have the net dropped yet. And then Jake says, 'Well, I've got to fine you fellers for conduct unbecoming to NASCAR,' and LD says, 'What do you mean, "unbecoming"? Chance and I probably just sold out every race for the rest of the season.' And Jake says, 'You know what I mean,' and then he fined Jake $10,000 and put him on probation until the end of the season for hitting me, and he fined me $5,000 for the helmet. Payable before qualifying starts at Pocono."

"Five thousand . . ." Nate issued a long, low whistle.

"Not only that," Chance added, "Jake told us not to bring him any team checks—he wants to make sure that we're paying this out of our own pockets. So I said sure, I'd write him a personal check."

"What'd LD say?"

"LD? He told Jake not to worry. He said that he'd pay the fine personally."

CHAPTER 8

Lake Concord, North Carolina

Its throat the deep, shadowed crimson of red velvet, the ruby-throated hummingbird whirred closer to one of the flower baskets that Cindy had hung at the corners of the multileveled, redwood deck. Hovering before a yellow trumpet-shaped flower, the tiny creature dipped its long, slender beak into the center of the petals, hung motionless for a second, then moved on to the next flower.

Chance smiled and looked out at the lake, where the orange presunrise sky was already painting the water the color of burnished bronze. Sunrises were one reason he and Cindy had decided to build their house on the west side of the lake. It provided them with a visible start to the day.

Of course, by the same token, Cindy had made certain that the master bedroom was built on the landward side of the house. Chance was a morning person. She, on the other hand, preferred not to be awakened by the first light of dawn.

Chance leaned back in the teak Adirondack chair, closed his eyes, and let the lake sounds—the lapping of water, the slight wind in the trees, and the all-encompassing birdsong—soak in for just a moment. Then, eyes still shut, he easily shifted to prayer.

Chance rarely prayed with words anymore, not unless he was praying with Cindy during their evening devotions or leading a prayer group at the track for SCM. Rather, he closed his eyes and began by meditating on the holiness of his heavenly Father, and of the unspeakable love shown by Jesus: God willing to become man and die for man's sins. Chance tried to imagine what heaven would be like—not the streets of gold and the gates of pearl, but the spectacle of billions of luminous creatures, from angels to saints, delighting in the opportunity to offer eternal praise to God, to bow and kneel at every mention of Christ's name.

Next, Chance collected one by one all of those thoughts and actions that he regretted since he'd last sat down with God. He began with the thrown helmet, then carefully laid out every act and every thought that might have displeased his Maker.

He moved to thankfulness next, and this took longer than anything. There was his salvation. There was Cindy. There were his parents, hers. There was the fact that he had the Bible, God's Word, readily available any time he wanted it. There were all his Christian friends and especially Brett and the others on staff with SCM. There was his job, and the way it had come almost easily, his team. There was Robert Vintner and his generosity with Chance and his family. There was the fact that Chance's parents got to drive the motorhome and be with him at nearly every race.

Chance thought of all the things that God had trusted him with—this six-bedroom, five-bath masterpiece of a house, carefully situated on a beautiful private lake in such a way that no other residence on the lake was visible from it. He thought of the growing nest egg of mutual funds, stocks, and CDs that Robert Vintner's money managers ran for him with as much care as if the fate of the world rested on their decisions. He thought of the mementos and memories that Cindy and he had brought back from their travels around the world. And then he thought of the truly important things: Cindy's health, his, the opportunities he'd had to share his faith with others. He wordlessly breathed his thanks to God for opening the windows of heaven on him and his wife.

And only after all this did Chance come to God in supplication. He asked safety for Cindy, his folks, her folks, their friends, his teammates, for Lyle and all on his team. He brought to his mind a driver friend who was struggling with an overly publicized divorce, and he asked healing on that situation. He remembered a young boy who had come to his autograph session on Saturday night in a wheelchair, and Chance asked God to restore strength to those crippled legs.

And finally, Chance asked God to give him the strength to stay in his will, no matter what.

A soft peace, like a blanket of warm mist, enveloped the young man, and he smiled and enjoyed the moment of this tender, ethereal hug. Then the birdsong and the soughing of the wind returned, and he reopened his eyes to the glowing predawn sky.

Chance lifted the screen on the slender Vaio laptop and pressed the power button. Moving the small silver computer to a more comfortable position, he waited until Windows had booted up and then he opened his Bible study program. He brought up the first chapter of the gospel of John, zeroing in on the opening phrase of John 1:14—"And the Word was made flesh and dwelt among us."

A few minutes later, he looked up from the screen as the sliding glass door opened behind him.

"Hey, early riser," Cindy said sleepily, gathering her nightgown against the early morning chill. "Am I bothering you?"

"You sure are," Chance said, setting the computer aside. "Now get over here and bother me some more."

Smiling, Cindy sat on his lap and wrapped her arms around him. She craned her neck to see his laptop screen, where he'd switched to an interlinear New Testament—line after line of Greek text, interspersed with lines of English.

"So what are you doing now?" Cindy asked her husband. "Studying to be a rabbi?"

"Wrong end of the Bible," Chance chuckled. He turned the laptop her way and began to explain the word study he'd been doing.

Three minutes later, he was still talking.

"So when you look at the original language of John 1:14," he concluded, "you see that the word translated in our Bible as 'dwelt' is actually a specific form of dwelling—dwelling in a tabernacle. And to the Jews of John's time, who were familiar with the excruciating detail their ancestors had gone through to build exactly the right tabernacle so they could get close to God—that word would have been like a flashbulb going off in their heads. Like 'I see; I don't need ritual. I just need Christ.'"

Cindy looked again at his notes on the glowing laptop screen.

"All this talent, and brains, too," she murmured, kissing his cheek. "I read the Bible, too, but . . . wow. You really get into this, don't you?"

"Like this?" Chance asked. "Only since we got married. I'd been reading Scripture every day since I was thirteen, and I decided that it was time that I better understand what I was reading, now that I was a husband and, God willing someday, a father. I mean, if I lead this house, I need to do the job right."

Cindy looked at him a long time.

"So," she asked, "you do this for me?"

"For you. For us. For the children God might bless us with, and for their children. For God—to show him I love him and appreciate all he's done for us."

She hugged him again.

"And most guys just go fishing." She grinned as she said it.

"Oh, I'm doing that tomorrow."

Cindy pantomimed pouring a drink on his head. "Mandie's here and she's getting breakfast going. You have time?"

"Lyle's coming by to pick me up at eight," Chance told her. He glanced at his watch. "I not only have time for breakfast, I have time to slip back upstairs."

"Oh no you don't!" Cindy said, jumping to her feet. "I've had two cold breakfasts in the last week!"

"So you're passing me over in favor of a waffle?" Chance asked, trying his best to sound wounded.

"No," Cindy said, kissing the top of his bare head. "I'm passing you over in favor of a Belgian waffle with fresh strawberries, hand-whipped cream, and . . . powdered sugar." She got to the sliding door and stopped.

"Besides," she said, "I'm driving over to the Danfords' at one to help Dottie, and Mandie and I have to make my momma's three-bean salad recipe and get it cooled down so I can take it with. And in between that, I've got to stop and talk with the interior decorator about the Caymans house."

"The Caymans house? Don't you think we ought to build it first?"

"I'm just getting some ideas so I'll know what to picture in the rooms as we talk with the architect," Cindy told him. "And after that, I've got a doctor's appointment this morning."

"Doctor? What's wrong?"

"Nothing's wrong." Cindy smiled. "Ladies aren't like guys. We don't have to be dying to go to a doctor. We just have to see them every once in a while for . . . girl things."

Two hours later, Chance was climbing into Lyle Danford's pickup. But it wasn't, he noted, just any pickup. It was an F-150 Lightning. He tried to remember what the top speed of these things was. He seemed to remember something to the tune of 150 miles an hour.

Chance reached over his right shoulder for the seat belt.

"What's the matter?" Danford grinned at Chance. "Don't trust my driving?"

"Your driving?" Chance asked. "Absolutely. But the driving of the yahoo coming the other way? Huh-uh. Besides, this thing will chime and beep at you every thirty seconds unless you buckle up."

"Naw, it won't," Danford drawled. "I opened up the computer and pulled the chip weeks ago."

Danford drove unbuckled, but sedately, down Chance's long white gravel lane and onto the asphalt private lane that circled the lake. As they passed the gatehouse at the county road, Danford shook his head.

"When I was ten years old?" Danford asked. "We was so poor that we didn't have a pot to . . . well, we didn't have a pot. My daddy drove a Buick so rusty that it whistled while you went down the road. But I remember us driving up to Randleman, to Richard Petty's farm, and seeing Lee Petty out there reading a newspaper, and my daddy asked if we could come in, and he said, 'Sure. Come on. I think Richard's down in the shop.' And he was and, poor as we was, he treated us like we owned the STP company, or something. And then about a year later? We drove down to Ingle Hollow and figured out where Junior Johnson lived, and his wife sent us over to his garage—it's right next to his house—and he took us in and showed us the whole place, even his engine shop."

Danford shrugged.

"Now I've got me a big old electric gate that makes it look like I'm livin' at Graceland, and you've got a rent-a-cop standing at the road outside your house. What's this world coming to, Chance?"

"We didn't get the guard until last year," the younger man replied. "But then one morning one of the drivers living at the other end of the lake was away, and his wife got up to make coffee, and she glanced up and there's some guy outside the kitchen window, pointing a video camera at her. She was still in her nightgown. And that's bad enough, but the next thought on everyone's mind was what could have happened if it had been something other than a video camera. So now we have a guard at the gatehouse, twenty-four/seven."

They drove in silence for a while, and then Danford started talking about some of the work he was doing on his land, planting selected trees and grasses to attract deer and wild turkeys.

"I got a couple of places that I rent up in Michigan during late deer season," he said. "But I figure that, this way, maybe I can get out during bow season and get a decent hunt in, even though we've still got to race on the weekend."

Chance nodded, thinking to himself that this was the most time he'd ever spent alone with Lyle Danford, without a PR person, or a reporter, or another driver or a crew member around.

That ended soon enough.

Robert Vintner Racing made its headquarters north of Charlotte, in a town called Mooresville, not far from Lake Norman, where many drivers and team owners made their homes. Lyle flipped on his turn signal and made the turn onto Rolling Hills Road.

From the outside, the RVR buildings were little different from the other squat industrial buildings that lined the nondescript side street: a UPS depot, a machine shop, a couple of warehouses.

Several other race teams were also on the same street. When mechanics and technicians signed on with a new team at the end of the season, the phenomenon was known as the "toolbox derby" because crew members could literally push their big red multidrawer toolboxes down the street to their next job.

But rather than being in one building, RVR was housed in three—one industrial-building-size "garage" for each of the two Nextel Cup teams and a separate building containing the engine shop, plus the chassis dynamometer and other big-ticket items that were used by both teams as they needed them. As the dyno building was neutral ground, it was where Robert Vintner kept his office and where the organization had its combination cafeteria and lunchroom. And that was where the two teams gathered for their Monday morning postrace meetings.

A projection TV was a permanent fixture in the room. The teams videotaped every pit stop with tiny overhead cameras mounted on booms above the pit stalls. The earlier parts of the Monday morning meetings were usually devoted to minute dissection of each stop, studying where time had been picked up and lost, and discussing how to best integrate one another's time-saving practices.

But as Chance and Lyle walked in, it wasn't a pit stop that was being played out on the screen. It was the broadcast tape of the race: Lyle's last pass and the accident that followed.

"Whup . . ." Danford laughed. "Maybe we better walk back out and come in later."

"Nonsense," Robert Vintner told him. Without his porkpie hat, the silver-haired team owner looked positively naked. He stroked his thick, bristly moustache and added, "It was our fault for not telling you that we made the cars a foot longer last week."

"A stretch Cup car," Danford mused. "There you go."

On the projection screen, Chance's car kissed Danford's wildly spinning Taurus almost nose-to-nose, crumpling both hoods, and then Chance swung around and backed into the wall as Danford spun down into the front-stretch infield, hit the outside of the pit lane wall, and caromed back into the grass.

"That's $100,000 to build a car, plus $100,000 in wind-tunnel time . . . times two," Vintner commented. "You ever think about that when you're out there, LD?"

"Never crosses my mind," Danford told him.

Vintner chuckled.

"Well, do you think it might cross it next time?"

Danford made a show of pondering the question.

"Not a chance," he finally said.

A couple of his crew members snickered.

Vintner looked at Danford, eyebrows raised.

"Lyle's right," Chance said. "We can't be doing spreadsheets on the racetrack, RV. You think about stuff like that, you'll slow down, and slow's not going to win you any races."

He paused, realizing that he had almost quoted his father verbatim.

Vintner shrugged.

"Well, you're right," he said. "You boys have got to drive it the way you see it. But if you drive many more like this, we're going to need us some deeper-pocketed sponsors. One of you had better bring me a Nextel Cup, come November."

"I will," both drivers said at the same time, and the whole room broke up in laughter.

The chitchat ended immediately. Monday was the drivers' one and only day at the shop, and their car chiefs and crew chiefs had a full morning planned for them. They both added their own comments about the pit stops, and then the teams retired to their own buildings.

The shops looked like any small manufacturing operation, only they were ultra clean: floors finished with an epoxy paint so well scrubbed and shiny that they looked wet.

Each driver sat with his car chief and crew chief to offer his thoughts on the chassis setup they'd run at Michigan, and to review the car he'd be driving at Pocono—an unusual track that had the characteristics of both an oval and a road course.

Then the drivers went outside and drove stop drills for their over-the-wall teams. The cars they drove were the ghosts of what fans saw on the track—bodies in gray primer with no numbering or decals, the only color on them the neon-striped hubs that helped the tire carriers slide the racing wheels into place.

These drills were usually driven by test drivers—up-and-comers or recently retired drivers who also drove many of the private test sessions. But there was no substitute for pit drills with the actual driver in the car. So Chance and Lyle took turns pitting at the practice wall that Robert Vintner Racing kept on the back lot, deliberately sliding the car in cockeyed, or too close to the wall, the way they might end up in an actual race, pitting on worn, hot tires. Then they pitted together, sometimes with Chance in front, and sometimes with Lyle, so the drivers could practice close-quarters exits, and the crewmen could work on concentration with the additional distraction of a second car.

The last item, and possibly the most important, was lunch. Lone wolf reputation or not, Lyle Danford always tried to eat lunch with his team when he was at the shop, and Chance had learned early on that this was a great morale builder. So he always did the same, even though it meant an extra hour away from home.

The two men talked shop all the way back to Lyle Danford's farm, a one-hour drive into the rolling hills outside Charlotte. Danford drove at a steady 55 miles per hour, braking early for the turns and signaling each one. Anyone watching would have thought he was just some farmer heading home after a run into town.

Chance looked Lyle's way as the older driver talked about gear ratios for Pocono. As he did, it dawned on Chance that this was a man he'd watched on television all through his high school years. Nearly twenty years separated them in age. There'd been a time when just meeting Lyle Danford would have been the high point of Chance's life.

And while they'd been teammates for four years now, this would be the first time they'd ever socialized outside of a business setting.

Danford had a reputation for keeping his private life extremely private. He had once told a *Sports Illustrated* reporter, "It just don't make sense to me to be all buddy-buddy with some guy during the week and then go out and try to kick his backside on the racetrack come Sunday. I got friends I hunt with and friends I fish with, but none of them drive Cup cars. It's just less confusing this way."

Chance knew Lyle wasn't a total hermit. If another driver was having a fishing tournament or some other kind of charity fundraiser, he could count on Lyle to show up and bring his checkbook. But the man was a notorious loner. And the fault, Chance realized, was as much his as it was Danford's. Chance had heard so many stories about LD's aloofness that it had never occurred to him to ask the man over for a day on the lake.

Yet here he was, headed over to the man's house for a barbecue. And Chance couldn't help but wonder why he'd been invited in the first place.

Danford turned off the highway and onto a county road made of freshly laid and striped asphalt. They followed this for a couple of minutes and then turned again. Now a brick wall was running to their left, a red brick wall eight feet tall, topped with white capstone, the tops of trees visible behind it.

It was the kind of wall a corporation might build to keep prying eyes away from a secret project, and it went on for a mile. Chance wondered what it cost to put up more than a mile of brick wall. A bunch, he decided. It would cost a bunch.

Then they got to a gate and it was as Danford had said it would be—big, imposing wrought iron. The mailbox alongside it had a number and nothing else. On one of the gateposts, a small brass plaque read, "Victory

Lane Farm," but that was it—there was no name. Passers-by might think it was simply an extremely successful horse ranch.

Danford keyed a remote control built into the truck's sun visor, and the two halves of the gate swung inward.

His driveway was a lane through woods so tall that it was like driving through a tunnel made of trees. The smells of fern and pine needles drifted in through the open windows as the truck's tires hummed on the concrete drive.

"You know," Danford said, "back before he passed, back when you was coming up in the Busch Series, my daddy said he remembered seeing your daddy race once, back in the seventies, over in Rossberg. Daddy said he was really good."

"He was," Chance agreed.

"So why didn't he stick with it?"

"Broke his back," Chance said. "He endo'd a sprint car on a little third-of-a-mile dirt oval up in Fairbury, Illinois. It put him in the hospital for two months, and took him out of farming for about seven, and that put a real hardship on his father, seeing as he was the only son. After that, he figured he'd better choose one or the other, either racing or farming. He'd already proposed to my mom, and farming seemed like the surer thing. So he hung up his helmet."

"Is he the reason you got into it?"

"Racing?" Chance thought about it. "Well, sure—I grew up wanting to race cars because there were all these pictures, all over the house, of my dad with this disco hair, holding a checkered flag and kneeling next to late-models, and modifieds, and sprint cars. And he's the one that bought me my first go-kart."

"But did he pressure you to go into it?"

"Pressure?" Chance shook his head. "No. Never. I started out doing it because I liked to go fast. And then I got into competition and I could see that I was good at it, and that was cool—having something where I could be better than everybody else. And after that, it was just a matter of moving up and trying to see just how good I actually could become. I mean, my mom and dad, they encouraged me, sure, even sacrificed to help me move up. But pressure? No. I never felt like this was something I had to do, whether I liked it or not."

Danford nodded, as if chewing on the thought.

"That's good," he finally said.

They came out of the trees into a wide vista of horses in tree-dotted pastures behind pristine white fences, rolling hills beyond. Resting atop a hill in the middle distance were a grand Tudor-style house and a number of long, low outbuildings.

In an outdoor arena marked with white-lettered placards, a lone rider in a black helmet was taking a big roan horse through a complicated dressage pattern. A farmhand looked up from the fence he was mending, recognized the pickup, and waved.

"Well." Danford grinned, waving back. "We're here."

CHAPTER 9

The rider in the ring turned their way as the men got out of the pickup. She galloped over, slid off at the driver's side, and wrapped her arms around Danford.

"Ugh!" Danford grimaced. "Girl, don't you wash this beast? You stink like a horse!"

"And you smell like a dirty old racecar, Daddy." The red-headed girl flashed a freckled smile and then noticed Chance coming around the front of the truck. She grinned broadly and shot her hand out.

"Hi! Remember me?"

"No," Chance said, grinning as he took the girl's hand. "I remember somebody named Angela, but she was about half your size."

"Just becoming womanly," the girl said, spinning on one paddock boot. "I'm fourteen now."

"Quit flirtin'," Danford growled. "He's way too old for you and he's married. Now where's your momma?"

"She's up looking at her roses with Mrs. Reynolds," the girl said. "I'd better go get Crimson cleaned up."

She led the horse away and Chance watched her go. "Fourteen, huh?" He shook his head and smiled. "LD, you're gonna have to get yourself a gun."

"Oh." Danford nodded. "I got a gun. A few of 'em."

They walked up the hill to the house and spent the better part of a minute following a stone walk around it to an immaculate formal rose garden. Cindy looked up, beaming, decked out in a wide straw hat and yellow-and-green gardening gloves. Beside her, dressed the same, Dottie Danford looked like her raven-haired older sister.

"Hi, honey," Cindy called. "Guess what? Dottie's giving me some cuttings to plant off of her prize Queen Victorias."

"Her what?"

"Her roses."

"Oh," Chance said. He looked around at the rose garden. "Do I have to plant them, or put up trellises, or anything?"

"Nope." Cindy shook her head. "Mandie and I can take care of this all by ourselves."

"Well, then." Chance smiled at Dottie. "Thank you."

For the next two hours, Chance and Lyle hung out. It was the same as hanging out with anyone else would be—if that anyone else happened to be a self-made multimillionaire.

They started in the garage, a barn-like structure that had been cleared to hold about two dozen cars on an epoxy floor every bit as spotless as those back at RVR.

Danford led Chance back to a red Mercury with a big number "16" on the door panels and roof.

"Remember this?"

"Only from TV," Chance said.

"This is the one," Danford told him. "The one I won my first Daytona 500 in. You win the 500 now, Daytona gets to rent the car from you for a year and puts it on display in the speedway museum. They didn't do that back then, but I was so proud I asked Buck Hansen—he was my team owner—if I could buy the car from him to keep it, just like this. And Buck says, 'LD, you think you got $25,000 to buy you a racecar just to look at?' 'Cause that was about what a Cup car cost back then, about twenty-five grand. And I waved that big old prop check at him, and said, 'Now I do.' And wouldn't you know it? That old Virginia gentleman turned around and gave me the car. Wouldn't accept a penny for it."

Danford swallowed, crow's-feet deepening at the corners of his eyes. "Buck died in that plane crash on the way back from Dover later on that year. That ol' boy was the last of a breed."

Chance ducked his head into the driver's window and took a look. The car had a dashboard that looked as if it had been put together with bits and pieces from Radio Shack, and the roll cage was different, with no Earnhardt bar. There was almost no headrest to speak of, and the rear window dropped steeply from the roof, with no access holes for wedge and trackbar adjustment. It was like going back in time.

They moved on and looked at other racecars from Danford's career. There was a midnight blue Bandolero car with a big red "35" on the side of it—sort of an undersized, high-roofed sports coupe of a racecar—but Danford walked past like it wasn't even there. After that, they got to a collection of hot rods—bucket Ts, and '32 Ford coupes, a tail-finned '57 Chevy riding on beefed-up Corvette suspension components, and a well-used 1968 Mustang fastback that looked remarkably like the one Steve McQueen had driven in *Bullitt*. Then Chance saw what was on the other side of the Mustang and it took his breath away.

"Ho-ly smoke. No. This . . . can't be . . . ."

"Original?" Danford asked. "You bet it is. A Ford GT40. One of the first models built for the LeMans race back in 1964. Next to old number 16, there, this here's the crown jewel of the garage. Check out the seat—it don't adjust. To make it fit, you've got to move the pedals. And this bulkhead here . . . what the—"

Danford was looking down at the ground, at an open tray of wrenches next to the sleek, low-slung sports car. Moments later, a door opened at the far end of the garage and a lanky young man in his early twenties came walking in, carrying a short length of steel-mesh-shrouded hose. He pushed up a pair of glasses and grinned.

"Oh, oh." He grinned. "Caught me. I noticed that the gas line was weeping last week, Daddy, so I called one of your guys at the shop and asked them to make up a new one. You going to take her out? I can have this on in half a heartbeat."

"Naw." Danford smiled. "Take your time and play with it."

Wiping his hand on his jeans, the young man turned to Chance.

"It's good to see you here, Mr. Reynolds."

"Chance. And it's Danny, isn't it?"

"Yes, sir . . . Chance. Yes, it is. I've always wanted to talk with you out when I see you at the tracks, but . . ." He shrugged.

"Yeah, I know." Chance grinned. "Race weekends are zoos."

Danny looked at the fuel line in his hand as if he'd just discovered it there, and then he looked up again. "You're staying for dinner?"

"I am," Chance told him.

"Awesome! I'll look forward to that!"

They exchanged a few more pleasantries, and then Danford led Chance out into the fresh, open air.

"Your boy Danny," Chance said. "He started in a few ARCA races a couple of years back, didn't he?"

"Sure did." Danford nodded. "But starting 'em was about all he could do. Never finished a one. The kid can find walls like flies find—" He caught himself. "I don't know." Danford shrugged. He watched a pair of horses grazing in the lush, green pasture. "Danny's been a good kid, a great kid, all his life. Always wanting to please, you know? And he wants to drive racecars so bad it hurts. So I've done what I could—shown him a few pointers, even sent him up to Buddy Baker's school a couple of times. And all the head-smarts, he's got that down pat. When he talks wedge and unsprung weight, you'd think you was talking to your car chief, back at your shop."

He paused to nudge a twig off the immaculate drive with his boot.

"But gut knowledge? The feel for a racecar? Boomer, it just ain't there. I mean, he knows that to win races you've got to take that car right up to the ragged edge of wreckin'. But try as he might, he just never has been able to figure out exactly where that is. He gets racing, and either he's slow, or he marches right on past the end of his side-bite. And I mean he wrecked hard a couple of times. So I finally told him, 'Son, you can only ring that old bell so many times, and you're about to use yours all up before you're twenty-one.' And you know him—he's the kind of kid you can talk to. He listens, and he knows I'm right. So he stopped tryin' to race. He's taking classes at UNC, studying to be an engineer, but I can tell it just breaks the poor kid's heart not to be racing."

Danford shook his head and took a breath. "So what do you think that old GT40 would go for now, if I was to sell her?"

Chance noticed the change of subject, but he didn't ask about it. "I don't know . . . I bet it'd be close to a million."

"Nine hundred grand was what one went for the last time they auctioned one at Harrah's," Danford agreed. "I paid ninety-five thousand for the one in there, plus a trailer full of spare parts, about ten years ago. That's what I tell Dottie when she harps on it. It ain't a car. It's a motorhead's certificate of deposit. . . . Hey, you like to shoot?"

Twenty minutes later, they were near the back of Danford's property, his old Willys Jeep ticking and cooling under the shade of an oak as Danford gestured at a group of silhouette targets—sheets of black steel cut out in the shapes of a jackrabbit, an antelope, a stone sheep, a deer, and an elk—on a hill across a shallow valley.

"Range is about 150 yards, which is what it's sighted in for," he said, holding out a Model 1894 .30-30 Winchester, the same rifle carried by John Wayne in countless Western movies. "You want to go first?"

"Thanks." Chance opened the little plastic case that Danford had given him and took out two orange foam earplugs, screwing them into his ears. He worked the lever-action on the rifle and raised it to his shoulder, resting his cheek on the cool, smooth comb of the stock. Putting the sights on the heart of the elk cutout, he took a half-breath, held it, and squeezed the trigger.

The rifle kicked, the crack of its report echoing like nearby lightning. With his exceptional eyesight, Chance caught the most fleeting glimpse possible of the bullet in flight, a bronzed streak jetting toward the target. The stock recoiled against his shoulder, and a metallic clang sounded from the far hillside.

"Got it," Danford said. "Low on the neck."

"I didn't allow for wind," Chance said. "Okay if I go again?"

"Sure." Danford nodded. "Empty the magazine, if you want. There's four more rounds in there, and we've got plenty more."

Chance worked the lever, chambering the next round, and reshouldered the rifle. Holding the sights just right of the softball-size white bull's-eye, he squeezed the trigger again.

Bang!

Clank.

"In the white," Danford said appreciatively. "Now show me that ain't luck."

Chance nodded, worked the lever, and shot again, putting another round in the bull's-eye. He lowered the rifle.

"Good shootin'," Danford said. "Keep goin', if you want."

"No, thanks," Chance said, handing the rifle back to him. "I think I'll quit while I'm ahead."

Danford nodded, depressed the loading ramp on the side of the action, and slid in three rounds to replace the ones Chance had fired. He chambered a round, shouldered the rifle comfortably, and squeezed off a shot, working the lever while the rifle was still at his shoulder, firing again, and again, and again, and again. After each report, a target rang, the sound drifting back as if a blacksmith was over there on the hill, working away. Watching through binoculars, Chance picked out small black dots in the white circles on target after target, until all five had been hit.

"Looks like you've done this before," Chance said as Danford lowered the rifle.

"You, too," Danford said, working the lever to clear the rifle's action. "You hunt a lot?"

"Used to," Chance told him, picking up the brass and handing it to Danford. "Back in Ohio, on my dad's land. It was an every fall thing until I got into Busch. Now, the last time I hunted . . . heck, the last time I shot . . . must have been six, seven years ago."

"Well, it don't look as if you've lost anything," Danford said, clapping him on the shoulder. "What say we go get a drink?"

Back at the house, Danford went behind the bar in his trophy room, where the wall shelves were lined with gleaming cups and statuettes. Three of the trophies were Nextel Cups—the award given at the end of the season to the Series' champion.

Danford bent and looked into the refrigerator.

"We got Coke, Seven-Up, Dr Pepper, some of that Code Red junk that my kids drink, lemonade, root beer, bottled water. . . . I'd offer you a beer, but we don't keep any in the house. I'm an alkie—been on the wagon longer than I can remember."

"Coke would be great," Chance asked. "In the bottle would be fine. And no apology's necessary. I don't drink, either."

The older driver glanced up from the refrigerator.

"You do AA?"

"Me?" Chance shook his head. "No. I've never been a drinker."

"This a religious thing?"

"Only partly," Chance said. He accepted the cold, green-glass bottle from Danford and took a sip.

"If you read the Bible literally," he continued, "it advises against being drunk, or making someone else drunk. But there are those who claim it actually recommends drinking in a couple of places—for medicinal purposes, or even to cheer a person up. Myself? I've always thought about all the times I need to have my wits about me: driving with Cindy in the car, or witnessing to someone, or even just talking with a sponsor or a fan. Guess I'd just rather not dull my senses."

Danford looked at him quizzically, tapping on the bar.

"Roll that back a second. The Bible tells you to drink to cheer up?"

Chance sipped his Coke again and nodded.

"It doesn't say to take a swan dive off the wagon, but it does say that," he said. "'Give strong drink unto him that is ready to perish, and wine unto those that be of heavy hearts.' Proverbs 31:6."

Danford grinned. "You memorized that?"

"I've memorized all of Proverbs," Chance told him. "Psalms, too. And all four of the Gospels. I'm still working on the rest."

"How about that?" Danford chuckled. "Now we know what to do with you if we can't figure anything else. We can stick you in a hotel room nightstand."

"There you go. Right next to the phone book."

"Okay." Danford nodded, setting down his empty bottle. "Come on. We better get the grill going before the girls decide to slice all that good steak up and make something fancy with it."

They went down a long hall to the kitchen, where a dozen thick New York strip steaks were already marinating in a shallow metal pan. Working with an ease that showed he knew his way around, Danford opened the big restaurant-style refrigerator and got out a dozen shucked ears of sweet corn. He set a tall metal pot on the stove, poured in a gallon of milk, and then added water until it was half full.

"Here's something half them snobs in chef's hats don't know about sweet corn," Danford said. "It don't taste right unless you cook it in milk. Course, you've got to watch it any time you boil milk. Get it a touch too hot and it'll skim up faster than you can say boo."

Chance nodded. Boiling corn in milk was the way his mother had always done it as well.

"Want to watch this while I go check on the grill?"

Chance gave the tall cooking pot a stir and then turned on his heel, taking in a full spectrum of copper-bottomed pans hanging over the stove, baskets full of fresh onions and apples, and a number of decorating details that he'd never seen before in a kitchen, outside of the magazines Cindy was always reading. Five minutes later, Danford was back in the kitchen, lowering the corn, in a cooking basket, into the simmering milk.

"All right," the host grinned, picking up the tray of steaks. "It's caveman time. Want to get the door?"

Danford opened the huge stainless-steel grill just the way he was, in blue jeans and a cotton work shirt, no apron and no cooking mitts. He didn't seem to notice the shimmering wall of heat that enveloped him as he worked.

"I got this rig from a fella that makes 'em one at a time over in Kansas," Danford said. "It's a charcoal grill. That propane, there, is just to start it—gets the coals ready in no time, and it don't leave a taste like lighter fluid can. And the grill's on a moveable rack, see? You can sear the steaks down low, close to the heat like this, and then, when you're done doing that, you can raise it up a few inches with this crank, here, and finish the cooking over low heat."

As he spoke, Angela came out of the house with the housekeeper and began setting a long glass-topped patio table large enough to accommodate twelve. Danny and the farmhand, both freshly scrubbed from their chores, began bringing cushions for the patio chairs out of a vine-covered storage shed next to the pool. Then Cindy and Dottie, changed out of their gardening outfits, walked out with a bowl of bean salad and two big pitchers of sweet tea.

That struck Chance as peculiar. No bell had been rung, no one had called anyone, and no instructions had been given. For all his laid-back appearance, Lyle Danford apparently ran his household according to a strict schedule, one that everyone knew and followed to the letter.

Almost everyone.

The kids were bringing out potatoes and sweet corn as Danford forked steaks off the grill, layering them onto a serving platter. He glanced around the patio and scowled.

"Where's Duane?"

"He ran into town to get some parts for his bike," Danny replied. "Said he'd be right back."

"He still got that rice-burner?" Danford squinted. "Thought I told him to sell it. If he don't, I'm gonna back the truck over it, next time I see it. How long ago'd he leave?"

Danny checked his watch.

"Uhm—about three hours."

Danford took the last steak off the grill and shook his head.

"Well, we ain't waiting for him," he said. "We've got guests, and even if we didn't, I'm not about to sit around waiting for that boy to grace us with an appearance."

He took a breath and smiled at Chance and Cindy.

"Hope you came hungry," Danford said, game face back on. He nodded at the table. "Sit wherever it suits you."

The housekeeper and farmhand accepted their plates and then excused themselves, receding back into the house. Everyone else took their places around the patio table.

Lyle grinned as he picked up a knife and fork.

"Uhm—Chance," Dottie said, quickly, "would you mind leading us in grace?"

Lyle put his knife and fork back down.

"Sure." Chance smiled. He bowed his head and prayed, "Father, we thank you for the way you take care of us. We thank you for the grace you showed in the sacrifice of your Son, and the faithfulness you show each day in attending to our every need. Please bless this food with which you've provided us, and this family that is so generous to share it. Please help all we do this day to glorify your name. In Jesus' name we pray."

"Aye-me—" Lyle began to say, but it was drowned out by the rattling whine of a road-racing motorcycle coming down the drive.

"Well, there's the blister," the host said, shaking his head. "Always shows up after the work's done."

The families had almost finished their salads when the Danfords' younger son came strolling in from the conservatory.

Chance and Cindy couldn't help but steal a look at one another.

Over the years, they'd gotten used to seeing Danford's kids dressed so squeaky-clean that they might have been made up for a JCPenney catalog shoot. Angela and Danny still were.

But this one looked as if he'd just stepped out of a grunge video.

His hair was spiked, frosted blond, with streaks of green and blue throughout. He had five earrings in his left ear, three in his right, one through his eyebrow, and a green frosted "love patch" of beard down the center of his chin. His baggy knee-length cargo shorts rode low, showing the plaid waistband of a pair of boxers, and his open plaid shirt showed a ripped gray CBGB T-shirt underneath. His boots looked like something a logger might wear, and when he walked, their metal cleats rang against the stone of the patio.

"Hey." Duane smiled. He had a silver stud in the center of his tongue. He kept his left hand stuck in his pocket and held out the right. Chance saw a red-eyed silver skull ring on Duane's ring finger and the number "88" tattooed onto the center two knuckles.

"How's it goin'?" Duane asked. "Remember me? I'm Dew."

"He's Duane," Danford muttered. "Can't be bothered to use both syllables."

"Good to see you again," Chance said, shaking the young man's hand. "You know my wife, Cindy?"

"Ma'am." The teenager nodded and shook hands with her—an odd southern courtesy, coming from a kid with a dog collar around his neck. He kept his eyes on the young couple. "May I join you folks?"

"Please do." Chance smiled at the young man. Despite his odd appearance, there was something about Duane that invited warmth.

As soon as Duane had shown up, Lyle Danford had settled into a visible funk. But his son seemed not to notice—or not to care.

Duane sat next to Chance and immediately began to talk with him about the racing season and how it had gone so far. His memory was impressive—he could recall, with detail, a pit stop in which a lug nut had jammed in an air wrench a month earlier. And his grasp of racecar tuning was more than evident.

"What kind of power-steering ratio," he asked, "is Andy setting you up with for Pocono?"

Chance looked up, surprised at the question.

"We were just talking about that this morning. It was the one thing we hadn't decided. I'm going high-middle. About seventeen to one."

"That's smart racin'." Duane nodded, forking a piece of steak. "Some of the old school think you set up for Pocono like a short track. And hey, you can get away with that in those shorter Busch races, but that second turn's a bear in those 500-milers. Third too, flat as it is."

"Well, thank you, the voice of experience," Lyle grumbled. It was obvious which member of the "old school" Duane had been referring to.

The teenager ignored the comment and went on about Chance's earlier career, right down to some of his sprint wins.

That was the way the meal went, and it made Chance more than mildly uncomfortable. His host, and the senior driver in Robert Vintner Racing's two-car operation, seemed considerably disgruntled, but Danford's teenage son prattled on as if he didn't notice it at all. Chance tried to include Duane's father in the conversation, but all he got were monosyllabic grunts. And despite the urban-grunge exterior, Duane seemed like a genuine, likable kid—courteous, attentive, and enthusiastic about having Chance and Cindy as guests.

Dessert was a homemade key lime pie. Chance found himself wondering how Duane could eat with a piece of jewelry running through the middle of his tongue. Then Angela and the housekeeper began to clear the dishes and Danford motioned to Chance.

"I'm stuffed," he said. "Care for a walk?"

"Sounds good."

They left the walled patio by a side gate and, skirting a pool large enough that it could have done justice to a country club, the two men walked side by side down a stone path and across the concrete drive to the barn. As soon as Danford slid the door open, he was greeted by a chorus of deep whinnies.

The barn's concrete center walkway was covered by thick rubber matting and flanked on either side by oaken stalls with polished brass fittings. A dozen horses looked out at them, ears turned their way.

"Wow," Chance said. "You've got yourself a regular herd."

"Oh, they ain't all ours," Danford said. "Some belong to little friends of Angela's—girls who could save up enough for a schooling horse, but not enough to board it. It helps them out and it gives Angie somebody to ride with."

He pointed to a gray-white horse with a delicate neck and wide nostrils.

"That one there's an Arabian," he said. "They've got one less vertebra than regular horses. You know that?"

"I didn't," Chance said, shaking his head. "We never kept livestock, growing up. Didn't have anybody to watch it on the weekends while we were off racing."

Danford nodded.

"Do you ride?" Chance asked him.

"Sure." Danford grinned. "This big, jet-black hombre down here. Midnight. He's mine."

They went to the stall and Chance looked up at the tall horse.

"Wow," he said. "He's huge."

"He's a thoroughbred," Danford explained. "Most of the horses that Angela and her friends ride are Morgans or quarterhorses, bred for maneuvering. This big, bad boy is made to cover distance."

Reaching into his pocket, he took out a red-and-white Starbrite mint, unwrapped it, and held it out to the horse, which nickered warmly and lifted the candy delicately off LD's open palm. It began crunching loudly.

"Don't tell Angela that I do that." Danford smiled. "She'd be out here with a toothbrush."

Chance laughed.

"So," Danford asked, keeping his face turned away, toward the horse. "What do you think of Duane?"

"He's a smart kid," Chance said. "Good conversationalist."

The horse stopped crunching and nudged Danford's arm with its forehead.

"If you ain't his old man, he is," Danford said, gently pushing the horse's head back. "Now . . . what do you really think of Duane?"

Chance patted the thoroughbred on its broad, flat cheek. "Well, he's different from his brother and sister."

"Man. Ain't that the truth."

Chance scratched the horse, waiting for Danford to say more.

"That junk in his ear and on his face?" Danford asked. "Started with one earring. Itty-bitty gold hoop. Showed up at breakfast one morning with it stuck in his left ear. Naturally, I was none too happy, but I said, 'Well, at least it's the left ear.' You know what they say—left is right and right is wrong. And the very next day, I come down to breakfast and now he's got this little fake diamond stuck through his right ear. And he kept adding more. Just to irk me, you know? When I saw the tongue, Dottie about had to sit on me. So finally I said I wasn't paying for him to do any more of that stuff to himself. I never gave any of these kids an allowance, but I paid them all for chores. I stopped that with him . . . cut him right off."

Chance pursed his lips, gazing down at his boots. He looked back up at Danford.

"I remember looking at pictures of you in the racing magazines when I was growing up," Chance said. "You had longer hair then—down over your ears and collar. What'd your father think of that?"

"Daddy?" Danford snorted. "He about had a fit. I used to sleep with one eye open, afraid he was gonna come in with a pair of sheep shears and shave me bald."

"And you outgrew that," Chance said. "Duane will outgrow this, too, LD. He'll pull the earrings out someday; I'd bet on it. And that stuff in his hair can be gone in one haircut."

"Yeah? What about the tattoo?"

"They can take 'em off with lasers now."

"I suppose," Danford agreed. He removed his ball cap and ran his hand back through his hair. "But what irks me worse is that number ain't any car I ever drove. Eighty-eight . . ."

"Uhm, LD . . . ," Chance said. He looked up at the beamwork of the barn, down the length of the empty aisle.

"Yeah?"

"That number . . . it's not eighty-eight. It's eight-eight."

Danford scowled.

"What's the difference?"

"Eight stands for 'H'—eighth letter of the alphabet. Eight and eight is 'H' and 'H'—Heil Hitler."

"What?" Even in the dim light of the barn, Chance could see Danford's face redden.

"It's a skinhead code," Chance explained. "Cindy and I saw that on TV last month—*20/20*, I think. Maybe *Dateline*."

Danford squeezed the top of the stall door as if he was trying to leave dents.

"I'll kill him."

"Now LD—"

Danford slapped the stall door and the horse stepped back, ears up, eyes wide.

"Don't 'now LD' me. You sound like Dottie. Next thing I know, you'll be tellin' me to put the little runt into 'time out.' My uncle—my daddy's older brother—he died in France, fighting the Nazis. And now my kid's got that bull . . . that stuff on his hands."

"I seriously doubt he's a Nazi," Chance said.

"Then what's this all about?"

Chance shook his head.

"I'm no shrink," he said. "But it seems to me that, usually, when a kid acts out like this, he doesn't like the way he's treated. So he tries to make sure his folks don't like the way he treats them."

Danford grunted in disgust. "Look around you, man," he said. "Did you have these kinds of things, growing up?"

"Not hardly."

"Neither did I. Heck. Neither did anybody. I mean, for Pete's sake, Disney World don't even look like this place. Now you tell me what that boy's lacking."

Chance said nothing.

Danford slapped his hand against the wood of the stall again and kept it there.

"You see that Bandolero car," he asked, "in the garage today?"

"Yeah," Chance said. "Danny's?"

Bandolero was a student series for teens and others learning to race. It hadn't been around when Lyle Danford was coming up; Chance either. But if Danford had been trying to show Danny the ropes, Bandolero would have been one way to do it.

"Nope," Danford said, his voice softening. "It's Duane's. I gave it to him three years ago, when he was fourteen."

Chance nodded, listening.

"And when Duane got behind the wheel of that sucker?" Danford smiled a tight-lipped smile. "That boy was like lightning in a bottle. This ain't just the proud poppa talking. I'm serious. I brought that car home and he practiced with it for a week, and then it took him all of three races to figure out exactly how things worked. After that, if they was havin' a Bandolero race and that kid of mine showed up, they might as well just give him the trophy up front and save everybody else the gas and the trouble. He was that good. And I hardly showed him squat, Boomer. He was a natural. Know what I mean?"

Chance nodded.

"What am I saying?" Danford shook his head. "Of course you know. But as soon as he turned sixteen and started driving somewhere other than on a racetrack, all of a sudden Duane didn't have time for the Bandolero car."

He held his hand out to the horse, calming it.

"I don't know," Danford grumbled. "Maybe it was not having Danny around the house to set an example. He started college, Duane stopped racing, and the next thing you know, I got an episode of *The Osbournes* happening right here in my house."

"Kids go through phases," Chance offered.

Danford shook his head. "It's more than that," he said. "Remember I told you I stopped giving him money? Well, about a month later, he comes home with that motorbike of his: brand-new, top-of-the-line. And when I asked him how he got it, he tells me he got a job. But I never seen a pay stub, never heard about where he's working. . . . And if he does have a job, it's got the strangest hours I ever heard of. Besides, who pays a kid enough to pay cash money for a motorcycle in a month? Somebody did, because I sneaked a look at his title, and it's full boat—no lien."

Chance whistled, despite himself.

"It gets worse," Danford said. "Mother's Day weekend, there's no race, right? So I'm home on a Saturday, for a change. And I go into his room to wake him up so we can go shop for something for his momma, and he's all crashed out on the bed with all his clothes on. Not asleep—he was out. Four sheets to the wind. And he smells like a bar, like cigarettes and stale beer and stuff, and that ticks me off enough, but then I noticed something. Right here . . ."

Danford touched the crook of his left arm.

"He was black and blue," Danford said, his voice breaking. "And there was a little hole, like a pin prick, with dried blood right in the middle."

"Did you ask him about that after he woke up?"

"I did," Danford said. "He laughed at me. Said he poked his arm movin' rosebushes for his momma. Said I was a paranoid old man. And his momma backed him up—said she did have him workin' in the garden for her earlier in the week. But . . . well, I don't know."

"Whoa . . .," Chance said softly, pursing his lips.

"Man!" Danford slapped the wood, hard this time, the horse snorting and stepping back. "You see what I got here? I got Danny, who'd give his right arm to be able to drive a fast lap without wreckin', who's willing to bend over backwards to please, and he's got no talent for it. And then I got Duane, who could be absolutely spectacular if he could get his head out of that noise he calls music and his parties, but I don't even know if he's . . . I don't even know if he's going to live long enough to do that."

Danford smiled a crooked smile. "I remember when little Angela was born," he said. "And the doctor told me I had a little girl, and I thought, 'Oh, oh,' because I always heard that daughters was the way the Almighty punished us for the ways we acted when we was coming up. But Angela has never given me anything but peace. It's her brothers that keep me awake nights."

The two men stood silent for a moment and the horse nudged Danford tentatively with its head.

"Tell me something," Chance finally said. "Have you talked this over with your pastor?"

"My pastor?" Danford shook his head, thin-lipped. "I'm kind of between pastors."

"How far between?"

"I don't know. Like since I was nine or ten."

"I see."

Danford looked at Chance out of the corner of his eye. "What about you?"

"Me?"

Danford poked Chance in the shoulder with a callused finger. "All the time I was growing up," the older driver said, "all the Christians I ever saw were these pasty-faced guys in white shirts and ties with their collars sticking up, and all they ever wanted to do was tell me I was going to hell. It made my . . . well, it made me tired. And Dottie's tried to get me into a church as long as I've known her, only I figured wherever she was going to take me was more of the same. But you ain't like that. You're a Christian, sure, but you're a man. You can drive, you can shoot, you fight back, you got you a pretty little wife that looks like she stepped off the cover of a magazine."

"What about Brett Winslow?" Chance asked.

"Brett?" Danford scowled. "He's okay, I guess, but you know me. I leave right after the drivers' meetings—never stick around for chapel. Heck, I've never done anything with SCM except to give them a check at Christmastime and send Angela off on camping trips with the kids' group. How would it look if the first time I show up to really talk with Brett, I got this problem in tow with me?"

Chance laughed. "You'd look like 99.9 percent of the people who come through a pastor's door—or a church door—for the first time."

Danford put both hands in his pockets and stared at the barn's clean-swept floor. "Heck, I think I know what Brett'd tell me, anyhow," he grumbled. "He'd say Duane was gettin' in with the wrong crowd. But, Boomer, I can't be there twenty-four hours a day, steerin' him straight. You know that."

"Then put him in with the right crowd."

Danford looked up.

"The race team, LD," Chance said. "They can keep him busy every waking hour he's not in school. And that way he's with you and Dottie at the track, on weekends, not hunting trouble around Charlotte. Surely you've thought of that yourself."

Danford took a deep breath, opened his mouth to speak, stopped, and then started again. "Yeah," he said. "Surely I have. And surely I've thought of what people would say if they saw Lyle Danford's kid running around the pits with rainbow hair and all that junk stuck in his face. Fact is, I haven't even recommended Danny to Robert on account of if I got one boy on the team, people might be wondering why I didn't do something for the other, and I didn't want to have to answer that question."

Chance looked at LD, but said nothing.

"Yeah, I know," Danford said, giving the horse one last pat on the cheek. "That doesn't speak too highly of me as a father, does it? Worrying about people's opinions rather than my own flesh and blood."

"I imagine that the team's got a dress code that covers the hair color," Chance told him, ignoring the question. "And if it doesn't, I'm pretty sure Robert would be happy to write one; same thing with the jewelry. And to cut down on any possible friction, why don't we do this—why don't I talk to Robert and ask him to put Duane on my team? We could probably have him trained and traveling with us by the time we go to Loudon."

The two men turned to leave the barn. Then Danford paused, looking Chance in the eyes. "That's good of you, Boomer. I'll owe you."

"It's no big deal," Chance said. "But you can repay me by doing what you were thinking about. Put Danny on your team."

"Fair enough."

They walked out into the sun.

"And LD?"

"Yeah?"

Chance put a hand on the older man's shoulder as they walked. "Do talk to Brett about all this. He's the chaplain, man. I'm sure he's better at this stuff than I am."

Chance and Cindy got home early that evening, while the sun was still low in the sky. Stopping Cindy's SUV at the foot of the driveway, Chance just sat for a moment and looked at his house in the slanting, yellow sunlight.

"What are you doing?" Cindy asked.

"I don't know," Chance said. "When I left here this morning it looked . . . bigger."

Unbuckling her seat belt, Cindy laughed and kissed her husband on the cheek.

"What are you going to do next, racecar boy? Covet Lyle Danford's wife?"

Chance turned her way and she kissed him right on the lips.

"Don't be foolish," Cindy told him softly. "I love my house. It's more than I ever dreamed of. I sat down with you and the architect. I designed and decorated every single room myself. You, Chance Reynolds, are a wonderful husband and a great provider."

"Hmmm," he said as she kissed him again. "I'd better park this. You feeling sleepy?"

"Later I will," Cindy teased. "Right now, I want you to buy me a sunset."

"A sunset?"

"Yep." She pointed toward the water. "From our boat. In the middle of the lake."

"Okay," Chance agreed. "One sunset. Coming up."

Ten minutes later, with Cindy curled up next to him, Chance was backing his Four Winns speedboat away from the canopied boat hoist. The sleek fiberglass boat was equipped with a Mercruiser V-8, capable of putting it up on plane in the blink of an eye. But Chance didn't do more than barely crack the throttle.

Partly that was out of courtesy to the neighbors. But mostly that was because he didn't want to break the mood, the soft, warm, unspoken communication between him and his wife.

They came about in the center of the hundred-acre lake. Chance cut the engine and moved forward to toss out an anchor. He moved back and the young couple settled onto the sofa-like seats in the rear of the boat, Cindy curling up in Chance's arms.

"Hey, there," she whispered huskily. "Wanna play 'Love Boat'?"

"Cindy . . ." Chance sat up. "The sun's not even down yet!"

"Okay," she said, putting his arm back around her. "We'll wait."

The sun touched the tops of the trees on the western shore, and Chance silently urged it to sink faster.

"I love my life, Chance," Cindy whispered.

"Do you?"

"Oh, yes." She nestled closer. "It's perfect. Totally perfect."

Tree branches crisscrossed the red face of the sun.

"I saw the doctor this morning," Cindy said.

Chance turned her face toward him.

"You said you were fine. . . ."

"I was. I am. And now I'm better than fine."

He searched her face, golden in the last light of day.

"How can you be better than fine?"

"When there's two of you."

Chance blinked.

"Two? You mean . . ."

"You'd better believe it," Cindy said, putting his hand atop her flat stomach and kissing him on the cheek. "You, driver, are going to be a daddy."

CHAPTER 10

Pocono Raceway—Long Pond, Pennsylvania

Jake Crockett stood scrutinizing the new coffeemaker that had shown up in the NASCAR transporter just that week, trying to find a place to pour in the water. Setting the pot down, the balding, bespectacled man tapped at the top of the black plastic and stainless steel machine, his ample belly bumping up against the countertop. He took a folding Buck knife out of his pants pocket and tried working the blade into one of the seams of the machine.

Nothing.

The old machine had been easy—a slide-in cup where you put the filter and the coffee, a little lid on top with a knob in the center that you lifted off so you could pour the water in, and one button to run the whole deal. Simple. This new contraption had one place to make coffee, another place to make espresso, a spigot for hot water, and a little black-tipped metal tube coming out of the side that looked suspiciously like something from the dentist's office. He tried lifting the machine up to check out the bottom. It wouldn't budge.

Mystified, Crockett reached around behind the coffeemaker. A thin metal pipe ran down the back and disappeared into the countertop.

"Well, I'll be smoked," he said aloud. "The son of a gun is hardwired."

Pouring the water back into a compact, bar-size sink, Crockett set the pot on the largest burner, found one of those little red buttons with "I/O" printed on it, wondered when it was that some genius had decided that "Off" and "On" were too simple, and pushed the button.

In seconds, black liquid began to trickle into the pot. Crockett bent forward and gave it a sniff.

Coffee. At least it smelled like coffee.

He looked at the food trays set out over the rest of the countertop. Bear claws. Doughnuts. Little tubs of yogurt with fruit on the bottom.

Patting absentmindedly at his belly, Crockett selected an apple, polished it against his pants leg, and scowled at the shiny red fruit.

His cell phone rang.

He looked at the plain gold Seiko on his wrist. It was five minutes shy of seven in the morning. The first Nextel Cup practice wouldn't be starting for another five hours. Qualifying wouldn't open for another nine.

"Wiley," he yelled through the open door at the front of the trailer. "When we get back to Daytona, you get me a different cell phone number, you hear me?"

Crockett pulled the little silver phone off his belt, flipped it open, and peered through the lower half of his bifocals at the incoming number. It was a "704" area code. A Charlotte number. Either that or a Charlotte cell phone.

Stabbing at the green button with his thumb, the president of NASCAR lifted the phone to his ear and rumbled, "Crockett," his gravelly voice one octave deeper than bass.

"Hey, there, JC!" The familiar voice rang tinnily from the speaker. "It's Danford. How you doin', man?"

"I'm in a meeting, Lyle," Crockett said, eyeing the apple.

"You're a lying sack, Jake." Danford laughed. "You're raidin' the snack bar, and you know it. Come on out to the back of the hauler. I got something for you."

"Got what?" Crockett asked suspiciously.

"Oh, for Pete's sake, Jake. Come on back and see."

The phone went dead.

Scowling, Crockett snapped the phone back into its holster and walked toward the sliding, deeply tinted double glass doors at the back of the NASCAR transporter.

Beep.

Beep.

Beep.

"What the . . . ?"

Crockett shifted the apple to his left hand and slid open the hauler door.

BEEP.

BEEP.

BEEP.

It was a truck. One of those pickup-size dump trucks that contractors use. Brand-new, by the looks of it. It was backing in a shallow arc toward the back end of the big transporter.

BEEP.

BEEP.

BEEP.

As Crockett watched, the bed of the truck tilted upward and a cascade of pink-orange metal ran jangling down onto the garage area tarmac. It flooded toward him and Crockett backed away, trying to slide the doors shut, but he couldn't—the stuff was already inside. He lifted a foot, shook it, and heard the plink of metal falling. A thousand profiles of Abraham Lincoln littered the pristine carpeting.

Pennies.

That's what they were.

Pennies.

The last of the coins came dripping out of the dump truck and the cab door opened. Lyle Danford got out, a Perkins Tools ball cap on his head, wearing jeans and a Ford Racing polo shirt, a clipboard in his hand, his cowboy boots crunching noisily in the foot-deep carpet of change as he slogged to the doors of the transporter.

"Mornin', JC." Danford smiled amiably.

"Are you nuts?" Crockett shouted. "What's this?"

"It's one million pennies," Danford said.

"Why?"

"Why?" Danford laughed. "Because one million pennies is $10,000, Jake. What's the matter? You miss that day in school?"

"Ten thousand . . . ," Crockett muttered.

"I'm paying my fine," Danford told him. "In person. No team check. Just like you told me."

Danford turned the clipboard around, holding it out.

"Sign here."

People were walking out of transporters and garage stalls all over the area, craning their necks to see what was going on. A few were already laughing. Two photographers in the ubiquitous khaki vests were edging closer and snapping pictures. A TV crew was quickly trotting their way from the media center.

"You idiot," Crockett grumbled, ignoring the proffered clipboard. "What the heck am I supposed to do with one million pennies?"

Danford made a show of thinking the question over.

"Well," he finally said, "you could do what I'm thinking. Or you can buy yourself a piggy bank. Better make it a big one."

"Welcome to pit lane at Pocono, where the forecast is blue sky, clear lakes, fresh pines, and, this weekend, NASCAR thunder."

Chance smiled for the camera and looked at the TV host. The guy had powder all over his face. Like a girl. Thicker than a girl. Like a Las Vegas showgirl. Chance could see it from three feet away. It looked ridiculous. Why was it you couldn't see that stuff on television?

"Our guest today is Chance Reynolds, driver of Robert Vintner Racing's number 43 E-World Broadband Ford Taurus, and number two and only 100 points off the lead in this season's Nextel Cup championship standings. And Chance, we understand that the leader in those standings, your Robert Vintner Racing teammate, Lyle Danford, made quite the splash at the NASCAR truck in the garage area this morning."

"Yeah." Chance laughed, getting in the mood for the sake of the cameras. "Old LD dropped a little change on Jake Crockett."

The camera light blinked off as videotape rolled and the host explained the obvious. Chance chafed in his firesuit, irritated at the fact that he'd had to put it on nearly two hours earlier than usual. But the pre-practice show ran for an hour, and there wouldn't be time to change after it; if he did, he'd miss part of the practice. If the car wasn't quick as it was, right off the truck, Andy would need as much track time as possible to dial it in.

The upside was that the embroidered shirts Perky brought to the track for him every weekend only showed one sponsor's name at a time, while the driving uniform bore logos for everything, from Goodyear tires and Foster Grant sunglasses to Coca Cola. And somewhere back at an ad agency in New York, or Los Angeles, or Detroit, people with stopwatches were watching this broadcast and clocking each "exposure"—keeping track, to the tenth of a second, of how long each sponsor's logo was on the screen.

Chance pushed his Ford Racing pit cap higher on his forehead and smiled as the little red camera light winked back on.

"And we'll get to the root of why Lyle Danford had to pay that fine in just a minute," the host said. "But first, Chance . . . Pocono is really the odd card in the Nextel Cup deck, wouldn't you agree?"

"I sure would," Chance said, glad that the discussion was back to racing. He launched into the discussion that the producer had prepped him on—a description of Pocono's unusual triangular track, followed by a simulated lap on a sponsor's computer game system. While a digitized racecar bobbed and weaved on a monitor in front of him, Chance kept up a patter, following along from the cheat-sheet he'd scrawled. Then he looked up and smiled as the director pointed at him.

"And that's a lap at Pocono," Chance told the camera. "Once you've done that, you've only got 199 to go, spring or summer, because both of the races here at Pocono are exactly 500 miles long. And after you're done, you can go home, put your feet up, and ask your friends if they got the license number of that eighteen-wheeler that hit you."

"And speaking of the truck that hit you," the host said with a grin, "when we come back, we are going to be talking to Chance Reynolds about this . . ."

The monitor showed video of LD's wounded racecar limping up the track and plowing into Chance at Michigan.

"No doubt an interesting week back at Robert Vintner Racing," the host said. "Is it civil war or peace pipe? We'll find out right after this."

Both men held their smiles until the camera light went off.

"Clear for ninety seconds," the unit producer said as the fill lights went down. A makeup girl came out and Chance waved her away.

"You're a natural at this, Chance," the host told him as the girl tucked a napkin around his shirt collar and touched up his forehead. "Good ad-libs. *Great* ad-libs. If you ever decide to hang up the driving gloves, you really ought to think seriously about looking into something like this."

"Well, thank you," Chance told him, cringing inwardly at the thought. "God willing, that won't be for quite some time, though."

Forty-nine hours later, Chance was hurtling down the short stretch for real: no game system this time. Cars jostled on either side of him, and the track ahead was a shifting mass of brightly colored spoilers.

He had qualified poorly—twenty-second out of the forty-three car field—but at least he had not been forced to use a provisional. Better still, Lyle Danford had qualified twenty-fifth and then come limping back into the garage area with a rod knocking loudly in his motor. That called for an engine change and, under NASCAR's one-engine rule, Danford had been shuffled back to the rear of the grid.

Coming out of the third turn for the first time, Chance got on the gas and realized that, despite the good speeds they'd posted during Happy Hour, he and his crew chief had guessed wrong on the gearing. He got a decent launch, but not nearly enough to catch up and run with the leaders. Then Pooch came on the radio and made his day.

"Inside," the spotter said. "Outside. Yellow's out. Race to the line. Clear low. Yellow's out—it's LD. He's smokin' bad. Yup—he blowed up."

"Pooch," Chance called back as he crossed under the flagman's stand. "Are you sure? Nothing he can't fix?"

"No way." Pooch chuckled. "His spotter's gettin' his ears melted. LD grenaded it. Almost lost it in the corner—he's oiled his tires. Now you just stay healthy and finish this."

CHAPTER 11

Mooresville, North Carolina

The fab shop erupted in applause as soon as Chance stepped in. Putting his two little fingers into the corners of his mouth, Andy Hofert let out a piercing low-country whistle and brought the room down to a dull roar. He stepped out where he could be seen by the whole race shop—nearly two hundred people, because the second shift had come in for this event as well.

"Last Sunday at Pocono," Andy told them, "we unloaded off the truck 52 points behind the gentleman in the dark blue racecar, and 227 points ahead of third."

Ragged cheers.

"But this young gun finished in fifth place last Sunday, and led a lap during green-flag pit stops to boot, while the aforementioned gentleman in the blue car completed the event . . . dead last."

More ragged cheers.

"That gave him 34 points for the effort, while Chance Reynolds . . ."

Whoops and applause.

". . . while Chance Reynolds received a total of 60 points for the day, and a 94-point lead when we loaded back up for the drive home."

A chant began: "Boomer, Boomer, Boomer, Boomer . . ."

"Gentlemen, I give you the driver of the number 53 Robert Vintner Ford and NASCAR's Nextel Cup Series points leader—Chance . . . Boomer . . . Reynolds."

Foot stomps joined the chanting.

Blushing red and wishing that he wasn't, Chance climbed up onto a mechanic's stool and raised his hands for silence. After a minute, he got a rough semblance of it.

"First of all, guys," Chance said, raising his voice so those in back could hear, "contrary to popular belief, I did not take the points lead in Pocono last Sunday."

Dead silence.

"You did."

Pandemonium broke out anew, and Chance held his hands up again. This time it took only thirty seconds to quiet the race team down.

"But guys, I want to remind you that this is June, not November," Chance said. "We've got a twenty-six-point lead— "

Cheers and a wolf whistle.

"But we still have twenty-one points races left to go. And two of those are road races, and we all know how I stink at those."

Everyone laughed.

"So it's not time to celebrate yet."

"Heck," said a bearded, gray-haired man standing at the fringe of the crowd. "I'm just happy I ain't workin' in the 35's shop this morning."

Laughter and catcalls.

"Okay," Chance said. "I can understand that."

More laughter.

"And I can understand getting pumped over this, because it's the first time in four years that we've had the points lead this far along in the season."

Still more cheers.

"But even more important, guys, is keeping the points lead."

The shop erupted again, and Chance realized that he was going to have to finish this talk in one breath if he was ever going to finish it at all.

"So dig down, build smart, give it everything you've got, and I guarantee you that I will do everything that I can to win races—and maybe even a road race! Let's get 'em!"

He climbed down off the table as the cheers began again, his face reddening all over again.

The reaction of his team couldn't touch what he'd heard in the motorhome on Sunday night.

He and Cindy had told his folks about the baby on Wednesday, as soon as they'd gotten to Pennsylvania, and that had put the elder Reynolds couple on cloud nine. But then, when Chance jumped ahead in the points race after Danford's bad luck, his parents had reacted as if it had happened as the result of sheer racing skill. He hadn't bothered to correct them. He'd just let them hug him and love on him.

The cheering died down. There was daylight streaming through an open door behind them, and when Chance turned, he saw it was Robert Vintner.

"Boomer," Vintner said, his face grave. "Can I see you out here?"

They weren't even out in the parking lot when Vintner stopped and put a hand on the driver's shoulder.

"Your momma called from Youngstown," the team owner told him. "They were taking the motorhome back to Chillicothe when your daddy started having chest pains. He's in the hospital, and he's awake and comfortable and all, but they think he might have had a heart attack."

"Hospital?" Chance reached into his pocket for his keys. "I've got to—"

"Sit tight," Vintner told him. "I've got a helicopter inbound for the shop right now, and they're prepping your jet at the airport."

CHAPTER 12

The helicopter wasn't one of the modern jet jobs that the teams usually used for airport shuttles from the racetrack. Those belonged to a charter company that traveled with the circuit, and they, like the team's second-unit transporters with the road-course cars, were all on their way out to California—to Sonoma, the next stop on the schedule.

So what the airport had sent instead was an older job, a genuine antique whirlybird with a derrick-like tail and a round, scratched, Plexiglas fishbowl of a cockpit. It shook just sitting on the ground, the passenger's seat was leaking stuffing, the seat belts were worn shiny, and the gray-whiskered guy at the controls was in a greasy pair of coveralls. He looked as if he should be turning a wrench on the aircraft rather than flying it.

Worse still, the next thing he did was confirm it.

"Lucky thing you boys called me when you did," he told Chance over the intercom as they rocked into the air. "I was just about to tear this sucker down."

"Why?" Chance asked. "Is it broken?"

"Broke?" The pilot laughed, pitching the cockpit forward as they gained speed. "Naw. It's just run out."

"Run out?"

"Due for an overhaul," the flier said as he banked west. "After ever so many flight hours, you gotta rebuild it."

"I see," Chance said. He looked at an ominous gap in the instrument panel where some gauge or another used to be. "Well, you're a real pilot, aren't you?"

"Real?" The pilot laughed. "Sure. Used to fly offshore hops to the drilling rigs off Loo-zee-anna back in the seventies . . . the first time the

Ay-rabs cut off the crude. Back when there was real money doing that. I barely get enough hours in every month to stay current anymore, but hey, this here run'll help."

Chance barely heard what the pilot said. He looked at his watch and his thoughts darted back to his family. Cindy was in her Expedition on the way to the airport. His mother had called her to tell her about Chance's dad, and Cindy had immediately jumped in the SUV and started driving. She'd phoned the race shop from the car, and Vintner had ordered the helicopter as soon as she'd told him the news.

Chance considered asking the pilot to step on it, then thought better of it. The old helicopter was not, as his regular pilot would have said, really an aircraft. It was a bunch of parts flying in formation.

They were about six miles out and could see the airport beacon when Chance glanced around, perplexed.

"Hey," he told the pilot over the headset intercom, "this isn't the way we came in before."

The pilot squinted in the harsh sunlight.

"Say what?"

"I haven't made a hop in from the shop in quite a while," Chance admitted, scanning the landscape and speaking more loudly, "but this isn't how we usually come."

The pilot spat something into a stained Styrofoam cup.

"Well, I don't see why not. It's the shortest. You said you was in a hurry. Ain't ya?"

Chance nodded. The pilot was crusty, but maybe he knew something the executive pilots did not.

They'd begun to angle in toward the airport when Chance spotted something else through the scratched and scarred Plexiglas. He blinked and looked again.

"You see those high lines," he said. "Don't you?"

The pilot squinted again.

"How's that?"

The power lines were very, very close.

"Wires," Chance said, pointing. "There!"

"Where?"

They actually missed the power line by inches with the skid tip on Chance's side. Chance could see that. But from the way the aircraft lurched, he knew right away that they had not done so on the left. Like an object hitting the end of a long, stretched bungee, the helicopter stopped abruptly, tilted, and then flipped sickeningly forward.

Most people would have screamed. Most people would have waved their arms or held their hands up, trying to fend off the crash.

Chance knew better than that. He didn't have a wheel to grab onto, so he hugged himself, tucked his head down into his shoulders as much as he could, and let out all his breath.

It looked as if they were still ten feet off the ground when he heard the rotors crack. Then all the noise in the world followed.

The next thing he knew was blackness.

CHAPTER 13

Charlotte, North Carolina

Cindy was peering down at him when he opened his eyes. A woman in a white coat was standing next to her. And on the other side of Cindy was Max Peters, the cardiac surgeon who traveled with RVR as team physician.

"I'm Doctor Farnia," the woman said, moving her finger so he could follow it with his eyes. "You're at Memorial Hospital."

"Yeah," Chance groaned. "I recognize it."

He'd wrecked hard at Charlotte before.

"Do you know what happened to you, sir?"

"Uh-huh. Helicopter crash."

The woman ticked something off on a chart.

"And do you know what day it is?"

"Monday," Chance told her. He pushed up on his elbows and turned to Cindy. "How's my dad?"

"Fine, by the sounds of it. They did an EKG and an echocardiogram, and they both came back normal. No sign of a heart attack."

"I had them fax me the test results and I concur," Max added.

Chance settled back onto his pillow.

"Praise God."

"No kidding."

"So what was it then?"

"Angina," Cindy said, smoothing his hair with her hand. "Sort of an early warning signal. They're keeping him on monitors overnight to make sure. Your mom said the doctor told him to take a month off, and your dad told the doctor to stuff it—no way was he going to miss seeing you race at Daytona. So the doctor said fine, he could go, as long as he let your mom do most of the driving down to Florida."

"Sounds like what I'd say," Max agreed, smiling.

"Good thing he was going to watch this week's race from home anyhow," Chance said as the white-coated woman passed a penlight in front of his eyes. The team didn't drive their own motorhomes out to the California or Phoenix races—they rented onsite, instead, from an outfit that supplied trailers to Hollywood productions.

Chance turned away from the penlight and looked at Max.

"How's the pilot?"

"He didn't make it, I'm afraid."

Chance sat silent, stunned. He was very bruised and scraped up—he could feel that. But everything seemed to be working, and nothing was in a cast. It looked as if he'd come through scot-free.

"Well, he's lucid," the doctor told Cindy, talking as if Chance weren't there. "And his pupils are dilating evenly. That's good. We'll want him here for observation overnight, though."

"Can I stay here with him?" Cindy asked.

"Sure." The woman smiled, Max patted Chance on the shoulder, and the two doctors left.

"Hawaii, Paris, the Bahamas . . . Memorial Hospital." Chance laughed. "Woo-hoo. I take you all the best places, don't I, girlfriend?"

"You do," Cindy said, climbing onto the bed next to him and kissing him on the forehead. "And you had me worried."

"Well, don't." Chance grinned, kissing her back. "I'm unbreakable."

Four days later, he was strapped into his racecar and building up speed on Infineon Raceway, the new name they'd given to the old Sears Point track. The car had been with the team for four years: every bit as long as Chance. With only two races a season on road courses, and with wrecks happening at only half the speed of an oval, the road-racing cars didn't get used up nearly as quickly as a speedway chassis.

Chance tossed the car into a right-hand turn and let it drift across the pavement. It was fun. And even though, of all the venues where NASCAR raced, Sears Point and Watkins Glen were the two where he was most likely to miss a top-twenty finish, Chance absolutely loved the challenge that a road course represented.

Chance still couldn't get over how he'd come through the helicopter crash with nothing but some bumps and bruises. The day after he'd left the hospital, he'd begun to see soft halos around objects—nothing major, but noticeable enough that he'd thought he might want to talk to Max about it.

Chance and Cindy had even flown up to visit his father, who was sitting up in bed when they got there and chafing for his doctors to decide on a drug and diet regimen so he could get out of the hospital and take the motorhome back to Chillicothe.

By the time Chance and Cindy had gotten home to North Carolina, the halos were no longer there, so Chance had decided that whatever had caused them was gone. He never had mentioned the problem to Max.

He glanced at the rearview mirror. Then he blinked and looked again. Something didn't seem right.

It wasn't the first time he'd felt that way. On the flight to California, Chance had seen bright red spots before his eyes as the airplane cabin had pressurized. But he hadn't thought anything of it. He knew blocked sinuses could have that effect.

Then they'd landed, and he had nearly walked into a coat rack in the airport, only seeing it at the last second.

He upshifted, and an image of Cindy jumped into his head. The California races were a travel marathon, so he'd asked her to sit the weekend out. She was at her parents' place, picking out nursery things with her mom.

Keeping the heel of his right foot on the gas pedal as he touched the brake with his toe, Chance stabbed the clutch with his left foot, upshifted again, and entered a turn. The red-and-white dragon's teeth marking the apex were there one moment—and gone the next.

Whoa.

That wasn't right at all. He turned his head as much as he could with the restraining straps, scanning the track ahead of him—there was this dark gray, foggy ball, just off center, in his right eye. He tried blinking it away. Nothing happened.

Chance keyed his radio.

"I'm coming in."

Andy was on the air in a heartbeat.

"What's up?"

Chance thumbed the mike button and thought for a moment. Everybody and their brother monitored these team frequencies.

"Meet me at the garage," he said.

He pulled into the garage area slower than usual, worried that he might clip a pedestrian, and drove the car straight into the team's stall, flipping off the main battery switch to kill the engine.

The window net came down from the outside.

"It sounded fine when you came in," Andy said.

"It is," Chance said, pulling off his helmet. "I'm not. I can't see."

"You what?"

"Get Max," Chance told him, tossing his gloves on the dash. "Hurry up. My eye's gone all screwy."

The team doctor was there quickly enough to help Chance out of the car. Standing in the garage, with the noise of air hammers and revving engines all around, Chance explained what had happened, and Max nodded.

"I've got a golf cart right here," the doctor shouted. "Get on. We're going to the infield care center."

Brett Winslow was waiting by the door as Max and Chance pulled up to the track medical center.

"Hey, Preacher." Chance grinned, putting up a good front. "You don't need to be here, man. I didn't even crash."

"No problem." The dapper chaplain smiled. "I was hanging out here anyhow. We were watching the Braves game on TV. What's cookin'?"

Chance dropped the smile and told him what he knew as they walked inside. A jumpsuited nurse helped Chance to an examination table, pulled down the top of his firesuit, and took his blood pressure and pulse. He felt something in his ear, brushed at it, and heard a voice say, "No worries, sir. I'm just taking your temperature."

Max bent low over Chance and peered into his left eye with a tiny bright light.

"Yuck," Chance said. "You had tacos for lunch."

"Shows what you know," Max replied. "I had tamales. Now the right."

The bright light moved to the other side and Chance saw a hugely enlarged image of Max's yellow-green iris. The gray spot was still there, hovering over everything.

Max turned and whispered something to another doctor, who took a look as well. He nodded.

"Okay," Max said to the nurse. "Let's get a cervical collar and back-board, and get him ready to transport."

"Transport?" Chance started to get up, but Max restrained him.

"Don't move around too much, Boomer," Max told him quietly. "You've got a torn retina."

It wasn't even a real operating room that they used, just a room with a big, bright, moveable light and a contoured vinyl chair, like a dentist's. Only this chair had a jig to immobilize his head, and instead of numbing Chance's teeth, the doctor, a young Asian guy with a long black pony-tail, put some drops in Chance's eye that made it impossible for him to move it.

"That's weird," Chance told him. "What is it?"

"There's a fancy name for it," the doctor said. "But basically, it's curare."

"Cure-are-ray?"

"Poison-arrow nerve inhibitor," the doctor said. "You know . . . blow-guns? The Amazon? Best paralysis agent known to medical science. Now I'm going to dilate your eye."

More drops went into Chance's eye and everything got very, very bright. The doctor turned the room lights down.

"Okay, Chance," Max said, leaning over the driver so he could see him. "What we're doing here isn't even really surgery. That is, there's no cutting involved. It's looking like you had some swelling from that helicopter crash, and it weakened the retina, on the back wall of your eye—weakened it so much that the normal movement of the eyeball in its orbit, plus possibly the Gs from the racecar, caused it to split and tear. The concern is that this tear could get bigger, so Doctor Niikura, here, is going to use a medical laser to make two extremely tiny burn spots on your retina at either end of the tear. It's a medical necessity. Without it, you can go completely blind in that eye."

"Burn spots?"

The Asian doctor leaned over him.

"You know how aircraft mechanics will drill holes at either end of a crack in a fuselage," he asked, "to stop the crack from spreading?"

"Sure. I've done that myself on my old Jeep's door panels."

"Well, this is basically the same principle."

"That I understand." Chance tried unsuccessfully to nod.

The doctor moved out of his field of vision, but kept talking.

"Dr. Peters, here, gave me a copy of your team treatment release, so we're okay on that end. You good to go? Any questions?"

"Uh . . . no. Fire away."

The doctor rolled a big, beige machine over to the chair and adjusted it until the head, terminating in a small dark glass dome, was directly over Chance's eye. The doctor stepped away.

"I'm over here at a control panel," the doctor told him. "We're looking at your retina on a video screen. The camera I'm using is calibrated so I can see the laser pulses with it. Okay. I've got your retina lined up."

"How does it look?" Chance asked.

"Like a torn retina," the doctor said. "Can you hold your breath for thirty seconds?"

Chance did as he was told, and the beige machine whined like a TV going on the fritz. After a second, it stopped.

"Okay, one more," the doctor said. "Take a breath. Hold it."

The unit whined again, and then the doctor was rolling it away. He came back and put more drops in Chance's eyes as a nurse undid the brace holding his head.

"These drops will reverse the effect of the dilation agent," Dr. Niikura explained. "Unfortunately, we don't have anything like that for the curare, so you'll just have to wait for that to wear off. Won't take more than an hour, but we'll keep you overnight, anyhow. It's SOP."

"That's it?" Chance asked.

"That's it," the doctor replied. "We're done here."

"Well, that was quick. I'm still in my firesuit."

"I'll go back to the track and get some clothes out of your motorhome for you," Brett said.

"Thanks, Preacher. I appreciate that."

Brett smiled—an oddly small smile—and nodded.

"So, Doc," Chance said, turning to look at the ponytailed doctor. "When can I get back in the car?"

"Oh. Well . . . you can't."

Chance started to protest, and then just shrugged.

"What the heck," he said. "We're at a road course. At least this way Robert can find himself an SCCA guy who knows how to make right turns. I wasn't looking for much in points from this anyhow, and neither is LD, so the standings shouldn't change. But I'll be ready for Daytona . . . won't I, Doc?"

The Asian doctor looked at Max, who looked at Brett. With eyeballs still immobilized by the curare, Chance had to turn his head to follow all the worried glances. Finally, Brett came over and took Chance's right hand with both of his.

"Boomer," he said. "You've got a torn retina, buddy. This thing they just did here has stopped it from tearing worse, but it didn't fix it, man. It's still torn."

"So when do we fix it?"

Chance turned his head to look up into Brett's eyes. He was surprised to see that the chaplain was tearing up.

"We don't," Brett said. "The injury you've got . . . well . . . there's no fix for it, Chance. Don't get me wrong; you'll still have plenty enough vision to drive on the street, read, do most anything. But racing? You're missing enough in that right eye to lose a whole Cup car on the track, man. You wouldn't want to drive that way."

Chance stared at his friend, disbelief etched on his face.

Brett swallowed, set his lips, nodded.

"This is it," he said finally. "You're done."

TURN TWO

CHAPTER 14

Charlotte, North Carolina

The music in the Zone Club was not so much heard as it was felt—deep, pounding bass producing a palpable thump in scarred tables and repainted walls. The entire room seemed to pulse with the drumbeat. Red strobe lights transformed faces into a series of bloodied still images, and a band played from a stage awash in theatrical fog.

To an outsider, the scene was total chaos, but to Duane Danford, the dance floor of the club was as familiar as his own room in his father's big Tudor house.

He found the guy he was looking for, the drummer from the band playing the second set. No wave; no nod. Duane simply looked at the dreadlocked drummer, made eye contact, and headed toward the restrooms.

Duane passed the Men's, kept going down the corridor, and pushed open the door to the Ladies'. The two girls at the washbasins didn't object; they just looked at one another and then left. And the single occupant of a stall flushed and departed immediately.

No other women came in—Duane had left a guy at the door to prevent that—and a few minutes later the drummer entered, nodded a greeting, checked all the stalls, and flipped a half-burned cigarette into the last toilet bowl.

"Let's do this quick," the drummer suggested. "Gig starts in twenty minutes."

"Hey." Duane shrugged. "I ain't in here to fix my lipstick."

He pulled a red bandanna-style handkerchief out of his back pocket and unfolded it on the counter of the sink. In it were a dozen half-inch pillows of white powder.

"How many you want?" Duane asked.

The drummer grinned.

"How 'bout a taste?"

Duane shook his head.

"You want free samples," he said, "go to Baskin-Robbins. You had a taste last Friday. Now, are you buying or are you blowing smoke?"

"Man! Lighten up, dude," the drummer tsked. "I'm buyin'. You know that. Gimme five. How much is that?"

"Same as last time," Duane told him. "Five bucks."

The drummer nodded and pulled a leather-covered money clip out of his shirt pocket, peeling off five $100 bills. He hesitated a moment and added another hundred.

"Make it six," he said. "I got a cousin comin' to visit."

"Southern hospitality," Duane said, and he handed the drummer six of the tight white plastic pillows.

The drummer left and a woman came in, a pretty redhead with a tiger tattooed on her thigh.

"Hey, Sly." Duane smiled.

"Hey, Dew." She smiled back. "Got six left?"

"Just barely," Duane told her. He handed her six of the little packages, took a dozen fifties in return, and the girl smiled and headed into one of the stalls.

Duane shrugged and left, stopping outside the door to hand one last pillow to his protection, a local high school fullback. He walked back onto the dance floor and stood pointedly in front of one of the band's speakers, music blasting him like the wind from a hurricane. In seconds he was joined by a guy in his twenties, wearing a black leather vest over his bare chest. The other man's head was shaved, and he had three blue tears tattooed onto his right cheek. "Burbank" was the only name Duane had for him; even though they'd been in contact for nearly a year now, Duane didn't know whether that was his first name, his last, or just the name of the place he'd blown in from.

"What's the word?" Burbank shouted the question—they had no fear of being overheard in the torrent of noise.

"I'm tapped," Duane yelled back. "You got more?"

"Meth?" The skinhead shook his head emphatically. "Cupboard's bare, dude."

"Man!" Duane kicked the floor in disgust. A crowd this size was usually good for three or four thousand in buys. He'd taken in just $1,200.

Less his costs, that came to just $600. Chump change, and Friday was the big night for this sort of thing.

"Make it up to you," Duane's supplier yelled. "Come on."

They walked down the corridor past the restrooms, the noise of the club diminishing behind them, until they got to a fire exit. Burbank hit the panic bar, and an alarm began ringing. They stepped out into an alley and the alarm stopped as the door clicked shut. Through the brick walls of the building, the ghost of the bass still thumped.

"What do you have?" Duane asked.

"Not here," Burbank said. "Let's walk."

They went down the alley, around a corner, and across the brick-paved street into a park. The path crossed a small footbridge and stopped by the side of a small pond, where Burbank looked around, nodded, and said, "Dew-man. How'd you like to make a move up?"

Duane looked at him, head cocked to one side.

"What sort of move?"

"The action you have," the other man said, scuffing the ground with the toe of his motorcycle boot, "that's okay for pocket change; buy you a bike and some threads and all. But what would you think about an opportunity to make some seriously thick green?"

"How thick?"

"Money-like-your-old-man-makes thick."

The seventeen-year-old laughed.

"Right," he said. "How am I going to do that?"

Burbank moved closer.

"Right now, you're the corner store," he said, his voice low. "What would you think about becoming the local distributor?"

"Distributor? You mean quantities?"

Burbank nodded, the tattooed teardrops seeming to move in the dim light.

"Sure."

Duane shook his head.

"Not my style," he said. "I like being the contact for people."

"Understood," Burbank said, moving closer still. "If you're the man with the magic, you do make friends, don't you? And you can still do that if you want. You just help a few bros to do the same."

"Why me?" Duane asked. He moved back a step. "Aren't there enough people selling crank by the bagful?"

"I ain't talking meth." Burbank laughed. "I'm talking skag."

"Skag?"

"Skag, smack, snow, eight, H . . ."

"I know what it is," Duane said. "Jeesh. I don't know, man. I don't even deal heroin, let alone move it in bulk."

"Opportunity knocks."

"Why me?"

Burbank motioned with his hand at the skyline.

"Because we can bring this stuff into Miami, but we got to move it places after that—Chicago, Detroit . . . and right here in C-town."

"And?"

"And that poses a challenge. Things are getting tighter every day," the skinhead said. "But I hear that you got yourself a gig that goes places like that."

Duane scowled.

"What? The race team?"

"Exactimundo."

The teenager shook his head and took another step back.

"I haven't even decided to do that yet."

"So," Burbank said, palms up. "Decide."

Duane shook his head again, thin-lipped.

"The guy that wanted me on his team is out injured."

"No matter," Burbank said matter-of-factly. "Just tell your dad's team owner you want the gig. You think he's gonna say no?"

"And I've got school in the fall," Duane added. "The team would be just a short gig for me this year, and I've already missed the only Florida run of the summer, down to Daytona."

"I work with very farsighted people," the man in the vest said, tapping Duane on the chest. "Get yourself in there, see how it works, and maybe we can get something happening for next year. You guys go to Florida in February, don't you?"

"Well, sure," Duane said, amazed that anyone would ask the question. "The season starts in Daytona. But that's school again—I'd be flying down with the old man, not riding with the hauler."

"So when do you get back there after that?"

"Same as this season—first week in July."

"Well, there you go." Burbank patted Duane on the shoulder. "Plan now, and do then. It'll be worth the wait. After all, you've got a whole semi to work with."

Duane laughed. "We'll need some room for the racecar."

"Oh, don't worry," Burbank agreed, grinning. "We won't leave the car behind."

"I'll think about it," Duane said.

"All I ask."

"And in the meantime," Duane said, "when can you get me another 200 grams of crank?"

"Wednesday," the skinhead said. "Meet me at the club."

The cop in the bushes a hundred yards away slowly lowered his directional dish microphone and stretched his leg. He was getting old for this line of work, just eighteen months away from retirement, now, and the ancient mortar wound, a souvenir from the week before the fall of Saigon, was acting up again. But the Ranger skills he'd learned in 'Nam—the tracking, trailing, and stealthy surveillance—were still useful, still paying dividends, decades later.

He waited until the subjects had left the park and then keyed the microphone on his tiny SWAT-style earpiece radio.

"You get all that?"

"It ain't live. It's Memorex," replied his partner in the van outside the Zone Club. "Who was that talking to Mr. Clean?"

"Don't know," the cop in the shrubbery said. "But we'll find out."

"Doesn't matter," said the one running the recording equipment. "We got us a sale on Wednesday. Felony quantity of methamphetamine, intent to deliver, intent to distribute. I take it we'll be there?"

"Only to observe," said the senior partner in the shrubbery, rubbing his leg. "Not to bust. Sounds to me like if we wait—if we're really, really patient—we'll get us a much bigger fish to fry."

CHAPTER 15

Lake Concord, North Carolina

Cindy dabbed the teabag with her spoon, bouncing it up and down in the cup of hot water, squinting at the cup. She'd never been a coffee drinker, just tea, but she'd switched to herbal as soon as she'd learned she was pregnant. But the herbal teas never turned the water all that dark—it looked like it used to look back in the old days, when Chance was still racing ARCA, and Cindy had reused teabags to stretch the grocery money.

The whine of a powerboat came faintly through the closed kitchen windows, and she looked up.

Boats on the lake were no rarity. Most of the families on Lake Concord were with the Cup series, and they all had the usual high-horsepower toys: powerboats, fishing boats, ski-boats, Jet Skis.

But this was Thursday, and the lake was usually deserted on Thursday—everyone gone to the track, which, this week, was . . .

Cindy glanced at the calendar.

. . . Michigan. They were back at Michigan again.

She spooned out the teabag, picked up the cup, and walked out to the deck, where the roar of the powerboat was much louder. Cindy went to the deck's edge and scanned the lake.

Chance.

She should have known it.

He had a couple of orange rubber buoys out on the water, and as Cindy watched, he ran toward them full throttle, boat banked over in a tight turn, bow aimed at the narrow opening between the orange spheres. The boat passed through, and the buoy on the right-hand side skipped sideways as it bounced off the hull. Cindy saw her husband slap the wheel with his hand and turn around for another try.

Cindy closed her eyes, wiped them with the sleeve of her robe.

Her husband had been at this for a month. If he wasn't out running an obstacle course on the lake with their boat, he was changing lanes on empty stretches of interstate, trying to see how close he could get to the centerline reflectors without clicking one with a tire. He'd loaded a racing game on the computer and spent hours at a time driving simulated races with his left eye closed.

All were different ends to the same means—trying to see if he still just might have what it took to horse a 3,400-pound racecar around a track in the heat of competition.

And, in each case, the answer was "no."

Cindy shook her head slightly, lips working noiselessly, as the boat raced back toward the buoys, striking the same one again.

Max Peters had been awesome, just absolutely awesome, the way he'd taken charge after Chance's injury. The same day that they'd stabilized Chance's eye out in California, Max had been on the phone with colleagues all over the country, seeking the best ophthalmologists in the business. But trips to Harvard Medical Center, Mount Sinai in Toronto, and even the Mayo Clinic had all resulted in the same diagnosis: an irreparable retinal tear.

They'd even gone to Switzerland and France, seeking treatments not yet available in North America, but the news had been no better. Any breakthrough that might help Chance appeared to be several years away, and as Chance had told Cindy, "Racing isn't the kind of business where you can take several years off; not if you want to be competitive."

And while Chance had tried to be sweet about the injury, even joked that it gave them an excuse for a second honeymoon in Paris, Cindy knew him better than that. The European trip had been a torture of expectations and disappointments, and, behind his brave smile, Cindy knew that Chance was hiding a shattered heart.

The boat roared back. Once again, it hit the nearest orange buoy.

Face wet with tears, Cindy picked up her cup and turned to go back inside. It would only hurt Chance worse if he knew that she'd been watching.

". . . trechete hina katalabete."

". . . run that you may win."

Chance set the slim brown onion-skinned volume down on the patio table and looked out at the lake, resting his eyes.

He glanced back at the Greek New Testament, shaking his head slightly. Chance had gone to his Scripture for refuge after yet another morning of frustration, yet there in First Corinthians, in the Greek *koine* penned by the apostle Paul some two millenia earlier, was yet another reminder of the thing that he was no longer able to do.

He picked up the text and read a few more lines until he came to *"adokimos genomai."*

"I become disqualified."

Chance set the book back down on the smooth teak table.

It had been back when he was racing ARCA that a speaker at a Bible study had mentioned that many words and phrases in the New Testament had nuances that did not come through in English. The Greek word *eremos*, for instance, was translated in the New Testament as both "wilderness" and "desert." But perhaps the most telling translation was in Mark 1:35, where *eremos* became "a solitary place." To God, a desert was a place void, not of water, but of relationships.

And when the apostle Paul advised the church at Thessalonica to pray "without ceasing," he'd used a koine medical term for a chronic, repetitive condition, such as hiccups.

Chance had become intrigued by such things. He'd even gone so far as to take a text-and-video course on New Testament Greek. And then, when Cindy had agreed to marry him, he had begun studying Greek in earnest, determined that, if he was going to head a family, he was going to get as close as he could to the teachings of Christ.

Now Chance could read Greek fairly well. And it had always brought him comfort to read the Bible in the language the apostles wrote. At least it had until recently. These days even God's Word seemed a constant reminder that he was off the racetrack for good.

He rubbed his temples. That was the other thing. Ever since the eye injury, reading—especially reading Greek—gave him headaches. The docs had said that would pass with time, but it hadn't. Not yet.

The cordless phone rang and the caller ID lit up: "RVR, INC."

He picked it up.

"Chance Reynolds."

"Chance! Robert. How are you?"

Chance smiled, despite his splitting headache.

"I'm good," he said. It was partially true. "Yourself?"

"Great, great. Say, I was wondering if you and Cindy would mind if I stopped by."

"We'd love it. Have you had lunch?"

"No," Vintner protested. "Don't go to any trouble. Hey . . . tell me. Is anybody out on your lake today?"

"On it?"

"Yeah. You know. In a boat."

"You want to go boating?"

"No. Just take a look for me, would you?"

Chance walked to the edge of the deck and looked both ways.

"Not that I can see," he said. "Then again, it's Friday. Most of the folks here are drivers and crew chiefs. Only owners get to lay around until Saturday morning."

"Ouch. . . . Okay. Well, I'll see you in about an hour, okay?"

"Sure," Chance said, wondering why Vintner was asking about the lake. "Fine."

Chance set the phone down and walked into the kitchen, opening the big stainless-steel refrigerator and getting out a carton of orange juice. He poured a tumbler, took a packet of Goodie's Headache Powder from his pocket, and stirred the yellow-white powder into the drink, ditching the used packet under some crumpled paper towels in the waste can.

Chance drank the orange juice down, scowling at the aftertaste, and rinsed his glass. He thought about it a moment, then washed it, rinsed it again, dried it, and put it away. He had the time.

Rubbing the back of his neck, Chance went back to the deck and studied his New Testament a little longer. He was just about to set the book down when he heard a distant buzz, far across the lake. It sounded like a lawn mower being run at about half again the normal speed.

Chance walked down to his dock and searched for the source of the sound. In a moment he had it, high in the sky. It was a distant, slow-moving, delta wing. It looked a lot like a kite, only there was a person seated beneath it, just in front of the blurred disk of a rear-mounted propeller. And instead of wheels, the noisy contraption had two white pontoons.

As Chance watched, the aircraft banked and dipped low, coming in over the water, only ten feet above it. He could see the pilot clearly now—sunglasses, bristly white moustache, the porkpie hat clamped atop his head by the band of an avionics headset, the hat's brim upturned in the slipstream.

Chance felt the brush of fingertips against his hand and looked down. Cindy was standing next to him, her hair tied back with a ribbon, a smudge of dirt on the side of her nose, her gardening gloves held loosely in her other hand. She squinted against the summer sunlight at the strange little airplane.

"Is that Robert?"

Chance nodded and lightly brushed the dirt off her nose with his fingertip.

The little plane circled back around and dipped closer to the surface of the lake, its polystyrene floats skipping like a stone over the chop. Then the engine noise dropped and the airplane flared, making a rocky water landing, the craft dipping forward and then righting itself. It turned and headed toward them, its unmuffled motor whining more loudly again. Ten feet from the dock, Vintner cut the engine and tossed Chance a line.

Pulling the airplane against the bumpers on the side of his wooden dock, Chance held it steady as Vintner unbuckled his seat belt and clambered off.

That was all he had to do—step off. There was no getting out involved, because there was no cockpit. Except for a little nose cone that contained the rudder pedals, the pilot's seat was completely open to the elements.

"New toy?" Chance asked.

Vintner smiled broadly and nodded. A pilot certified to fly single-engines, multi-engines, even jets and helicopters, his fondness for all things aeronautical was legendary around NASCAR.

"I don't know, Robert," Chance said, fingering the purple wing fabric as his team owner fixed a painter to a cleat on the dock. "It seems to me that I've got lawn furniture built more solidly than this."

"That's why they call it an ultralight," Vintner said.

"You came all the way out from the airport in this?"

Vintner grinned and nodded.

"How did you take off?" Cindy asked, looking at the airplane's plastic pontoons.

"In-line skate wheels built into the floats," Vintner said.

"Your airplane's made out of roller-skate parts?" Cindy asked him.

"Just the landing gear."

"Well, that's cool," Chance told Vintner, looking the plane over. "I didn't even know that you had a seaplane rating."

"I don't," the older man said. "With an ultralight, you don't need one. You don't even need a pilot's license. The engine is just twenty-two horsepower. Made by Kohler."

"Kohler . . . ," Cindy mused. "Isn't that the company that makes sinks and toilets and bidets and such?"

Vintner just gave her a blank look.

"Well, how many water landings have you made with this thing?" Chance asked.

"Counting this one?"

"Uh-huh."

Vintner scowled and looked skyward.

"One."

"I thought so." Chance laughed. "Come on up to the house, man. We need to get you out of the sun."

Vintner's protests aside, Cindy and her housekeeper pulled together a quick lunch of cold ham sandwiches, leftover potato salad, and lemonade, and he finished every bit of it. Then Cindy and Mandie went back outside to work on Cindy's roses, and Chance and his team owner retired to the study.

The room was high-ceilinged, with a view of the lake through tall Palladian windows. Across the room from the massive mahogany desk, a sofa and two reclining chairs were arranged in a broad alcove that served as Chance's trophy room. Several bowls, golden loving cups, and cut-glass sculptures adorned the shelves, but the center was conspicuously empty.

"That space for what I think it is?" Robert asked.

"Yeah," Chance replied, not looking at it. "The Monday after I took the points lead, Cindy came in here and made room for the Nextel Cup. Didn't say anything about it—just did it. You know, to show her confidence in me. I guess I can move everything back now."

"Heck," Vintner said. "You're still only six hundred points back of second. People have made up worse deficits than that. Old LD has the lead, but it's down to less than a hundred and fifty points this week. He hasn't driven for beans since you've been gone."

"Nobody left to push him around the track." Chance grinned.

"Yeah," Vintner agreed. "Something like that."

The team owner walked over to the trophy that Chance had won for the night race at Daytona, flipped the switch, and smiled as the lights came on around the precious-metal model of the racetrack.

"So tell me," Vintner said, still looking at the trophy. "How is it?"

Chance took a breath, then checked himself. He'd never, ever lied to this man.

"It's hard, Robert," he admitted. "Very hard. I mean, I've been trying to stay busy, but everything I do reminds me of what's happened. I wax Cindy's SUV, and I think of the guys back at the body shop, waxing the car before they put the decals on. I hear a jet fly over, and I think of flying to the next race. I went into the shop last week and signed all that stuff that people had mailed in to get autographed—all the hats, and pictures, and die-casts, and whatnot. And I signed everything, but as I did, I kept asking myself, 'Why bother? They probably don't even want it anymore. I'm not . . . somebody.'"

"Yes, you are," Vintner said sharply. "And I've heard of one-eyed drivers before. We can get our own doctors to speak up for us, petition NASCAR—sue 'em if we have to."

Chance closed his eyes, grimaced, reopened his eyes.

"Oh, Robert," he said. "That is so, so tempting. And there's part of me that's saying, 'Heck, yes!' But the fact is, the Cup doctors are right. If I went out there less than a hundred percent and put somebody in the wall and hurt them or killed them? I'm selfish, but not that selfish. There's no way I could live with that."

Vintner worked his lips and put the trophy back on the shelf.

"Well, Boomer," he finally said, "this stinks."

"Don't I know it."

Vintner waited, obviously working up to something.

"I know it's not my business," he said. "But were you ready for something like this? Financially, I mean?"

"Ready?" Chance opened his hands, closed them, and sat down on the sofa. "I don't know how you can be. Don't get me wrong; Cindy and I have been careful with our money. But after my folks worked so hard to bring me up, get me going in the racing business, we both agreed that they should share in what we have, so we put together a fund, and I've been paying 20 percent of what I make into that. At first, my dad said, 'No way,' but he finally let us do it after I told him it was for Mom. And we built this house, and it's paid for and all, and we've got a time-share down in Daytona. . . . I guess I'll sell that now. Then there's some property we bought in the Caymans—so we could build a winter house? I might be able to hold onto that. But a lot of what we have is tied up—not 'liquid,' as the bean counters say. There's a couple of Ford dealerships I'm invested in. There's stocks and mutual funds. And while I can cash some of that in, now's not the best time. It was bought for long-term; we'd lose money."

Vintner nodded and sat on the other end of the sofa.

"And then we've got the lease on the jet," Chance continued. "I'm still on the hook for that, even though we aren't flying it."

"Let me help you sublease that," Vintner suggested.

"You know somebody?"

"I know a couple," he said, winking.

"Thanks," Chance said gratefully. "That would really help."

"You still taking your flying lessons?"

"No," Chance said. "Couldn't pass the medical. Not like this."

"Well, that stinks, too."

A distant hum began, and cool air began breathing down on them from the ceiling vents.

"Listen, Boomer," Vintner finally said, "I still have you on the roster as the driver of record for the 53."

Chance turned, brow furrowed. "You don't have to do that."

"It's best. It gives us a known name on the list, and your contract says we pay you, injured or not."

"I won't hold you to that."

Vintner squinted. "With a baby on the way? No, sir. There ain't no way we're leaving you high and dry."

"Well, I appreciate that."

They fell silent again. Both men knew that the driver's salary was only a small part of the typical driver's actual income—that winnings, appearance fees, promotional fees, licensing fees, and royalties made up the lion's share. But since they both knew it, neither mentioned it.

"How're you coming with your suit against the helicopter charter company?" Vintner asked.

"Well, their insurer is fighting it, of course. My lawyer says we've got an open-and-shut case—the pilot's blood alcohol was high enough that he wasn't legal to fly. He wasn't drunk, but he must've had a late night. Still, the insurer is trying to say I insisted on going in the way we did. We can't prove I didn't—no cockpit voice recorder on that old eggbeater. But even if I did, he was the pilot in command, so we'll win. It'll just take time. Maybe years."

The hum stopped and the air went still.

"Sue me," Vintner suggested.

"What?"

"Sue me. I was the one that called that charter service."

"Robert . . ." Chance stood, hands out to his sides. "They were the only service flying."

"But still, I called them," Vintner insisted. "So I'm responsible. But I can't just say that and pay you straight out; I got partners. If you sue us, though, I guarantee we won't fight it."

Chance looked down at Vintner. The older man had an untanned line on his forehead where the hat usually sat. It made Chance think of his father.

"And if you say another word about me suing you," Chance told him, "I guarantee that I will toss you out of my house."

"All right." Vintner nodded. "Then I've got another proposition."

Chance sat back down.

"Shoot," he said.

"Well, you know we've been playing musical chairs with drivers for your car. We even put Pooch in the car at Daytona and Loudon."

"I saw that," Chance said, glad to be talking about racing. "And he didn't do bad, from what I've read—top twenties both places."

"Yeah, but his wife is screamin' bloody murder about us puttin' him back in a car. She's not even that crazy about him spotting. He'll be fifty-eight years old, come November, and they got a house down in Florida that he's supposed to be fixing up."

"Uh-oh." Chance laughed.

"Uh-oh, indeed. You don't cross Trixie, not unless you want you a face shaped like a frying pan. So I got a couple of Truck guys that I'm gonna give some seat time to at the Bristol night race, and at Darlington, Richmond, New Hampshire, Dover, Martinsville, and Phoenix. I'm sendin' roses to Trixie to see if she'll let us run Pooch one more time at

Charlotte—he drove test for us there last month. But for the other four races—if you're positive you ain't comin' back . . ."

Chance put his hands up, and Vintner continued, "I'm thinkin' of bringing Gage Grissom up from Busch."

Chance thought a moment.

"That's smart," he finally said. "Gage has been running good, but he's far enough back in the points that you aren't robbing him of a title chance in the Busch Series. And that gives him a restrictor race at Talladega, a short track at the Rock, and intermediates at Atlanta and Homestead. Plus there's no Busch race the weekend of Talladega, so he can start with his head clear. And it still leaves him eligible next year to compete for Rookie of the Year. Yeah. I like it."

"My thoughts exactly," Vintner said.

"So what's your proposition?"

Vintner sat up.

"I want you to help Gage make the transition," he said.

"Well." Chance scowled. "Cup races are longer than Busch races, and the cars are faster, but I think Gage is ready."

"It's not just that," Vintner insisted. "Gage is just twenty-two years old—same as you were when you got into Cup, but you were an old twenty-two. He's not. He's single, a party guy, stays out late. He's rough-cut. And the sponsor side? Personal appearances and such? What he's done in Busch ain't half of what he'll see in Cup."

"You want me to nursemaid him?"

"I want you to mentor him," Vintner said. "Steer him past the land mines. Be his friend. I wasn't planning on bringing this kid up until I had a third Cup car, and we're at least two years away from that. I'd feel a lot better about it if I had somebody like you coaching him."

"Sure," Chance said without hesitation. "I'll do that."

"There's a good second salary in it for you."

Chance stood up and looked out the windows at the lake—at water, sky, and nothing.

"Forget it," he said. "You're already paying me a salary."

"Forget you," Vintner barked. "You could earn the first salary sittin' here fishin'. If you're doing a job for me, I'm paying what it's worth. You got that?"

"Fine," Chance said, offering Vintner his hand. "Come on. I'll help you wind up the rubber band on your airplane."

CHAPTER 16

Bristol Motor Speedway—Bristol, Tennessee
AUGUST

Trying the best he could to remain incognito behind a dark pair of metal-framed Foster Grants, Chance walked briskly through the tight and crowded infield of the second shortest track in the NASCAR Nextel Cup circuit. Walking to the side of RVR's number 53 hauler, where two crewmen were wrestling a tall green nitrogen bottle out of its compartment, Chance found who he was looking for.

He had to look twice to make sure he was right.

Duane Danford's hair was back to just two colors—brown with blond highlights. He'd cut his piercings down to a single diamond stud in his left ear. A pair of mechanic's gloves, complete with the team number embroidered on the backs, covered his tattoo, and his E-World Broadband team uniform was crisp and spotless.

"Hey, Dew."

"Chance!" Duane didn't even bother with a handshake; he just threw his arms around the driver and hugged him. "Man—where you been? I haven't even seen you since you got me this gig."

"Oh, I think you got it on your own merits."

"Right." Duane rolled his eyes. "Don't worry, my old man made it clear how I made the team. And I appreciate it, Boomer. So what're you doin' here? Saddlin' back up?"

Chance blinked, glad for the sunglasses.

"No," he said. "Not this time."

"When, then? Soon?"

Chance didn't say anything.

"Oh, man." Duane scuffed at the ground with his shoe. "That's bogus. I've heard talk, but I was hoping it wasn't true."

Chance shrugged.

"I'm just here to watch a guy who's running in Saturday's Busch race," he said.

"So you'll be around? Sweet! Maybe we can hang."

"I'd like that," Chance said. "In fact, that's why I'm here. SCM is having a Bible study at seven o'clock tonight, in their assembly center. You know where that is? In the drivers' paddock?"

"Yeah. Sure."

"Think you can make it?"

"Seven?" Duane made a show of thinking about it. "I don't know. We've got a lot to set up tonight. But I'll try. Okay?"

"Sure," Chance said. "All that I ask."

As Chance walked away, a crewman stopped wrestling nitrogen tanks out of the hauler, looked at the teenager, and scowled.

"Why," he asked Duane, "did you tell him that? We'll be set up by five. This might be our only night off this week."

"I know it," Duane agreed. "And you think I'm gonna blow it on a Bible study? Dream on."

Sitting in a cramped alcove at the front of the SCM assembly center, Brett Winslow checked the columns on his newsletter one last time, and then clicked the little printer icon in Microsoft Word.

"In Jesus' name I ask it," he muttered, quite earnestly. "Please. . . ."

After a moment's hesitation, a putty-colored HP LaserJet printer, three years older than the vehicle in which it sat, clicked and whined to life. In Brett's tenure as chaplain, this particular piece of office equipment had been dropped at least four times during setups, and even if it hadn't, it was already far beyond its projected life expectancy. It was no wonder that it was temperamental. But printed paper began sliding from the slot in its top.

"Thank you, Father," Brett breathed, absolutely sincere. He waited to make sure the first page wasn't a fluke and then walked out into the assembly center itself.

Setting up the SCM assembly center was just possibly the fanciest piece of precision driving that happened at any track, any week. The "center" was composed of two NASCAR transporter-type eighteen-wheelers that arrived at every track loaded with four golf carts, a complete portable children's playground with safety fence, lawn furniture, literature tables, a collection of fitness equipment, and a giant awning. And after all of these things were unloaded, the two trailers had to be jockeyed into place so they were perfectly parallel and less than half an inch apart. Doors were slid open between the two, and a foam insert, a steel threshold, and a fifty-three-foot piece of vinyl roof flashing were plugged into the gaps. Glass doors were fitted to one outside wall, steps were folded out, and—voilà—a small sixteen-by-forty-foot auditorium was ready for its congregation.

Usually the assembly center sat in the infield. But here at Bristol, it had been set up outside the track, as SCM always set up in the drivers' motorhome paddock, and Bristol was too small for an infield paddock. This made it a little harder to get to, but at least conversations did not have to be shouted over the roar of engines on the track.

Outside the center, Astroturf, patio furniture, and a portable white picket fence defined a small awning-shielded "front yard" in which members of the racing community could take shelter from the hectic pace of the track. And when Brett saw who was sitting there, he lost all semblance of poise.

"Chance!" He half yelped the name, leaping down the assembly center steps as the driver rose to meet him. "Man! It is so good to see you! What are you doing here?"

"Studying Joshua," Chance said, indicating his open Bible and his laptop computer.

"Sure, sure." Brett nodded. "But what brings you to the track?"

"Just doing a little scouting for Robert."

Brett nodded again. He knew better than to pry into a racing team's business. He glanced at the open laptop.

"That's a lot of notes," he said. "All yours?"

"Yeah," Chance replied as they settled into a pair of patio chairs. "I've been noting all the parallels between Moses and Joshua: crossing water on dry ground; sending out spies; interceding before God; the last wills and testaments."

"Wow . . . " Brett nodded.

"And people always want to dismiss this, saying that Joshua becomes, in effect, the new Moses. But I can't agree."

"You can't?"

"No. I mean, both led Israel, but Moses was the deliverer of God's laws, while Joshua reflected on them and was their mediator—he's really the more inspired of the two leaders."

Brett nodded, his eyebrows arched.

"And the holy ground episodes? Moses and the burning bush—that's clearly God the Father. But after the manna ceases? When Joshua meets the commander of the army of the Lord? The fact that he is a military commander, like in Revelation, the presence of the sword, which later is likened to the Word in the New Testament? . . . I know some people say that the commander is an angel, but I don't believe it. I think the signs show that he is the preincarnate Christ."

Brett sat up straighter.

"Where have you been reading this?"

"In my Bible." Chance shrugged.

"No." Brett shook his head. "I mean, what commentaries?"

"Commentaries?" Chance pursed his lips. "None. Why? Am I that far off base?"

"Not at all," Brett told him, sitting back. "In fact, nowadays, most Christian Old Testament scholars would agree with you. But you just figured something out, Chance, that I didn't grasp until my third year of seminary. And even then, I didn't get it until my Old Testament prof pounded it into my head. Fine work, man. Really. Very fine."

CHAPTER 17

So God exists in three persons," the speaker was saying. "Father, Son, and Holy Ghost."

Chance risked another glance at the center's glass doors. He'd waited outside for Duane for as long as he could, and the guest Bible teacher, a pastor from a local church, had started exactly on time, so he'd had no alternative but to come inside.

"And you may fear God the Father and pay lip service to his Son, but you are not Christian unless you are indwelt by the Holy Ghost."

At least he didn't say "Ghost-ah." They'd had one of those the year before—"sin-ah, Ghost-ah, Hell-ah, SAY-ved-ah."

"The Bible says that we can be recognized by our fruits," the speaker continued. "Yet, if you try to do God's work without the Holy Ghost within you, you might as well try taking your racecar out on that track over there without a single puff of air in the tires."

A couple of people in the group looked at one another and smiled.

"Inspired means 'breathed in,'" the speaker said. "If you read a word in the Bible, it was placed there by an inspired person, and by inspired, we mean full of God, full of the Holy Ghost, like a functioning tire on that racecar; not flat, but full of air."

More smiles.

"So what's it going to be? Are you going to run fully equipped, or with no air in your tires?"

Somebody coughed, and the speaker frowned.

"Because tonight, beloved, you have an opportunity, if you've never done so before, to change your life. . . ."

And as the invitation proceeded, Chance prayed for hearts to be changed, and two of the twenty-plus men in the room went forward for a word with Brett.

"Thank you very much for your message, Pastor," Chance said, shaking the man's hand. "I enjoyed it."

He had waited until almost everyone in the place had left before coming up, biding his time to see if Duane would show up at all.

He hadn't.

"Why, thank you," the speaker said, beaming. "Say, you're Chance Reynolds, aren't you?"

"Why, yes, sir." Chance smiled. "I am."

"Well, you certainly have some fans among my grandkids. And my daughter says that she even lets them get on the Internet and listen to your radio conversations with your crew, because you never curse."

"I try not to," Chance said, laughing. "I know that, right after I got married, my wife used to take a Sharpie and write on a piece of tape; 'And GOD's listening, too!' And she'd stick that on my dash. So I guess the credit goes to her; she trained me."

The speaker laughed and Brett joined in.

"Say," the speaker said, looking around. It was just the three of them now. "I was noticing something tonight. Every time I said 'no air in the tires,' I was getting this . . . well . . . this strange reaction. Did you notice that?"

"Yes, sir," Chance said. "I did."

"Well? Why is that?"

Chance looked at Brett, who nodded back at him.

"Well, sir," Chance said, "that would be because, generally speaking, there is no air in the tires."

"What? You mean they're solid?"

"No, sir." Chance shook his head. "It's just that air is too hard to predict in terms of expansion. If you fill tires with humid air and they warm up, it might expand considerably, while dry air might not expand nearly as much. And we need to precisely control tire pressure, because that's how you calibrate the spring rate of the tire."

"Spring rate . . . of the . . . tire?" The speaker got this deer-in-the-headlights look.

"So to keep things constant," Chance said, forging on, "we don't use air at all. We inflate our tires with nitrogen."

"Nitrogen? But that would blow up!"

"No, sir." Chance shook his head. "I believe you're thinking of hydrogen. That's another reason for choosing nitrogen. It's safer."

"Really. Well, I'll be . . . uh . . . darned."

They spoke a little longer, standing on the Astroturf outside the center. Then Brett's assistant pastor took the speaker back to his car in one of SCM's golf carts.

Watching him go, Brett chuckled.

"Well," he said, "now he's got a new piece of trivia."

Chance grinned. "Hey, he meant well, and besides, how many people outside our sport would know that?"

Brett looked at him a long moment. "Exactly. Hey . . . you got a minute?"

"Sure. What's up?"

Brett went back into the assembly center and came out with a manila envelope.

"The Holy Spirit—the 'air in my tires'—told me to give you this. So if you don't want it, take it up with him, okay?"

"Okay. What is it?"

"An application for Shepherd University."

"Shepherd University?"

"A Bible college," Brett said. "You went to junior college, right?"

"Just barely. I never got a degree or anything. But my folks thought that, until I got signed with a for-real racing team, I should get some foundation laid down for schooling, in case I had to go on to a four-year college and get a regular job. So I did the fundamentals . . . you know . . . the whatchamacallits."

"Required classes."

"Right. About killed me, but I did it."

Brett tapped the envelope.

"This would probably be a whole lot more user-friendly. Shepherd is designed for folks who have full-time jobs with churches and such, so most of it is on-line; that, or on interactive CDs. You really only meet on campus two times a year for a week at a time, and a person with your insight and grounding could, I think, get a bachelor's in theology in no time at all. Maybe even within a year."

Chance squinted.

"A bachelor's in theology? What would I do with that?"

"Nothing." Brett shrugged. "Or anything. Do you remember that trip that RVR took to Ford Motor Company, the one that you invited Danielle and me and little Kyle along for?"

"Sure."

"Danielle and Kyle thought the trip to Greenfield Village was the best," Brett said. "But the part I remember was talking to the head of Ford's Human Resources operation, because I asked him what he'd done his college work in, and he said, 'Geography.'"

"Geography? Really?"

"Yeah. I think you were over driving cars on the test track or something. Anyhow, I remarked on how odd that was—after all, it was the only degree he had—and here he was, making all the major personnel policy decisions for a global company. And he said no, it really wasn't. And then he brought out these press releases—all these biographies of Ford vice presidents—and he showed me how the head of Ford of Mexico had majored in Chinese history and Renaissance art. And how the vice president of marketing had been a music major. And I'll never forget what he said next. Remember, this is the guy who hires and fires for one of the biggest companies in the world. And he said, 'I think everyone that can should get an undergraduate degree in something they truly love, so they'll never regret not having had the chance to study it. And if they want an MBA later on, why then they already have that bachelor's to stand on.'

"And Chance, you know, every time I walk in to visit a guy in his transporter, it seems to me that he's got his nose stuck in a hunting magazine, or a fishing magazine, or a boating magazine, or watching a movie or boxing or a ballgame on TV. But you? You've always got your nose stuck in a Bible. And every time I've seen that, I've thought of what that Ford guy said to me, and I've wanted to tell you this. Then, last week, I sent to Shepherd for an application for one of the guys in our youth ministry and for some reason, I asked for a second one, too. And now I know why. If you've got time right now . . . well, I just thought you might like to have a degree in something you love."

"Well . . ." Chance looked at the crest on the envelope. "Thanks."

"You don't owe me an answer," Brett told him. "I just wanted you to know what's available. But there is something else I wanted to ask you about."

Chance looked up.

"What's that?"

"Are you going to be at Richmond?"

"Me? Uh . . . yeah. I've got this thing I'm working on for Robert."

Brett beamed.

"Great! The fellow I had lined up for our Bible study called me this afternoon and said he had to bail. His assistant pastor fell off a ladder and busted both ankles. How would you like to take his place?"

"Me? Lead a Bible study?"

Chance knew that most of the guest speakers were published theologians.

"I saw what you were working on today. And Cindy used to email me those word studies you were doing."

Chance stared at Brett.

"She what?"

"Oh, for Pete's sake, Chance." Brett laughed. "She was proud of you. And with good reason. You've got lots and lots of Bible smarts. You just might be the first Bible study teacher these guys have ever had who knows . . . really knows . . . what's going on inside their heads. So. You'll do it?"

Chance's first inclination was to refuse. He didn't feel qualified. Then he remembered all the prayer with Brett, all the times that Brett was there to talk to, the trip to the hospital in the helicopter.

"Sure," he finally said. "I'll be happy to."

"Outstanding! I'll put a notice in Sunday's bulletin."

They shook hands and Chance headed back to his loaner car for the drive to his motel. His head was already spinning with thoughts for the Bible study.

It was only as he was driving away that he wondered once again what had happened to Duane.

CHAPTER 18

"So . . . you live around here?"

Duane had to shout to be heard over the sound of the band, but then again, Duane was accustomed to shouting over the sound of bands. And even though the night was quite young, the bar had packed about three hundred bodies into a room with seats for a third that many.

"Heck, no," the girl shouted back. "I'm from Chicago. My folks just drag me down here every August. You?"

"I'm with one of the race teams."

"Really?" Her eyebrows shot up. "You a driver?"

Duane hesitated a moment. This brunette was pretty cute. He wondered just how big a lie she'd swallow.

"No," he finally said. "Just a wrench."

"And you travel all over with the team, huh?"

"Oh, yeah," he said, ignoring the fact that this was his first race weekend as a member of the 53 team—or any Cup team, for that matter—and that his duties consisted mainly of pulling the gas cart back and forth between the fueling station and the pits.

"Well, then, Dew . . . that's what you said your name was, right?"

"Uh-huh."

"Well, Dew, you got anything better than this weasel-spit they call beer?"

Duane looked around. He reached into his pocket and pulled out a tiny rectangle of aluminum foil, no larger than his thumbnail.

"Wow . . .," the girl cooed. "Is that what I think it is?"

"If you're thinking 'The Real Thing,' well, yes, it is," Duane told her. Methadrine was good for business, but for picking up girls, he'd never found anything better than cocaine.

"And here I was just hoping for a little weed." The girl smiled. "Sweet."

She looked around. "I can't do this out here," she said. "Is it okay if I just take it back to the Ladies'?"

"Sure." Duane nodded. "Want me to go with you?"

She laughed, her dark hair swaying. "It wouldn't get us a second look back in Chicago, Dew," she said. "But I really don't think that would fly down here in Tennessee."

Duane looked around. There were a lot of cowboy hats, despite the heavy grunge rhythm of the band. "You're probably right," he agreed. "But save some, okay? That's a full gram, and it hasn't been stepped on. Not once."

She rubbed the back of his hand seductively with her fingertips. "You wait here," she said. "I'll be right back."

Duane ordered another beer, amazed that the bartender didn't ask for an ID. Then again, judging from the faces around him, it looked as if the drinking age in this county was something like fourteen.

He sipped the beer, then another, and chased away about five people who tried to take the girl's seat.

"My girl's sitting here," he told yet another guy, a kid in a NASCAR T-shirt.

The guy looked at the seat.

"No purse," he said, his speech slurred.

"She took it with her."

"Okay," the drunk said, staggering away. "No prob—"

Duane looked around for the Ladies' room door. He couldn't see it from where he was sitting. And the drunk had been right—the girl's purse was gone.

He thought about asking somebody to go in and check on her. Then he realized that he had never even gotten her name.

Duane had one more beer before he conceded that she had walked out the back door with his gram of coke. She'd probably moved on down the road and sold it by now.

He looked at his watch and shrugged. It was half past ten, and he was due back at the hauler, pressed, dressed, and shaved, at five in the morning. Time to hit the hay.

Duane got back into the team car that he'd borrowed from one of the tire carriers and started back toward the motel. Then, on a whim, he swung off onto the main highway and headed out to the track.

There was a Tennessee state trooper at the intersection, and Duane held his breath, hoping to contain the smell, but the cop didn't care about that. He just took one glance at Duane's NASCAR credentials and waved him through.

Ditto at the gate that crossed the track. A sleepy rent-a-cop stopped the car, squinted at the hard-laminated team pass, and said, "Well, they sure are working you late, aren't they?"

"Naw," Duane said. "I'm just stopping to get my jacket."

"Good idea. They say it's going to be pretty brisk, come morning."

Duane drove back by the team's transporter and didn't even get out. He just sat there. There was a security guy walking the garage area with a flashlight, but he'd seen his buddy at the gate clear Duane, so he didn't bother him.

After a minute, Duane started up the car, turned on the headlights, and left. He knew that every track was different; and each one had its own security procedures. But what he'd just seen had verified what he'd suspected—that while fans could expect to get their coolers and even their binocular cases checked on the way into a racetrack, he could come and go unimpeded, as long as he was with the show. No one had so much as glanced at his backseat, let alone the trunk.

It was a very useful thing to know.

CHAPTER 19

Duane saw Chance Reynolds coming and did his best to try to fade into the early morning hubbub of garage-area activity. It was hard to hide in a red-white-and-blue uniform with your name stitched on the back, but Duane was one of hundreds of such people in the infield, and there seemed to be several additional hundreds of race fans walking through. He slipped his metallic gold Gargoyles down from the top of his head onto his face, and stooped as if inspecting the immaculately painted wheels on his fuel cart.

Chance walked right on by, less than twenty feet away, his lips moving as he walked, and Duane watched him from the corner of his eye. Chance was a cool guy, and he looked like he might even be fun to hang with, but Duane hadn't gone to the Bible study, and Chance was, after all, his father's friend. He didn't need the third degree, especially not after being shut down by that brunette.

Chance kept going, heading toward where the Busch teams parked their haulers. The coast looked clear, but Duane decided to go check out pit road for a while. He started heading that way, wondering as he did so why Chance's lips had been moving like that. Probably a cell phone, he decided: one of those ear-bud headsets.

Chance didn't even think twice about praying as he walked. He'd done it for years. He prayed while he was walking, prayed while he was fishing, prayed while he was driving his street car; prayed on the track. Once, as he prayed while driving in a qualifying race at Daytona, he'd keyed the mike button by accident. To his surprise, Pooch had chimed in at the end with a somber baritone "Amen."

This morning, he was praying for guidance, something he did often, as he had known for decades that God's judgment was much better than his own. Robert Vintner had asked him to guide Gage Grissom, to mentor him, and Chance had agreed, but he had no sooner done so than he had realized that, if Gage wanted a mentor, it was Gage who should be asking, not Vintner.

So now Chance was apprehensive. He was going to know in just a very few minutes whether this was a terrible mistake or a workable idea, and he wanted it to be workable because he didn't just want to hang around the world of racing. He wanted to be useful. He wanted desperately to drive that racecar again. And if he couldn't do that himself, he wanted to be instrumental in the life of the person who did.

Apprehensive. Chance reminded himself that, in the thousands of verses of Scripture he'd committed to memory, there wasn't one that counseled apprehension. Quite the contrary. So he took a breath, he went on praying, and he slid open the mirrored solar-glass doors on the back of the fifty-three-foot lowboy trailer. Blinking at the change in light level, he walked into the trailer's air-conditioned interior.

Robert Vintner Racing's Busch Series transporter was a well-maintained hand-me-down from one of RVR's Nextel Cup teams. The layout was identical—a low ceiling separated Chance from the car bay, set up to transport both a racecar and a fully prepped backup car. On the lower level, most of the trailer was a long corridor with counters and storage compartments on either side, a virtual parts store and machine shop on wheels. And at the far end—the front of the trailer—was a lounge area where conferences were held, and where a driver could change clothes, nap, or hole up for some quiet time away from the crowds. Chance tapped on the door and looked in.

"Hey, Gage."

Peering at a pre-practice roster, firesuit open to his waist, the young driver looked up, scowling at the interruption. Then he saw who it was.

"Boomer!" The kid's face lit up like a lightbulb. He was freckled, with green eyes and flaming red hair. Only his strong, square cleft chin saved him from looking like a hopelessly youthful Ted Koppell. Chance knew in a heartbeat that Grissom's race-shop nickname would have to be something like "Rooster," or "Red."

"C'mon in, man!" Grissom said, picking up the racing magazines that littered the U-shaped leather couch. He took his pit cap off the seat, looked for a place to hang it, and tossed it on top of the bulkhead-mounted TV. Then he grinned again.

"Man, you must be psychic or something," he said. "Here I am—I'm supposed to be getting my head clear for this Busch race—and all I can think of is how much I hope I don't screw up a few weeks from now, when I strap myself into your racecar."

"Not my racecar," Chance said, taking a seat. "Yours."

"That's kind of you," the kid said. "But I know I'm just fillin' in until you're knitted up."

Chance cocked his head and looked at Grissom. The kid was in earnest. Vintner must not have told him anything yet about this ride being permanent.

Then again, that made sense. At the press conference they'd held, they'd just told the media that Chance was on medical leave due to lingering vision problems. So that's how Robert must have handled it with Gage. No need to add any more pressure to the young driver's life. Or maybe Robert was still hoping for a miracle. Deep down inside, Chance had to admit that he was hoping for one himself.

"Well," Chance said instead, "when I'm knitted up just might be a while. So treat it like it's yours."

That opened an awkward silence of perhaps five seconds. Chance wasn't sure what to say next.

"Man," Grissom finally said, sitting back down again. "I can't believe you're here, sir."

"Whoa! I'm not that old! It's 'Chance.' Or 'Boomer.'"

"Okay." When the kid blushed, his freckles nearly vanished. "But I can't believe you're here . . . uh . . . Chance. I wasn't kidding that I was thinkin' about you. I've been thinking of calling you for days."

"Really?" Chance sat up. "Why's that?"

Grissom shrugged.

"I know a lot of the guys up and down the garage area," he said. "You know, from the weeks when Busch and Cup both run at the same track, like this week. And you know what they say. Opinions are like . . . well, everybody's got one. And nobody's afraid to share theirs around Cup. But I've never found a single person here that had a bad thing to say about you. I mean, they respect you on the track. You drive hard, and you're as competitive as they come. But everybody, and I mean everybody, says you're a great guy."

"Hey, you keep that up, I'm gonna have to leave."

"I hope not," Grissom said earnestly. "I need you around."

"Why's that?"

"Because . . . well, hey, I wouldn't tell just anybody this, but I'm landing in Cup three years before I thought I would and about two years before I'm ready. And I could sure use the help of somebody who knows the lay of the land."

Pretending to move a magazine, Chance turned away, bowing his head, and mouthed, "Thank you."

Then he turned back to Grissom and said, "Well, I'm sure available. I've been rattling around that house of mine like a BB in a boxcar. It'll be a blessing to be of some use."

There wasn't one thing fake about the kid's smile.

"That's great!"

"Then let's start with basics," Chance said, leaning toward him. "You've met Andy, right?"

"Yeah," Grissom nodded. "Hoss. Super guy. Smart."

"Well, if you understand that," Chance said, "then you're halfway home. Andy may not say much, but when he does, you'll want to listen. Now, there's only three things you need to remember about working with this race team . . ."

CHAPTER 20

Lake Concord, North Carolina

Leadership experience.

Chance scowled at the college application and scratched his head absentmindedly. There was the Willow Creek Leadership Summit that he and Cindy had attended with Brett and Danielle up near Chicago the year before. Or at least they had attended part of it. He'd had to run to the airport Friday morning and fly out so he could qualify. But he'd been there a couple of days. They'd even asked him up on stage. He supposed that counted.

He wrote it in. He remembered a few infield services where SCM had asked him to deliver his testimony. He wrote that in as well.

What else?

"Leadership" made him think about his brief time on top in the Nextel Cup points race. These days, he didn't like to even think about the points standings. He'd logged onto NASCAR.com on his computer in the den that morning, and the standings roster had shown him still in the top thirty, even after being out of the running for eight races—soon to be nine. He'd had one heck of a season going until he got hurt.

Watching himself plummet through the standings was like getting reports from the bank that somebody else was writing checks on his account. Actually it was worse; in this case, there wasn't a thing Chance could do about it.

He shook the thought out of his mind and turned back to the application form. The gray fog-spot of missing vision danced over the page until he turned his head slightly.

Why do you wish to study with Shepherd University?

Chance thought about the question and then wrote, "To come to a deeper understanding of God's Word."

He looked at what he'd written, then he changed the period to a comma and added, "and to use that understanding to lead others to a more meaningful relationship with Jesus Christ."

There. That about covered it.

"Chance?"

He looked up and smiled at Cindy. She was wearing white bib overalls over a pink top. She looked cuter than the proverbial button.

"Hey, sexy." He smiled.

She pursed her lips.

"Now you get your mind right off of that," she said, trying and failing to act stern. "Gage is here. And you know what? He's even sweeter than he looks on TV."

"Now you get your mind right off of that," Chance joked back, standing and kissing her. "That boy's young enough to be your—"

"My what?" She squirmed out of his arms and stood, arms akimbo.

"Your . . . uh—brother."

Cindy rolled her eyes.

"Dottie's coming by in ten minutes to run me in to the doctor," she said. "Your folks are landing at Charlotte this afternoon at one. Want us to go pick them up?"

"Naw. I'll get 'em."

"You sure? That's just two hours from now."

"I'm sure. This way you and Dottie can have lunch and do some shopping or whatever you want."

"For maternity clothes," Cindy said. "Yecko. They make women look like pears wrapped in tissue paper."

"You'll be a very sexy pear," he told her, kissing her atop her head.

"Gage," she said, "is waiting."

"Yes, ma'am."

He followed an original-Audubon-print-decorated hallway to the front of the house, where he turned, crossed the entry foyer, and stepped into the living room. Gage was sitting there in an E-World knit shirt, his pit cap on one knee, looking at a coffee-table book of Ansel Adams photographs.

"Hey, Gage."

"Hey!" The kid shot to his feet. "Thanks for asking me by. Man, Boomer. This is some house."

Chance chuckled.

"It's Cindy's house," he said. "She just lets me sleep here sometimes."

"She's a pretty lady."

"You need to tell her that. Bein' pregnant has added like a quarter inch to her waistline, and she thinks she's Dumbo."

Chance took a second glance at the shirt.

"Did you have an appearance today?"

The kid blushed.

"This?" He touched the logo. "No. The shop FedExed me a bunch of shirts and hats over the weekend, and Robert wanted me to sit in on the team meeting today. I just wore this to . . . you know . . . try to fit in."

"I see." Chance nodded. He usually wore just a plain shirt at the shop. "How'd the meeting go?"

Gage's face clouded.

"Let me guess," Chance said. "LD?"

"Yeah." Gage nodded. "Listen . . . I don't know if you guys are friends or whatever, but Chance, I've got to tell you. The man was a total jerk. I mean, I said hello and went over to shake hands with him, and he just walked right on past me to talk to his car chief about something. And then later on, when we were reviewing a stop he made? I asked him about why he called for four tires instead of two, and he looked right past me like I was a ghost or something. I gotta tell ya, Andy and Mr. Vintner and Pooch and the rest of them were as nice to me as could be. But LD? My momma would say he needs an education in the social graces."

Chance nodded.

"I hear you," he said, "but don't take any of that personally. First, on that tire call, you were right, which means LD was wrong, and being wrong is not his long suit. And second, if you're new in the shop, the first thing old LD tries to do is see if he can scare you to death. And that's not just drivers. He does that to engine builders, body hangers, suspension guys. Heck, he does that to the trade school kids they hire to sweep up."

"Really?" Gage asked. "Did he do that to you?"

"Absolutely."

"But he doesn't act that way now."

"No, he doesn't," Chance agreed, thinking that he hadn't seen much of LD since Sonoma.

"So how did you get him to stop?"

"Easy." Chance grinned. "I just whipped his backside on a racetrack. It was my first Talladega race, as a matter of fact. I won it and he finished eleventh. He didn't talk to me for a week afterward, but when he did, he was actin' decent."

"Oh, great. So he's gonna treat me like dirt until I beat him? Man. I'll be eighty years old."

Chance took a long look at the young driver, his head cocked.

"Tell you what," he said. "You want a Coke?"

"Got any RC?"

Chance laughed.

"You are a southern boy, aren't you? We're fresh out of Moon Pies, but I think we got us some RC in the kitchen. C'mon."

They bypassed the dining room, using the shortcut that Cindy had asked the architect to design in—a short cabinet-lined hallway with swinging doors at either end.

Gage turned and took in the kitchen—the shiny pots hanging from the rack over the island counter, the big stainless-steel refrigerator, the commercial-quality convection oven, and the hood-topped range.

"You're not married, are you?" Chance asked.

"Married?" Gage shook his head. "No."

"But you've got a girl. Am I right?"

"Yes, sir. We got engaged just as soon as Mr. Vintner gave me the call to move up to Cup."

Chance nodded. It sounded familiar. He opened the refrigerator, bent forward, and looked in.

"We've got something here called 'RC Draft,'" he said. "Is that the same as an RC?"

"Are you kidding? That's the good stuff."

Chance pulled out two frosted cans—the RC for Gage and a Diet Vanilla Coke for himself.

"Thanks." Gage smiled.

"Don't mention it. Let's get some air."

They walked downstairs through the family room and out onto the big, multilevel deck. Both men ignored the teak chairs and stood at the railing, sipping their soft drinks and looking out over the lake. A slow shimmer of ripples danced the length of the water and disappeared around the bend.

"Tell me something, Gage," Chance said. "Do you want to win?"

The younger driver looked his way, surprised. "Well, sure," he said. "Doesn't everybody?"

Chance shrugged. "Not necessarily," he said. "Some people love racing a whole lot more than they like winning. Not many of them make it to Cup anymore, but the fact remains that there are a whole lot of people in the world driving racecars who are content just to sit behind the wheel and turn fast laps."

"Not me," Gage told him, shaking his head.

"I didn't figure it," Chance told him. "Robert wouldn't have brought you up unless you were hungry for wins. But are you ready to drive for one every single time?"

Gage's face reddened just a bit. The squint in his eyes could have just been the morning sun, but Chance figured it was the beginnings of irritation. He hoped so.

"Of course," Gage said, and yes, he did look irritated. "Why?"

"Because if you want to win, you are going to have to finish ahead of forty-two other drivers who also want it—every single Sunday," Chance told him. "And 999 races out of a thousand, one of those drivers is going to be Lyle 'Lone Wolf' Danford. He usually qualifies, and even if he doesn't, the man's got more provisionals than Kellogg's has got corn flakes. So if you have any hesitation about racing him, you'd better put that aside right now, or you might as well not even climb into that racecar."

Gage nodded, silent, head down.

Chance was quiet as well, thinking about what he would say next. He knew that this was all new for Gage. Even the trip to the race shop would have been a new experience. Most Nextel Cup teams were located near Charlotte, giving them access to the local talent pool and, in the days before FedEx, the Holman and Moody racing parts that made up so much of a Cup car. But Busch teams were located all over the map, and RVR kept theirs in Allen Park, Michigan, practically on Ford Motor Company's back porch, giving the lower budget team access to the automaker's engineering expertise.

"You need to remember," Chance said, "that the engines for both cars—the 35 and the 53—come out of one shop, and Doc and his people never know who's getting which block, so they build them just as consistent as they possibly can. We share wind-tunnel data, spring data, shock data, aero data. Old LD has got a gem of a crew chief in P. T.

Sloane, but I wouldn't trade Hoss for him and three others just like him. Our over-the-wall guys were within a thousandth of a second of LD's in the last pit-crew competition, and the way they've been working out ever since, you'd think they got beat by half a minute. True, LD's probably been racing longer than you've been breathing, but your reaction times are going to be a whole lot quicker. You've got a shot at beating him every time you roll out onto a track, and you've got to believe that if you're going to race him. So do you?"

Gage nodded. "I guess so," he said.

Chance looked at him. "Don't guess, Gage. Know it. Half of doing is knowing that you can. I mean, think of it, you're from Gulf Shores, and you're making your Nextel Cup debut in your home state. When you walk out for driver intros at Talladega, they're gonna shout the grandstands down. Use that. Know you can do it, and you'll be Superman."

The kid nodded and Chance glanced at his watch.

"Tell me something," he said. "Do they have that expression down in 'Bama—'blowin' off some stink'?"

Gage grinned.

"They don't," he said. "But I've got Yankee cousins. I know it."

"Well, do you want to? My mom and dad are flying in over to Charlotte. Want to help me pick them up?"

"Sure." Gage grinned. "I'd be honored."

The stakeout van, a white Dodge of the type used by tradesmen all over the country, was idling in the park next to the high school parking lot, its two occupants glassing the two acres of crowded asphalt with powerful, shock-protected marine binoculars. As they watched, a black Mustang pulled to the curb outside the school and parked. Both cops moved their binoculars slightly to focus on the driver.

"Man, oh, man," the older cop said. "Is that who I think it is?"

"Sure is," the younger one said. "My twelve-year-old's got posters of him all over his bedroom."

In the shadow-surrounded eyepieces of their equipment, the men watched as Lyle Danford rubbed his close-trimmed goatee absentmindedly, put on sunglasses and a Charlotte Hornets ball cap, and slid down slightly in the Mustang's bucket seat.

"Trying to stay inconspicuous," the older cop murmured.

"I'll see if I can get some shots of the back plates," the younger one told him, setting down his binoculars and picking up a 35mm Nikon with a large, squat telephoto lens.

"Don't let him make you."

"Never happen," the younger man said as he stepped back between the seats and opened the van's sliding side door.

The older cop checked his watch and made a note of the Mustang's arrival. Five minutes later, the van's sliding door opened again.

"It's a rental," the younger one said. "Hertz barcode sticker."

His colleague nodded.

They watched in silence for another ten minutes. Then the distant ringing of a bell drifted across from the school and through the open windows of the van.

"Let's look sharp," said the older man.

A small flood of teenagers in jeans, T-shirts, polo shirts, and cargo shorts came running out into the lot, climbing into pickups, vans, used sedans, and the occasional PT Cruiser or VW Beetle. Few carried books; it was the first day of school—orientation day. Regular classes wouldn't start until later in the week.

The men trained their binoculars on the corner of the parking lot, where motorcycles were crammed into a cordoned-off area.

"There he is," said the older one. They watched as Duane Danford came walking out of school, pulling on his helmet, and got aboard a yellow Kawasaki Ninja. Still watching through his binoculars, the older cop leaned forward and started the van's engine.

The bike weaved through departing traffic to the street, where it hung a sharp left and then rocketed away down the asphalt. The Mustang pulled away from the curb, and the van, just now exiting the park, followed at a discrete distance.

The older cop looked at the speedometer and frowned; they were already running twenty over the limit.

"I dunno," he said, glancing around at the big, bulky van. "Seems to me that this boy's daddy's got himself a much better vehicle for following that bike."

They kept up their surveillance, following the distant Mustang and the more distant Ninja until both the motorcycle and the car got onto the state road into Mooresville. They drove into an industrial park, the bike turning off onto Rolling Hills Road. The Mustang's brake lights flickered for a moment, but it drove right on past.

The older cop pulled off into a parking lot, made a U-turn, and headed out the way they'd come.

"Hey," the younger cop said. "We're breaking off?"

The older one nodded his head. "No joy," he said. "The kid's going to work."

"Well, what about the father? Do you think he could be in cahoots on this?"

The older cop pursed his lips.

"Not a chance," he said. "He's just a worried-sick daddy trying to keep tabs on his boy when he can." He was silent for a moment. Then he added, "I hope it works out for him."

"If it does, two months of surveillance goes into the dumper."

"I don't care," the older cop said. "I still hope it works out."

Although he'd picked them up after flights more than a dozen times, Chance always got a kick out of the Ellis Island expressions that his mom and dad wore in airports. Nate Reynolds was a highway-travel kind of man, far more comfortable with truck stops than ticket counters and departure lounges. And as for his wife, well, Marilyn Reynolds had asked time and again exactly what it was that kept the plane up in the air, and she had never been satisfied with the answers that flight crews gave her.

They came around the security checkpoint pulling their wheeled carry-ons, and Chance stepped in, picking up his mother and swinging her around like a girl in a '40s movie.

"Stop that," his mother giggled. "I'm already queasy from that big old airplane. I swear that pilot hit every bump in the sky."

Chance kissed her on the cheek and shook his father's hand. "Do you need to stop at the baggage claim?"

"Everything I got is in here," Nate Reynolds told him, nodding at the carry-on bag. "I think your mother's got about thirty or forty suitcases checked."

"I have *two,*" Chance's mother insisted. "Two suitcases and a shoebag. And who is this nice, quiet young gentleman?"

"I'm sorry," Chance said. "Mom and Dad, this is Gage Grissom, the fellow who's driving the 53 come Talladega. Gage, these are my folks, Marilyn and Nate Reynolds."

"Ma'am," Gage said, shaking hands. "Sir. Can I help you with your bags?"

"What a gentleman!" Marilyn Reynolds exclaimed. "You must be from the South."

But Nate Reynolds just looked at the young man silently, noting the team shirt and the pit cap: a shirt from Chance's team and a cap like Chance once wore. And as Chance took the carry-on bag from his father, he could see the hurt etched there, deep within the older man's eyes.

CHAPTER 21

Victory Lane Farm—Norwood, North Carolina

Jack, Jim, Johnny, and Hiram were all old acquaintances of Lyle Danford's, but he couldn't say that a one had ever been his friend.

He'd stopped on the way back from returning the rental car, intending to buy himself a pint of one of the four—just a pint in the flask-shaped bottle, the smooth, curved bottle that had once worn white impressions into the hip pockets of his jeans. And then he'd walked out with not a pint, but a full, sealed fifth of Jack Daniels: good southern whiskey—Tennessee whiskey, distilled in a dry county. Imagine that.

Of course the guilt had clouded over him just as soon as he'd gotten back into his truck. He'd made the pledge to Dottie while she'd still been pregnant with little Angela, her belly full of the promise of that unborn life, her face full of her grief over the ultimatum that she'd had to deliver. They'd been building the house back then, driving over in the evenings from the old place to see the progress after the swarms of contractors had gone home—that is, to see it on those nights when he could manage to stagger out to the car.

And he'd argued with her over it at first, feeling cheap even as he'd done so, but working out of that deep well of pride he'd sunk into over the years. He'd told her that he wasn't drinking every night, that he never drank before a race, that he had it under control. But then she'd shot that videotape, shown it to him while he was sober.

The video camera they'd had back then had been this prehistoric, ungainly VHS thing, so huge that it'd had a carry handle built into the top. But he'd been too drunk to even notice his pregnant wife standing there with that big, black camera, its red "record" light glowing, taping the whole thing while he berated seven-year-old Danny, shouting at him, towering over him, using the sort of language one rarely even heard around a race shop.

She'd played it back for him late the next morning on the big TV in his den, the one he usually watched his race tapes on. In his mind's eye, he could still see the pictures: the weaving, red-faced parody of the race-day-morning Lyle Danford, ball cap back on his head, screaming the riot act at a second grader for leaving a toy on the kitchen floor. Dottie'd known what to show him on her tape, the menacing finger waving in front of the poor kid's nose, a close-up of Danny's normally cherubic face twisted in abject fear, cringing at the stumbling, slurring giant before him.

But it was the sounds that had truly scared him sober: Danny's howling, terrified remorse; three-year-old Duane hiding in the next room, shouting, over and over again, "Don' hut my bruddah . . ."—and worst of all, clearest of all, because the microphone was right there on the camera—his pregnant wife's sobs as she'd bravely recorded the evidence.

And all that had happened fourteen—nearer to fifteen—years before. A decade and a half. Nearly a third of his lifetime.

There hadn't been any AA. No Twelve Steps, no doctors, no Yankee shrinks charging surgeons' wages just to listen. His pride had been too large, his self-esteem too weak, for anything such as that. Instead, he'd simply gathered up the bottles, amazed at their number. He had fifths stuck in boots, in closets, in car trunks. A pint had been tucked away—convenient, sly, and secretive—in the bottom of a toolbox, under the socket-wrench tray. He'd searched them out, found them all, and then put them in the trash on pickup day, waiting until he could hear the garbage truck whining at the first house down the road so he wouldn't be tempted to sneak one back inside.

He'd been surprised at how difficult it had been to quit. It wasn't a physical thing; he never had the shakes, no DTs, no hallucinations of crying angels. But he'd become comfortable with the feel of the tumbler, smooth and heavy in his hand . . . as it was now. It had been a way to unwind on the flights home, a way to oil the nerves on the too few hours when he was off and apart from the publicists and the reporters and the personal appearances and photographers.

He pictured the face, Danny's face, on that horrible tape, and then he swirled the amber liquor in his glass, remembering the smooth, languid feel of it. He'd brought it outside, to the darkened patio, to pour it, but even here with a light breeze, he could smell the smoky, sharp liquor, feel it inviting him back.

Dottie's sobs . . .

How was it that a thing that made you feel so good could make you act so bad? What was it that was so seductive that a man was willing to sacrifice his family for a feeling?

Danford lifted the heavy glass and smelled it, sensing the sharp, familiar bite as the fumes wafted into his nose. He remembered Duane grinning for the track photographer, the trophy in one hand and the checkered flag in the other, kneeling in front of the midnight blue Bandolero car. Then Danford saw his son in his mind's eye as the boy was today, all the defiant pins and rings, walking around with hatred tattooed into his knuckles.

Lyle Danford could put up with the look. For all his youth, Chance Reynolds had been exactly right—the look could change in a New York minute. But, way down deep inside, Danford knew it hadn't been a rosebush that had put those marks in the crook of his seventeen-year-old's arm. He knew that neither his wife nor he had paid for that motorcycle and that his younger son couldn't have either—not by any means even remotely legal.

And he knew that a white Dodge van had followed the two of them from Duane's high school all the way to the turnoff to RVR. You didn't have a granddaddy who grew up running bootleg whiskey and not know how to check a mirror every few seconds, taking note of those things that did not change with the scenery.

The van had not been fancy—no big flashy chrome wheels or stripe jobs or smoky tinted windows—so Danford figured it hadn't been gangbangers. And it had followed him expertly, keeping its distance and allowing other vehicles to get between it and its quarry, which meant it had to be the law. As soon as Danford had determined that, he'd begun to entertain this conflicting set of thoughts.

On the one hand, he didn't want his son to get arrested, didn't want him sent to jail—didn't want that sort of frightening stuff for Duane, and didn't want that sort of publicity for himself. He hated himself for so much as thinking the last part. But hate it or not, it was true.

And on the other hand, he knew that he couldn't talk the kid out of the path that he was taking; it was like talking to a wall. Nor could Dottie, although at least she seemed to have a bit more tolerance for all the outlandishness. So maybe getting busted and thrown in the slammer, possibly even serving some jail time, would be good for the kid. Scare him straight. And if that kept Duane from ruining his life, maybe it was worth the bad publicity.

Not maybe. Definitely.

Thinking those sorts of thoughts gave Danford a headache, the dull kind of headache that had steered him to the package liquor store.

He'd made his purchase furtively, and the woman who sold him the bottle had not, to his great relief, been a race fan. She'd just slid the bottle into a tall brown paper bag, handed him change for his fifty, and told him to have a nice night.

Right.

He smelled the liquor again. He wasn't going to kid himself—wasn't about to tell himself that it was only going to be a sip. If he drank it, he knew that he was going to drain the heavy, cut-glass tumbler, drain it in a single deep draught. But maybe he could stop with just the one drink. He hoped he could. Surely, after fifteen long, hard years, he had at least built up that much strength of character.

He wet his lips with his tongue, lifted the tumbler an inch closer, and then stopped, listening.

There. He heard it again. The high-rev whine of Duane's road-racing motorcycle, faint on the breeze, but coming closer. Setting down the tumbler, Danford walked around the house, through his wife's rose garden. A full moon was out, so he stood in the shadow of a trellis, listening and watching.

In a moment, Danford could see the twin headlights of his son's Ninja, far down the long front lane. The sound of the four-stroke engine slowed, and Duane rolled right past the house, coming to a stop and killing the engine just outside the garage.

As Danford watched, the side door to the garage opened, and a man walked out and stepped into the light from the sodium vapor lamp burning over the driveway.

Danny.

Lyle Danford's elder son came out, a socket wrench in his hand, and said something to Duane as the younger boy stood next to his motorcycle and took off his helmet. Danny laughed at something Duane said, and then the two of them walked back into the garage together, Duane putting his arm around his older brother's shoulder.

Danford watched and wondered.

Danny and Duane, buddying around with one another—who'd have thought it? Yet he'd just seen it with his own eyes.

What was it Chance Reynolds had told him? "God is faithful to give you what you need, if you'll only acknowledge that he's the source, and that he knows better than you."

Danford looked at the garage and realized that he didn't know what he needed. But he knew what he wanted. He'd known that for years.

A son who listened. A son he could be proud of. A son who could build on what he'd started. A son who could demonstrate that the things Lyle Danford did—that ability to work magic with a racecar—was something resident deep within his very genes.

And now that he thought about it, Danford had to admit that maybe, just maybe, the Almighty had answered that prayer before he had even uttered it.

But he'd answered it with *two* sons, not just one.

Danford turned and walked back through the darkened rose garden, back to the patio, where he'd left the tumbler.

He lifted the glass and smelled the smoky whiskey once again.

His troubles weren't over. Of that much, he was certain. He still had more questions than answers when it came to Duane. And there was still the specter of those undercover police and whatever dark activity it was that had set them on his younger son's trail.

Taking the tumbler with him, Lyle walked across the patio to his big stainless steel barbecue grill. It was still uncovered after the evening meal; the nights were still warm enough to dine outdoors on his evenings home. He opened the grill's cover, blew softly on the ash-whitened charcoal briquettes, and was rewarded with a soft, red glow, like the eye of an awakening dragon.

Danford poured his drink on the coals, raising clouds of steamy smoke. He blew once again, and the alcohol in the liquor caught fire, blue flames leaping up into the rising smoke. He went back to the patio table, found the fifth of Jack Daniels and poured the contents of the bottle into the grill as well, the blue flame climbing the stream of whiskey as he poured until finally it jumped into the bottle and traversed it in a circle of pale fire, consuming the last of the liquor with a muted, flat pop.

He slid the bottle down into the ash bin and then watched the grill as the liquor burned. The blue flames moved in the evening breeze. They looked like devils, dancing on the corpses of the whitened, spent coals.

CHAPTER 22

"All right, Dad, what is it?"

Chance Reynolds asked the question as matter-of-factly and as privately as he could, standing with his father out on the darkened deck, watching the full moon rise over the still waters of the lake.

"What's what?"

Chance Reynolds turned the cup of hot cider in his hand and looked at his father, saying nothing.

His father sipped his own cider, buying time. And then finally, in a voice choked with emotion, he told his son, "It's me. I'm the reason for all of this. I'm the reason you can't drive anymore."

Chance turned, free hand on the railing, and faced his father. "How do you figure that?"

"Son, I know the story. I know that you were coming to see me when that helicopter went down."

"And you figure that makes it your fault?"

Nate Reynolds nodded.

Chance sighed, setting his cup down on the broad deck railing.

"Dad . . . ," he said. "First of all, you didn't choose to have that chest pain. It just happened to you. Second, you didn't ask me to come—I'm a grown-up and I came of my own choosing. And third, you didn't have anything to do with that helicopter going down."

Eyes wet with tears, Nate Reynolds nodded.

"But still," he insisted, "if I hadn't gone to the hospital, if you hadn't come—"

"What?" Chance asked. "I would have been okay? How do you know that—know it for a fact? If I'd stayed there like I'd planned, maybe I would have driven pit practice, and the throttle would have stuck and I would have wrecked right there in the parking lot and blinded myself—totally—for life. Or even if nothing happened at the shop, I might have been hit by a truck or a train or whatever on the way home and killed. Do you remember what you told me when I was just starting to race, and I used to say things like 'if only I hadn't tried that pass'? You told me yourself that 'if only' are the two most dangerous words in the English language. And you were right."

Nate Reynolds looked down at the steam rising out of his cup.

"Dad," Chance said softly. "If this is the worst thing that ever happens to me, then I will have been a very, very fortunate man. I'm not blind. I can still drive a car on the street, I can still read, I can still see Cindy every morning when I wake up. I'm looking forward to seeing the birth of our baby. I can do everything I did before except fly an airplane and drive a racecar."

"But racing was your life!" Nate objected. He shook his head. "And you love the Lord so much. How could he let this happen?"

Chance looked his father right in the eyes. "I've been down that road," he said. "And I'll be frank, there are times—like three o'clock in the morning—when I find myself going down it again. But that's just me sulking, not God talking. And I can tell you how he allowed this to happen. Do you want me to?"

Nate Reynolds nodded.

"Well, first of all," Chance began, "Ephesians 6:12 tells us that God is not the only spiritual power active upon this earth—that verse talks about the 'rulers of the darkness of this world.'"

Nate nodded again.

"Second," Chance continued, "God gave people free will, and that includes that pilot's freedom to try to fly a helicopter even when he was not in any shape to do so.

"And third, God is constant, but he's not passive. Do you remember in the Old Testament how God would dwell over the tabernacle?"

"Sure," Nate Reynolds said. "A pillar of smoke by day and a pillar of fire by night."

"That's right," Chance said. "And the Bible tells us that the children of Israel spent forty years wandering in an area that you or I could walk across in a month or two, easy—especially if God provided the food and water, as he did for the Israelites. So it stands to reason that they might have stayed in one place for a year or more. They would have had time to really set up housekeeping. Yet when the cloud lifted over the tabernacle, they had to move, and follow, or they would no longer be in the will of God."

"So what's that got to do with you?" Nate asked.

"Easy," Chance told him. "For the past four years, it's pleased God to have me drive a Cup car. But maybe now he has a different purpose. Maybe I can better please him by doing something else."

"What's that?"

Chance grinned. "That's the exciting part," he told his father. "I don't know yet."

Nate nodded again. But he still did not look convinced.

CHAPTER 23

Richmond International Raceway—Richmond, Virginia

The racecar, crimson red in the morning sun, emblazoned in gold print with the brand name of a Midwestern lunch meat producer, broke free of the pack and tore down the gently curved, 1,290-foot front stretch. It rode midway up the fourteen-degree banking through the first two turns, exiting the second turn high on the curve, and drifting up to within inches of the wall. The big V-8 engine roared as the racecar accelerated again and then entered the third turn, the red air dam settling to within millimeters of the track as the car squatted from the banking and the braking.

Standing on the observation deck high atop RVR's Busch team trailer, Chance pivoted on the balls of his feet, following the car through smoke-gray Foster Grants. He wore a radio headset with one cup displaced, back behind his ear, so he could both listen to the radio and carry on a conversation at the same time. Beside him, Andy Hofert and Robert Vintner were similarly set up.

"He's carrying too much speed into his entries," Chance commented. The two men with him nodded in agreement.

They watched the car run another full lap in clean air. After that, Chance keyed the "talk" button on his radio.

"How's she feelin', Gage?"

The airwaves were silent as the car completed a turn, and then the young driver responded.

"Terrible tight in, tight high, loose out," he said. There was a pause, and then the young driver came back. "It ain't the car, is it?"

"No, it's not," Chance responded, pleased that the rookie was willing to own up to his mistakes. "Your entries are too hot; you need to back up your braking point a good fifty, sixty yards. And you're getting on the throttle at the right place, but you're opening too fast. This place doesn't have that much banking. You need to work that pedal like you've got an egg under your foot. Take your time. This is just practice. There's no money riding here."

The kid braked earlier for the next turn, and the car settled low on the track. But the back end hopped under wheelspin as he came out, and by the next turn he was back to braking too early. Then he caught up to a pack of slower cars and began the tedious process of snaking his way through them.

"Ask Skipper if he wouldn't mind putting in a little more throttle cable," Chance told Andy. He phrased it that way because, regardless of the fact that Chance and Andy were here at Robert Vintner's request, Nicholas "Skipper" Anderson was the crew chief of the RVR Busch car and, as long as they were at the track, his was the final word on anything that did or did not happen to the car.

Andy nodded and headed down the ladder to the garage area.

"Come on in," Chance radioed the driver. "I'll buy you a pop while Skipper tweaks."

"You go ahead," Vintner told Chance. "I'll just stay up here."

Chance nodded, thankful that the team owner was wise enough not to pressure the young driver too much. Putting the headset back on over both ears—he knew that both the media and the fans wouldn't bother him if he looked as if he couldn't hear them—Chance swiftly descended the ladder and trotted across the open tarmac to the team's stall in the garage.

In seconds, Gage's racecar was pulling in, the brilliant red paint abruptly losing its luster as the car went from the bright sunshine to the shadow of the garage.

The crew jacked the right side of the car up even as Chance was unfastening the window net, dropping it down inside so he could help Gage unclip the restraints on his helmet. He pulled the steering wheel off of its hub and set it on the dash, careful not to crimp the wiring to the radio and the kill switch. Then he took Gage's driving gloves while the young driver unfastened his seat harness.

By now, the hood was up and three crewmen were bent over the engine compartment. The tire handler was measuring the wear to the car's right front tire, and Chance could tell by the way the man shook his head that the carcass was overheated and worn—when you came into a turn too fast, that right front tire took most of the abuse.

Chance stepped back and fished a Coke and an RC Cola out of a cooler as Gage emerged from the car window. He looked like a man crawling out of a manhole. The young driver swung his legs out and Chance handed him the open RC.

"So what are you up to tonight?" Chance asked Gage.

"Tonight?" Gage asked, surprised at the question. "I don't rightly know. Some of the guys, we like to go party with the fans in the infield on Thursday nights. That way we've got a day to recover."

"Well," Chance said, glad to distract the young driver and get him thinking about something besides his driving, however momentarily, "I'm talking at SCM tonight at seven. Why don't you come by before you head to the infield?"

"SCM?" Gage asked. "You mean the chapel people?"

Chance nodded.

"I don't know," Gage told him. "I'm not much for religion."

"Neither am I." Chance laughed. "Come on by."

"Well . . . okay." Gage nodded, puzzled by the comment. He leaned over to see what the crew was doing under the hood.

"Skipper's putting a longer cable between the pedal linkage and the throttle linkage," Chance explained. "That'll add more flex and slow down your throttle response just a touch."

"What's next?" Gage asked, shaking his head. "Bungee cord on my foot?"

"Now come on," Chance said, putting his arm around the driver's shoulder as they walked to the front of the car, away from the press of fans and media gawking through the open garage door. "Lots of guys in Cup dampen their throttles, particularly at a flat track."

"Yeah," Gage agreed. "But this ain't that flat. And besides, I've never needed that before. I don't know what's got into me."

"I do," Chance said simply.

"What's that?"

"You've got RVR's Three Musketeers—RV, Hoss, and me—looking over your shoulder and watching your every move. It's got you screwed in about a turn and a half too tight. Am I right?"

The red-headed driver waited a moment, then nodded slowly.

"This isn't an audition," Chance told him. "You've got the ride. Next month at Talladega, you're going to be driving the 53, and you are going to have every resource of RVR behind you. That's settled. Done deal, case closed. It was decided weeks ago."

"I know."

"Your head knows," Chance agreed, tapping through the other driver's unruly red hair. "But your heart still thinks it's sittin' on the bubble. And that's got you trying to drive fast when you know as well as I do that speed is not what wins races. It's quickness—getting around the track in less time than anybody else. To do that, you've got to be super smooth through the turns. You enter them hot, you burn up time trying to get settled, and the clock just tick, tick, ticks away."

Gage shook his head again.

"No," Chance said flatly.

"How's that?"

"Get 'I can't' out of your noggin," Chance told him. "You can, or you wouldn't even be here in the first place. So start thinking 'I will' instead."

Grissom looked at him quizzically.

"We're not here to judge you, Gage," Chance assured him. "We're here to see the way you and Skipper like to run things, and to listen to how you like to be spotted, so Andy and I can get things right next month at Dega when you drive for us in Cup. We're the ones deep on the learning curve here, not you. So don't go worrying about proving stuff to us. Drive the way you know how and show us what you like. Now we'd better get you stitched back in. Skipper needs him a good set of scuffs for you to qualify on this afternoon, and what he just pulled off ain't it. And remember . . . SMC, tonight at seven."

Back atop the transporter, the late morning sun warm on their backs, Chance, Andy, and Robert watched Gage's red Busch car turn a few more practice laps. None of the three had a stopwatch, but they didn't need one to tell that the young driver had smoothed right out, steadily moving up through the other cars. When Skipper joined them, puffing from the climb up the ladder, he handed Robert a printout. The team owner read it and then looked up at Chance.

"Gage is faster by three miles an hour than anything else out there." Robert grinned. "What the heck did you tell him?"

Chance shrugged.

"The truth," he said. "I told him he was good."

"Well, keep tellin' him."

The other three men returned to the ground while Chance stayed on the observation deck, watching Gage run the rest of his practice. Skipper had figured—and Andy had agreed—that twenty laps would be just enough to wear away all but an optimum skin of usable tire rubber. It would leave the tires perfect for ripping off two quick laps during that afternoon's qualifying session.

The red car was halfway through its lap schedule when Chance felt another man's footsteps on the aluminum deckplate. He turned and smiled when he saw it was Lyle Danford, but Danford returned only the weakest semblance of a grin.

"The kid's fast," Chance said, by way of a conversation starter.

"Thanks to you, from what I hear," Danford grumbled. "So what do you do next? Put him over your shoulder and burp him?"

Chance decided to drop the diplomacy.

"All right," he said. "What's eating you?"

"Oh, I dunno," Danford said, settling onto the triangular seat built into the corner of the deck railing and nodding in the direction of the front stretch. "Only about three dozen cars, come Sunday, if I so much as blink while I'm out there."

"Come on, LD." Chance grinned at the older man. "You've been the points leader since when? Texas?"

"I have," Danford said with a shrug. "And I'm down to a sixty-seven-point margin. I'm holdin' on by my stinkin' eyelashes."

Chance looked straight at his former teammate, the gesture futile as both men were wearing dark sunglasses.

"That's not how I'm used to hearing you talk, Lyle," Chance said.

"Well," Danford replied, looking up at Chance, "this ain't much the way I'm used to feelin' either."

That's all he said, but immediately Chance had the gist of it. "It's your boy, isn't it?"

Danford nodded slightly, and immediately Chance began to feel guilty about not hunting Duane down the day after that Bible study.

Chance found a collapsible chair—a high-tech metal and canvas job—and pulled it close to Danford.

"Tell me," he said.

So Danford told him. He told him about following Duane, about the white van that had tailed the two of them.

"So the van . . . ," Chance asked. "Charlotte vice?"

"Feds," Danford said. "I've got a couple friends on the force; I've done fundraisers for them for years. And they tell me that the city has asked the federal government for help in addressing gang-related drug sales. So they've sent in what they call 'Mobile Enforcement Teams'—specially trained cops who deal exclusively with dope and gangs."

"FBI?" Chance asked.

"Worse," Danford repeated. "DEA. The same folks who fight the cartels down in Central America. Now they're after my boy, and Boomer, I've got to tell you, I'm starting to think he's in so deep that there might not be anything I can do to save him. I mean, I can't talk to him. I can't even ground him, because he'll just wait until I'm gone and then high-tail it out of the house. My daddy would have whupped him, but . . . well, you and I have talked about that. Heck, these days, if I lock him in his room, the authorities are apt to come by and lock me up. So there isn't anything left that I can do."

"'I can do all things through Christ which strengtheneth me,'" Chance quoted softly.

"Say what?"

Ignoring the question, Chance took off his sunglasses and looked straight at Lyle Danford.

"Tell me something, Lyle," Chance said. "Do you pray for your kids?"

"Huh?"

"Pray for them. Do you ask God to guard and guide them?"

"Well, I don't know. Not in so many words, I guess, but yeah, I . . . well, I hope for them. I ask the Almighty to keep 'em out of harm's way. At times like this, you'd better believe I do."

"And is anybody listening?"

Danford sat up straight and took off his own sunglasses.

"Man," he said. "That's a heck of a question to be coming from a guy who calls himself a Christian."

Chance shook his head. "I'm not asking if there's a God who hears your prayers," Chance told him. "I'm asking if your prayers are getting sent to God."

"Well . . . why wouldn't they be?"

Chance hesitated. "I guess I'm just asking," he said, "if Lyle Danford is a guy who calls himself a Christian."

Danford looked at Chance, saying nothing, for three long, slow seconds. Then he pulled off his cap and slapped the aluminum railing.

"What is this?" He looked left and right, as if he was expecting more people. "I come to you like a friend, asking for advice, and here you are trying to convert me or something." Danford rose to his feet and started for the ladder. "You're being like all those gawky, do-gooder door knockers that used to come around and wake me up back when I worked nights at the mill. I didn't need that then, and I sure don't need it now."

Danford turned at the top of the ladder and offered one last angry glare. Then he disappeared down the ladder, the roar of stock cars flooding in to fill his absence.

CHAPTER 24

Now wait a minute, Boomer," said a man sitting halfway back in the rows of folding chairs crowded into SCM's traveling assembly center. About half were the padded, chocolate-brown seating that SCM carried around the country as part of its equipment. The rest were scuffed, metal, black and gray specimens borrowed from the track's media center. And even those had proven insufficient to the task—about ten guys were standing against the walls, some having given up their seats to the five or six drivers' wives in attendance. The evening had turned cool, but all the bodies in the room had lifted the temperature several degrees.

"I've always heard," continued the man, who wore a Mobil One Henley-collared shirt, and whom Chance recognized as a tire carrier for one of the Cup teams, "that one of the requirements for the end days would be the conversion of the Jews. Like in all of Israel finally recognizing the Messiah. Heck, I've even read books based around that. Are you saying that's not biblical?"

A few people nodded as the crewman spoke, and Chance nodded as well, letting him know that it was a worthy question.

"Certainly, the Bible makes it clear that there will be Jews who come to Christ," Chance agreed. "In Revelation, there is talk of the hundred and forty-four thousand judges who are 'sealed' from all the tribes of Israel. But as far as Israel coming, as a body, to Christ—no. Jesus made it clear in John 6:58, and in several other places, that salvation is not a matter of who you are, or what country or group you belong to, but what you believe and where you place your faith. In fact, if you go to the Old Testament, you'll see over and over again even there that God does not promise to save all of Israel, but only a 'remnant.' Look at Jeremiah 31:7."

There was a whisking of onionskin pages all around the room as those who had brought their Bibles turned to the reference.

The sound of turning pages died down.

"'For thus saith the LORD,'" Chance read from his well-worn Bible. "'Sing with gladness for Jacob, and shout among the chief of the nations: publish ye, praise ye, and say, O LORD, save thy people, the remnant of Israel.'"

He saw a few heads turn toward the sliding glass doors of the center, and when he looked that way, he saw why: Lyle Danford and his two sons had come in. They made their way to the far wall. A couple of the younger crewmen made motions to make room for them, but Lyle shook his head and shooed them back to their chairs.

"Even if you can trace your lineage back to one of the twelve tribes, or back to Abraham, for that matter . . . God's not impressed by pedigrees," Chance explained to the study group. "Ultimately, we all come from Adam, and God knows that he made him out of dirt."

From his seat in the front row, Brett Winslow chuckled and, hearing that, a few of the other men decided that it was okay to laugh in a Bible study, so they joined in as well.

"Listen," Chance said. "Those of you who've been coming to these studies for several seasons now can see that we've got a pretty good crowd here this evening, and more than a few folks who may be here for their very first time. And that's great. We hope we'll see you over and over again, and we hope you'll bring your buds. But I don't think we'd be acting responsibly here this evening if we didn't do something that we don't often do at our Bible study, and that's talk, here and now, about God's gift of eternal life and how to receive it.

"I know that every single person here is a hard worker," he continued. "The Busch Series and Nextel Cup are the top of the heap in American racing. You don't get here without working hard, and as for the drivers' wives here tonight . . . well, between running a household and riding herd on us, that's like working two jobs in one."

More chuckles.

"So we're all hard workers. We got where we are by knuckling down and putting in the long hours, crazy hours, and it's natural to think that anything worth having is going to be gained that way. But we're not talking about something natural here tonight. We're talking about something supernatural. You can't earn it, no matter how hard you work. You can't buy it, no matter how much you're worth. All you can do is accept it. We are all paupers in the eyes of God."

The room was so quiet that Chance could hear a light rain beginning to fall, pattering against the rubber-coated metal roof of the assembly center.

"I'm not about to lie to you," Chance told the men and women crowded into the assembly center. "You can search the Scriptures, and you won't find a single place where Jesus buttonholes somebody and says, 'All right, here's what you need to know: there's these four spiritual laws . . .' That's just not the way he ministered. He was more into the kind of ministry that you see in the garage every week, the kind that the folks here at SCM do so well—what Brett, here, refers to as 'the ministry of hanging out.'

"But we live in a world where everything moves amazingly fast, folks. And I'm not going to belabor the obvious—most of the people here make their livings in either cockpits or pit boxes. There's facts that go along with that life. And guys . . . ladies . . . you've got to be ready. I don't care whether you're sixteen or seventy-seven. You've just got to. The Bible says, 'Now is the accepted time . . . now is the day.' And man, that might have been written nearly two thousand years ago to people in a foreign country, but I've got to tell you: it applies to you. You personally. Eternity is coming. Sooner or later, it's coming. Get it settled now."

The rain was coming down now in earnest: a thousand tiny hammers pulsing on the roof of the crowded, wordless assembly center.

"By God's standards, I'm a sinner," Chance said. "If you've told a lie—just one—then you're a sinner, too. If you've ever thought of telling a lie—just once—then you are, too. Those aren't my standards. Those are God's. And step one is admitting what you are according to those standards.

"Sin—even one sin—digs you into a hole," Chance continued. "And you cannot, I don't care who you are, dig yourself out. You don't have the tools. You can't buy your own way out. You don't have anything God needs or wants.

"But there is somebody who can buy your way out, and that somebody is God's Son and God himself—Jesus Christ. When Jesus allowed himself to be crucified—and that's what he did, because what God does not allow does not happen—he took your place and my place and accepted your due and my due for your sins . . . and mine. He said, 'Look, you can't afford this, so I'll pay.' And he paid with pain, and humiliation, and every last drop of his blood.

"You can react to that one of two ways," Chance told the group. "You can be prideful and turn your head, think it doesn't apply to you or lie to yourself that you're going to handle things by yourself . . . or you can graciously accept what is being given to you freely. And God has a way of doing that, too. He asks that you acknowledge that Christ's sacrifice, and that sacrifice alone, is what pays your sin debt. And he asks that you take whatever's been occupying Number One in your life and replace it with the Lord Jesus Christ."

The rain increased to a constant, cacophonous downpour against the roof.

"There's no secret prayer for doing that, no magic chant, no rite or sacrament or ritual," Chance said, raising his voice so he could be heard over the roar of the rain. He bowed his head and closed his eyes. "But right where you are, right now, you can tell God, in your own words, what you just realized, or recommit yourself to what you've realized anew, and get this settled. Right now. This minute. Do that now."

As Chance spoke the last words, he opened his eyes and looked up. All around the crowded little hall, heads were bowed and lips were moving noiselessly in prayer. Even Danford's sons had their eyes downcast out of courtesy to the decisions being made around them. But among all of the people gathered there, only one did not have his head bowed, and that was Lyle Danford. He was gazing back at Chance with a look so blank, so void of expression, that he might have been playing poker with the guys back in the transporter, communicating not the slightest bit of information about the hand that he had been dealt.

CHAPTER 25

Chance ended the Bible study at eight, just as he had announced he would. He knew time was precious to almost all of the people in his group.

But that had not stopped a good dozen of them from coming forward to thank him. Most of the rest had begun to leave, getting as far as the broad awning outside of the assembly center, where the rain, still pounding steadily on the roof and pouring off the canvas in torrents, stopped them in their tracks, causing a press that extended all the way back into the center.

On the other side of a small crowd of people waiting at the sliding glass doors, Chance could see Gage Grissom, head bowed and eyes closed, facing Brett Winslow, whose head was bowed as well, the two of them obviously praying together.

"Well, amen," Chance whispered.

Then he looked for Danford. The driver and his sons were no longer standing near the back of the assembly hall. Nor were they in the line of people waiting to get out.

Shaking hands and acknowledging further thanks, Chance squirmed his way through the knot of people at the wide sliding door and made his way out onto the steps, leading down to the sheltered area under the big tent-like awning. The rain was even louder out here, the taut canvas reporting every single drop like a drumbeat. And the heavy tempo of the weather seemed to make it even more imperative that he find Danford. Chance knew that it must have taken a lot for the older driver to come to the study, let alone bring his sons. Something deep inside was urging Chance to acknowledge that.

He scanned the crowd standing around on the Astroturf, but he didn't see Lyle Danford's familiar profile among them, didn't see the blond-on-brown pattern of Duane Danford's race-weekend hair.

Lightning lit the motorhome paddock, and that's when Chance spotted them. From the steps, in the single moment of that blue-white flash, Chance could see three figures hurrying away. Tucking his Bible under his arm and pulling his coat collar up over his head, Chance trotted down the steps and dashed out into the rain, after them.

Shouting would have been futile. Thunder was shaking the air around them, and rain was rattling off the roofs of the motorhomes parked in the paddock, beating on the asphalt and splashing into newly formed puddles, drumming steadily against the jacket over Chance's head. So he simply ran after the three of them, planting his feet carefully so he wouldn't slip on the wet asphalt, and by the time he caught up with them, they were already under the awning next to LD's huge Prevost bus-chassis motorhome, the two boys standing there, dripping, while Danford fished the keys out of his jacket pocket and unlocked the door.

"Hey, Boomer," Danford said simply, not surprised to see him there. "Come on in and get yourself dried off."

Chance followed the three into the motorhome, which glowed with recessed lighting and smelled of rich hardwoods and leather. It was amazingly spacious on the inside and this, Chance knew, was because this particular model came with slide-outs—sections of the motorhome interior that could cantilever out, away from the chassis, adding more room while it was parked. Chance and Cindy had considered that themselves when they'd gotten their own Prevo coach, but Chance, who had grown up sleeping in a pickup camper on race weekends, had balked at paying nearly $800,000 for a place to bunk at the track. Apparently, Lyle Danford hadn't shared this hesitation.

Danford ducked into the lavatory area and came back with four bath towels, tossing two to the boys and handing a third to Chance.

"Thanks," Chance said, meaning it. The thick terry cloth towel was wonderfully warm—the towel bars on these top-of-the-line coaches were water heated, he remembered.

Already, the squall outside had begun to diminish. While lightning flashes still showed every now and then between the motorhome's miniblinds, the thunder that followed was more delayed and muted, and the raindrops on the roof had dwindled to a steady patter.

"You guys are more than welcome to bunk here for the night," Danford told his sons. "Save you having to go out in the slop."

"Thanks," Danny told him, "but the team's got the two of us in one room at the Quality Inn—it'd be a shame to waste it. And besides, we've got a crew meeting at breakfast tomorrow."

"Understood." Danford nodded.

"But I will make a pit stop before we go," Duane added, ducking into the motorhome's black marble lavatory.

Waiting until the door closed, Danford turned to his eldest son.

"Now you get that boy's backside into that hotel room and you keep it there, do you hear me?"

"Yes, sir," Danny said somberly.

"You want a pizza, that's fine—you go ahead and order one in," Danford told him. "You want to see a movie, order one up on the TV. But don't let him get out on the town. Sit on him if you need to. I got enough headaches comin' this weekend. I don't need to be hunting for Duane all over Richmond. You read me?"

"Yes, sir," Danny repeated. "Don't worry, sir; I promise. We'll get in and we'll stay in."

The lavatory door opened and Duane came out, all smiles. He stepped up and shook Chance's hand.

"That was a fine talk, man," he said. "You go to school for that?"

"I'm starting to," Chance told him.

Lyle Danford arched his eyebrows.

"Awesome," Duane told Chance. "Catch you in the morning."

"Good night, sir," Danny said, and the two of them headed back out into the night, the doorsteps whirring back into place and locking after the door closed behind them.

"What about you?" Danford asked Chance. "You want to stay here, instead of driving back to the hotel? That couch folds out into one heck of a bed. Got a goose-down comforter in the cabinet."

"I appreciate the offer," Chance told him. "But I'd just have to drive back to the hotel in the morning to change, anyway."

"Well, have a drink before you go," Danford said. "Coke?"

"Anything would be fine."

Danford opened the refrigerator, rummaged for a moment, and came back with two Cokes and a Saran Wrapped tray of sandwiches.

"We got roast beef, ham, turkey, and cheese," Danford said, peering through the plastic wrap.

"Roast beef sounds great."

"Want it heated?"

"Cold's fine."

"Then I'll join you," Danford said, handing Chance a sandwich and taking one for himself. "I keep the ham sandwiches around for Duane. He crumbles cheese curls on top of the mayonnaise before he eats them. Can you imagine that?"

"Just barely."

"Well, have a seat."

Chance looked at the leather sofa, touched its buttery smooth surface tentatively, and put his towel down on it before sitting in his damp jeans. Danford felt the fabric of his own jeans, shrugged, and then settled onto the loveseat facing him.

"That true what you said? You're studying to be a preacher?"

"Not exactly to be a preacher, no." Chance told him about the conversation with Brett and about the advice to get a degree in something you loved.

"And besides," Chance concluded, "most of the course work is on the Internet. I'll study some before I turn in tonight, back at the hotel."

"What do you do? Read the Bible on computer and take quizzes?"

"A little. But most of it is theology, and hermeneutics—that's the study of interpreting Scripture. I passed their basic Greek test, so I'm taking an independent-study course in advanced Greek, plus an introduction to Old Testament Hebrew. The counseling course looked interesting—I figure if I'm going to be a father, that might come in handy. So I'm taking that, too, this term. Things like that."

"Man. Sounds like you've got time on your hands."

"Well, when all this goes away"—Chance waved his hands to take in the motorhome, the track, the millions of dollars' worth of racecars and support equipment sitting just a few hundred yards away—"time is what you end up with plenty of."

"I never finished high school, myself," Danford muttered, lifting the bread of his sandwich and squeezing a little packet of yellow mustard onto it. "I did the GEDT after I met Dottie, though. She's been to college. Studied art."

"No kidding?"

"Sure. She still paints when she's not outside, messing with her roses. I'm gonna build her a studio, back of the house, for Christmas."

Both men fell silent then, because both realized, simultaneously, that it would take the income of an active, competitive driver to make a gesture like that as a Christmas present, and only one of them could afford to do it any longer.

"Probably a good thing for me that you're taking that counseling course," Danford finally said as he picked up his sandwich.

Silently praying a blessing over his food, Chance put some horseradish on his roast beef. Then he looked up.

"From the way things went today," he said, "I'd say I'd better take the whole thing before I go and try applying it."

"Naw." Danford shook his head. "That was just me. I told you we was poor when I was a kid, right?"

Chance nodded, even though he found it hard to believe that a man with Danford's wealth had ever been poor.

"Well, we was," Danford said. "Daddy drank a little, so he never really got ahead. He worked at the textile mill when they needed him and did odd jobs when they didn't. We pretty much lived paycheck to paycheck. Anyhow, one time when he was roofin' to get by, he fell off a ladder, carrying a bundle of shingles. Messed up his back bad—he ached until the day he died, although he went back to the mill when they called him, a month after the accident. But for three or four weeks there, there was just no money coming into the house. None whatsoever. And we got us some door-knocking Christians that came by . . . I think I was about thirteen at the time . . . and Momma and Daddy were gone to the doctor, so I screwed up my courage and I told these church folks, 'Listen. We need us some help. We ain't got no food here.' And you know what they did?"

Danford looked up over his sandwich and Chance shook his head.

"They offered to pray with me," Danford told him. "That's what they did. I mean they didn't give me a dime, didn't offer me a crust of bread. They didn't even give me directions to a soup kitchen. They offered to pray. Here my whole family's ribs was showin'—I had two little sisters in the house and you could tell that they was hungry—and all they want to give me is a 'God bless ya.' The very next day, I lied about my age and went to work in a poultry-processing plant—only place I found that would hire me. I let 'em pay me my first day's wages in chicken. And to this day, I tend to go just a little bit sour when folks hand out God instead of solutions."

He bit into his sandwich and shook his head.

"I'm sorry, Lyle," Chance said sincerely. "They . . . I . . . should have been giving you help, not talk."

Danford shrugged and shook his head. "Who knows?" He took a bite of sandwich, chewed it, and swallowed, washing it down with a sip of Coke. "If somebody had stepped in and cared for us back then, maybe I wouldn't have started working when I was thirteen, and I might never have developed my world-famous competitive edge."

He grinned broadly. "So maybe it was all for the best."

Chance sipped his own Coke. "Maybe so," he said. "But you're my friend, Lyle. And friends help friends."

Danford smiled kindly. "I went off half-cocked earlier," he said. "The reason I showed up tonight . . . well . . . I figure if I know somebody with an in with the man upstairs, I shouldn't ought to waste that. I was hoping maybe you'd pray for me."

Chance took a breath.

"I do pray for you, Lyle," he finally said. "Every morning and every night."

The seasoned driver looked at Chance—with not the impassive poker face that he'd shown in the assembly hall, but the face of a man who was genuinely touched. Then, just as quickly, the look went away.

"So," he asked. "About Duane: what advice do you have for me?"

Chance thought for a moment.

"If," he began, "you're really certain he's got the law after him . . ."

Danford nodded.

"Then it seems to me that you have two choices," Chance said. "One would be to cooperate with the police, give them all the information you have, and see if they can stop Duane before he gets too much further over his head."

"I've thought about that," Lyle said. "What's the alternative?"

"To keep so close an eye on him that he never gets into another situation where the police would be interested," Chance said. "What we've done, getting him on the race team—"

"What you've done," Danford corrected him.

"Whatever. That's a good start. But it's not enough. You're going to have to keep him on a pretty short leash."

"I got his brother watching him," Danford pointed out.

"That's a step," Chance agreed. "But his brother's not his daddy. It's not his responsibility. It's yours."

"Maybe you haven't noticed," Danford pointed out, "but I seem to be . . . what do you say . . . persona non grata with my youngest son."

"But the Bible still makes it clear that you're the one God's holding accountable for him," Chance replied. "I'm not saying it's going to be easy, LD. If he keeps resisting your authority, you just may have to put together enough evidence of suspicious circumstances—and I think that motorcycle title is enough by itself—that you can hire a good, Christian, family lawyer. You might have to go to court and get an injunction requiring Duane to be with either you or Dottie when he's not in school or at work. I'm no lawyer, but I'm pretty sure that you can get a judge to issue an order like that on a juvenile. One that says that if he breaks that rule, he's in the pokey, no questions asked."

"Man," Danford mumbled, "wouldn't the tabloids just love to get hold of that for a human-interest story?"

"Better that than the news that he's serving twenty years in the penitentiary," Chance said. "Or that he's gone and hurt somebody or killed them in a drug deal."

Danford picked up his Coke, set it down, and said nothing.

"We're talking worst-case scenario here, Lyle," Chance added quickly. "Duane may have attitude by the yard, but he's not stupid. On the contrary, he strikes me as an exceptionally bright kid. I don't think you're going to have to get a restraining order on him. I think that just the knowledge that you could do it would be enough to really cool his jets. And deep down inside, this might be something he's really wanting anyhow—somebody to sit on him a little and show him that they love him."

"Love him?" Danford leaned forward. "That boy's got enough for any ten kids. I've never denied him a thing."

"Well, sometimes," Chance replied, "denial is love."

Danford leaned back and shook his head.

"Boomer," he said. "I've raised three kids. Yours is still in the oven. And I reckon I just might know a little more about this parenthood thing than you think."

"Well," Chance pointed out, "you asked."

"And you answered, and I thank you."

Chance said nothing. He'd known Danford long enough to recognize when he'd pushed the man as far as he could go.

The two men ate their sandwiches and drank their soft drinks.

Chance looked at his watch.

"That was good, LD. Thanks." He got up. "Now, I'd better get back to the hotel. You need to get your rest, and I've got that studying to do, and I need to call Cindy at her mom's."

"Call her from here if you like," Danford said, nodding at the cell phone in its charger on the motorhome's black marble counter.

Chance grinned. "These aren't the kind of calls you make in front of company."

Danford shook his head and got to his feet.

"I keep forgetting you two are so young," he told Chance. "So, just how far along is Cindy now?"

"A little under five months."

Danford grinned.

"Man," he said. "You'd better get back to your hotel and get you some rest. Four or five months from now, you're gonna wish you'd gotten more."

CHAPTER 26

Foothills Medical Complex—Charlotte, North Carolina

The ultrasound image didn't look much like a baby at first. It looked more like a radar picture of a rapidly developing weather front. But then, as the doctor pointed out hands, feet, arms, legs, head, the image made sense, and Chance and Cindy gazed at the screen in nearly reverent wonder while the doctor moved the flashlight-like imaging head across Cindy's swelling abdomen.

"Looks as if this youngster understands that you don't want to know the gender until the time comes," the doctor commented. "We've got a leg in the way from this angle; I couldn't tell, anyway."

"I'm pretty sure it's a boy," Cindy said, smiling. "I'm getting way too big to be carrying anything feminine."

It was exaggeration, of course. From behind, it was almost impossible to tell that Cindy was pregnant.

"Let me get a picture of mother and child," Chance said. He raised the little brushed-aluminum digital camera that he'd bought the morning after Cindy had told him about the pregnancy, and took a shot: Cindy's beautiful, beaming blue-eyed face, with the monitor clearly visible in the background.

Chance looked at the image on the little screen on the back of the camera, and then showed it to Cindy, who smiled. She was a remarkably good sport about his determination to document just about every aspect of her pregnancy. They had shots of her shopping for maternity clothes, shots of their Lamaze classes, shots of the two of them converting what had been their third spare bedroom into a nursery with pink and blue wallpaper dotted with white lambs.

Chance had already filled up most of a CD with digital photographs, and they were only two-thirds of the way through the pregnancy. But both sets of soon-to-be grandparents loved it. Cindy's mother already had a PC—she used it with her sewing machine for embroidery—but Chance's folks had actually gone out and bought a computer so they could get email and see the updates that he sent.

Cindy's doctor pronounced her "healthy as a horse and still as pretty as a picture." Then the two of them got in the Expedition and drove across the small medical campus surrounding Charlotte Receiving Hospital to see Chance's ophthalmologist.

There, as Cindy sat and watched, Chance went through the same routine that he'd endured approximately every two weeks since Sonoma. He'd actually gotten used to having his eyes artificially dilated. The ophthalmologist examined his retina, and then did something he hadn't done before—he had Chance put his head against the brow band of a special video camera and recorded what he was seeing during the eye examination.

"Let's take a look," the doctor had suggested, seating the two of them at a table in front of a large flat-screen computer monitor. Then he'd begun running the video he'd shot, and Chance couldn't shake the similarity of that situation to what they'd experienced earlier in the morning at Cindy's obstetrician's office. In both cases, it was the two of them, holding hands and looking at a screen while a physician explained what they were seeing. Only in Cindy's case, it had been a hopeful and exciting visit.

"So," Chance asked as the doctor put drops in his eyes to relax the dilation agent. "How am I?"

"Good," the doctor said. "I'm ready to call the situation stable. We can cut the visits back to every three months, if you like."

Chance nodded. "And the literature," he asked. "Any new studies?"

"New?" The doctor shrugged with his hand. "There are new studies every day. But as far as something that can help you right now? I never like to say 'never.' But I have to admit that, in every case I've seen or read of like this, what you've got after stabilization is the best you're ever going to get. Dr. Peters and I will keep looking, but I wouldn't get my hopes up if I were you."

"'For with God, nothing shall be impossible,'" Cindy whispered.

The doctor looked up.

"That's the Bible," she said softly. "The gospel of Luke."

The doctor nodded, but said nothing.

Cindy slept while Chance drove the two of them home. She was nodding by the time they got to the main highway and sound asleep a few minutes after that. It was a new characteristic of her pregnancy. She'd become like a cat, always finding the warmest seat in a room and curling up and falling asleep instantly, waking refreshed after twenty minutes, and then nodding off again an hour or so later.

Not that Chance minded. He knew the rest was good for her, so he welcomed it.

Besides, it made him feel good to be driving while she slept in perfect faith that he was there to keep her safe and sound and comfortable. He looked at her, watching her chest rise and fall slowly with the breaths, looked at her face—flawless, right down to the strong cheekbones and the perfect natural symmetry of her nose—and felt his throat go thick with emotion.

One blue eye winked open and looked back at him.

"Hey, handsome," she purred. "You keeping an eye on the road?"

"My good one." Chance nodded.

The tires hummed on the pavement.

"I love you, Chance."

He squeezed her hand.

"I love you too, sweetheart."

"And God's going to make this work out," Cindy added.

"I know he will," Chance agreed. "But I think I need to be doing something as well. . . . If I can't drive, I mean."

He fell silent and now it was Cindy's turn to squeeze his hand.

Chance gulped quietly.

"I guess I'm thinking that it's finally time for me to figure out what I'm going to be doing next year," he said. "To get ready to move on to whatever job I'm going to be doing next."

"You're drawing two salaries now."

"Until the end of the year."

"But I thought Robert said you had a place with RVR."

"He did, but I'm not sure RVR has a place with me. I mean, if he makes me a crew chief or a car chief, first of all, somebody has to go, and he's got really exceptional people in all four of those positions. It wouldn't be fair to them or the teams to have me coming in and bumping out a good guy. And second, who would I be working with? Either LD, which would be a constant reminder of who used to be his teammate, or Gage, which would be even worse—having the guy he's replacing breathing down his neck for the rest of his career. And it would be the same thing if Robert made me a general manager. His heart's in the right place, but I really think I need to be looking for something else, you know?"

"In racing, though . . . right?" Cindy asked, both eyes open now.

"Oh, sure, in racing. I mean, what else do I know?"

CHAPTER 27

Talladega Superspeedway—Talladega, Alabama

The reality of the situation truly sank in when Chance saw his car with rookie stripes.

Although his name was still painted above the driver's side window of the distinctive, red-white-and-blue E-World Broadband Taurus, two long, yellow, horizontal rectangles had been added to the rear valance. They were there to warn other competitors that the driver of this particular entry was in his first year of NASCAR Nextel Cup Series competition.

To Chance, who had lost his own rookie stripes three years earlier, it was like a trip back in time. And that was good, because it helped him remember what Gage Grissom was going through. He remembered going into the first turn for the first time at Atlanta and having three seasoned veterans pass him—foom, foom, FOOM—on the inside, their tires distorted by the side-bite, their front air dams erupting in dots and dashes of dust as they ground the uneven bits away against the pavement. The cars he had driven in the Busch Series had helped to prepare him to a certain extent, but Cup cars sported an extra hundred or more horsepower and a longer wheelbase, and those two facts made all the difference in the world.

There was that plus the fact that qualifying was always a crapshoot to a certain extent. You could practice with your qualifying cylinder heads, your qualifying intake, and your qualifying exhaust system—all the crew chief tricks to make a fast car go faster—but you couldn't control the fact that the track might be ten degrees warmer by qualifying time. That difference could make a loose car tight or a tight car completely unmanageable.

And you couldn't control your qualifying time. The qualifying order was determined by drawing numbered "pills"—that was what the folks around NASCAR called them—out of an old-fashioned hand-cranked bingo drum. While crew chiefs had any number of superstitions that they observed during the qualifying draw—wearing a special T-shirt under one's uniform shirt, or carrying a rabbit's foot, or avoiding people who were eating peanuts—what it all boiled down to was randomness, pure and simple.

Then there was the fact that you could not, for all practical purposes, tape up a car in practice to the extent one would for actual qualifying. Blocking off airflow to the radiator for that long a time was just like asking the engine to blow. So you practiced with a little tape on the grill, and qualified with it all on. The idea was that the crew chief had enough practical experience and wind tunnel data to know what difference those few pieces of tape would make. But a rookie driver would not.

Chance knew all of this and spoke of none of it to Gage. In fact, as there had only been two Busch races in the month since the September Richmond race, his conversations with Gage had been few and, for the most part, technical. He hadn't even had an opportunity to ask the young driver about the decision he'd made at the SCM Bible study, even though Gage had come to the Saturday morning Busch chapel service at both Dover and Kansas. Unlike the Bible studies, the chapel services were fairly public events, attended by media and even some well-connected fans. And despite the fact that the Bible called on Christians to be unashamed of Christ, Chance knew better than to come up to a new Christian in front of others and say, "Hey, I saw that you got saved in Virginia. Outstanding!"

Chance had tried calling Gage a few times, but the two men were on separate timetables. With the news that he was moving up to Cup, Gage's appearance and interview schedules had picked up. What with Cindy's and Chance's doctor visits and the shopping they were doing to finish the nursery, it seemed as if they were always away whenever Gage called back. And neither man carried his cell phone regularly enough to be reached dependably.

So the talk they'd had this morning had been more of a performance than a conversation. Chance had been very matter-of-fact, letting the rookie ride on the confidence that he had made dozens of qualifying runs before in Busch competition. Then he had left Gage in Andy's capable hands while Chance drove one of the team golf carts through the tunnel to the back of the grandstand and took his place high above the press boxes, one of just a handful of people standing on the long spotter's platform.

Andy had drawn the fifteenth qualifying spot, about one third of the way into the order. It wasn't as late as Chance would have liked—the car would run best on a slightly cooler track—but it was late enough that there would be good rubber laid down on the groove, providing not only better grip but a broad black stripe for Gage to follow around the tri-oval.

The qualifying record at this track, set by Bill Elliott in 1987, was almost 213 miles per hour, and it was in absolutely no danger of being broken today. That same year, Bobby Allison's car almost went over the catch-fence in a spectacular airborne crash. So from 1988 on, all Cup racing at Talladega and Daytona—the two true high-banked super-speedways—had been done with restrictor plates. These were thin metal plates that choked off part of the airflow to the intake manifold and dramatically reduced a car's horsepower. Drivers uniformly hated restrictor-plate racing—it changed the racing from an edge-of-the-envelope experience to something more like an aggressive commute on the interstate. It reduced throttle response and it tended to bunch cars up, creating lots of potential for "the big one"—a wreck that would collect a number of cars all at once. But it did reduce the number of crashes in which cars went airborne, and it kept the energy at a level that the catch-fences could contain.

Still, even though no record was on the line today, and even though the speeds would be kept down to 185 to 187 miles per hour, the first dozen cars out on the track all had been very competitive, turning lap times within a tenth of a second of one another.

As Chance watched through his binoculars, the thirteenth car in the qualifying order—a locally sponsored racer hoping to make the big time—ran his warm-up lap and then, going into Turn One on his first timed lap, blew the motor in a plume of blue-gray smoke. The car oiled the track from that point until the backstretch, where the driver was able to pull down onto the apron for the coast back into the pits. This in turn required NASCAR to take to the track with oil-dry and sweepers, followed by jet dryers to blow the residual oil-dry compound out of the racing groove.

That took fifteen minutes. And Gage, Chance knew, would already be buttoned into the racecar, waiting his turn to take to the track. Waiting to go out was always a butterflies-in-the-stomach experience. Waiting out a delay could be absolutely unnerving.

Chance touched his radio, keying the headset's boom microphone. "They're just about done here, Gage," he assured his driver.

Gage's voice came back in a burst of static.

"Does it look like they've got it all up?"

"Yeah," Chance told him. "But you'll want to run in the lower groove. That's what everybody's used so far, so that's what they've cleaned the best. There'll always be at least a little bit of oil-dry left high on the track until ten or twelve cars have run by it. You've only got one car left ahead of you. I'll tell you how that goes."

"Sounds good."

The safety crews left the track and the fourteenth car in the qualifying order, another rookie, came roaring out of the pits, using every bit of track that he could to get up to speed in the warm-up lap. Then he took the green flag for his attempt, and Chance could see right away that he was running too high. Sure enough, he got into Turn One too hot, lost traction on the dusting of oil-dry compound that remained high in the turn, and spun, backing the car into the wall at nearly 150 miles per hour.

"Sit tight," Chance told Gage, down on pit road. "We got a wreck in One."

The driver of the wrecked car was okay—the window net came down almost immediately—but the rear quarter of the car had disintegrated against the wall, littering the track with debris. Ten more minutes were spent towing away the wreck and sweeping up the track, and Chance could almost feel Gage growing warmer and warmer in his firesuit as he waited for his turn to go out. Finally the safety crews came back in and the yellow lights around the track stopped flashing.

"Just follow the groove," Chance advised as Gage fired the engine and came roaring out of the pit lane, winding through the gears to build momentum. The shifts were abrupt, with no lull between them, and Chance knew that Gage, like all Cup drivers, was shifting without touching the clutch, not willing to waste even a millisecond of engine power. In the grandstands at Chance's feet, a crowd of more than 80,000 fans was standing and cheering, knowing that there was an Alabama boy at the wheel, making his Nextel Cup debut on the 2.66-mile, steeply banked tri-oval—the biggest track in NASCAR.

The red-white-and-blue car with the orange "53" on its roof flew around the track for its warm-up lap, the front air dam pressed right down to the pavement by the airflow. But as soon as Gage crossed the starting line, Chance knew that he was running far too close to the wall, and as the car dived into the turn, the extra speed induced by running downhill across the thirty-three-degree banking was enough to get the car loose. Gage fishtailed through the first turn, caught it, and then fishtailed again in Two.

"Okay," Chance told him on the radio. "Lift."

"What?"

Even over the radio, the confusion was evident in Gage's voice.

"Lift," Chance repeated. "All the way. Trust me. I want you to slow down as much as you can without flat-spotting the tires. Then, when you get to Four, I want you to make a U-turn well before the start-finish line and bring her back all the way around to the pit road exit."

"You want me to run a lap *backwards?*"

Chance grinned.

"Nothing in the rulebooks that says you can't, Gage."

Out on the track, the engine noise died to almost nothing as the young driver lifted off the accelerator obediently.

The car motored slowly around the final two banked turns, turned down the banking to the pit lane entrance, and then started back the other way, slowly running clockwise on the 4,000-foot backstretch.

"Okay," Gage radioed. "I'm going back. Mind telling me why?"

"Here's what we're doing," Chance said, glad for the rookie's trust. "You're still on lap one, because you haven't crossed the start-finish line yet. Your time is going to be huge, but that doesn't matter, because it wasn't going to be competitive anyway. So what we're going to do is run it over again and use it as another warm-up lap—it won't count as a lap until you actually cross the line. And then we're going to clip off a quick one and stay right in the middle of the groove and get you a spot up near the front. Okay?"

"Gotcha," Gage replied.

"Drop down to the pit exit and make your turn uphill into the end of the front stretch, just before One," Chance advised the driver. "That'll let you use the banking to get yourself up to speed."

"Will do."

The E-World Taurus pulled down onto the pit lane exit and then started its turn up the track. The crowd, on its feet, roared its approval, understanding what the rookie was up to. The noise in the air was almost palpable.

"Okay," Chance said, "through the gears and drop the hammer. Your tires are warm now. You can keep it floorboarded through every turn as long as you stay right in the groove. You can do it. Go."

Gage got the car up to speed quickly and stayed there, the engine howling at full power as he swept around the track. He passed under the flag stand and his average lap speed—"71.383 MPH"—flashed up on the scoreboard, raising a titter from the stands. But he was running full bore now, and the car was right in the middle of the black-fogged section of track that defined the racing groove. The car didn't bobble or jump one iota. It just rode around the first two turns of the huge, banked tri-oval in a perfect arc and then shot down the long backstretch, exiting the second turn perfectly square.

The crowd was jumping up and down now, cheering him on, and Gage rode at full throttle into Turn Three, something that would have been madness at most speedways, but was possible here because of the wide track and the incredibly steep banking. He let the car drift with the groove until he was almost touching the concrete wall on the Turn Four exit, and then he flew down the front stretch. The engine roared until he was a hundred yards past the checkered flag. After that, he shut it down, popping the shifter back into neutral and saving the power train for the race.

The lap speed—"186.501 MPH"—flashed up on the scoreboard, and the crowd erupted in screams and yelps as "53" appeared in lights at the top of the position column.

"Spectacular run, Gage," Chance told the driver. "That's good for the pole."

Of course it didn't last. There were still thirty-five cars left to make qualifying attempts. The good news was that Gage was now definitely in the race without having to resort to a provisional. Even if every single car that followed him was able to beat his time, he would still qualify thirty-sixth, one step above the last spot that could be won on the basis of lap speeds.

But the vast majority of them could not so much as touch his lap speed. Even so, an hour after Gage's run, the Home Depot Chevrolet came out and bettered his speed by a slim three-thousandths of a mile per hour. Then Lyle Danford, third to last in the qualifying order, clipped off a first qualifying lap at 186.701 miles per hour. He shut the engine down at the line, not even bothering to run the second lap.

That put Gage third in the field for his first Nextel Cup start—right behind Danford in the starting grid.

CHAPTER 28

Chance pulled the folding chairs off the metal trailer four at a time and handed them to Brett Winslow, who arranged them in rows in the empty inspection garage, leaving a center aisle running down the middle of the rows.

Outside, plainly visible through the four open garage doors, NASCAR officials were running cars through the prerace inspection in the morning sunlight, fitting templates over roofs and hoods and deck panels, running calipers over spoilers and fender metal, checking hood pins with magnets, and generally looking for the myriad other ways that an innovative crew chief might try to win an unfair advantage over his brethren.

Prerace inspections were almost always done outside, weather permitting. The cars had already undergone a fairly thorough inspection in order to get their qualifying stickers, and ambient light was better for the general once-overs that the cars were given the morning of the race. The post-race inspections were a different matter—NASCAR would take the top finishers into the garage and tear them down right to the crankshafts, measuring and weighing everything to make sure the vehicles were completely within the rules. But on race-day morning, the racing organization's only use for the inspection garage was for the mandatory drivers' and crew chiefs' meeting. And SCM had long since worked out a congenial relationship with NASCAR—if NASCAR would let SCM set the garage up for chapel, NASCAR could use SCM's seating and sound system for their drivers' meeting.

In the back of the big, open fifty-by-one-hundred-foot garage, Brett's youth pastor and one of the guys from the physical therapy unit were setting up the sound board. It was an elaborate affair with dozens of sliding switches and meters, in truth, more than was needed for Brett's brief twenty-minute weekly message. But SCM used a top-of-the-line sound system for the benefit of the recording artists who often volunteered to come in and lead worship.

On the weeks when no outside talent was coming in, Brett sang. And unlike most men who liked to sing, Brett actually had a pretty good voice—one that somebody would actually want to listen to. He often sang as he was driving or working in his cubicle in the assembly center, and he usually sang, or at least hummed, as they got things set up for the services. But this morning he wasn't doing either one. Chance noticed that.

"You're pretty quiet this morning, Preacher," he said.

"Huh?" Brett looked up. "Oh . . . just lost in thought, I guess."

"Running through your message?"

"Yeah. Something like that."

But there was something about Brett that didn't look right, either. Chance watched him out of the corner of his one good eye and then it struck him; the chaplain wasn't smiling. And that was downright remarkable. Brett Winslow was *always* smiling—a smile of joy when he was singing, a smile of camaraderie when he was talking with you, a smile of comfort when he was dealing with a worried or bereaved family. But this morning he was perfectly straight-faced. Chance had never seen him that way before. Not once in four years.

Much as he wanted to, Chance didn't pursue the topic. He'd gotten far enough along in his counseling studies to know better. When Brett wanted to talk, he'd talk. So Chance held his peace and set up chairs.

Later that morning, after the drivers' meeting, as crew members and wives were coming in to join the drivers for the service, Brett had a shadow of a smile back on his face even though he was still nowhere near his usual buoyant self.

But after the soloist—a music major from Alabama State—had sung "Heart of Worship," Brett was back "on," and he delivered a brief but powerful message on "the God of lost causes." He talked about how the father of the demon-possessed boy in Matthew 17 was at his wit's end when he came to Jesus, and how Jesus fixed things then and there. He talked about Lazarus. He talked about parents in the New Testament who'd lost their children—the widow in Nain, the leader of the synagogue—and then had them restored by Christ.

"And I tell you with all my heart that I love the people in this room," Brett said. "I truly do. You're like family to me. I see you more than I do some members of my natural family. But I don't love you a thousandth . . . a ten-thousandth . . . as much as the God who bled out his life in love for you. And he is the one you should turn to before your back is against the wall, and he is the one you must turn to when there doesn't seem to be any way out. You talk to him in the language that Jesus gave us in Matthew and Mark—in prayer and fasting—and he will listen. You have his word on that."

As he listened to Brett's words, it struck Chance that maybe his old friend had put together this message especially for him, because no one knew more about Chance's situation than Brett. The more Chance thought of it, the more he was sure of it, and it brought tears to his eyes just to think it. Then he looked around the room and noticed that nearly half the people there were wiping their eyes, and he was no longer so sure that it had been for him, and him alone.

His inclination was to have a word with Brett after the service, but about a dozen people had apparently felt the same way; there was a line waiting up front. And Chance could see Gage making his way out the side door. He wanted to talk with the rookie one last time before he got dressed to drive. Taking a final look in Brett's direction, Chance set off at a trot after Gage.

"You good to go?"

"As good as I'm gonna be," Gage began. Then, seeing the look in Chance's eyes, he said, "No. I take that back. I'm good. I'm ready."

"There you go."

With Gage in the lead, the two men walked down the transporter corridor to the lounge, where Gage's driving clothes had been set out. At the doorway, Gage turned, head cocked.

"Is everything okay?"

"How do you mean?" Chance replied.

"Well, just now—out in the garage area, on the walk from the chapel service to here. You kind of blew by me like I wasn't there."

Chance nodded.

"That was intentional, Gage," he admitted. "I've been kind of ducking the press while this eye thing gets completely figured out, so, although people have seen us together, talking, I've not given any interviews about what we're doing. And since I haven't been talking, the tendency is going to be for the media people to report on what they see, as opposed to what they've heard, and I don't want it to seem like you're driving the car, but I'm pulling the strings. Because that's not the case and that's not fair to you."

Gage shrugged. "Who gives a flying rip what they think? Besides, I wouldn't have qualified worth squat if you hadn't been there, coaching me."

"I just reminded you that you had the option to rewind—"

"Which I never would have had the nerve to do if you hadn't told me."

"Okay." Chance nodded. "But as for giving a rip, you really need to, Gage. This racing deal is a whole lot about image. Especially when you're new. Guys like LD can afford to have attitudes; the sport grew up around him. But if you start out with a chip on your shoulder, that'll scare people off, including sponsors."

Gage listened, saying nothing.

"Gage, you are genuine," Chance said. "The real deal. I can tell that. Don't hide it. I know a lot of young racers who think they have to act wild to fit in. They don't. Two hundred miles an hour strapped into a ton and a half of metal is plenty wild enough. I mean . . . you made a decision at that chapel service in Richmond, didn't you?"

Gage glanced up quickly.

"Did Brett tell you that?"

"Absolutely not. Nobody respects a man's privacy more than Preacher. But I saw you praying with him."

"Yeah," Gage admitted. "I did. But I'm not really sure it took."

"Why's that?"

Gage glanced around, making sure they were alone.

"I dunno," he muttered. "I mean, the night of that Bible study, I felt so . . . well . . . changed. . . ."

Chance nodded.

"But then, just three days later," Gage continued, "my girlfriend and I had a blowup, and I wound up sore at her—had this attitude the rest of the week. And then, later that week, when she was gone visiting her sister, some of my buds came over, and the next thing you know, we had a party going, and I'm making out with some chick that showed up for the party. I didn't even know her name. I mean, we didn't . . . you know . . . do anything, but still, I sure wasn't thinking of Janet. Or maybe I was, and I was trying to get even. And I ended getting blasted out of my gourd."

Gage took a breath and leaned back against the bulkhead, eyes on the ceiling.

"And by the time we got to the Dover race, man, I was back to the same-old, same-old," he muttered. "Going out and finding a kegger and drinking myself stupid. . . . Chance, I haven't been to another Bible study. I almost didn't even go to chapel this morning except I was already there after the drivers' meeting, and you were there and . . . I dunno . . . I guess I was trying to get on God's good side before this race. Does that all sound like the attitude of a Christian to you?"

Chance smiled.

"It doesn't sound like the attitude of a mature Christian, no," he agreed. "But let me ask you something. Is that the first time you ever had a blowup with your girl?"

"No," Gage admitted.

"And getting drunk. Was that the first time that ever happened?"

Gage managed a lopsided grin. "Not hardly."

"But was it the first time you ever felt bad about those things?"

Gage cocked his head, pursing his lips.

"It's the first time I ever felt this bad," he said. "Yeah."

Chance smiled. "Somebody, I'm not sure who, once wrote, 'There is a hole in the human heart that only God can fill.' And that was you before you made that decision, Gage. An empty-hearted man. But when you said 'yes' to Christ, that hole was filled. By God. Every Christian carries God, the Holy Spirit, inside."

Chance touched his chest with his fist. "And that's what's different, Gage. Without God, every blowup looks like the other person's fault, and getting drunk is just getting drunk. But when you have the Holy Spirit inside of you, the Bible says that those sorts of things 'grieve . . . the Spirit.' And what you're feeling now is conviction over having done that. I'd say it 'took' just fine, Gage. And the way you feel now is proof of that."

"So what do I do about it?"

"What we just did. The Bible says it's good for Christians to bare their faults to other Christians. And it says we should pray about them too. Want to do that?"

Gage glanced over Chance's shoulder, down the empty corridor.

"Sure," he said, looking back at Chance.

The two men bowed their heads.

"Gracious Lord Jesus," Chance prayed, "you died one death for all sins, and we thank you for that. We thank you for putting the unseemly side of ourselves under your blood, so it will not be held against us. We thank you, our Creator, for knowing that we are weak. We thank you for the comfort of the Holy Spirit, and we apologize from the very bottom of our hearts for our offenses. We humbly claim your sacrifice as our payment for those transgressions, and we ask you to help us do better each and every day and walk more closely with you. In your precious name we pray."

"Amen," Gage said.

"You're God's child," Chance assured Gage. "Have confidence in that."

The rookie nodded.

At the far end of the transporter, Duane Danford came through the sliding glass doors, took a tire gauge out of a drawer, looked up, and smiled.

"Hey, Chance." He nodded. "And CT, you go get 'em today."

Duane went back out the way he'd come in.

"CT?" Chance asked.

"That started yesterday," Gage said with a sheepish grin. He pointed to his red hair. "I've got this, and I'm from Alabama. Next thing you know, Abe, the gas man, decides I'm 'Crimson Tide.'"

Chance laughed until he hurt.

Gage's Alabama roots did him proud during driver introductions. As he walked out, waving, to shake hands with the grand marshal, all 138,000 people in the grandstands rose to their feet, roaring as if they were trying to be heard in Selma. Binoculars to his eyes, Chance could see that the kid was blushing, all the way from the spotters' stand, high atop the grandstands.

Then, as soon as Gage had made the walk to the racecar, they were down to business. Chance saw Brett walk up next to the car and put his arm around Gage's shoulder. The two men bowed their heads, and Chance tried to pray with them, but he was distracted by a regret—a melancholy at being up there on the stand and not down in the car. Then a crewman handed Gage his heel cups.

It all seemed to go more quickly for Chance, watching it from atop the grandstand. They did their radio check, with Pooch checking in from his station atop the hauler, where he could get a better view of the backstretch.

"Gotcha, Gage," Chance confirmed. "Go with God, buddy."

Then the engines fired and the field was moving.

Chance was just about to remind Gage to just take it easy and hold position for the first fifty laps when a new voice came on the radio. It was the color commentator for the NBC racecast, asking Gage how he felt in the moments before his first Nextel Cup start.

"Good, BP. I'm lookin' forward to it."

The pace car doused its lights, and Chance stayed quiet, letting the kid—the driver—concentrate. The field circled the track like a pair of multicolored caterpillars. The pace cars pulled off, and Chance trained his binoculars on the flag stand.

"Get ready," he radioed Gage. "Green flag! Green!"

The air reverberated with the thunder of forty-three unmuffled race engines at full throttle. Like a wave crashing down the front stretch, the field accelerated past the starting line and into the first turn.

"Looking outside," Chance advised his driver. "Still looking. Stay tucked. He'll find a hole behind you. On your bumper. Clear."

The field began to form a rough, elongated wedge. At its head, LD, Gage, and a Chevy were running single file. Behind them, a cluster of a dozen cars was running double- and triple-wide. And in the middle of the field, cars were running four-wide for as long as the straightaways would allow it.

"Man," Gage's voice crackled over the team's FM frequency, "all I can see in my mirror is 'Home Depot.'"

"That's cool," Gage told him. "You'll need five or six cars working together to really start to pull away here. Just stay tucked."

"I'm tuckin'," Gage replied, and Chance laughed.

The field circled the track three times, two more cars joining the single-file group up front. Slowly they began to creep away from the other thirty-eight cars, the aerodynamic advantages of five cars running nose-to-tail overcoming the horsepower constraints imposed by the restrictor plates.

On the fourth lap, Gage got back on the radio. "I'm running hot," he said simply.

"Where's the gauge?" Andy asked immediately from the pits.

"Two-thirty-five," Gage replied. "And climbing."

"You seeing any steam, Chance?" Andy radioed.

Chance glassed the car carefully, looking near the right side of the windshield, where the cooling-system overflow was.

"Nothing yet," he replied. He kept the "talk" button down and said, "Drift about half a car high on the straights and get some air on the grille, Gage, but don't let the 20 get below you. We'll need to run her this way until Hoss can pull some tape off on the first stop."

"Ten-four."

Gage popped up for a quick breather out of the next turn and then tucked back in again. But breaking the draft like that slowed the front group's progress away from the rest of the field. Chance could almost sense the tension from the pits; all the car needed was to have a two-inch strip of duct tape pulled away from the front grille, just a little more air on the radiator to keep the engine from overheating. But the team couldn't afford a stop just for that—they'd lose too much track position unless they waited until a regular pit stop.

"Listen," Gage radioed again. "I think I'm stronger than LD. I'm keeping up with him even when I break the draft. How about I lead us until we can pit and fix this?"

Chance nudged Catfish Lebeau, Lyle Danford's spotter, who was standing next to him on the platform. Lebeau looked his way and Chance put one hand in front of the other, pantomiming a pass. Lebeau spoke on his radio for a moment, and then shook his head.

Gage nudged him again, and Lebeau lifted his headset.

"Gage is running hot," Chance yelled into his ear over the roar of the passing field. "Needs clean air. How about letting him ahead?"

Lebeau spoke into his radio again, and again he shook his head.

"LD wants the front," Chance told Gage.

Gage stayed quiet through two turns. On the backstretch, the radio crackled again.

"Then I'll race him for it," he said.

Chance groaned.

"Wait 'til you start catching lapped traffic," he warned the rookie.

"I ain't got that long," Gage told Chance. "These guys behind us are gonna get organized, and when they do, they're gonna catch us with me breaking draft all the time like that."

Chance took a breath and watched the field. The rookie was right; four of the cars behind the lead pack had already lined up single file to start their own breakaway.

"Got enough to take him on the outside?" Chance asked his driver.

"Probably not," Gage replied after a moment's pause. "I'll have to go inside."

"Never happen," Chance warned him. "LD'll shut the door."

"He's leaving enough room going into the corners," Gage insisted.

"Not if he sees you coming."

The radio crackled for a moment.

"I'll just have to take him so quick he can't stop me."

Chance shook his head, a useless gesture while he was talking on the radio.

"Okay," he reluctantly agreed. "Drive it the way you see it."

The rookie ran one complete lap without popping out to get air on his grille. Then he let a twenty-foot gap open up between Danford's car and his own, building up a little room in which to get a run on the leader. Coming into Turn One, Gage drifted about half a car width high and then, using the steep banking of the track to assist him, dove low, toward the apron.

Immediately, Danford reacted.

"Outside." Chance warned his driver. "He's dropping."

But the rookie had too much momentum; he was committed. The red-white-and-blue Taurus got a nose inside of Danford's midnight blue car, and then Danford came down and hit Gage's right front fender with his left rear wheel. It was the only part of the leader's car that wouldn't damage his aerodynamics or spin him out.

But Gage had no such assurances. The rookie's car angled down, dropping its left front wheel off of the banking onto the flat apron. This rotated the car even more sharply, and that was all she wrote. The red-white-and-blue Ford began a long, drifting slide up the track, smoke boiling from all four tires, the car rocking in the slipstream even though the roof flaps were wide open. On the track behind, cars bottomed their air dams, tires smoking as they braked.

In less than a second Gage had backed heavily into the wall, crumpling the rear end almost all the way to the window, the back of the car erupting briefly in flame as the fuel line broke. The car dropped back down the track and got into the wall again as one of the following cars clipped his left fender. Behind them, the high-banked turn erupted into tire smoke and collisions.

"On the brakes and hold them," Chance advised Gage. "Fire's dying. Keep yourself up on the wall. Don't let it roll back down."

There were cars running down on the apron until another burning wreck blocked that route. Other cars were broadsiding into the wall. The field, running two wide, was trying to funnel into a remaining racing lane that was only one car wide, and the field was paying the price. The only cars spared from the carnage were the twenty-five backmarkers able to brake in time—and Lyle Danford, running scot-free by himself down the backstretch.

"Okay," Chance told Gage. "We're clear. Drop your net if you're all right. You're still burning. Better bail."

Chance trained his binoculars on his old racecar, its crumpled nose now pointed almost directly at him halfway through Turn Two. For ten long seconds, nothing happened. Then, finally, he saw movement inside the car, the window net coming down, and Gage's helmet emerging from the window as the driver squirmed out. The car was still smoking heavily. A narrow river of coolant was running from under the air dam, down the steep banking to the apron. And half of the right rear tire was visible outside the fender, a sure indication of a broken trailing arm.

Chance lowered his binoculars, took a breath, and turned to head for the stairs. He wouldn't be needed on the spotter stand anymore. Not for this race.

CHAPTER 29

Victory Lane Farm—Norwood, North Carolina

Unless you arrived by helicopter, you couldn't just drop in on Lyle Danford. The big wrought-iron gate at the foot of his mile-long drive made sure of that. But Chance had buzzed the house from the gate. Then he'd driven up through Danford's private pine forest, coming out into the opening where the house stood, surrounded by maple trees aflame in their autumn foliage. Yet there was still no sign of Danford as Chance got out.

Puzzled, he stood there a moment, and then he heard it: the rumble of a diesel engine coming from the far side of the house. He followed the path around to the side, through Dottie's rose garden and onto the patio, the engine sound growing louder as he walked. And there, beyond the pool, was Danford, shirt off in the Indian-summer sun, gold Ray-Ban aviators over his eyes, working the levers of a huge yellow Caterpillar bulldozer, scraping the ground in a near corner of his backyard to a reasonable semblance of levelness. As the muscles in his back and arms moved, the 'dozer growled and belched black smoke, the conical cap on its exhaust pipe bouncing and nodding.

Chance waved to him and Danford shut the engine down, its grumbling ceasing abruptly, the rustling of the wind through the maple leaves ebbing in to take its place.

"Chance Reynolds," Danford said amiably, smiling behind the sunglasses, stripping off a pair of deerskin chore gloves. He took a red T-shirt from the back of the bulldozer's seat, wiped his face with it, and then pulled it on. There was a gold Marine Corps crest—an eagle atop an anchored globe—on the front of it.

"LD." Chance looked at the scraped, scarred clay of what once had been a gently undulating back lawn. "Don't stop your work on my account."

"This?" Danford climbed down off the rig and waved a dismissive hand at it. "Naw. This ain't work. I just like moving the earth around. Contractor's showing up tomorrow to start on that studio I'm makin' for Dottie. He'll probably take one look and grade it all over again."

Chance grinned. "I doubt that."

"I don't." Danford shrugged. "He's an ornery little tarheel cuss who thinks he's the only one that can do anything right. Besides, even though I got everything under the sun right here, he brings his own equipment with him and he charges for it by the hour."

"Then why put up with him?"

"Because he's the best stinkin' builder in Carolina. He won't cut corners, and he'll put up exactly what Dottie wants, and not its second cousin. And when he gets done with it, it'll laugh off a hurricane and outlast the house."

"Think so?"

"Know so. He did our addition a couple of years ago." Danford fished two Cokes out of a galvanized bucket of ice and tossed one to Chance.

"I'll put up with irritation," Danford continued, "if that's what it takes to get the job done."

Chance laughed. "Are you trying to tell me that you're patient?"

"And what's so amusing about that?" Danford twisted the cap off his Coke and settled into a patio chair, nodding for Chance to take the one next to him.

"Oh, I don't know," Chance said, sitting down. "I guess it just makes me think of a prayer I read in my studies, something attributed to Augustine, I think: 'Lord, grant me patience, but grant it at once.'"

Danford smirked and nodded.

"So, Boomer," he said, taking a sip of his Coke, "what brings you all the way out here?"

"I just thought I'd check in and see how you and Dottie are getting on with Duane."

"That's why you stopped in, to see how we're doin' with Duane?"

"Yeah."

Danford took off his sunglasses. "That's the only reason? Nothing else?"

Chance stopped in midsip.

"What else," he asked, lowering the bottle, "would there be?"

A half grin grew slowly on Danford's face. "Oh, I don't know," he drawled. "Maybe to bust my chops about spinning little Howdy Doody out at Talladega."

Chance paused, squinting up at sunlit maple leaves.

"Is that what you did?" he asked. "Wrecked him?"

Danford's face grew into a full grin. "I dunno, Boomer. What do you think?"

Chance cocked his head. "What do I think? I think you've gotten a heck of a lot better at that stuff since Michigan."

He sipped his Coke.

"Well." Danford shrugged. "Practice does make perfect."

"Of course," Chance said, "at Michigan, we'd both gotten the white flag. I was racing for the win. You put Gage into the wall on what? Lap six?"

"We were goin' into lap seven, actually, and I *knew* you came here to bust my chops over it."

"He wasn't even racing you, Lyle. Not really. He was running hot. He was just trying to get some clean air on his grille."

"He pulled inside me on a turn, Boomer. That's racin', in my book. And if he's torqued about it, then maybe he oughta be over here standing up in his own size sixes and tellin' me about it himself."

Chance set his Coke down.

"You know, Lyle, I went down to the infield care center after the wreck."

"Sounds like something you'd do."

"Yeah. It was standing-room only in there."

"Oh, I get it." Danford set his own Coke down. "You not only want to bust my chops about Opie, you want to get on my case on behalf of the entire rest of the field. Is that it?"

"And you know how it is," Chance said, ignoring him. "The rest of the guys, they know this is Gage's first race, and after the docs got done with them, they stop by to see how he's doing, and to a man, he apologizes to every single one of them."

"Oh, gee." Danford rolled his eyes. "Ain't that sweet."

"And then," Chance continued, "when it was just him and me, Gage looks me straight in the eyes and says, 'I shouldn't have moved when I did. I should have waited. I should have listened to you.'"

"Well, what do you know?" Danford shrugged. "It sounds to me as if the boy can be taught."

Crossing his arms, Chance looked Danford straight in the eye.

"Lyle," he said evenly, "you just don't get it, do you?"

"Get what?"

"That he doesn't even know that you wrecked him. He thinks he was the one that did something wrong. He thinks he broke some Nextel Cup code of behavior or something, that he screwed up his shot at the big time."

"Maybe he did."

"Throw that bull some other direction, Lyle. The kid trusted you. He thought you were a teammate. What you did wasn't even foul driving, man. It was just plain mean."

Danford arched his eyebrows. "That what you told him?"

"Not yet." Chance shook his head. "Then again, I doubt that I'll need to. He's probably seen the race tapes by now. I guess he wasn't at the shop meeting this morning?"

"Naw. Pooch is driving your car this weekend at Charlotte, and Robert's giving some seat time to a Truck driver at Martinsville—the Busch Series is running in Memphis that weekend, and your boy wonder has to run there 'cause Robert's trying to keep his Busch car in the top ten."

"Listen to you—'boy wonder.'" Chance huffed. "What have you got against Gage?"

"Got against him?" Danford shrugged. "Nothin'. I just got no use for him, that's all."

"Sell that to the magazines, Lyle. I know you better."

"Oh," Danford smiled. "That's right. You're taking that counseling course at the Bible college, aren't you? How's that going?"

Chance said nothing.

"Come on, Boomer. Try it out on me. Tell me how I'm compensatin' for an abused childhood or something."

Chance looked at the house, making certain they were alone.

"Come on," Danford goaded him. "Tell me."

"Let's talk about Duane."

"Duane?" Danford laughed. "What's this got to do with Duane?"

Chance crossed his arms. "Everything, Lyle. Don't you see that?"

Danford pulled his head back an inch or two, frowning.

Chance lifted his hands, palms up.

"You've got an incredibly talented kid who could be a great driver, but is courting trouble instead," Chance said. "And Gage is an incredibly talented kid who is a great driver, and he's courting greatness instead of trouble."

"Are you sayin'," Danford asked, his voice too low, "I'm jealous?"

"I'm saying you're upset," Chance told him. "I'm saying you're a man who likes to be able to fix things, and this thing with Duane isn't fixing all that easy. Another guy might work that out by putting his fist through a wall. You did it by putting Gage into the wall."

Danford rolled his eyes skyward.

"Can't you see that, Lyle?" Chance asked.

"Oh, man. It's Billy Graham meets Doctor Phil."

"Well, you asked." Chance took a breath.

"Lyle," he continued evenly, "Gage didn't take my car away from me. My eye did. But car or no car, I'm your friend. I'm still going to be here for you and Dottie—and Duane."

Danford ran his thumb over the surface of his Coke bottle, saying nothing. The wind picked up for a moment, and the leaves rustled.

"I want to help, if you'll let me," Chance continued. "Will you?"

"Well," Danford said, "it's like I said. I'll put up with irritation, if that's what it takes to get the job done."

Danford sniffed, just once. Then he got up and walked to the edge of the patio, looking out at the idle bulldozer and at the scraped, scarred ground that was going to become his wife's Christmas present. He put his sunglasses back on and said nothing, so Chance walked up beside him and stood there.

"You know," Chance finally told him, nodding at the bulldozer. "I've always wanted to try my hand at running one of those."

Danford looked at Chance and managed half a crooked grin.

"Just keep it pointed away from the house."

CHAPTER 30

Mooresville, North Carolina

The forty-eight hits of blotter acid rested in the pocket of Duane's work shirt: four dozen precisely metered droplets of liquid LSD placed evenly onto a perforated three-by-five sheet of blotting paper with smiley faces stamped on its back. Even in a resealable plastic bag, the $1,200 worth of drugs was so thin that it didn't make as much as a bulge.

That was the beauty of acid, Duane thought as he spread green floor-sweeping compound over the floor in Robert Vintner Racing's car 53 fabrication shop. It was super portable. Twelve bucks' worth of coke—that was an incriminating lump in your pocket. But the same amount of blotter acid wasn't any bigger than an index card. And if he ever got stopped, it was every bit as flammable. Which was why Duane, who had never smoked, and never intended to, also had a butane lighter in his pants pocket.

Duane picked up his broom and began to push the sweeping compound across the floor. It looked like shredded green pencil eraser and smelled like bubble gum. Not that he liked or disliked bubble gum. That was just what it smelled like.

The downside of LSD was that, as powerful as it was, it was still strictly a recreational drug. Duane had only tried it himself a couple of times—once when he was out camping with his buds and once when his folks were gone to the annual NASCAR awards banquet—but he remembered both trips vividly. Each one had started out with about an hour of a mild high, followed by several hours of intense hallucination. The second time, it had looked like everything was covered with pulsating Juicy Fruit gum wrappers. He never had figured that one out. And then, both times, after he had come down, he had crashed—slept solidly for almost twenty-four hours.

It wasn't something that you could do again right away the next day. In fact, hard-core use was about once a week. Which meant that, even if he had forty-eight hard-core acidheads on the hook—which he did not—twelve hundred a week was about all he was going to get out of it, and that was just a thousand, once you accounted for the price of the product. A thousand dollars was chump change for the amount of risk involved—college kids bragging to other college kids about tripping, word getting around. Loose lips.

Speed freaks were a lot more low-key and they dropped more cash per transaction. Plus, they bought six days a week. For some reason, there was this blue-law mentality in the South that virtually kept him from being able to make a sale on Sunday, yet Duane knew that crank moved like popcorn every other day of the week.

But Duane hadn't sold any speed in nearly a month. He'd gone out to his Ninja after school one afternoon, and there'd been a plain white matchbook wedged under his gas cap with a note penciled on it: "Page me—B." So Duane had ridden to a pay phone, where he'd called Burbank's pager number and keyed in the payphone number and a pound sign. Two minutes later, Burbank had called him back.

"Stay away from the club, dude," Burbank had told him, not even bothering to say hello. "It's scorching."

"Cops?"

"Yeah, but not local."

"So you want me to meet you someplace else?"

"Negatory, man. I'm leavin' town for a while."

"But I've got buyers lined up."

"You and every other dealer in town," the voice on the other end of the phone had said. "But everybody's in the same boat, dude. Charleytown is drying up until this thing blows over. No worries, man; droughts drive the price up. When business starts in again, we'll make it up, and then some, on the back end. I'll call you."

And with that, the line had gone dead.

So Duane had been reduced to buying blotter acid from a guy who had a brother that was a chemist up at Duke. It was strictly kid's stuff. Duane wasn't even sure that it was really LSD. The word was that diluted rat poison had much the same effect.

But he'd learned the next day that Burbank had been smart to chill out like that. Duane had stopped in the school parking lot to talk to a girl—just somebody from his algebra class that he was thinking of asking out. And as they'd spoken—comparing notes on a new hip-hop CD—Duane had noticed that there was a yellow lineman's tent on a utility pole at the edge of the school property: one of those rubberized canvas shelters that the power company guys used to stay dry while they worked in crummy weather. Except it had been a beautiful day, not a cloud in the sky. Nothing but a light breeze.

And when that breeze had lifted the tent flap for a moment, Duane had gotten just a glimpse of a guy holding something that looked like a small satellite dish. It had been pointed at him.

Directly at him.

Still sweeping the shop floor one-handed, Duane checked his shirt pocket, feeling the thin plastic bag with the card of blotter inside, and then patted his pants pocket, finding the reassuring oval tube of the butane lighter. Maybe Burbank was being paranoid. Maybe the power company guy really had been a power company guy. But lately it seemed to Duane that his parents were snooping after him all the time, showing up at the mall when he was there, finding excuses to walk into his room at odd hours. Maybe he was being paranoid.

"Hey, Dew."

The teenager jumped, his broom clattering to the floor.

"Sorry, guy!" Chance Reynolds put a hand on the teenager's shoulder, steadying him. "I didn't mean to startle you."

"Oh . . . Boomer." Duane grinned, completely red in the face, and retrieved his broom. "Man, I was way off in the ozone there. I didn't think anybody was working back here, that's all."

"Well, take a breath."

"I'm cool." Duane tilted his broom upright and leaned on it. "So what brings you into town?"

"You."

"No joke?"

"No joke."

Duane nodded at the edge of a body-hang table and sat down on it. "What's up?"

Chance started to sit, then stopped.

"You hungry?" Chance asked. "Want to hit the Steak 'n Shake?"

"Well . . . I'm working, here, Chance. I can't just take off."

"It's okay. I talked to Andy."

Duane squinted at Chance. "What's this about, man?"

"Humor me, okay? Cindy has been out with your mom all day shopping for baby monitors and the next round of maternity clothes. And I'm flat-out starving."

They went to the restaurant together in Chance's car, which he considered an advantage: Duane wouldn't be as likely to storm off in a huff if he didn't have his motorcycle waiting just outside the door.

"Get food," Chance urged him. "I want to eat, and nothing feels more miserable than eating by yourself, you know?"

"Well," Duane said, "I had a pretty good lunch at school, but I'll get something."

Turning to the waitress, he said, "I'd like a double cheeseburger with bacon, fries, chili, a vanilla shake, and a water, please, ma'am." Then he turned back to Chance, who was laughing so hard he was bouncing.

"What?" Duane asked.

"A cheeseburger and a chocolate shake, please," Chance told the waitress. Then, grinning at Duane, he said, "Sorry, Dew. I guess I just forget that you're still a teenager."

Duane pulled his head back an inch or two—a brief moment in which he looked exactly like his father. Shrugging, he said, "I guess that works out to be a compliment."

"Believe me, it does. So what year are you in school now?"

"Junior." Dew grinned. "One more year and 'Hello, world.'"

"When I was your age, absolutely no one mistook me for someone older."

"Except for on the track, from what I hear."

"Well, you're no slouch on the track yourself, from what I hear."

"All right." Duane sat up straight. "I knew it. You've been talking to my old . . . my father."

Chance cocked his head. "Why wouldn't I be talking to your dad? We've been racing together for what? Four years?"

"Yeah?" Duane looked back defiantly. "And do you think he talks to me about you?"

"Well . . . sure. Doesn't he?"

"Okay." Duane shrugged. "Maybe he does. But you don't live in our house. He's not invading your space."

Chance laughed. "He's put me into the wall something like three times over the last four years. I'd say that counts as an invasion of my space."

Duane just looked back at him blankly, saying nothing.

"All right," Chance agreed, "it's not the same relationship. He's my teammate—my friend—not my father."

The milkshakes came, two frost-covered metal mixing cups filled with milkshakes so thick that spoons stood upright in them.

"So what's he like?" Duane asked, pouring his shake into a glass.

"Who?"

"Your father."

"Mine?" Chance poured his own shake, trying to keep a big blob of ice cream from sliding down and making a mess. "He's . . . great. Other than Cindy, I'd say he's my best friend in the whole world."

"Really?"

Chance thought about it for a moment. "Yeah," he said. "Really."

"That's cool." Duane was stirring his shake, but he was looking at Chance, not at the shake. "Tell me about him."

So Chance told him. He told Duane about the evenings building racecars together under the sodium vapor lights in the pole barn back in Chillicothe. He told him about the long heart-to-heart talks on the drives back from races. He told him how his father had once driven all night to get to an ARCA race in Phoenix after he'd seen that Chance had not qualified well, just to be there to encourage him.

"Wow," Duane said when Chance had finished. "I've seen your dad at races, but never for more than just to say 'hi.' I wish I'd talked with him more. He sounds . . . really outstanding."

"He is." His throat tightened as he said that, and he wiped his eyes.

"And I guess that's the difference between you and me," Duane said. "Sounds as if when you were growing up, your folks were really paying attention to you. At the Danford household, it's all about the old man. He stands still and the world turns around him."

Chance shook his head. "I don't know if that's a fair comparison, Duane. My dad farmed. As long as the weather wasn't being contentious, he set his own schedule. He said himself that it was a blessing that he got the time to spend with me. Your dad's blessing has been different. It's been longevity in a career where most folks don't last much more than a decade. Look at me; I was a ball of fire for four years in Cup, and now I'm sidelined. Permanently. When you race for a living, it's a pretty concentrated lifestyle."

"It was his choice," Duane pointed out.

"True," Chance agreed. "But how you view a situation really depends on how you look at it. I mean, you look at my dad, and you see a dedicated guy who really invested in his son."

Duane nodded.

"Yet two years ago," Chance continued, "I got interviewed by this little pipsqueak from one of those lifestyle magazines. And he tried to twist it around as if my dad had forced me into racing—'living vicariously' was how he phrased it. Like my dad hadn't made it in racing on his own so he'd ridden me hard until I succeeded."

Duane's eyebrows went up a notch or two.

"Man," he said, "that's bogus. What'd you tell him?"

"I told him that if that was the way he was going to write, then he'd better be ready to write the next one with broken fingers."

"No way!" Duane laughed.

"Okay," Chance agreed, shrugging. "Not in so many words. But he got the message. If a reporter wants to take a shot at me, that's fine. I'm a public figure and that makes me fair game. But you don't go gunning for my family. Not without consequences."

Duane nodded and tried his milkshake.

"That's cool," he said. "You're willing to step out, take some heat for your family."

Chance nodded slowly.

"Your dad's the same way," he told the teenager.

Duane looked down at the tabletop and didn't look up. "You think so?"

"I know so."

"So why is it you and me are having this talk, and not me and him?"

Chance stayed deliberately silent until the teenager looked up.

"Because," Chance told him, "he doesn't think you'd even listen to him, let alone talk."

Duane sipped his shake again. "Yeah," he admitted. "He's probably right about that."

Chance stirred his milkshake with the straw.

"So," he asked, not looking up, "why the changes? I thought you enjoyed racing."

"I did. Still do."

"So why'd you stop driving?"

Duane said nothing for a moment. Then he asked, "Why did your father help you with your racing?"

"My father?"

"Yeah."

"Well," Chance replied, startled by the question, "because he saw I had a talent. He wanted to help me. He wanted to give me a shot."

"And why did he want to do that?"

"Well . . . because he loved me."

"Exactly."

Chance cocked his head and looked the teenager in the eye. "I'm not following you."

Duane smoothed his paper placemat, patted it twice, and looked up at the ceiling for a long, slow moment, light glinting off the diamond stud in his left ear.

"Your father put you in a racecar because he loved you," Duane said, his voice breaking. "And my father put me in a racecar because he loves . . . I don't know. Himself. Or racing. Take your choice."

Chance shook his head firmly. "I don't believe that."

"You don't?" Duane's eyes flashed. "Then look at Danny."

"Danny?"

"Sure, Danny. The poor dude spent years turning back-flips, trying to turn into a race driver."

"And your father spent years trying to help him."

"Well," Duane said, hands up, "it might have been a great idea to ask Danny if that was what he wanted, first."

"Wasn't it?"

Duane took a breath and then forced a smile for the waitress as she set their food on the table.

Without asking—almost without thinking about it—Chance bowed his head and said, "Father, we thank you for this food, this day, and this talk. Please bless them all, in Jesus' name."

"Amen," Duane said, to Chance's surprise. Then he continued, "What Danny wanted was to make Lyle Danford happy. And when he couldn't do that behind the wheel of a racecar, my father put him on the back burner in about half a heartbeat. Man, Boomer, don't you get it? We're not his kids. We're the organ-grinder's monkeys. And just as soon as we aren't useful to him, he drops us out of his life."

Chance sighed and pushed his plate back an inch or so. "Duane, racing has been your father's life for longer than you've been alive. It's what he knows. It's the way he knew to help you guys. But when Danny didn't show an aptitude for driving, your dad wanted him out of it for his own safety. And that's proof he cares about him."

"Oh," Duane rolled his eyes, "the old 'I wouldn't want my kid to do this; he might get hurt.' And you know what? Everybody in this sport seems to say that, but then they're all tickled pink when the kid follows them into it."

Duane scowled at Chance, and the sounds of clinking glasses and distant conversations filled the silence.

"Maybe," Chance said, "we'd better eat before it gets cold."

They ate in silence for a few minutes and then, as Duane was polishing off his cheeseburger and fries, Chance said, "You're turning eighteen next summer, right?"

"Yeah," Duane said, swallowing. "August seventh. Why?"

"Because you'll be old enough then."

"To do what? To drink in North Carolina?"

"That too, I guess." Chance laughed. "But no, I was thinking of going over the wall."

Duane set his shake down. "You mean in a pit stop?"

"Sure." Chance nodded. "I was talking to Andy Hofert. He's thinking of having you practice with the team, maybe have you start out at first as a sub for one of the tire carriers."

"Too cool."

"I thought you'd say that," Chance said. "Of course, a move up like that . . . it comes with some responsibilities."

"Such as?"

"Such as having all your wits about you, all the time," Chance said. "When you go over the wall, it's not just your safety that's at stake. There are six other guys out there, plus the Cup officials. If one person screws up, any of them could get hurt. You want to make sure you're not doing anything that could jeopardize that."

"Like what?" Duane asked, leaning back from the table.

Chance took a breath. "Like putting something up your nose besides your finger."

"Oh, yeah," Duane said, nodding his head. "You most definitely have been talking with my father, haven't you?"

"Your father?" Chance shrugged. "He's got a pretty good idea that you're doing a lot more than using."

Duane said nothing.

"Well?" Chance arched his eyebrows. "Are you?"

Duane wiped his lips with a paper napkin.

"What I do," he said, "is my business."

"Not really."

"Yeah? How's that?"

Chance tapped the tabletop lightly. "You might turn eighteen in August, but until then, you're a minor, Dew. Your dad's not only responsible for you. He has a lot of latitude as to what he can do to keep you safe."

Duane laughed—his father's short, barking laugh. "Like what?"

"Like getting a court order to restrict your movements, if need be."

The teenager's eye's flashed. "He told you that he'd do that?"

"I suggested that he do it," Chance told him. "If he has to."

"Fine." Duane smiled thinly. "If he wants to play that game, I'll play it. And then, come August, I'll be long gone."

"And old enough to prosecute as an adult."

Duane said nothing, his poker face as effective as his father's.

"You know," Chance told him, "back when I was your age, there were a few of us country kids that used to drive out in the summer to a friend's house, next to the Ohio River. The road followed the river for a while. And there was this one turn—well, I'm not sure how the custom got started—but we had this thing that whoever touched the brakes first was chicken. So one time, I get the bright idea of disconnecting the switch from the brake pedal. So the brake lights won't come on, you know? And we get to that turn, and I'm not showing any brake lights, so the guy behind me is bound and determined that he's not going to touch his, and, of course, he lost it—spun out and busted right through a guardrail, he was going so fast. He put the car back end first into a phone pole, which was a good thing, because it kept him from putting it in the river."

Duane said nothing, but the look in his eyes showed his interest.

"Nobody got hurt, beyond a few bumps and bruises," Chance continued. "But the guy's car was totaled. And it could have been way worse. There were five kids in that car."

"So why are you telling me?" Duane asked.

"To make a point," Chance said. "That we all seem to do dumb things. They may seem crafty at the time, but . . . and sometimes they have consequences that could be dangerous—harmful—to others."

"I'm not hurting anybody."

"The law doesn't see it that way, Dew. If you sell to somebody, and then they go out and T-bone a busload of schoolkids while they're high, it's not inconceivable that you could be charged as an accessory to manslaughter. If you sell to somebody and they overdose and die, you could be charged with murder. It's a felony just to possess certain quantities of most of this stuff, let alone sell it. And your dad thinks the law is onto you."

Duane looked down at the table.

"That's not news to you, is it?" Chance asked. "Look, Dew, I'll be the first to admit that I'm not privy to everything that's going on between you and your father. But whatever it is, I'm certain that getting busted and sent to the pen is not going to be the solution."

"Why? Because it would embarrass him?"

"No. Because it would ruin your life."

Duane continued to look down at his plate, dabbing a French fry over and over again in a little puddle of ketchup.

"In Richmond," Chance said, "after the Bible study, you complimented me on the lesson. Did you mean that or was that just talk?"

"Well . . . sure . . . I meant it."

"Then let me give you another quick Bible study. In Matthew, also in Luke, Jesus points out that you cannot love him . . . you cannot serve God and . . . well, the word in Greek is *mammonas:* things that we want so badly that we will do unethical things, ungodly things, to get them."

Duane said nothing, but his head moved up and down minutely in the slightest suggestion of a nod.

"So who—or what—are you going to serve, Dew?"

Duane grinned nervously, his face reddening.

"We–well, Boomer," he stammered, "I'm not sure that's a decision I'm gonna make over a plate of fries at Steak 'n Shake, you know?"

Chance felt his eyebrows rise a bit.

"Not deciding is a decision, Dew," he told him, his voice low. "If you don't decide to go with God—and faith in Jesus is the only way you do that—then you're automatically allowing things to rest the way they are, in sin. And God can't accept sin in his presence."

"Are you telling me," Duane asked seriously, "that the devil is the default?"

Chance laughed. "I never thought of it that way, but yeah, I guess the devil is the default."

"Whoa!" Duane pursed his lips, looked at his watch, and clasped his hands together atop the table. "Listen, Chance, I don't mean you any disrespect—"

"And none's taken."

"Great. But it sounds like you're steering this toward . . . well . . . toward what I don't want to rush into, you know?"

"I understand," Chance said. "So long as you realize that it's not the kind of thing that you want to wait too long on." He reached into his jacket pocket and brought out a small paperback book with racecars on the front of it. "I'd like you to take this with you."

"Okay. What is it?"

"It's something SCM put together," Chance told him. "It's the New Testament and Psalms, plus an explanation of God's plan for us. And there's a section with testimonies from some of the guys who race Cup—I'm in there, in fact."

"Sweet," Duane said, accepting the book.

Chance glanced up.

The kid looked absolutely genuine.

After he'd dropped Duane back at RVR, Chance turned his cell phone back on. In a matter of thirty seconds, it beeped to let him know that he had a page. Thumbing the button to get to the proper screen, he found the call-back number: it was Brett Winslow's cell phone—the one that he used when he was traveling on the race circuit. Chance hit "Call Back," and the SCM chaplain answered on the second ring.

"Hey, Preacher," Chance said, "it's Boomer. What's up?"

"Chance!" Brett had a gift for making you feel like your phone call was the high point of his day. "Thanks for calling back, buddy. Listen. You're going to be in Atlanta this weekend, right?"

"Sure. What do you need, another Bible study?"

"No, I've got that covered. Actually, I was hoping you might come in and do the message on Sunday."

"The chapel service?" Chance could feel his own heartbeat. "What . . . won't you be there?"

"I will, but I have some meetings with the SCM board. It'd be a real blessing to me if you could do it."

"Well, sure, Preacher. If you want, why, I'd be honored."

"Great! I'll see you on Sunday! God bless."

"You, too."

Chance flipped the phone shut, wondering what he'd just gotten himself into.

It had been near the end of the shift when Chance had dropped Duane back at the garage, so Duane had finished his sweeping and put his broom away. Then he'd gotten his helmet out of his locker and walked out to his bike.

He looked at the six-month-old motorcycle, its yellow finish even richer in the mercury vapor lights of RVR's parking lot. The Ninja looked fast just sitting there.

Duane slid the SCM New Testament under the elastic cargo net on the bike's pillion seat and thought about what Chance had told him. What was that Greek word he'd mentioned? *Mammonas*. That was it.

And how had he described it?

" . . . things that we want so badly that we will do unethical things . . . to get them." That's what Boomer had said. And the Ninja sure seemed to fit into that category.

Duane unbuttoned his work shirt, took out the little zip-top plastic bag, and slid the card of blotter acid out of it. It had no smell, nothing to suggest the potent qualities of the chemical it contained. He took out the butane lighter, flicked it a light, and then looked at the silly little smiley faces stamped on the back. It looked so innocent, so harmless. He held the flame of the lighter closer to the card.

Then he slid his thumb off the lighter. The flame winked out and the card became a dim rectangle in the light of the parking lot. He put the blotter acid back in its bag and buttoned it away.

After all—torching twelve hundred bucks' worth of product? For some lame principle?

What kind of loser would do that?

CHAPTER 31

Atlanta Motor Speedway—Hampton, Georgia

Have you ever noticed," Chance asked, "how, when racers talk about 'luck,' the only luck they're ever referring to is bad luck?"

Somebody in the back chuckled.

"Like when you're leading the race on the last lap, and a tire cuts down, or the fuel-pressure needle starts to flutter, even though your crew chief assured you that you were good for six more laps."

More chuckles.

"Or if the tranny lets go, or you drop a valve and have to finish on seven cylinders, or the guy ahead of you checks up, and you get in the marbles and end up backing it into the wall. What do you say when the guys from NBC or Fox stick the microphone in your face? 'Bad luck.' That's what you tell them. 'Racer's luck.' But let the guy ahead of you run out of gas, or cut down a tire, or get together with somebody else, and that's not a matter of luck at all. No, sir. If you squeeze through by the hair of your chinny-chin-chin and manage to come out ahead . . . even if you did it holding your breath with your eyes closed . . . that's not luck. That's steely-eyed, stone-cold experience!"

Now the whole group was laughing.

And it was a sizable group.

In a way, Chance was glad he hadn't learned just how large the group would be until a couple of hours earlier. The week off had done wonders for Gage's nerves, and he hadn't needed a rewind to qualify well—not spectacularly, but in twelfth, still in the front half of the field and comfortably ahead of LD, who'd had to use a provisional. Still, even though there were larger tracks than Atlanta on the Cup circuit, there were none faster, so the team had used every asset it had to fine-tune the racecar during Saturday morning practice and Happy Hour. That hadn't put Chance at the NASCAR inspection garage until an hour before the drivers' meeting, and he'd been surprised to see twice the number of chairs that they usually set up for chapel, with extra chairs set in rows outside every one of the open garage doors.

"Who are you expecting for chapel," he'd asked Brett, "the President of the United States?"

"No." Brett had smiled. "We're expecting you."

"Well, Preacher," Chance had turned and took in the seating, enough for more than three hundred people. "Looks like you're being overly optimistic."

"Not at all," Brett had assured him. "You know how we put flyers on all the transporter doors on Saturday, to publicize the service?"

Chance had nodded.

"Well, we got so much feedback from people wanting to hear you that I'm wondering if we have enough seats."

"Novelty value?" Chance had asked.

"I wouldn't say so," Brett had assured him. "These folks are your friends, Chance. They respect you. And they know you understand them. I think they just want to hear you preach."

And by that point, it had been too late for Chance to back out.

"And it's the same way when you get together with somebody out on the track." Chance continued. "I mean, if you're driving with your thumb on the mike button so you can't hear your spotter, and you don't look before you switch lanes, and you wreck yourself and the guy next to you, that's not 'brain fade,' that's just 'a racing deal.'"

More laughter.

"But let the guy next to you do the same thing and, if you're feeling particularly articulate, you might inform the TV people that 'he ran out of talent.' Otherwise, you're apt to just tell them, 'He wrecked me,' or to say the sort of thing that gets you a note from the sponsor."

Now there was nervous laughter. After all, this was church, even though it had garage doors and concrete. As Chance looked out over the crowd, smiling, assuring them, he stopped and gulped as quietly as he could. There at the back, near the wall, was Brett Winslow, and next to him were Dr. Jack Nobles and Sylvester Trapp.

The two men were known to everyone who regularly attended the Speedway Christian Ministries services. In fact, for all intents and purposes, they *were* Speedway Christian Ministries.

Dr. Nobles was the SCM chairman, who oversaw SCM's activities in more than a dozen North American racing series. Thirty years earlier, he'd also been the founding chaplain in SCM's first series ministry—this one. With snow-white hair that looked sculpted onto his head, not a follicle out of place, he was a pleasant combination of dignity and gentility. He was wearing what he always wore: a charcoal gray suit with a white shirt and tie—possibly the only tie in the entire garage area. The closest he had ever come to explaining why was one chapel service, when he'd deadpanned, "I used to be a Boy Scout. I believe in bein' prepared. This way, if the Lord was to call me home this instant, all you boys would have to do is put me in a pine box, dressed just the way I am, and say to one another, 'Don't he look natural?' "

Sylvester Trapp was so outspoken that the press had once christened the two-time champion "Motormouth." But only those very close to the racing community knew that the hound-dog-eyed driver and Regina, his wife, had approached Dr. Nobles with the idea of putting together a ministry to travel with the Cup series. Fewer still knew that the Trapps had written the check that had started SCM and seen it through its crucial first few months of operation.

Knowing this, Chance took a deep breath and went on preaching.

"Fortunately, this is a small community," he said. "And while you get grudges every now and then, ultimately everybody here realizes that we've got to get along. It's a tricky business we're in. You don't want folks driving mad. So if two of you go into the wall and it was you that made the $400,000 mistake, you try to even things out. You take the guy fishing. Or you invite him and his family over to your place for a barbecue."

He looked straight at Lyle Danford, who grinned broadly, his face reddening not the slightest little bit.

"So why is it," Chance asked, "that I can get over the fact that somebody busted my racecar and took me and my sponsor's logo off the track twenty laps into the race—that somebody cost me who knows how many championship points—but let my wife invite the in-laws over without asking me first, and I give her the silent treatment for three full days, which in our business is the same as a week? Or I get so torqued over the way my kids dress, or the music that they listen to, that I deprive them and me of the love that is such a precious part of childhood—and parenthood?"

Around the big garage, heads nodded slowly. And, seeing that, Chance forgot about who was standing by the wall, and went on speaking what God had placed in his heart.

CHAPTER 32

"Looking high. Outside. He's fading. Hold your line. Clear."

Chance lowered his binoculars and watched the familiar red-white-and-blue NASCAR Taurus inch away from the five-car pack behind it. One car length. Two. Three.

"Fuel's not an issue," Chance heard Andy remind his driver over the radio. "Go for it."

Gage didn't reply, which was understandable. There were just twelve laps to go, and he was hooked up—the car performing perfectly on four fresh tires picked up during a caution-lap pit stop eight laps earlier. That had turned the event into a twenty-lap sprint and Gage—who, like Chance, had grown up around little county fairground bullrings—knew how to race sprints.

Chance watched his driver turn a lap and said nothing. There was nothing to say. Not one of the cars on the track had a hope of catching him. Then the radio crackled.

"My water temp's rising," Gage said.

"Where is it?" Andy replied.

"Only 225 right now," Gage radioed back, "but it's going up."

"Boomer?" Andy's voice sounded anxious, even in the headset. "You see any steam?"

"Looking," Chance replied. "No. No steam yet."

Then, on a hunch, he focused the binoculars on the front of the race-car as it rounded the third turn. A bit of white blocked most of the car's oval grille.

"Got it," he said. "Hot dog wrapper on the grille."

"Water temperature's 235," Gage radioed.

Silently, Chance fumed. Trash on the track was frustrating, but it was also inevitable when you crowded 200,000 people into one piece of real estate. Lowering the binoculars, he checked the track ahead of their car. There was only one other competitor remotely near them, the brown-and-white number 88 Taurus, making good speed, but out of contention, having had to go into the garage area for repairs forty laps earlier.

Mind racing, Chance found the 88's spotter and spoke with him.

"Two-forty," Gage said tersely over the radio. It was about as hot as the radiator could get without boiling over.

"Okay," Chance told him. "The 88's ahead of you. He knows you're coming, but I've asked him to hold his line. Tuck up behind him and draft just as close as you can."

"That'll take what little air I have off the radiator," Gage protested.

"I know," Chance said. "Let's do it now, before it gets any hotter."

Then, knowing that the 88 had a sponsor who would spring for a bumper camera, and understanding that, with Gage leading, there would be a TV crew hanging around Gage's pit, Chance said, "Hoss, who's there from NBC with you? Matt?"

"Yeah," Andy replied, obviously puzzled. "It's Matt."

"Ask him to see if his producer can give us a shot from the 88's bumper-cam when we pull up tight to him, will you?"

"Uh . . . okay." There was a moment's pause, then he said, "Yeah. He says they'll do it."

"Great. Gage, close up just as quick as you can."

Gage's car closed rapidly on the other Ford and then slowed minutely, inching in behind him. Chance followed the cars and then, lowering his binoculars, looked at the big JumboTron television screens that faced the grandstands, carrying the network race feed. Sure enough, as Gage drew in closer, the picture changed to a shot of the red-white-and-blue Taurus' front end, rounded and slightly distorted by the wide-angle camera lens. The waxed paper hot dog wrapper looked like a big square of translucent white tape, held firmly over the racecar's grille by the 200-mile-per-hour slipstream.

"Move on in," Chance urged Gage. "Closer. Closer."

On the JumboTron, Chance could see the edges of the hot dog wrapper beginning to lift and ripple.

"Just a little closer," Chance told Gage as the two cars rocketed nose-to-tail down the backstretch.

The JumboTron image showed the wrapper flapping and wrinkling. Then it dropped out of the picture, and the crowd roared with joy, understanding what had just happened.

"Okay," Chance radioed Gage. "Grille's clear. Pass him high. You'll be a little tighter, now that that grille is clear."

"Gotcha."

The number 53 Taurus pulled next to the lapped car and they ran side by side down the front stretch.

"That did it," Gage confirmed. "Needle's dropping like a rock. Down to 220 already."

"Motor sounds good," Andy replied as the two cars passed the pits. "Go ahead . . . drop the hammer."

From then on, it was nothing but turning laps. Gage had a quarter-lap on the field, and nothing but open track ahead of him. When he took the checkered flag, there wasn't a single seat occupied in the grandstands—everyone was on their feet. And to Chance, watching his racecar turning doughnuts on the painted grass in front of the pit lane, it was positively surreal, like watching a movie rather than being at an actual event. Then, when the car headed for Victory Lane, it was only as the other spotters patted him on the back and rubbed his neck that Chance realized his face was streaming with tears.

CHAPTER 33

Lake Concord, North Carolina

"Psychoprophylaxis."

Without even thinking about it, Chance divided the word into its Greek roots: psycho from *psyche,* the mind, and prophylaxis meaning "to prevent." Mind prevention.

Hmm.

He lowered the book on Lamaze childbirth to rest his eyes, and Cindy smiled back at him from across the den. She was curled up with a Brandilynn Collins paperback, or rather she was reclined with it. Cindy's habit of curling, catlike, in a chair had given way in recent weeks to a preference for the flat out, fully reclined position of the den's hopelessly macho leather La-Z-Boy: a piece of furniture hitherto used only by Chance. Cindy had adopted it about the same time that she had gone to slip-on sneakers exclusively, on the grounds that they were much easier to put on in her advanced state of pregnancy.

From what Chance had learned so far in their childbirth classes, psychoprophylaxis—the principle that was core to the Lamaze method—was based in large part on the theory that the mind only has one gate, so if you fill it up with something other than pain, such as a concentration on breathing and pressure, then childbirth could be absolutely pain-free.

Frankly, Chance was skeptical. Under the same theory, if you tickled yourself with a feather when the throttle on your racecar stuck, then the collision with the wall wouldn't hurt.

It didn't seem too likely.

Then again, at least he was involved, taking the classes with Cindy. When Chance had asked Lyle Danford if he and Dottie had delivered any of their children by Lamaze, the crusty North Carolinian had looked at him out of the corners of his eyes and shaken his head.

"Boomer," Danford had told him pityingly, "you can no more have that baby with that little gal of your'n than she can strap in on Sunday and drive that racecar with you. Both of them are what you call your 'individual endeavors.' In either case, the best the two of you can ever do together is to share in the results of the labor."

Like much of what Danford said, it had been both outrageous and utterly true. So, rather than seeing himself as Cindy's Lamaze "coach," Chance had taken to picturing himself as her spotter. He could almost see Pooch in a delivery room, headset on, chanting, "Outside, outside, he's got a head out on ya. Don't back off now—BREATHE!"

"What are you thinking of, handsome?" Cindy asked him.

"Spotting," Chance told her. And then the doorbell rang and saved him from having to explain.

"That'll be Gage," Chance said, getting up.

"I'll get you two some lunch," Cindy said, raising her chair back.

"You'll stay right here and relax," Chance told her back.

"Okay," she told him, theatrically batting her eyes. "I'll be an obedient wife."

Chance laughed. "That'll be a first," he said.

Gage was grinning ear to ear as Chance opened the front door.

"Good meeting at RVR this morning?" Chance asked, laughing.

"Was it ever!" Gage shook Chance's hand. "Like Times Square on New Year's! Man, I wish you could have been there."

"I wish I could have been there too, Gage," Chance told him as they walked down the hall. "But Robert and I think it's better that I stay clear of the briefings. I want the team to focus on you."

"Well, still, I missed you," Gage told him as they entered Chance's study. The young driver looked at the wall of trophies, his eyes brightening, and then he said, "Hey! I was in the hot seat on *Stock Car Week* on the Horsepower Channel today."

"I'll watch it tonight when it airs," Chance promised as they sat down. "How did it go?"

"Oh, man, I about had to deflate my head to get out of there. Those guys were awfully complimentary."

"With good reason. You beat the best of the best yesterday."

"Yeah, but you know how that show is. You get interviewed by a panel of active drivers. And those guys are like you," Gage said, pointing with his open hand toward Chance's wall full of trophies. "They've each won a bunch of times."

"True," Chance agreed. "But none of them ever won his second time out in Cup. Nobody ever had, until yesterday. You've got a place in the record book, Gage."

"It's your place," the young man said. "If you hadn't told me how to clear my grille, I would have been toast."

"I just did what a spotter does," Chance assured him. "I gave you some advice."

"Well, I appreciate it." Gage brightened again. "Hey! Perky got me a booking on *Letterman!*"

"No kidding! When?"

"Tomorrow," Gage said. "And then I'll stay over in New York and do *Good Morning America* the next day. Perky thinks she'll have some radio stuff for me to do Thursday morning, too."

Chance nodded, but he didn't say anything.

"What?" Gage asked.

"It's . . . oh, never mind, Gage. I don't want to rain on your parade."

Gage leaned nearer.

"No. Tell me. You haven't led me wrong yet."

"Well . . ." Chance pursed his lips. "Vivian's the best at her job, but it's up to you to say 'when.' And it sounds to me as if she's got you working every day this week."

Gage grinned. "I don't mind."

"Well, that fiancé of yours might mind. The limelight is great, but you don't want to live there."

Gage laughed.

"As if it's possible," he said, "to get too famous."

"It is."

"I don't see how."

Chance paused, clasped his hands, and rocked forward.

"Okay," he said. "Let me show you."

The two men walked over to the desk, where Chance turned on his laptop, brought up Dogpile, and typed in a string of words. In a moment, he'd found the site that he was looking for, and clicked on it. He clicked again, and turned the computer screen toward Gage as a picture came in, block by block.

"Recognize him?"

"Sure," Gage said. "That's Jason Larkin. I remember watching him race when I was a kid. He died back in the nineties didn't he?"

"That's right. He crashed in practice at Daytona."

"Well, it's not the best picture. His hair's messed up, and his eyes are closed."

Chance nodded and clicked a key. Another picture filled the screen. It was a man's back this time, the man being held on his side by two latex-gloved hands, the fingers of the left hand deforming the flesh of his buttocks.

"What's this?" Gage asked.

"Jason Larkin," Chance said. He clicked again and another shot came up. This time, Larkin was on his back. The photo showed him from his knees on up.

"He's naked!" Gage said. "He's . . . man, he's not covered up at all. What's going on here, Boomer?"

Chance clicked an icon on his toolbar, and a screensaver—a scenic shot of a mountain range—came on.

"Those," he said, "were Jason Larkin's autopsy photos. I've never looked beyond what you saw here, but I understand that they get worse. A lot worse."

"Autopsy . . ." Gage looked back at the computer, mouth open. "But they can't put that stuff on the Internet!"

"It's a public record," Chance said. "Larkin's family has had lawsuits going through the courts for years, trying to block sites like this, but judges were afraid it'd set a bad precedent. And people look at it—maybe like we just looked at it, to be outraged. But they look at it. That's why it stays up there."

Gage didn't say anything.

"Gage," Chance said, "as you get better known, people will take more and more of you, as much as they can, until there's nothing private left, if you let them. For your sake—and for the sake of that girl you're marrying—you need to guard against that."

"Well, I can understand that," Gage agreed. "But it's just that, I'm hot right now and . . ."

Chance tapped a Bible on his desk.

"And to stay hot, you need time to decompress," Chance told him. "A day of rest. It's right. It's God's way. And it's healthy."

Gage nodded.

The phone on the desk rang—a distinctive triple chirp.

"That's Cindy on the intercom," Chance said. He pushed a button on the console and said, "Hi, babe."

"Hi, honey." Behind Cindy's voice, Chance could hear the sound of the treadmill—she was determined to stay in shape throughout the pregnancy. "I don't want to disturb you guys, but I wanted to make sure you don't forget, Chance, the architect is coming by to show us the drawings for the Caymans house in an hour."

"We'll be done by then," Chance promised her. "Love you."

"Love you."

"The Caymans house." Chance smiled as the speakerphone went silent. "I swear that Cindy's more interested in building that place than she was in building this one."

"Well, I hear it's nice down there."

"It is. Expensive—expensive to build, at least. We're building on Little Cayman, so all the supplies and the workmen will have to come in from Cayman Brac, next island over. But it'll be a nice place when we're done."

Gage nodded pleasantly. "I'd like to see it."

"We'll have you down," Chance said. "After it's done."

CHAPTER 34

Rockingham, North Carolina

"We have been exhaustive and thorough, visiting the leading eye surgeons throughout the United States and Europe, and they have been consistent in their opinions that there is presently no surgical solution for my injury and may, in fact, never be one," Chance read from the script Vivian Frankel had prepared for him. Then, setting the script aside, he looked up at the roomful of reporters and television cameras and continued, "And so today I am regretfully announcing my retirement from the racetrack. Driving has been great for me, and it will be hard to leave it. In fact, Robert Vintner has offered to keep me on as the driver of record through the end of this season. But this announcement has really been inevitable, ever since Sonoma, and I thought it best—for my sponsors, for RVR, and for myself—to take care of it now, well before the season ends."

There was a moment of stunned silence, and Chance realized that Perky had done an excellent job of keeping the details of Chance's injury away from the media until the team was ready to announce it.

But he was glad they'd finally done so. Chance always noticed English words that were lifted almost directly from Greek, and one of those came to his mind now—*catharsis:* to cleanse. To come clean. It felt good to finally have this out in the open.

Hands shot up all around the media center.

"Marty." Chance nodded at a TV reporter in the front row.

"Boomer, you said that you are retiring from the racetrack. But it's obvious that, while your situation keeps you from driving, it's not slowing you down in any other respect. So are you going to stay on in racing in some other capacity?"

"I hope so." Chance laughed. "This is really all I've done since I was a kid, so it's a little late to start learning how to mow lawns."

The room erupted in relieved laughter.

"So the answer to the question is 'yes.' Robert and I have talked about several other capacities in which I can serve RVR, and we really don't have anything to announce, mostly because I don't know what I want to do yet. Cindy and I just want to start our winter break early—like Monday—and relax and think things over. When we know what I'm doing, you'll know."

"So," the TV reporter continued, "will you still be spotting for the team here and in Phoenix and Miami?"

"No," Chance told him. "Our regular spotter is Pooch Gibson. I was more coaching than spotting anyhow, and Gage is obviously so good that he doesn't need much coaching, and we have a guy who's driven Phoenix a lot running that race for us, so I'm going to give the spotting job back to the man who's best at it, and that's Pooch."

"Is Gage the new driver of record for the 53 car?"

The questioner was in the back, and Chance couldn't see who it was, but it didn't matter, because Perky answered for him, "We'll have an announcement on a permanent driver in a couple of weeks, at Homestead, and because nothing's been signed, we really can't comment until then. Until that time, we're going with the drivers we've announced, race by race, and if you need that release again, just see me after we wrap up here."

Robert Vintner had known what he was doing when he'd given Chance a set of keys to his motorhome and told him to help himself to it after the press conference. The whole meeting, from Chance's statement to the conclusion of the question-and-answer session that followed, had taken no more than half an hour, but it had left him as exhausted as if he'd just climbed out of the car after a 500-mile race.

Then, mere minutes after Chance had slumped onto the couch, a knock came at the door.

For a moment, he debated not answering it. He and Perky had agreed to defer any follow-up interview requests until after the team had announced Gage as his permanent replacement. But quite a few reporters had the credentials to get into the drivers' paddock. While there was an unwritten rule that media never came to a motorhome unless invited, he knew that there was a first time for everything, and the last thing he wanted to see today was another camera lens.

The knock came again. Grunting, Chance got up and walked, stocking-footed, the six feet to the door. But when he opened it, he was greeted not by ESPN or the Horsepower Channel, but by Brett Winslow, Sylvester Trapp, and Dr. Jack Nobles.

"Guys . . . wow. Come on in. Sit. I'm glad to see you."

"Chance," Brett and Dr. Nobles both said at once.

"Boomer," Trapp said, shaking his hand as he stepped inside.

"Can I get you guys a soda or a bottle of water?"

"No, thanks, man," Brett said. "We just got done having coffee over to the SCM trailer."

"Well, again," Chance said, "I'm glad you're here."

"You know why we're here?" Dr. Nobles asked.

"I assumed to cheer me up," Chance said. "Why? Nobody's dead, are they?"

The three men looked at one another.

"No." Trapp chuckled. "Although, these days, the first thing I do every morning when I get up is check myself, just to make sure."

They all laughed and Chance sat with the three men in the motorhome's living area. Like Lyle Danford, Robert Vintner hadn't stinted when it came to his home away from home. The space available would have sufficed for twice as many people.

"So what's up?" Chance asked.

"Chance," Dr. Nobles said, "SCM needs your help."

"Why, uhm, sure," Chance said, surprised at the comment. "How much do you need?"

"No, no." Dr. Nobles laughed. "I may be the first preacher since Moses and Aaron to turn back an offering by saying it, but no, Chance, it's not that. We're not here for your money. The racing community has been very kind to SCM in that regard."

"Then what is it?"

Dr. Nobles turned to the Nextel Cup chaplain.

"Brett," he said, "why don't you tell him?"

"Sure," Brett said, clearing his throat. Then, with his face absolutely grave, he said, "Chance . . . it's my boy. Kyle. About two months ago, he started complaining of headaches and blurred vision, and at first, Danielle and I just thought he might need glasses. I mean, he's only five, but some kids need them then. So we took him to an optometrist when we got back to Charlotte the last time, and he referred us to an ophthalmologist, and he referred us to another specialist and, to make a long story short . . . Well, Kyle's got a cancer. It's behind his eye, pressing on the optic nerve."

"Man, I could tell something was up, Preacher," Chance said. "I just knew you weren't yourself. But the Lord has put me face-to-face with some of the best eye surgeons in the world. I think I can point you to the right people."

"No." Brett shook his head. "It's not that, either. We've got a great team of oncologists, up at Duke. They've already started him on chemotherapy to shrink the tumor. That's why Danielle hasn't been traveling with me lately. That'll go on for a few weeks, then they'll rest him and let him recover, and then they'll start radiation. And that'll be the tricky part. Kyle's still growing, of course, and while the doctors are very hopeful that they can stop the cancer and save his eyesight, there's a considerable risk that the radiation could keep the bones in his head from forming properly. That means the radiation has to be done in small doses, and he has to be monitored constantly. So we're looking at a lot of doctor visits—daily doctor visits—for at least the next year. It's going to be practically a full-time job for Danielle."

"Wow." Chance took a breath. "Can Cindy give her a hand?"

"You both can," Trapp said.

"Well, sure." Chance nodded. "What can we do?"

"Chance, I'm accepting a pastorate at a church in Chapel Hill so I can be there for my family on a day-to-day basis," Brett said. "I'm resigning as SCM's Nextel Cup chaplain."

Chance said nothing, stunned. Out on the track, the sound of a stock car engine wound by as the Cup drivers began Happy Hour.

"That's why we're here, Boomer," Trapp told him. "The ministry needs you. We want you to take Brett's place."

CHAPTER 35

Lake Concord, North Carolina

A preacher?" Cindy felt queasy for a moment and put her hand out to the kitchen island, steadying herself. "Chance, you're not a preacher."

"That was my thought, exactly," Chance told her. "But then Jack pointed out that I was well on the way with my studies. He said I already have Bible knowledge to rival many of the pastors he's known over the years."

Jack. All of a sudden, he was calling Dr. Nobles Jack, as if they'd been pals for years.

But the name gave Cindy an idea. "Well, what about Dr. Nobles? I know you want to help Brett and the ministry and all, but Dr. Nobles founded SCM. Certainly he could be chaplain until they found a replacement."

"I don't know, hon. He's pushing eighty, and he's arthritic. And chaplaining SCM can be pretty physical at times. Brett sets up and takes down the chapel seating pretty much by himself. Besides, they aren't looking at me as a stand-in. They want me as the permanent chaplain."

Cindy's heart sank. Chance was smiling the way he'd smiled when he'd told her that RVR was moving him up to Nextel Cup. And obviously he expected her to react the same way—to melt into his arms and tell him how wonderful it was. But she couldn't bring herself to do it.

"Chance," Cindy said, her voice on the edge of breaking, "you said that you were going to find something in racing."

His smile faded.

"But I have, sweetheart." He held his hands out, palms up. "Don't you see? All my life, I've been around racing, and all my life I've wanted to honor God. And now God's put it together so I can do both."

Deep inside of Cindy, the baby kicked, and she grabbed for the counter again. There was a moment's silence, and she thought about the unbuilt house in the Caymans, about this house that they were standing in, about the community she had found with the other women whose husbands drove, or managed teams, or were crew chiefs.

Chance's face fell. "Oh, honey," he said, "I'm doing this all wrong. I should have talked it over with you first."

"Should have?" Cindy felt the color rising in her face. "Should have? You . . . you've told them 'yes' already, haven't you?"

Chance stood there, saying nothing.

Hot tears welled in Cindy's eyes. "Haven't you?"

Chance reached out to her, and she stepped back, feeling the tears tracing down her face.

"Oh, honey," Chance said softly. "Of course, I said that I'd have to talk it over with you."

The baby kicked again.

"Is that what we're doing?" Cindy's voice was breaking as she wept, and she hated that it was doing that, but she forged ahead. "Are we talking? I don't hear you talking to me about anything. I hear you telling me. Chance . . . do you even know what this position pays?"

"Well, sure."

Cindy was sniffling now, and she hated that even worse.

"Well," she said, "I know what Brett was being paid. Danielle told me once. Chance . . . you earned more in a single weekend than Brett earned in a year. Much more."

"That was when I was driving."

"There's other things on teams. Andy Hofert has a nice house. P. T. Sloane and his wife take nice trips. And their kids . . ."

She put her hand on her belly.

"And their kids," she said, "go to nice schools, and . . ."

Then she was crying harder, and she felt his arms around her, and for just a moment she wanted to melt there, there in the place where she had always felt safest. But anger flashed within her again, and she shook her head and pushed him away.

"'One flesh,'" she told him, the words hot in her mouth. "You know so much Bible. . . . So did you forget that? That we're one now? Since when did you ever get the right to take us into ministry?"

She turned and found her keys on the hook by the door, felt Chance's hand on her shoulder, and shoved it away.

"Don't!" She hated the way she sounded even as she said it. Still, that didn't keep her from adding, "Leave me alone! Don't follow me!"

And with that she rushed into the garage, the baby heavy within her. She climbed into her SUV and wondered where it was that she was going.

"I appreciate your coming over, Lyle," Chance said. "But man, I feel so stupid. You just clinched the Cup yesterday. I shouldn't have called. You don't need to be running around the country, holding my hand on my day off."

"Oh, I've clinched the Cup before." Danford shrugged, looking out through Chance's den windows at the lake. "And sure, it's a big honor, and it's good money, but in the end, you realize that everybody and their brother—from the magazine editors to the pop companies—are just trying to make a buck off your smile. That's what they wanted me for this afternoon—another stinking photo shoot. And I've got to tell you . . . standin' there, sweating in a firesuit while some sissy photographer waits for the light to get right? Given a choice between that or a day at the lake, I'd say I'll take the lake every time. Besides, it's partly my fault that Nobles asked you."

Chance turned to face him.

"How's that?"

Danford shrugged. "I may not have been to a chapel service or a Bible study prior to this year," Danford said, "but I've written a pretty good check to SCM every Christmas. I guess I thought of it as an insurance premium with God—yeah, yeah, I know. But, back in the day, I actually wrote one of the checks that helped old Trapp get SCM through its first year. So he came and talked to me when Brett got the news about his boy. He asked me who I'd want for a preacher, and I said you, and he said, 'Huh. That's what Brett said, too.' And I've got to tell you, Boomer, it's what most folks have said. You know that expression, 'There's no substitute for seat time'?"

Chance nodded.

"Well, it applies here, too. Don't get me wrong. Brett's a good man. But he don't know—gut know—what we're all up against every weekend, week in and week out. You do. And while I'd give half my right arm to see you back in a racecar, if that ain't in the cards, then this is where I'd want you. You got the perspective."

They looked out the windows at the lake.

"Anything like this ever happen to you?" Chance asked.

Danford chuckled. "Yeah. When I got into racing. I was still working over to the textile mill when Dottie and I got married. And when I come home and told her that I was running a guy's car up at North Wilkesboro that weekend, she put her foot down and said she wasn't going to be married to any gone-every-Sunday racecar driver."

"So what did you do?"

"I bought her a chair and a mirror." Danford grinned. "And I told her that she could take her pick. She could stand behind me and support what I chose to do, or she could sit in that chair and watch herself starve, because I was done welding mill machines for a living. She came around after a while."

Chance just looked at him.

"Yeah, I know." Danford shrugged. "Not your style."

"Cindy's been gone for three hours," Chance said, standing up. "And she's pregnant. I have to go find her."

"No, you don't."

Chance just looked at him again.

"She passed me going the other way when I come here," Danford said. "She was on our road. So I'd say she's with Dottie right now."

"Don't you think we should head over to your place?"

"No." Danford shook his head and looked back at the lake. "I think we should get your boat out and go fishing."

"A mirror and a chair?" Cindy asked, forehead furrowed.

Dottie Danford laughed. "Girlfriend, it wasn't even a nice mirror. It was just some tacky, tall, pine-framed closet mirror that he picked up down at Wal-Mart, and the chair was this dented, scratched, old folding chair that I swear he brought home from the VFW."

Cindy laughed despite herself, knuckles to her lips.

"What'd you do?"

Dottie rolled her eyes.

"I decided that I was going to get all pious on him, you know?" She shook her head. "So I pick up the Bible my grandmother left me, and I sat down in my rocking chair, ignoring him and pretending to read. I mean, I'm not even seeing the words because I'm so teared up. But then I started thinking . . . if Lyle's really the man God set aside for me, and if God knew where Lyle was heading all along, then was I really being the voice of reason? Or an obstacle? And if I was being an obstacle, was that what I wanted to be to the man I'd joined my life to? Plus, I figured if God wanted him out of racing, he'd take him out. So I said, 'Okay.' And it's worked out."

She arched her eyebrows and sipped her sweet tea.

Cindy was silent for a minute, maybe more. Then she looked up, eyes wet again.

"Do you think that's what God did with Chance—took him out of racing?"

Dottie smoothed her friend's hair.

"Honey," she said. "I don't know. But I think God's still on the throne. What do you think?"

"I think . . ."

Cindy paused and wiped her eyes.

"I think I'm so hung up on that Caymans house that I'm forgetting about what goes inside it," she said.

Cindy twisted her wedding ring on her finger. She touched her belly, smiling at what she felt there.

She got up.

"I think . . ." She smiled weakly. "I think I'd better go see Chance."

TURN THREE

CHAPTER 36

Daytona International Speedway—Daytona Beach, Florida

Chance Reynolds sat in a lawn chair under the awning of his motorhome, gazing at a wallet photo of Cindy holding little Nathaniel. Taken just eight hours after the delivery—Cindy had insisted that he wait until after she'd had a sponge bath and combed her hair—it showed his young wife beautiful and beaming. And the shutter had caught Nathaniel at the start of a yawn, so it looked as if their tiny infant son was laughing.

One month ago. That was all the longer it had been, even though it seemed as if a lifetime of change had come into his and Cindy's lives. There'd been so many things to conclude, so many to set up, but God had worked things out.

Mandie, for instance. Having a full-time housekeeper had made sense when Chance had been driving. And Chance and Cindy could even justify it a little longer with a new baby in the house. But not for long.

But then Mandie had come to them, tearfully saying that her daughter would be needing her help over the summer in the catering business she'd opened, and would they mind letting her cut back to one or two days a week after Memorial Day?

And it all had gone that way. Robert Vintner had been as good as his word on the leased jet; an Indy Car team had picked it up almost immediately. There'd been a list of Cup people looking for condos in Daytona, so that had been easy to sell, and he hadn't missed it for a minute. Cindy's folks were staying with her and Nate back in Lake Concord, and since the series chaplain had to be available at the track twenty-four hours a day, a motorhome was Chance's only logical choice for lodging, even during the two weeks at Daytona for the start of the season.

A sizzle and a small flash of flame snapped Chance back to the present. Tucking the photo back into his Bible, Chance grabbed a spatula and moved his two hamburger patties away from the flame-up.

"C'mon," he muttered to a gas grill so new that the inside was still shiny. He blew out the flame sputtering on the ceramic blocks, and then blew it out again when it came back. "Knew I should have bought a steak."

But a steak didn't make sense when you were dining alone, and hamburger was lots cheaper. That was something he thought about all the time, now that he was eighteen years and counting away from Nathaniel's first college bill.

Someone tapped the horn as they drove by and Chance waved with the spatula. It was a Ford loaner, a red Explorer, but the windows were tinted, so he wasn't quite sure who he was waving at; whoever was driving was wearing the ubiquitous pit cap and sunglasses of the off-duty NASCAR team member. Probably some driver. Probably on the way to a sponsor dinner—one of those VIP meet-and-greets. It was fashionable to complain about those, but a plate of banquet hall chicken and a Caesar salad didn't sound all that bad to Chance right now.

The Explorer backed up and the passenger's window came down.

It was Gage.

"Boomer!" The young driver beamed at his former mentor. "You bachin' it this week?"

"Yeah." Chance grinned, hoping he didn't look as lonely as he felt. "Cindy's home with the baby."

Gage leaned over and opened the passenger-side door.

"Well, c'mon," he urged. "Ford's havin' a banquet over to the museum. I'll buy you dinner."

Chance glanced down at the burgers. They looked a little dry.

"I appreciate that," he told Gage. "But I've got some folks that asked me to come by and see them. . . . Duty calls."

"Well," Gage looked at the grill, "save some room, man. I'll bring you dessert."

Chance laughed. "I'll do that."

The Explorer pulled away.

Lights were winking on in the motorhomes staged around the paddock area. Most were dark bronzes and burgundies, the colors favored by the people who bought Prevos and other high-end rigs.

Chance's own motorhome was a Bounder, in the cream-white hue that was common to most budget RVs. It was a good rig, and his father had helped him to select the best one that SCM's budget would allow.

But the fact remained that the sticker cost on his Bounder wouldn't buy a bathroom for a Prevost. And during Speed Weeks, most drivers just used their motorhomes as rec rooms and dressing rooms; they slept in condominiums and hotel suites. A few even had second homes near Daytona.

"You're coveting, pilgrim," Chance whispered to himself. He scooped the two hamburger patties off his little grill and slid them onto a foam plate, where each one immediately cracked in two.

Bowing his head, he thanked God for his food.

"Hey, man. Are you Dew?"

Duane looked up from the tires he was unloading from his handcart. The guy who'd spoken to him was wearing the stained white coveralls of the sanitation workers who serviced the speedway, a paper garage pass dangling in a plastic credentials holder from the fabric waistbelt of the uniform.

"Yeah," Duane said, squinting in the half-light of dusk. "I'm Dew. Who're you?"

"Your hands, man," the man told him, ignoring Duane's question. He was dark-haired, and his voice sounded Latin. Cuban, maybe.

"What?"

"Your hands, man," said another man in a sanitation uniform. This guy was bigger. Stockier. "Show them."

The bigger man picked up one of Duane's larger wrenches and held it, club-like.

Duane showed them his hands.

"The gloves, man," the skinnier one told him. "Take them off."

Duane did as he was told, and the skinny guy reached out and turned his right hand over, tilting it toward a light on the corner of a nearby garage, looking at the tattoo.

"Yeah," he said to his companion. "This is the hombre."

"So you know who I am," Duane said. "Now, who are you?"

"You don't want to know," the bigger one said. His accent was different—almost French.

"He's right," the skinny one said. "All you need to know is that the B-man said you were our guy."

"'B-man?'"

"Burbank," the bigger one said, the displeasure evident in his voice.

"Oh," Duane said. "Sure. I was wondering when I'd hear from somebody down here."

"Well, now you're hearing," the skinny one said. "You're back here in July, right?"

"That's right," Duane said. "First week in July. The Pepsi 400."

"Chilly," the skinny one told him. "We're gonna have a little product for you to take back up north. When you go back, yes?"

"Absolutely." Duane nodded. "How much will you have?"

"Two hundred and fifty."

Duane's jaw dropped.

"Ounces?"

The skinny guy shook his head, grinning.

"Kilos," he said.

Duane figured it out in his head.

"That," he said, "is like 550 pounds."

"Hey," the big one smirked. "You're good at math, man."

Duane ran his hand back through his hair. "Man," he said, "are you nuts? That's a lot of skag."

The skinny guy shrugged and looked up at the hauler.

"Hey," he said. "The trucks—they are big, no?"

"Yeah," Duane said. "But 550 pounds . . . we're not talking there about anything that you could slip under the tray in a toolbox."

"Listen," the big guy grumbled. "Are we wasting our time here or what? Do you have a way of moving this for us or no?"

Duane thought for a moment.

"Yeah," he told the two men. "I got a way."

"Chilly," the skinny one told him. He handed Duane a slip of paper with a number written on it. "That's a beeper number. Don't lose it, okay? You get down here in July, the first thing you want to do, you call that number. From a pay phone, and not here at the track. Comprende? Five minutes later, no more, we'll call you back. We'll do the business."

CHAPTER 37

Darlington Raceway—Darlington, South Carolina

That was fantastic, Gage," Chance said.

SCM's golf cart double-bumped over a utility cable taped to the dark asphalt path.

"It wasn't me, Boomer," the young driver said, shaking his head. "It was you."

The chaplain took the next turn and glanced at his young friend. It was too dark to make out Gage's face.

"I beg to differ," Chance said. "You're the one that gave his testimony."

"Yeah," Gage agreed. "But from what I hear, SCM used to consider themselves fortunate if they got a couple hundred people to show up for these fan services."

Chance drove in silence for a moment. What Gage had just said was true. SCM had a separate pastor who traveled with the series and worked with local churches on fan outreach. But ever since that minister had asked Chance to come out and speak on Friday nights, and ever since Chance had begun bringing drivers and crewmen along with him, the services had swollen. The season was still young, yet SCM's outreach team had seen more decisions for Christ so far this year than they had in the previous five seasons combined.

"In the end it's all God, Gage," Chance finally said, waving hello to the fans lined up at a chain-link fence, waiting to glimpse a driver. "But God often works through people. You listened when he called. And I know how crazy your appearance schedule is."

"Thanks." They passed through a pool of light and Chance could see Gage's smile. "It was weird, though. I wasn't half as nervous on *Letterman* as I was tonight."

Chance held up his hard-card as they passed the guard shack at the paddock entrance.

"Of course," Chance said. "There was more at stake tonight."

He stopped the cart in front of Gage's motorhome.

"Six hundred," Chance said as they shook hands.

"Pardon?"

"Six hundred," Chance repeated. "We have volunteers taking rough counts during our invitations in the outreach ministry. That's how many folks came forward tonight."

Gage's hand froze in midshake.

"Six hundred?" He looked stunned.

"At least." Chance grinned. "And the Bible tells us that heaven breaks out in celebration over just one."

Chance was still grinning as he headed back to the Bounder. This was the second race where Cindy and little Nathaniel had been able to come along. The next two races, Tennessee and Texas, would be too far to take a two-month-old along. But on these shorter runs—the last week in Georgia, and this week in South Carolina—it had been feasible for them to travel as a family, and Chance was loving it. It was, he hoped, a wonderful picture of how things could be in the future, once Nathaniel was a little older.

Chance was getting the hang of this now. He'd learned how to budget his time so he could perform all of his duties and still have time for folks who needed counseling, and he had worked out the logistics for being where he needed to be on race days. Brett had come clean with him and told him how it was that the former chaplain had always been able to beat the ambulances to the infield care center. He had, he'd told Chance sheepishly, generally gone there just as soon as the field had left pit road; he usually just found a gurney and took a nap.

Between tips like that and the miracle of TiVo—which allowed Chance to record races so he wouldn't lose track of his congregation's work life—Chance was getting the knack of handling his new life. Having his family with him made it complete.

Chance pulled up in front of the Bounder and walked in as quietly as he could, not wanting to wake Nathaniel. Cindy was back in the bedroom, lying on the queen-size motorhome bed and holding the tiny sandy-haired infant as he slept. When Chance looked in on them, she smiled and got up, laying Nathaniel gently in his crib, taking care to put him on his back before covering him up.

"Hey, Preacher," she said, smiling and pulling the bedroom door partway shut.

"Hey, sexy," Chance said, hugging her. He marveled at how quickly she'd regained her figure; she was already back into her old jeans.

"Max Peters called," she said, hugging him back. "His number's next to the cell phone, on the counter."

"Okay," Chance said, walking back and picking up the Post-It note. "What's up? Is anybody hurt?"

"No. He said it's no emergency. But he asked for you to call him right away, no matter when you got in."

"Well, okay," Chance said.

He dialed the cell phone.

"Hey, Boomer, thanks for calling," RVR's team physician said after the phone's second ring.

"Hi, Max," Chance said. He'd had cell phones with caller ID for years, but it still spooked him when people did that. "What's up?"

"Are you going to be back in Charlotte on Monday?"

"Monday?" Chance pulled out his PDA and tapped on the calendar icon. "Yeah. I'm dropping Cindy off at the house before I go to Bristol. Why? You need me?"

"I do," Max said. "I need you to take an airplane ride with me up to Duke University Medical Center."

"Well, sure," Chance said, tapping the appointment in. "Who's having surgery?"

"Maybe you, eventually," Max said.

Chance scowled at the phone.

"Huh?"

"There's a doctor up there, Chance," Max said. "He's been working on a new procedure—just got FDA go-ahead to use it on humans."

Chance felt his heart quicken.

"What kind of procedure?"

He heard Max take a breath.

"Retinal reunification," the doctor finally said. "I've sent him your files, Boomer. We spoke late this afternoon. This guy thinks that maybe—just maybe—he can fix your eye."

CHAPTER 38

Duke University Medical Center—Durham, North Carolina

"Don't worry about my last name," the doctor said as Chance stumbled over it. "Most Americans can't pronounce it, and I'm not that crazy about it. My friends call me Jerry."

For some reason, that one bit of dialogue put Chance immediately at ease, which was saying something. The trip in to the Medical Center had involved a chopper hop from Raleigh-Durham Airport, and Chance still wasn't all that crazy about riding in helicopters.

And while the doctor's name did look as if the label-maker had gone haywire on his Duke University badge, and he appeared vaguely Middle Eastern, he spoke with almost no accent.

"Before I go any further, I would like to perform just two or three quick tests," the doctor said. "Nothing invasive—just looking and measuring. Is that all right with you?"

"Uhm, sure," Chance said. "Go for it."

It didn't take long for Chance to discover that the doctor's definition of "invasive" differed from his own. While the examination began with the same sort of visual inspection that Chance underwent on a regular basis, it soon proceeded into a series of physical tests, several of which involved the application of instruments directly against Chance's eye. By the time an hour had passed, he'd been poked in the eye so many times that he was starting to feel like the loser in a Three Stooges episode.

Then the last test was concluded and the doctor, together with three of his residents, excused themselves, leaving Chance and Max alone in the examination room.

"Well, gee, Max, that was really fun," Chance quipped, rubbing his eye.

"They've got to be thorough," Max said. "Jerry's got a lot riding on this, too, you know? The FDA watches outcomes very closely on new procedures like this. If the first ones aren't successful, it can stay in clinical trials for a long, long time. And didn't your mother ever tell you not to rub your eyes?"

"She should have warned me not to take trips to the hospital with strange doctors."

"I'll assume you're talking about Jerry," Max said, stepping over to the magazine rack and flipping open a copy of the *New Yorker*.

"Assume what you'd like." Chance slipped his phone off his belt and checked it: no messages. Then he took a *National Geographic* from the magazine rack, leafed through it for what seemed like an eternity, and checked his phone again. He was surprised to see that fewer than ten minutes had passed.

Finally, just when he was about to ask Max if he wanted to take a walk and see if they could find a coffee shop within the medical complex, there was a tap on the door and a nurse looked in, asking them to join the doctor in his office.

"I know you're anxious, so let me get right to the point," the doctor said. "There are hundreds of conditions that could preclude the use of our procedure, but none of them seem to apply in your case. We believe that you are a candidate."

Chance felt warm and even a little light-headed. He was only vaguely aware of Max patting him on the back.

"That's great," he finally managed to say.

The doctor smiled and opened his desk drawer, taking out a small plastic case.

"This," he said, "is a spatular sonic transducer, which just means that it is a thin device that emits very low frequency, very powerful, highly directional sound waves."

He opened the case and used a pair of tweezers to remove something that looked like a small metallic postage stamp with two thin wires leading from it.

"This is a prototype, and it's one of fewer than fifty in the whole world," the doctor explained. "We designed it here at Duke, in cooperation with the engineering school and the computer science department. The way it's used is pretty straightforward. I administer drugs that deeply relax the web of muscles that encircle your eye, then I slip a pair of these transducers onto either side of your eye, align them so they are parallel to the tear, and I manipulate the torn retinal material by pulsing it with sound waves, through the wall of the eye, while watching the retina on a special monitor. You've made up a bed by yourself before? Lifting and resettling the sheet until it lies flat?"

"Sure," Chance said.

"Well, we do the same thing with the torn tissue in your eye," the surgeon told him. "We use the vibrations of the sound waves running through the vitreous body to lift and settle the retinal tissue until it lies flat, the way it was originally. Then I micro-sear it with a very fine surgical laser—just a series of three or four dots, like the two you have now, only much, much smaller. Once I'm done, I slip the transducers out, we bandage the eye to retain it while the drugs wear off, and that's it."

"What's the recovery time?" Max asked.

"A week, no more," the surgeon told him. "We will ask Chance to wear a patch during that time. After that, he can begin to use the eye normally."

"My vision will fully recover?" Chance asked, surprised.

"That's the hope," the surgeon said. "Of course, there are risks: a whole laundry list of them. I'll give you the documentation to go over with Dr. Peters, here. This procedure is not something you want to undertake lightly. Worst case, you could end up totally blind in that eye. But our trials to date indicate a 52 percent chance that you would recover normal sight."

"Fifty-two . . . ," Max murmured. Then he fell silent. Through the insulated windows, Chance could hear the muffled sound of a helicopter coming into the Medical Center's pad.

"Two-point-three percent," Chance finally said.

"How's that?" Max asked him.

"Two-point-three percent," Chance repeated. "That was the odds of me being the one who wound up in the winner's circle every time I strapped myself into a car for a Cup event. Yet I strapped myself in every Sunday that they were racing."

He turned to the surgeon.

"I'll do it," Chance said.

The doctor's eyebrows shot up.

"You don't have to decide now," he assured Chance. "Take some time and think about it."

"Not necessary," Chance told him. "I'll do it. When can we schedule a time?"

CHAPTER 39

California Speedway—Fontana, California

"Aargh . . . ," Chance said.

The garage full of Nextel Cup Series regulars laughed at him. Their chaplain did look like a pirate, even though his eye patch was white gauze, rather than black cloth.

"I apologize for the dramatic appearance," Chance said. "But as you probably know, I had a second procedure last week to further stabilize the injury to my eye, and the doctors don't want me using it again until it's healed back up."

He felt bad saying that. What he'd just said was true, but it was a half-truth, and it felt wrong to be doing that, especially in a chapel service. But he and Cindy had talked it over, and they'd decided—and Max had agreed—not to discuss the matter with anyone in any further detail, not even with Chance's parents.

The Duke doctor had been right. The laundry list of possible complications had been just that, and while he had pronounced himself pleased with the way the procedure had gone, one of those possible complications was a postsurgical infection that could leave him blind and possibly even result in a need to surgically remove the eye.

The Nextel Cup Series was a pretty tight-knit community. Chance knew that there were a lot of people in the sport who cared for him deeply. It just didn't make sense to get them thinking one way and then risk disappointing them. So, under the pretext that no news would be good news, Chance had deliberately understated what Jerry and his medical team had done for him up at Duke.

His flock was smaller than usual this Sunday. Although he still got crowds that were consistently much larger than the ones that had attended services in previous seasons—a lot of fans came to stand in the back, just for the novelty of seeing a former driver preach—most drivers did not bring their wives and families to the California race and, without the urging of that female conscience, some of those guys went back to their haulers after the drivers' meeting and used the chapel slot as a time in which to sneak in a half-hour nap—a recharge before getting changed for drivers' introductions.

But the ones who were here were really here, hanging on his every word, reacting to every syllable. So he did something he hadn't done before. He mentally set aside the talk he'd prepared and simply spoke.

"If you don't believe that the Bible is an exhaustive reference for how to get through this disconnected drama that we call life," he said, "then I refer you to the fact that none other than Jesus himself speaks out on eye surgery in the seventh chapter of Matthew and the sixth chapter of Luke. That's where our Savior tells us that, before we get ready to take a speck of dust out of our brother's eye, we'd better prepare by yanking the ceiling beam out of our own.

"Which of course is really a caution on the practice of performing character surgery. Because when we presume to tell others how to shape up, we are arguing from a highly fallible position unless we are perfect. And folks, perfection has walked this earth one time, and one time only."

From then on, Chance just spoke as he was led. There wasn't a script, an outline, or, as far as he could tell, a point. All he knew was that, twenty minutes later, when he'd finished, there was a long line of people waiting to thank him and shake his hand.

"Thanks," he told Gage when the rookie got up to him. "But to tell you the truth, I'm not even sure what I said."

"Remember when you told me about the Holy Spirit?" Gage asked him. "I think that's who was talking this morning."

"Wish I'd heard it."

"No joke," the young driver said. "Next time, run a tape."

And when Duane got up to him, having waited and let all of the drivers step ahead of him, all the youngest Danford had to say was, "Thank you, Preacher-man. That was . . . that was true."

Lyle Danford took second at Fontana and came within a hairsbreadth of winning. It was a dramatic departure from the way his season had gone to date—after winning the championship the year before,

Danford had been struggling to find top-ten finishes ever since Daytona. But it also meant that Danford had to stay on at the track for interviews and his crew stayed on as NASCAR tore down his car in the post-race inspection.

So, since the helicopter livery was running a constant stream of shuttles out to the airport, Chance and Duane found one with some room and rode out ahead of Lyle and Danny, who was helping to babysit Lyle's car through inspection. It saved Chance and the younger Danford from having to wait around the track, and it gave them some quiet in the private Johnson Controls lounge out at the airport.

"So how's it been going for you?" Chance asked Duane as they settled down at a table with two cans of Coke and a basket of popcorn.

"Me?" Duane straightened up a bit. "Good, man. School's goin' . . . well, it's going okay. And with the team? I've been practicing with the over-the-wall crew, getting ready. And I've got to tell you, Boomer, slipping that wheel onto the hub and all five wheel lugs at the same time, in one quick movement? You talk about something that looks simple and takes forever to master."

"Like hitting a golf ball, from what I hear," Chance agreed.

"Hoss has been great, though," Duane said. "He doesn't gripe. He pumps you up. He makes you want to do better."

"Don't I know it," Chance said. Then, after he'd let that sink in a moment, he asked, "So are you?"

"Am I what?"

"Doing better."

"Oh, sure," Duane said. "We're already in the low fifteens on our practice stops."

"That's not what I'm asking about," Chance said.

Duane just looked back at him, his face blank.

Chance took a breath and held it.

"Is that what you want, Dew? You want to dance?"

The teenager looked down at the floor.

"Are you concentrating on school and racing?" Chance asked. "Or are you into something . . . uh . . . extracurricular?"

Chance had to deliberately stop himself from asking "or are you *still* into something . . ."

Duane still didn't say anything.

"What's your dad been saying?" Chance asked.

"My dad?" Duane laughed. "Oh, he made a lot of noise about grounding me. And I guess you two talked, because he mentioned that court order. That was in the off-season, though. But just as soon as Daytona came around, and his points started heading for the dumper? I don't even know if he realizes that I'm living in the same house."

"So what?" Chance asked.

"What does that mean?"

"It means you've got a good head on your shoulders, Dew. Your dad's not riding you—okay, I've got an opinion on that. But I also know that you don't need to be ridden to know what's right from what's wrong."

"This is what? A pep talk?"

"It's straight talk. Tell me something. Have you looked at that New Testament I gave you?"

"Some." Duane shrugged.

"Dew." Chance leaned forward. "If you're waiting for *me* to ride you, that's just not going to happen. Jesus died for you, man. He took pain for the way you live your life. He stepped in to kick the doors of heaven open for you. If that doesn't excite you . . . if that doesn't get your heart going and make you want to make a move . . . Well, either that's amazing to you, and the most wonderful thing you ever heard, or it's just words."

Duane looked back at him, a glimmer of pain in his eyes.

"Listen," Chance said, "I remember that talk at Steak 'n Shake. And I'll be the first to admit that my relationship with my father and your relationship with yours are like night and day. Point taken. But I don't have to have had your experience to offer an opinion on it—otherwise I'd have to live a thousand lifetimes before I could counsel anybody on anything, and obviously that's not how it works. But I can tell you one thing, Dew. If I had friction with my father, even if I was hopping mad at him, I can't for the life of me see how my going to jail—or my going to hell—would make the situation even the least little bit better, in my mind."

Duane's face reddened for a moment. Then it passed.

"Why," the teenager asked, "are you talking with me? My father is going to be fifty years old the year after next, Boomer. Fifty. Half a century on this planet, and he still thinks he's the center of it. And yet everybody seems to accept the situation—the fact that he never bothered to grow up."

There was the scream of jet engines outside on the tarmac as one of the other teams lifted off to head back to Carolina.

"You're entitled to that opinion," Chance said. "But let me ask you this: if you don't think your dad ever grew up, and that troubles you, then doesn't that place the onus on you to act just a little bit more mature?"

The teenager's face reddened again and stayed that way.

"You're not just some kid, Duane," Chance said. "God put the stuff between your ears to make you a man, capable of making a man's decisions a lot sooner than most guys. Why not use what he gave you?"

Duane stared back at him. Then he opened his carry-on bag and took out a textbook.

"Excuse me," he said, the chill evident in his voice. "I've got to study for my chem class. We've got a test coming up tomorrow."

As soon as Lyle and Danny showed up, they all got onto the plane. LD was still pumped from his strong finish in the day's race. Danny just looked tired—run out, as if he hadn't slept in days.

Chance and Lyle took a pair of the recliners, facing each other, at the front of the passengers' compartment. The boys went into the back, where Danny nearly collapsed onto the couch, slipping a seat belt loosely around his waist, while Duane plugged in a pair of ear-buds.

"MP3 player," Lyle grumbled, shaking his head. "You ever hear the junk that kid listens to? It sounds like a train wreck."

"Your dad probably said the same thing about what you listened to when you were his age."

Danford nodded. "My daddy was probably right," he said.

The plane took off and climbed smoothly to its cruising altitude, where it leveled into pillow-soft flight. Danford's jet was crewed by a pair of executive pilots who considered even the slightest bit of turbulence to be an affront to their professional dignity. After the seat belt light had gone off, the copilot came back and got a tray of chips, salsa, and sandwiches out of the galley sideboard. Chance heard both boys thank the man respectfully, but when LD got up and went back to get two roast-beef sandwiches, he reported that Duane had his nose buried in a book, and Danny was out like a light on the couch.

"Poor Danny." LD shook his head. "Lately, it seems like, every time I see him, the poor kid's wore out. He has to try so hard to do the things that just come naturally—used to come naturally—to Duane. If only I could combine the two."

"You know," Chance told him, "I think that's at least the second or third time I've heard you say that."

"Well, it's true."

"Still, it's a little odd."

"How's that?"

"The way you say it," Chance said. "'If only . . .' That's usually not how I hear you talk."

Danford nodded.

"My daddy used to tell me," he agreed, matter-of-factly, "that 'if' is an excuse."

"Exactly."

Danford glowered back at him, his jaw set. Then he took a breath.

"I don't have to explain this business to you, Boomer," he said. "You know how it is, particularly when things ain't clicking. It don't leave a lot of time to be nursemaiding your family."

"Lyle," Chance said, leaning toward him, "understand that I mean you well when I say this, but . . . that sounds like another excuse."

Danford kept things in check this time.

"Listen," he said. "Dottie and I have been keeping a pretty close rein on Duane lately."

"Close enough?"

"Why?" Danford asked, his face reddening again. "What do you know?"

"Know? I don't know anything," Chance told him, keeping his voice low. "Not for sure. But I sure know that there are some things that Duane just doesn't want to talk about."

"Well, like I said, we got him on a short leash. And I got his brother keeping an eye on him."

"And you know what I think of that."

Danford took a deep breath.

"What do you want me to do, Boomer? I ain't the one that's actin' out here, you know? I ain't the one that needs to straighten up. And I got a job to do, and I don't need to tell you how hard it is to do it. I mean, there just ain't enough hours in the day to get a race team back in the hunt again and deal with every single one of the parenthood issues. I feed Duane. I clothe him. I keep a roof over that calico head of his. I try to show him what's right and wrong. I don't see how I'm gonna be able to do much more than that; not unless you expect me to hang up my helmet like—"

He stopped talking and looked down at his sandwich.

"Like what?" Chance asked him. "Like I did?"

"I didn't say that," Danford said, still not looking Chance in his one uncovered eye. "It wouldn't be fair to say that."

Chance said nothing. He'd let his ire come up, and he was willing it back down again. He resettled the patch on his eye and took a deep, slow breath.

"You know, this thing that happened with me," he told Danford. "My eye. Getting knocked out of the car. I've got to admit it: I had me some 'why me' moments right after it happened, after I realized that I was done racing. But now that I've got a little distance on it, I can see that what I'm doing right now is a heck of a lot more important than what I was doing in that racecar."

Danford looked at him and shook his head slowly.

"Boomer, I'm forty-eight years old," he said. "That's already pretty long in the tooth for what I'm doing for a living. And I'll tell you the truth, if I hadn't done well last year, I might be able to see stepping back from all this. Concentrating on being a daddy. If this season don't finish with us in the top ten, I might still consider that. But the way I've got to look at this is that I don't have much time left where I can do what I do, and make the money that I make, and secure a future—not just for Duane, but for Dottie, and Danny, and little Angela. And for myself, for that matter. I mean, am I concerned about my kid? You bet I am. I'm losing sleep, worrying about him. But right now, I've got to do what I'm doing, and Danny's going to have to wait."

Will he? Can he? Those were the obvious questions, but Chance knew better than to wound Danford further by asking them.

"I'll get us another couple of Cokes," he said instead, getting up and walking back to the galley.

Danny was still sleeping, and Duane was still reading. Chance turned to open the door to the small refrigerator, then he turned back toward Duane, glancing at him with his one good eye.

He hadn't been mistaken. Duane wasn't reading his chemistry textbook any longer.

No, the text that was absorbing all his attention was a paperback with racecars on the cover.

The SCM New Testament that Chance had given him.

Parked just within the opened door of a dark hangar, the white van was all but invisible, its occupants dim shapes within the shadows. But the carefully chosen location gave them a clear view as Danford's private jet glided in from the starlit sky and taxied to Charlotte's private aviation terminal.

"So how do we know," the junior cop asked, breaking the silence, "that this isn't a load coming in right now? I mean, think about it: you've got a private jet, coming in from the West Coast. And we know that Burbank is from the West Coast. For all we know, there could be a suitcase full of smack in the baggage compartment."

"It's a possibility," his partner agreed.

"So what are we doing watching from here? Why aren't we over there, checking?"

"Because," the senior cop said, watching the plane through the cumbersome night-vision binoculars, bracing his elbows on the van's steering wheel, "that might be a possibility, but what's coming down in Florida in July is more than a possibility. I told you, we turned the Haitian. He's ours. We got him on felony possession, and we can deport him in a heartbeat. He's not going to give us any bull. If he says they're moving more than a quarter ton of snow through the Danford kid this summer, then they're moving it, and you know as well as I, that will be a history-books-caliber bust."

The younger man scratched his unshaven cheek.

"So we wait?"

The older cop lowered the binoculars and looked at the younger man. "Are you kidding? Of course we wait."

CHAPTER 40

Duke University Medical Center—Durham, North Carolina

The doctor leaned close, so close that Chance could smell the Listerine Breath Strip the man must have taken just before walking into the consulting room. Against the thin skin around his eyes, Chance felt the cool steel of the forceps that the surgeon was working under the tape of the patch.

"No difficulties?" The doctor kept working as he asked the question. "The patch stayed in place the whole time?"

"Yeah," Chance told him. "I did what you said, I was careful when I showered, and it stayed on just fine."

More cool metal as the doctor used the forceps to lift the edges of the patch.

"Well," the doctor said as he worked, "I know that we shaved your eyebrow before the procedure, but they grow back pretty quickly, so this is probably going to hurt a little. Keep your eye closed."

"You're the man, Jerry," Chance murmured.

There was a sound like pulled Velcro, and the remains of Chance's eyebrow felt hot, cold, and painful, all at the same time. Light, red and angry, flooded his eye through the closed eyelid.

"Yow!" Chance touched the area gingerly. "Maybe you're not the man, Jerry."

"You oughta try having your legs waxed," Cindy chuckled as she bounced little Nate on her knees.

"Keep the eye closed," Jerry told Chance. The surgeon kicked his stool over closer to the wall and slid the bar down on a rheostat. The room lights dimmed.

"Okay," Jerry said. "Take a look."

"Hmph," Chance said, blinking. "Bright . . ."

The doctor lowered the rheostat further.

"Your eye has been closed and covered for a week," he said. "It's going to be quite sensitive to light for the next few minutes. That's to be expected."

Chance blinked again and turned and looked at Cindy. He covered his left eye and looked at their son.

"Hey," Chance said. "How about that?"

"What?"

"Nate. He's all there."

Nathaniel emitted a startled "Ah!" as his mother hugged his father.

"Any distortion in your vision?" Jerry asked.

"Well," Chance said over his wife's head, looking around. "There is this . . . it looks like . . . You know when you're in a dark room and somebody opens a door off to your side, and you can't see the open door but you can sense the light? Almost like it's behind you?"

The doctor nodded. "That's excellent," he said.

Chance cocked his head, questioning.

Jerry pulled a piece of facial tissue out of a dispenser in the counter and folded one corner up.

"When your retina was torn, part of it was lifted, and occluded," he said. "By that, I mean that light entering the eye would not strike it, because it was in the shadow of the lifted retinal tissue. See?"

Chance nodded.

"So, just as the rest of your eye is sensitive right now because it has been deprived of light for a week, that particular portion is ultrasensitive, because it has been deprived of light for . . . how long?"

"Nine months," Chance told him. "Roughly nine months."

"There you go," Jerry said. "It's been in the dark for three-quarters of a year. That part of your eye is as sensitive as a newborn child's."

"So why is that good?" Cindy asked, turning her face away from Chance's shirt and wiping her eyes.

"Because it shows that the lifted tissue did not become necrotic—it didn't die," the surgeon told her. "If the photosensitive cells—the rods and cones in the retinal tissue—had been separated from their blood supply, then they would have perished in a matter of minutes. I didn't think that had happened; the tissue did not appear necrotic in our visual examination. But I couldn't be completely sure until now."

"Hmm." Chance blinked again. "Is this the way it's going to be from now on?"

"Not at all," Jerry assured him. "In a week—no more—everything will normalize and that effect will go away entirely. But you'll want to wear sunglasses, even indoors, for the first couple of days. Did you bring some with you, as I asked?"

"Yes," Cindy said, holding up a dark drawstring bag. "Oakleys. He has a whole drawer full of them."

The surgeon's eyebrows went up.

"Sponsorship deal," Chance explained.

"All right." Jerry grinned. "We have sunglasses here, just in case you forgot yours. But we get ours from the pharmacy. Yes, Oakleys will be fine."

CHAPTER 41

Lowe's Motor Speedway—Harrisburg, North Carolina

With a flip of his boot tip, Chance downshifted the Harley. He slowed enough to fish his NASCAR hard-card out of his jacket and flash it to the security guard at the tunnel entrance.

The motorcycle boomed and thundered through the corrugated tunnel under the track, the sound lessening immediately once he'd ridden out the other side. It was a gorgeous May afternoon, the sun warm through his thin leather jacket, the air clean and invigorating.

It had been a treat to be able to wake up in his own bed this morning with Cindy beside him, have breakfast in his own kitchen with his son, and then ride the bike in to the track. That was what was so great about Lowe's. Harrisburg was, for all practical purposes, Charlotte. Ninety percent of Nextel Cup lived within an hour of the track. From Lake Concord, the track was actually only about half the drive that it would be to downtown.

And in May, when Lowe's hosted the All Star event one weekend, and the Coca-Cola 600 the next, it was like homecoming for the folks in Nextel Cup. With no need to rush off to another track between the first weekend and the next, and with crews sleeping at home and able to spend evenings with their families, the hectic pace of Nextel Cup lessened just a bit and left everyone that much more congenial.

Chance rode the motorcycle up to the SCM assembly center and hit the kill switch, silencing the V-twins' mellow thunder. He put the bike on its kickstand and, helmet under his arm, walked through the ministry's outdoor gathering area, nodding and saying hello to the volunteers. In the little cubbyhole that served as his office at the far end of the assembly center, he picked up a short stack of messages, mostly housekeeping items, like a reminder that the new shipment of folding chairs would be in that afternoon. But on top of them all was a note from home—Cindy calling to let him know that Robert Vintner had been trying to reach him.

Chance unclipped the cell phone from his belt. Sure enough—a call had come in on that as well. He just hadn't heard it over the noise of the motorcycle.

Chance began to dial Vintner's cell phone, then stopped. The garage area was just a two-minute walk away. And he could do with a stretch of his legs after the hour-long ride into the speedway.

Of course, the two-minute walk took more like ten. People stopped Chance every few feet—some to ask for prayer, some to report prayers answered, some just to say hello. A few fans with garage passes recognized him and asked for autographs, and more than one uniformed crew member told him how he was looking forward to the weekend's message. Just as Fontana was one of the most sparsely attended chapel services, the Charlotte weekends—where just about every driver's family would accompany him to the track—would be standing-room only, even with the extra chairs.

Finally, after a dozen conversations and twice as many handshakes, Chance got to the RVR trailers. The haulers for the 35 car and the 53 were right next to each other and, on a whim, Chance tried the 35 first. It was the right guess—Robert was standing next to the workbench, going over a prep sheet with P. T. Sloane. The team owner looked up, scowling at the interruption, and then flashed into a grin when he saw who it was.

"Boomer! Good to see you, man! Cindy said that you were out terrorizing the countryside on that motorbike of yours."

"That's me. Marlon Brando all the way. Whattaya got?"

Vintner laughed and turned back to Sloane.

"Good thinking, PT," the owner told Danford's crew chief. "Set 'er up, and we'll go with what we had planned for next weekend."

Then, looking up, he said, "Come on back, Boomer. You want a coffee or anything?"

"I'm good," Chance said as they went back into the tucked-and-rolled leather lounge at the far end of the trailer.

"So you're riding the Harley again," Vintner said as they sat. "No more trouble with the blinker?"

"No," Chance said. "The vision slipped in that eye from 20/10 to 20/15, but the surgeon said that was just because of scarring."

"Still," Vintner said, "slipping to 20/15 sure doesn't sound like anything to cry about."

"I'm not," Chance assured him. "So what's up?"

"What are you up to a week from Thursday?"

"A week from Thursday?" Chance took his PDA out of his jacket and tapped the calendar. "Driving the motorhome up to Dover. Why?"

Vintner looked out into the corridor of the transporter. It was empty, but he shut the door anyhow.

"Trixie Gilbert had surgery yesterday," he said. "Gall bladder."

"Oh, man," Chance told him, crestfallen. "I didn't even know. Cindy and I should have been there."

"Naw," Vintner said. "You know Trixie. She didn't want a fuss, so she swore Pooch to secrecy. Only reason he told me was that he knew I'd have to find another spotter for this weekend and the next. It's just the two of them, you know, so the nurse duties sort of fall to him."

"Well, now that I know, do you think she'd mind if Cindy and I dropped in tonight?"

"If we asked, yes. If you just do—of course she won't mind. She's over to Memorial Hospital."

Chance nodded and made a note in the little silver PDA.

"So, you need my help in finding you a spotter this weekend?"

He didn't volunteer himself. He knew that he'd be needed at the infield care center, just in case there was trouble.

"Nope. We've got that all covered."

Chance looked back at the PDA.

"Wait," he said. "You were asking about the Thursday after next. What's Pooch got to do with that?"

"Thursday is when Pooch is supposed to be driving test on the 35 over in Kentucky."

Chance nodded. That made sense. NASCAR allowed Nextel Cup teams to rent race venues and test only a few times a year—in fact, the number had recently fallen from seven sessions a season to just five. So the better teams sought out "clone tracks." Those were tracks where the Series did not race—so testing there did not count against one's total—but where conditions closely approximated those of the actual race venues.

Kentucky Speedway was one such track; while the Busch Series raced there, Nextel Cup did not. Yet the Busch Series crew chiefs had noted that Kentucky's track conditions were practically identical to those at Kansas Speedway. And while the Kansas race did not come around until the end of September, teams preferred to finish their testing well before that. The late-season races could be critical to a team's points standings.

"So how can I help?" Chance asked. "Want me to find a driver?"

Vintner locked eyes with him for the space of one breath.

"You know what I want, Boomer."

Chance broke eye contact, looking down, then back up again.

"You want me to drive test for you," he finally said, his voice low.

"Of course, I do," Vintner told him. "You're the perfect sub for Pooch. I wouldn't want to say it in front of him, but you're actually more than perfect—you're better than him."

"Now—"

"Now, nothing," Vintner continued, his hand up. "When I had you and LD driving for me, I was the envy of every multicar team owner out there. I mean, I've known guys with two-car teams where the drivers couldn't even agree on what chassis to run, let alone come to some sort of accord on right-side camber and shock valving. But Boomer, I've got to tell you, I pulled the prep sheets on both cars for the last two years, and you and LD were so close to identical that it was scary. You're the perfect driver to test for him. The only place where you didn't agree was on road courses, and that made sense, because neither one of you was worth half a hot hoot on a road course."

Chance laughed. It was the only possible reaction, because what Vintner had just said was absolutely true.

"So what do you think, Boomer? We're in a tight spot here. Can you help us out?"

What Vintner didn't say—what he didn't need to say—was that Robert Vintner Racing and Robert Vintner himself had helped Chance Reynolds and his family out quite a bit over the years. Lining up the eye surgery—a trick that Chance knew had to involve several pulled strings—had only been the most recent episode.

"We'll use a team jet to get you from Charlotte to Cincinnati, and we'll keep it there and fly you from Cincinnati to Dover when you're done," Vintner quickly added. "Take Cindy and the baby with, if Cindy wants to go. And don't worry about your motorhome. I'll have the crew drive it up to Delaware for you, and it will be set up and waiting for you when you get there."

Chance laughed. "Aren't you getting a little ahead of yourself? I mean, I pulled out on disability. You can't get track insurance. I can't even get back into a Cup car without a doctor's sign-off."

"You've got one," Vintner said, putting a manila file folder on the table in front of him. "Actually, you've got two. You've got one from Max and—just in case anybody gets snippy about our outfit's own doctor signing you off—one from some fella whose name looks like somebody leaned their elbow on the keyboard."

Chance pursed his lips and crossed his arms.

"And if it's the pay you're thinking about, don't worry," Vintner said. "I'll make it worth your while."

"Now, Robert, you stop that. You paid me two salaries last year."

"And you earned them," Vintner told him. "Don't sneeze at money, man. Remember, you're a daddy now."

Chance blinked, hoping he wasn't tearing up.

"Okay," Chance said. "Enough. Uncle. I'll drive your test."

"Great!" Vintner grinned.

The team owner rubbed his walrus moustache and cocked his head.

"What?" Chance asked.

"Well, I was just thinking. You had two wins last season. And that's one more than you need to make the All Star this Saturday."

"And you already have two cars and two drivers in it."

"Ohh, we got more than two cars," Vintner said. "I'm willing to bet that we've got an extra set of wheels back in Mooresville, somewhere."

It was deliberate understatement. Andy Hofert and P. T. Sloane each hauled two completely prepared, track-tuned racecars to every single Nextel Cup event. That made a total of four RVR cars in the garage area at this very moment. In addition, each of the RVR teams had anywhere from twelve to eighteen racecars in various stages of preparation back at the shop, just half an hour away. If he ever needed to, Robert Vintner could fill the average suburban strip-mall parking lot with about $6.5 million worth of state-of-the-art racecars.

"And," Vintner added. "I think I might be able to scare up a single-race sponsor with—oh, I don't know—maybe about one phone call. Seeing as you're already qualified."

Chance slowly pushed the file folder back across the table.

"Forget it, Robert," he said. "If this whole deal is a prelude to getting me to make a comeback, then I'm not interested."

Vintner just bounced his eyebrows a couple of times.

"I'm working for a different boss this weekend," Chance told him. "I'm . . . Robert . . . I'm seeing God change lives, man. Don't get me wrong; what you do is important. Really important. What I do wouldn't even be possible if it wasn't for what you do. But what God wanted me to do four years ago, and what he wants me to do today are just two entirely different things."

"And you're sure of that."

"I'm positive."

"Okay," Vintner told him. "My turn to say 'uncle.' But you'll drive the test in Kentucky, right? We'll be hurtin' if you don't."

"Now let's see." Chance made a show of mulling over the idea. "Do I want to drive an RV all the way up to Delaware, or do I want to fly there and get some seat time to boot?"

He grinned.

"Yes, Robert," Chance told his old boss. "I'll drive your test."

CHAPTER 42

Kentucky Speedway—Fort Mitchell, Kentucky

Three generations of Reynolds men grinned back at Cindy from the tiny LCD screen of the digital camera.

Or at least two were grinning: Chance, in the racecar's seat, and his father, standing with his arm draped over the roof. Five-month-old Nathaniel, being held up to the window by his firesuited father, had a look of total rapture on his face that, at his age, was either unqualified astonishment or a slight case of gas.

"One more," Cindy told them. The camera's strobe stuttered for a moment and then flashed.

"Okay," Chance said as he handed Nathaniel to his father. "Now you'd better get this young man back in the van before I fire up. I'd like him to still be able to hear when he gets to kindergarten."

Just getting into the car had been something of a shock for Chance.

Some things had been startlingly familiar. His firesuit, sent along with the hauler from RVR's shop in Mooresville, had been his old E-World Broadband uniform. Or rather it had been his old livery stitched onto a brand-new firesuit—obviously one of the spares they'd had left in stock when his accident had taken him out of the running. And the suit, the track, the look of the car—which had been left in gray primer, nothing in color but the car numbers required by NASCAR—all brought him back as if it had been just a day or two, and not nearly a year, since he had last been in a Nextel Cup car.

But climbing through the window had been trickier than before. There were more things in the way. The seat was radically different—made from Kevlar, rather than aluminum, with a tub-like projection that rose up on either side of his legs to help contain them in a crash.

"Wow," he'd told P. T. Sloane as the crew chief helped him strap in. "I can't see squat to my right side."

"Don't I know it," the gruff, heavy man told him. "New rules—NASCAR extended the head restraint on the right-hand side. Helps ya keep from hyperextending your neck in a side impact. Andy cut a peephole into Gage's, but LD said it don't make no difference, seeing as you can't really turn your head anyhow. He figured that as long as we have to have it, we might as well make sure it's sturdy."

Chance nodded his head, something he could still do because he hadn't yet put on the helmet and its tethers.

"Besides," PT had said, "we'll have a spotter up on top the grandstand for every second of the test. NASCAR's requirin' 'em now, you know, for all practices, and we're using one even when you're the only car running, just to make sure nothin' blindsides you."

"Sounds good."

And now, helmeted and cinched down, Chance was glad for the extra spot of vision he'd regained in his right eye because it felt like half of it was blocked by the new safety equipment. That wasn't really the case: the new restraint really only blocked part of his peripheral vision, and the rearview mirror had a pane in it that gave him some clue as to what was happening out his Plexiglas right-side window.

Still, he was glad that he'd had a lot of experience with the HANS device before combining it with the new seat and head restraints. It had allowed him to get accustomed, by degrees, to a loss of freedom of movement and vision that he had taken for granted back in his sprint-car days. Had all of this just been thrown at him all at once, it would have been downright claustrophobic.

"Radio check. Welcome back, Boomer."

The spotter for the day was Guy Rappleye, a Craftsman Truck Series driver Chance knew from those weekends when Truck was the Saturday event before a Cup race.

"Thanks, Rapper," Chance said. "But I'm not back. Just visiting."

"Well, it's great to have you. Good signal. Ten by ten."

The window net went up and PT whirlygigged a finger. Just seeing that made all the hair stand up on the back of Chance's neck. He hadn't realized how much he'd missed this—he was positively giddy with excitement.

Taking a deep breath, urging his heart rate back down, Chance checked the center switch and made sure the battery circuit was live. Then he turned on the ignition and lifted the starter toggle.

Like a dog shedding water, the racecar shook as the big V-8 engine rumbled to life. Crewmen began disconnecting the start-cart, and Chance turned on the cooling fans that would keep the brakes and other vital parts within operating temperature for the stop-and-go cycles of the test. He flipped another switch and cool, filtered air began to flow into his helmet from a tube connected to his chin bar.

"Track is clear. Track is open," his spotter called.

"Car's clear," PT radioed. "Whenever you're ready, Boomer."

Chance eased the car into first and then rested his left leg against the side of the seat-tub, shifting without the clutch through the next two gears, and then grabbing fourth as he passed the pit road exit line.

He held the car low through the first two turns, just as he would in a race. The tires had good grip—they were "scuffs" that had been run for several laps during a practice at Charlotte.

Chance kept the RPMs several hundreds below the red line for the first lap, and then he dropped the hammer for the second, following the regular racing groove, a smudge of smoky rubber that followed the fastest conventional line around the track, the car fighting back in the turns, but controllable.

For a moment he just wondered at the fact that he was back on a racetrack. The grandstands may have been empty, the infield nothing but rutted grass, but Chance couldn't have been more pumped if he were leading the final lap of the Daytona 500.

"Speak to me," PT radioed, shattering the reverie. "What's she doing?"

"Tight," Chance said. "Tight in, tight through the middle, tight out. Terrible tight. We're too soft, right front."

"Air pressure?"

"I doubt it. I think we're talking shocks, maybe spring rubber. But I'll give her a couple of laps to make sure."

He did that, enjoying the old familiar sensation of speed and control, even though the car was fighting him into every turn.

"Still tight," he radioed the crew chief. "Definitely right front. You can try a spring rubber, but I think we need a stiffer shock."

"Okay," PT concurred. "Bring her in. Flaky suspected this. He's got a new shock valved and ready."

So Chance completed the first laps he'd run in a Cup car in nearly a year and brought the car to pit road, the feeling as natural as walking, as natural as breathing. He shifted down to second gear at the entrance and put the tach needle exactly at the RPM calculated to leave the car at 55 miles per hour—the pit road speed limit at Kansas. Up ahead, he could see a crewman with a radar gun and another with a stopwatch, timing him two different ways to make sure the car chief had not been off in his calculations. Behind the wall on the empty pit road, Cindy and his parents were beaming, waving.

And as Chance pulled into his spot smartly, hitting his marks right on the dime, he left the face shield down on his helmet.

After all, he knew the guys on LD's team pretty well, but not so well that he'd want them to see his face wet with tears.

The day, which would have been one solid, prolonged chore for a full-time Nextel Cup driver, had been perfect—absolutely perfect. It hadn't been a race. Chance had rarely run more than twenty laps at a time. And it hadn't been until late in the afternoon when he'd run with two other cars driven by a couple of Truck Series drivers, drafting and gauging the effects of aero push, that his had not been the only car on the track.

And just that, that he'd been out on the track, that he'd had that . . . that experience once again. That his father had been there to see him firsthand and know, know without reservation, that Chance had not lost something irrevocably because of his love for the older man. Those things had made the day far more than worth it. They'd left Chance ecstatic that he'd come to run this test.

They'd had a break in the middle of the day while PT changed differentials and engines. It had been a window in the middle of the day, long enough for the five of them—Chance, Cindy, his folks, and little Nathaniel—to drive back across the river to Skyline Chili. They had the sort of lunch that had punctuated Chance's childhood during the rare summer weekday trips to Reds games: hot dogs with cheese, served on bakery-fresh buns, and topped with Cincinnati's signature chili. Chance had forgotten about that chili, with its fine-ground beef, just as he had forgotten his father's joyous smile. It had been good to visit both once again.

The last thing Chance had done was a qualifying test. Taped up, the car had become a different beast, and they'd had to come in twice, once for a track bar adjustment, and once to add half a pound of pressure to the left rear tire.

But with those two adjustments, the racecar flew. There was no other word for it.

"She's hooked up," was all Chance had radioed during his warm-up lap. Then he'd run a lap at speed, crossing the finish line and cutting power to the engine just as steam began to jet from the overflow.

"That'll do," PT had drawled over the radio. "Seein' as that's the best time ever."

"No joke?" Chance had asked him. "We never tested faster here?"

"Son," PT had told him, "ain't nobody has ever tested faster here. If we'd a had us a NASCAR scorer in the box, that lap you just busted would be a track record."

So the day had ended on a very high note. Then they'd flown to Dover on RVR's smaller jet, a Citation 10 that was so much like the plane Chance had leased that it was eerie. And as the plane circled before landing, Chance had looked across the aisle at Cindy, asleep in her seat, and then at little Nathaniel, asleep as well in a car seat that had been securely strapped in. The whole day—the testing, the success of it, the flight up—had held for Chance the odd feeling of something foreign. It was, he'd decided, like the end of a tropical vacation. When you come back from something exotic and wonderful, and then you have to make the transition back to your regular life.

It was dark when Vintner's driver dropped them off at their motorhome in the paddock at Dover Downs. Dark, and they were tired. Cindy had immediately headed back to the bedroom to put little Nathaniel down for the night in his crib, while Chance went up front to make sure the blinds had been pulled for the windshield.

They had. And the LEDs on the dashboard showed that the vehicle had been properly leveled, was running on external power, and the freshwater tank was being replenished from an outside tap. He was turning away when a glint of light drew his eyes to the half-open ashtray.

He opened it all the way and found a single-edge razor blade. Curious. Maybe whoever had driven the motorhome up had used a box cutter for something and had changed the blade.

Chance picked up the blade and headed back to the galley to put it into the trash. Little Nathaniel wasn't old enough yet to be getting into things, but it didn't hurt to cultivate good habits early.

Chance got to the galley and was opening the lower cabinet door, where the trash can was, when yet another reflection caught his eye.

It was a mirror this time, a rectangular mirror no larger than a paperback, its surface smudged as if someone had run a wet fingertip back and forth across it. He picked it up and walked into the bedroom.

"Honey," he asked, holding the mirror up, "is this yours?"

Cindy gave it a glance and shook her head.

"Must belong to whoever drove this up for us," she'd said. "If it was somebody traveling with his wife or girlfriend, she'll be missing it, come morning."

Shrugging, Chance headed back to the galley. Then he looked once again at the mirror, and then at the razor blade, and an image, one that he had seen a hundred times on TV cop shows, came into his head. He could almost picture someone using the razor blade to finely chop a white powder, to arrange the powder in thin lines that one could snort up through a tightly rolled dollar bill.

Heart sinking, Chance took the cell phone off his belt and pushed the speed-dial button for Robert Vintner.

"Boomer!" The team owner was obviously on cloud nine. "Hey—PT emailed me the test results. Looks like you guys got her dialed in, all right. That was one heck of a lap, man!"

"Thanks," Chance said. "Hey, I'm over here at the motorhome."

"Everything okay?" Vintner asked. "Set up the way you like it?"

"Yeah. Sure. I was just wondering, who drove this up here for us?"

"Lyle Danford's boy. Danny."

"Danny, huh? Anybody ride up with him?"

"Yeah. I think his brother came up with him. The kid that works on your old team. Duane."

CHAPTER 43

The two policemen—one a Kent County sheriff's deputy and the other a crime scene investigator from the Delaware Bureau of Investigation—had had the couth to drive in quietly, no lights or sirens. And with the two of them, plus Lyle Danford and his two sons, Robert Vintner, Cindy, and Chance, it made for quite a crowd in the Bounder's little sitting area.

But no one was sitting. The deputy was writing notes at the counter, and the CSI man was running a penlight over the little catchall bin atop the engine console. Vintner was looking worried, the Danford boys were looking nervous, and their father was looking just plain ready-to-strangle-someone angry.

He wasn't mad at Chance. When Chance and Vintner had come to see him at his motorhome, just six stalls down from where SCM had set up in the paddock, Danford hadn't argued a bit when Chance had said that, seeing as he had reason to believe a law had been violated, he felt ethically obliged to notify the authorities. In fact, Danford had seemed relieved at the prospect.

"That's overdue," was what he'd said.

They hadn't gotten a lot out of the boys. Duane had taken one look at the cop cars and clammed up, glaring tight-lipped at his father and not saying a word. And Danny had told his father, "Daddy, I was just driving the motorhome like Mr. Vintner asked me to. I didn't know what was going on back here. You've got to believe me."

"I do," Danford had told him.

Then, turning to Duane, he had said, "And you, boy, have just run right out of leash. I don't even know if I've a mind to bail you out."

The CSI man had both Duane and Danny run cotton swabs over the insides of their mouths, dropping the swabs into miniature test tubes, which he sealed, labeled, and initialed. He had the boys turn out their pockets, and then he looked at their arms, between their fingers, and into their eyes, holding the penlight before their pupils and then taking it away. He bagged both the mirror and the razor blade, and then the deputy took Duane and Danny outside to take their statements.

"Listen," the investigator told Chance, Lyle, and Robert once the boys were out of earshot, "you were right to call us. This does appear suspicious. But I've got to tell you, this mirror has been pretty well licked up, and there doesn't seem to be any residue left on the blade. I'll take them in and test them, but I doubt we'll have anything more than a trace sample of cocaine, maybe amphetamine."

Chance and Danford exchanged a glance.

"Well, ain't a trace enough?" Danford asked the investigator.

"Not against any half-decent defense lawyer," the man told him. "If I had everybody here turn out their pockets, I could come up with trace samples of cocaine."

LD took a step forward, eyes squinted.

"Now just you hold on, mister," he said. "These are good folks. They ain't druggers."

"Exactly," the investigator agreed, leaning back just a bit. "And yet, if anybody here has, say, a hundred-dollar bill in their pocket? Nearly 90 percent of all hundred-dollar bills in circulation test positive for cocaine. That's a fact. It's that prevalent. So even if this mirror and this blade test positive, we certainly won't have enough to pursue possession. And regardless of what anybody did on the way up here, nobody's high now. Both of those young men look sober and react normally."

There was a whir and a hiss as the motorhome releveled itself.

"What are you saying?" Danford asked.

The CSI man nodded in the direction of the uniformed cop.

"I'm going to recommend to the deputy that he not make an arrest," the investigator said. "The swabs I had them run? That's for DNA, but the most it can tell us is that some male member of your immediate family licked his finger and then ran it over the mirror. Could be one boy. Could be the other. Could be you. Licking a mirror is suspicious, but it's not against the law. Even your run-of-the-mill public defender could get this thrown out by morning."

Danford buried his hands in his jeans pockets, staring down at the floor.

"I never thought I'd be saying this," he said. "But if you could just run Duane in, hold him overnight, maybe it'd scare the kid straight."

"I hear you," the investigator said. "But Delaware's pretty adamant on civil liberties. The deputy, there, could get a derogatory for making an arrest on insufficient evidence. We'll do all we can. We'll process whatever we can on what we've got. But I can tell you right now that, while it looks suspicious, it won't be conclusive. All that's going to come out of this here is a report."

Lyle turned to Chance.

"Maybe that would be enough for what you said," he told the chaplain, his voice low. "For going to court, getting an order, makin' Duane stay with either his mother or me when he's not at work."

The investigator nodded his head.

"That's an excellent idea," he said. "If that was my boy, that would be the first thing I did once I got back to Carolina."

CHAPTER 44

Michigan International Speedway—Brooklyn, Michigan

"You won this race last year, didn't you?"

"Yeah, Duane," Chance said, "I did. And you're changing the subject again. Are we going to talk, or what?"

The teenager put his hands behind his head and stretched.

"Talk?" Duane shrugged. "Sure. We'll talk. I don't have much of a choice. The judge said that, until I turn eighteen, I've got to be one of three places—the high school, the shop, or in the company of one of my parents. And she also said I had to take counseling with a professional of my parents' choice, and the old man chose you. So here I am. And talking about you winning here is not changing the subject."

"How so?"

Duane leaned forward.

"I remember that race," he said. "The old man almost wrecked you once, and then he did wreck you on the homestretch."

"And your point is?"

Duane tapped the desk in Chance's tiny cubicle at the back of the SCM assembly center.

"That Lyle let-us-bow-down-and-worship-him Danford will run over anybody and anything that gets in between him and what he wants. I mean, this weekend, the only thing he's thinking about is that, if he places in the top five and the 24 car misses the top ten, then he takes the points lead. He's not thinking about his family, and he's sure not thinking about me. I'm a problem that he took care of with a court order and third parties—such as yourself."

Chance began to respond, but then he took a breath. He glanced at the clock on his computer screen and then turned back to Duane.

"Tell me something, Dew," he said. "Do you love your mother?"

Duane scowled.

"My mother? Of course. Everybody loves their mother."

Chance nodded.

"And how about your sister?"

"Angela?"

"Yes. Angela. Do you love her?"

Duane scowled again.

"Sure."

Chance lifted his head.

"How much?"

Duane just looked at him. Out on the track, there was the roar of racecars practicing.

"Let's say the house is on fire," Chance said. "Angela's trapped upstairs. You can get her out, but you can't do that and get yourself out as well."

"Why not?"

"Work with me," Chance said. "I'm being hypothetical here. It's your life or Angela's. Who do you save?"

Duane shrugged.

"Angela."

"Do you mean that or are you just saying it because it seems like the right thing to say?"

"No." Duane was getting a little red in the face now. "I mean it."

"Okay." Chance nodded. "How about if it's your life or Danny's?"

"Danny. Definitely, I save Danny."

Chance nodded again, not looking at Duane anymore.

"And you'd die for your mother, too?"

"Of course," Duane said. "Why?"

Chance looked him right in the eyes.

"Because it doesn't add up, Dew."

"What doesn't add up?"

"You say that you love your mother and your brother and your sister enough to die for any of them. And yet you are willing to allow this chip that you're carrying on your shoulder—this thing that you have between you and your father—to make all three of their lives absolutely miserable."

The roar on the track died down and stopped. Duane didn't say anything.

"Duane," Chance said softly, "you say your dad's selfish. I won't argue with that. But he's not the Lone Ranger here, you know? And being stubborn just makes things worse. Isn't it time to change?"

The teenager just sat there for thirty long seconds. Then, silently, he nodded.

Just at that moment, the door to Chance's tiny cubicle of an office opened. It was SCM's youth pastor.

"Oh, man," the youth pastor said, "I'm sorry. I didn't know you were . . . But listen . . . Chance . . . you've got to come quick."

Chance got to his feet.

"Sure," he said. "What's up?"

The younger pastor looked at Duane and then back at Chance.

"Spit it out," Chance told his colleague. "What's up?"

"We need to get you to the care center," the young man said. "It's LD. He just hit the wall. Hard. It looked bad."

Chance saw Danford at the infield care center, but couldn't do much beyond that. The security guard had stopped Duane at the door, but Chance got in, and when he did, a cluster of doctors and nurses were already gathered around Lyle, cutting the top of his firesuit off, taking his blood pressure, and placing a cervical collar around his neck. After several minutes, Max Peters broke away from the cluster of doctors and took Chance by the arm.

"He's coming to," Max said. "But we're going to fly him into the ER at University of Michigan Hospital and do a CAT scan, at least. Maybe an MRI. I'll fly with him. I've already asked the helicopter livery to send a chopper to take you and Robert over there."

So the blue-and-gold University of Michigan Life Flight helicopter had come in and taken Lyle and Max away, and then a second chopper had landed.

"Where's Danny?" Chance asked Robert Vintner over the *whap-whap-whap* of the blades.

"He was driving over from the hotel when the wreck happened," Vintner yelled back. "We tried calling, but the cell service is spotty. Too many hills."

"Okay." Chance grabbed Duane by the arm. "Come on," he told him. "You're coming with us."

Robert sat up front, next to the pilot, and Chance and Duane got in the back. The helicopter lifted off and immediately set off in a beeline, east by northeast, for Ann Arbor. Looking Duane's way, Chance took off his headset and motioned for Duane to do the same.

"This way they can't hear on the intercom," Chance told him, speaking loudly over the sound of the helicopter's jet turbine. "Private conversation. Okay?"

Duane nodded.

"You said you wanted to change," Chance said as woodlands and lakes flashed by hundreds of feet beneath them. "Did you mean that?"

Duane nodded again.

"That's good," Chance told him. "Wanting to change—that's what the Bible calls 'repentance.' Where you take whatever has been leading you through life and replace it with something better."

A third nod.

"So," Chance asked him, "what are you going to do?"

"I . . . I . . .," Duane stammered. He wiped his nose with the back of his hand. "Boomer . . . Listen. There's a part in the back of that New Testament you gave me. It talks about asking Christ into your life?"

Chance nodded, his heart thumping.

"If I do that . . .," Duane asked, eyes shiny with tears, "if I do, will God make sure that my old . . . that my dad's gonna be okay?"

Chance closed his eyes, thin-lipped, and shook his head.

"God does not negotiate, Duane," he said, looking the teenager straight in the eyes. "We're all offered the same gift. It's a take-it-or-leave-it thing. Will he listen more closely to the prayers of his children? Absolutely. I believe that with all my heart and soul. But you need to accept it for what it is . . . eternal life, not a bargaining chip. Not a ticket to talk to God. God loves you, Dew. But he won't honor anything that's not genuine. It's got to be a heartfelt desire to come to him . . . to accept his Son."

Duane bit his lip and turned to look out the window. Houses—the square ranch houses of suburbia—were scrolling by beneath them. They crossed an interstate and the helicopter banked.

Duane turned back, wiping his face with both hands.

"Say I've got that desire," he said, his mouth close to Chance's ear. "Say I do. What do I do next?"

Chance closed his eyes and breathed a silent prayer. He reached into his jacket and took out a pocket Bible, held it where Duane could see it, and opened it to Titus 3:5.

"NASCAR has a regulation that a driver can't get back in the car with a concussion," Max told Chance and Vintner and Duane in the hall outside the ER examination room. "And I've examined Lyle, as have the doctors here, and we're unanimous in our opinion that he does not have a concussion. Frankly, I don't think he was knocked out by the crash. I think he passed out from the pain."

"The pain of what?" Duane asked, his voice small.

"He's got two cracked ribs," Max said. "Those aren't life-threatening in the least, but they can be unbelievably painful, especially for the next few days. That, plus we found a hairline crack in his left ankle. We can tape that for races and put a walking cast on it weekdays."

Max turned to Vintner. "I'll be frank," he said. "LD can drive. I can't order him not to. But he is going to be in a world of hurt every moment that he's in that racecar tomorrow. I can't imagine how anybody, not even Lyle Danford, could drive a race in that condition."

"Can he hurt himself worse by driving?" Vintner asked.

"If he wrecks, absolutely. But just by driving? No. Not if we keep him taped."

Vintner looked down the hall, where a pair of white-coated doctors peered at a chart together before disappearing into an examining room. He turned back.

"Then it's his decision," he finally said.

"That it is," Max grumbled. "Well, let's go see the man."

They filed into the room and Danford smiled weakly at them from the examination table. He was sitting up, with broad strips of adhesive tape across his ribs.

"How're you feelin', LD?" Vintner asked.

"Feeling? I ain't feelin' nothin'. These ole boys got me so shot full of painkillers I could probably fall off this building and walk away from it."

"I've told them about your situation," Max said.

Danford nodded.

"And I've told them you're cleared to drive. Even though, as your physician, I hardly recommend it. You can't drive on painkillers. You'd have to do it unmedicated. And it would not be pretty, believe me."

Danford nodded again. He touched his taped chest gingerly.

"I drove with one cracked rib before," he said. "Felt like somebody was twisting a knife in my side every time I turned the wheel. And this ain't one. It's two."

"You want to sit out?" Vintner asked.

Danford scowled and shook his head.

"I can't, Robert. You know that. It's the points lead. We can't get it if I don't start."

"No man on earth could drive for 400 miles with the kind of injuries you have," Max objected.

"I don't have to drive for 400 miles," Danford replied. "Just a few. Maybe just two and a half."

"How's that?" Max looked puzzled.

"NASCAR rules." Danford grinned, wincing. "To get credit for a race, all I got to do is start it. Start it, run a lap, and then pull off. Although I'd try to run until the first yellow, if I could. Then I could get out—"

"And we could finish the race with a substitute driver," Vintner said, nodding.

"But not just any substitute," Danford said. "We need us a top-five finish tomorrow. We don't want to take some hit-or-miss guy who couldn't qualify on Friday and put him in my driver's seat. We need us somebody spectacular. A guy that can be in the hunt."

He turned to look at the Cup Series chaplain and grinned, his hand still on his taped ribs.

"What do you say, Boomer? As a favor to a friend? Will you drive my car tomorrow?"

CHAPTER 45

"For this my son was dead and is alive again,'" Chance read aloud. "'He was lost and is found.'"

He closed the Bible and looked up at the crowd that packed every square inch of Michigan International Speedway's big inspection garage. Several people smiled back at him, and he nodded.

"We all know that story from Luke," he said. "The Prodigal Son. That's him. And if you know Jesus as your Savior, that's you, too. That's me. And yesterday, as we flew into University of Michigan Hospital to check on his dad, that was Duane Danford."

There was a moment of murmur in the crowd, then somebody, a tire carrier from Chance's old team, stood up and began clapping. In seconds, the whole garage was on its feet, applauding and whistling—everyone but Duane Danford, who sat in the front row, face reddening around his smile.

Chance held his hands out for quiet, and the crowd settled down.

"I don't usually announce converts in chapel," he told them. "But Duane wanted you all to know this. And this young man asked me if he could have a moment in the service this morning, and I said he could have all the time he wanted. Duane?"

The applause began anew as Duane got to his feet in his E-World Broadband crew uniform. He walked to the front, the applause continued, and he turned his back for a moment, wiping his eyes. Finally he turned to face the crowd again, and a silence settled over the garage. He moved the microphone on the lectern and cleared his throat.

"I'm glad you're all here," he said. "I want you all to hear this, even though . . ."

He stepped back to wipe his nose and several men shouted encouragement.

"Even though I wanted to speak to one man," he continued.

Chance looked to the back, where Lyle Danford was standing with the help of a pair of aluminum crutches. Chance saw the driver take off his sunglasses and smile.

"Dad," Duane said. "Daddy . . . I . . ."

He closed his eyes, worked his lips, opened his eyes again.

"You work hard," he said. "Every week . . . and I know why you do it. It's for Mom, and for Danny, and for Angie, and . . . and for me. Especially since Boomer, here, got me on the 35 crew, I've gotten to know just how tough your job can be. And I know it's even harder when you're worried about us . . . about me."

LD closed his eyes, and Duane was silent for a moment.

"I just want you to know how sorry I am," Duane forged on, "for how much of a pain in the . . . for all the trouble I've been. Man . . ."

The teenager shook his head. "I just wish," he said, "that I could take it all back."

There was another moment of silence, but Chance saw LD mouth the words, "You have."

Duane gulped.

"So I just want you to know," he told his father, "before you climb in that racecar today . . . Man, I'm going to work so hard to be somebody that you can be proud of."

There was a clicking sound, metal against metal, as Lyle Danford worked his way forward through the tightly packed folding chairs, his crutch legs bumping up against them as he moved.

Duane looked at Chance, who nodded, and the teenager left the lectern and met his father halfway, throwing his arms around him. The crowd stood and applauded again, and Duane helped his father off to the side. After everyone had settled back down, Chance stepped up to the microphone.

"I don't have a message for you this morning," he told the sea of faces. "Or rather, I do, but you just heard it. In the fourth chapter of Ephesians, verse 24, the Christian is commanded to 'put on the new man, which after God is created in righteousness and true holiness.' Folks, we've seen that done here this morning. If you haven't done so yet, then I just want to invite you and tell you that now is the time. And if you have done that, but you've wandered away . . . well, the light is on, the door is open, and the welcome mat is out. I can't think of a better time than this to come back. Can you? Let's pray."

The uniform that Chance had worn in Kentucky had been cleaned and then air-expressed to Michigan along with his helmet, gloves, and driving shoes. Now the uniform and shoes were laid out on the bed in his Bounder, and he had this odd déjà vu feeling about beginning that old prerace ritual. It was something he'd thought he'd never do again.

But here he was. Robert Vintner had personally tracked down Dr. Jack Nobles by phone, explained the situation, and convinced the SCM founder to fly up for the day on an RVR jet. Dr. Nobles had gotten there just after the chapel service, full of support for the way his chaplain was helping one of his flock, and he and Chance had barely updated one another before it was time for Chance to change. The old chaplain would stand Chance's regular post in the infield care center.

Chance reached for the uniform. Then he stopped and knelt next to the bed.

"Father," he prayed aloud, "I'm doing what I'm doing today to help a friend and to glorify you. Please . . . please help me to keep it that way. To glorify you. Not me. In Christ's name I ask this. Amen."

Then he put on the firesuit, its tailored form fitting him with the ease of a second skin.

Perky had done what she could to quell the rumors, putting out a press release and holding a media center briefing in which Vintner had explained that Chance would be suiting up just in case he was needed as a substitute, that this was a favor from him to a friend and the team, and a one-time circumstance, and that Chance remained committed to his ministry.

Still, the photographers and the reporters descended on Chance like hungry piranhas the moment he walked onto pit road. Photoflashes and microphones surrounded him, and twenty people asked questions all at the same time.

"All right," Chance said, holding up his hands. "All right. Let's take a moment and get this settled. As Perky told you, LD is pretty banged up from yesterday's crash. He's still aching, and I've suited up to relieve him if necessary."

A guy from Fox Sports crowded closer with his microphone, asking, "Will it be necessary?"

"With Lyle Danford?" Chance chuckled. "Who knows? The man's got a pain threshold about ten stories high. Personally, I think all I'm going to get, dressed up like this today, is a case of heat rash."

The reporters laughed and Chance laughed with them. A small part of him believed that what he'd said just might actually be true despite what LD had told him at the hospital.

"So, Boomer," someone else said, "the team announcement said this was a personal favor."

"That's right."

"But obviously, you're cleared to drive, and we understand that you drove a test in Kentucky last month. So are you coming back?"

Chance shook his head.

"I never left," he said. "I'm still here, but the priorities have changed. What I'm doing here is not like taking a color-commentator gig until the injuries heal. I was called into ministry. It's a vocation, not a vacation. God put me here. You don't up and quit on God."

Nobody said a thing, and Chance was glad for the media training he'd had as a driver. He knew he'd just given the TV people their "sound bite."

"Listen, guys," Chance said. "I need to do my regular chaplain duties and work the grid, and I'd appreciate some privacy while I do that, okay? Take whatever pictures you need now, but please . . . please . . . give me some space after that."

The photostrobes flashed again, and then Chance walked away from the center of the media scrum and began working his way down the starting grid, exchanging a few words with each driver. For the most part, the journalists honored his request, but when he got to Lyle Danford, and the veteran winced as he tried to lift his leg to get into the car, Chance looked pointedly at P. T. Sloane and the two of them lifted Danford up and slid him into the car.

That was just too good for the cameras to pass up, and a ring, three photographers deep, quickly formed around the car.

Chance helped where he could, assisting Danford with his restraining straps and harness, trying to keep the driver from aggravating his cracked ribs.

"Don't you go being a hero," Chance told Danford. "You understand me?"

"Don't you go far from that wall," Danford told him, grunting at the pain. "First chance I get, I'm pitting this sucker."

Danford got his chance earlier than anyone had expected. Six laps into the race, one of the front-runners cut down a tire and hit the wall, coming down and taking out three other cars in the lead pack, including the points leader. Danford, who had started at the rear of the field in his backup car, had not yet passed a soul.

"Okay," P. T. Sloane yelled, as Chance was not wearing a headset. "He'll come in when pit lane opens. We'll do no service on this stop, understand? Just the driver change. We don't want to fall a lap down. Now gear up."

Chance nodded, checking his restraining straps, working his earpieces into his ears, donning a set of heel protectors, and finally putting on his helmet and cinching it tight. He put his driving gloves under the left epaulet on his uniform—the first time in two decades of racing that he had actually used the epaulet for anything. Then he got atop the pit wall and waited. He wondered about getting into the car with the helmet on; he'd never done that before.

As it turned out, he needn't have worried. Hurt or not, Danford hit his tape marks in the pit box with pinpoint accuracy. Two tire carriers pulled down the window net, unstrapped Danford, and literally carried him back over the wall. As for Chance, the gas-can man simply picked him up and put him into the car with the ease of a baker sliding a loaf of bread into the oven. Then it was a flurry of connections, straps, and buckles as they secured him into the car.

"Test, test, test," Sloane's voice came over the radio.

"Got you," Chance said tersely.

"Okay. Checklist. Let's not miss anything. HANS straps . . ."

Chance's head got jerked back an inch or so.

"Check," PT said. "Harness—check. Steering wheel—give her a yank . . ."

"Check," Chance said, twisting and tugging the wheel to make sure it was seated on its hub.

"AC hose?"

"It's running," Chance said. "I can feel it."

"Gloves on?"

"Check."

"Okay. Window net's going up. Ugh—there. Buttoned up. Car's clear. Get on out of here!"

Tires smoking, Chance left the pit box, keeping the car in second at the prescribed point on the tach until he'd cleared pit road. Then he ran it out in third and caught fourth as he was exiting Turn Two.

"You're good," a familiar voice said in his ears. "Field's a hundred yards back."

"Pooch!" Chance yelled.

"Ouch. Yeah. Who else?"

"Who's spotting for Gage?"

"His brother—the kid who drives ARCA. We flew him in last night. No way would I miss this, Boomer."

"Well, good to have you, buddy," Chance radioed as he flew down the backstretch, closing the gap between himself and the back of the field.

"All right, do the reunion later," Sloane said on the radio, all business. "LD briefed us on the car. We're a touch loose, even for him, and that's *loose* loose. So here's what we do. Go by this time, and then pit on the next lap. We're running dead last right now, so as long as we don't get lapped, it don't hurt none to fix things. LD had to hit the binders pretty hard when the field checked up, so we're going to put fresh rubber on all around, pop the spring rubber out of the right rear, and fuel it. How's the windshield?"

"Perfect," Chance said.

"That's cool. We leave the tear-off on. Stay on this time by."

Chance closed in at the rear of the field, downshifted to third, and matched the pace of the car ahead of him. He circled the track one more time, and then dropped to the entry lane as Pooch called, "Pit, pit, pit" over his radio.

It was like riding a bicycle. It all came back. Chance rolled down the pit road at exactly 55 miles per hour, jinked into his box, and slid to a stop with the crew swarming over his car. The car went up on the right side, stayed there a moment, and then went down. It rose on the left side and he brought the RPMs up on the engine. As soon as the jack dropped, he popped the clutch and shot down pit road.

"Hurry," Pooch urged him as he entered the track at Turn Two. "NASCAR says the pace car's coming in this time by."

Chance got the car into fourth and floored it down the backstretch.

"That's it," Pooch said. "Stay low in your turn. Green, green, green. Green flag! Stay low and start working it."

Four completely fresh tires made Chance a veritable Superman for the next two laps. He held an insanely low line, almost running on the apron, and passed half the field in the space of five miles.

"Okay," Pooch said. "Clear high. Grab the groove. Let's cool off that rubber and save some, okay?"

Careful, consistent driving and world-class spotting helped Chance to miss the next spin, a rookie in a Dodge who littered body panels down the front stretch and brought out a second caution. This time, Chance stayed on, shuffling steadily to the front as the cars ahead of him pitted. Finally, he crossed the flag stand right behind the pace car and got his five points for leading.

"We're hooked up," he told the crew chief. "I'm a little tight, but that's fuel load. We're light and the spoiler is catching some air. As soon as we fill and pull the spoiler down, we'll be perfect."

"Copy that," Sloane said. "We show you good for fifteen laps. Let's roll the dice and stay out."

It worked. Twelve laps later, there was another yellow for debris on the track—an unusually high number of yellows for Michigan, where races had been known to run caution-free, but Chance was not arguing. He pitted with the rest of the field, took right-side rubber and fuel only, and got back on in fourth place—an incredibly fast stop.

"Okeydoke," Sloane said. "Here's the deal. Field's lost four cars. The 24 is just back on the track now. That makes him thirty-ninth, and from the sounds of it, I'm sayin' he dropped a valve. So he's just turning laps.

You're number four. If you can stay where you are, we get the points lead, no prob, when this thing's all over and done with. We got a hundred laps gone, sixty left. We'll need one more stop to make it, and so does everybody else. Just don't you bend it, boy, y' hear?"

"Yes, Dad," Chance ribbed the crew chief.

It was only then, as they were just turning laps, running down the counter, that it finally sunk in to Chance that he was back in a Cup car, in a race, very near the front, with 200,000 fans on their feet and several million—including his folks back in Chillicothe—watching on TV. But there were no tears this time. Just awe at the fact that he was there at all.

"Thank you, Lord," he breathed, as the car tore into a turn on the high groove, the one that was kindest to the tire rubber.

And in the end, it was the pit calls that made the difference.

"Boomer," P. T. Sloane said. "Try one lap in the low groove."

"Go," Pooch chimed in. "You're clear."

So Chance ran one full lap down close to the apron, then Pooch called him clear and he went back up to his high line.

"How'd that feel?" Sloane asked him.

"Good," Chance said. "We've still got great side-bite."

"And you're two-hundredths faster down there," Sloane said. "So here's what we gonna do. Pit window's coming up. Gage is down two laps, so Hoss is pittin' him first and givin' him four tires. When he's back out, you two try to hook up—stay low and draft on him all you can. I figure we got us eight laps of fuel, and we're gonna run seven and then see if a yellow comes out. If it don't, we pit and get right-side rubber and one can of fuel."

"That's stretching the left-side tires quite a bit, isn't it?" Chance asked.

"That's why they call it a sport, Sport."

So Chance caught Gage on the backstretch and the two of them drafted for six laps, their two cars repeated on the JumboTrons facing the grandstands as they ran down the miles. Then, on the sixth time around, yellow lights began flashing all around the track.

"Floorboard her," Sloane ordered. "Race back to the line."

"Clear!" Pooch called.

"Where's the wreck?" Chance asked as he dove for the bottom of Turn Two.

"Ain't no wreck," Pooch drawled. "The 24 blowed up. About three hundred yards behind you. He's oilin' the track. Just run high as you exit Four, and you'll stay out of it."

Chance caught the lead car, a red Monte Carlo, as they entered Turn Three, and he had four car lengths on him as they came out of Four. Tail jinking as he fought to keep the car on a straight line, he kept the hammer down all the way to the line and then lifted.

"Change of plan," Sloane radioed. "We're gonna do four tires and one can of fuel."

"But," Chance objected, "if the rest of the leaders just take two, that'll put me down to—"

"Eighth," Sloane said. "Sixth, if we're quicker than snot. But there's sixteen laps left in this thing, Boomer. I figure ten, maybe twelve of them green. Good driver can work his way up on four fresh tires. You feelin' like a good driver today?"

Chance thought it over. "Give me four."

Pit lane opened, and Chance used rear brake bias to slide into his pit box, bringing the car to rest with the nose canted out. Everything seemed to slow, and he looked at his mirror, watching for pit lane traffic behind him. There was nothing near as the left-side jack came down, so he nailed it, missing the rear tire carrier in the next box by a mere fraction of an inch.

"Twenty-nine in two," Pooch reminded him, keeping him from speeding on pit lane. The red Monte Carlo jumped out of its box as Chance neared the end of the lane and the two cars roared side-by-side across the exit line.

"Hang on," Pooch called. "NASCAR's checking the camera. Okay. You got him by a whisker. Pull in ahead of the eight. You're in fourth place, driver! Outstanding!"

The pace car looked tantalizingly close. Three cars were ahead of Chance in the field. He got on his radio.

"How many tires did these guys take?"

"Just two," Pooch replied. "All three. You the man."

"Now you lay back on that restart, Boomer," PT reminded him. "Open up some space and get you some running room."

So he did and, when the track went green, he had third place by the time they'd finished the front stretch. There were still two cars ahead of him, but it had become, as P. T. Sloane would put it, "a fishing derby"—all he had to do was reel them in. Chance ran low, lower than his competitors could run with two worn tires, and he'd caught them both within four laps. After that, it was showtime—he ran the main groove without lifting at any of the corners. By the time he'd taken the white flag, he was half a lap ahead of the field.

The fans were on their feet, and the grandstands looked like a wind-tossed sea: people jumping up and down. Hands, hats, and programs waved. On the JumboTrons, a twenty-foot-tall image of his car floated, the track whizzing by under it. He scanned his gauges, looking for a high coolant temperature, a low oil pressure, a fuel pressure drop—anything that could set the boot to this.

It didn't matter, he realized. He was coming out of the fourth turn. He could blow up at this point, and he'd still coast past the flag stand half a mile ahead of everybody else.

But he didn't blow up. He roared across the finish line at 9,200 RPM, as fast as the limiter chip would let him, and the waving, cheering grandstand absolutely erupted.

"Yeah," PT said simply over the radio. "That'll work."

Chance slowed and dropped low while every single driver left on the track rolled by him, giving him high sign after high sign.

Finally, when he was the only car left out there, he considered doing doughnuts in the infield, then decided against it. This wasn't his racecar, and he remembered the story about Rusty Wallace, who, after winning a sprint race in St. Louis, had totaled a car during the post-race celebration. No need to add to the shop's workload. So he contented himself with dropping the window net, pulling low on the track, and then turning around and running a lap clockwise, waving out the window to the standing, cheering fans.

Every single crew member of every single team was lined up to slap him five as he rolled down pit road toward the winner's circle. And that was the part that choked him up—seeing that rainbow of uniformed humanity, lined up to wish him well. When he got into the winner's circle, he just sat for a moment after he'd pulled the helmet off, willing his heart rate back to normal. And that's when Lyle Danford leaned in through the window, cracked ribs and all, and gave him a big hug around the neck.

"Robert's got a man to drive your motorhome back to Charlotte," he said. "You and Cindy and the baby are flyin' home with me. We've got us about two hundred people back in Charlotte that want to say howdy tomorrow morning."

CHAPTER 46

Outside Mooresville, North Carolina

Chance had suspected it. But the inevitable was confirmed as he was driving the Mustang up State Route 136, toward the shop; the cell phone rang and it was Perky.

"I'm glad I caught you," she said. True to her nickname, she actually sounded glad. "I just wanted to remind you that you're due at the studio in Charlotte at eleven-thirty."

"For what?"

"For what? Did you forget already? *Nextel Notebook,* on the Horsepower Channel. They tape at noon, and they always have the race winner as their first guest."

Chance drove in silence for a moment.

"No, thanks," he said. "Get me off, okay?"

"Get you off?" Now Perky did not sound glad. "Chance, I can't get you off. *Nextel Notebook* has a NASCAR license. They automatically get the winner. That's a condition of competition. When our team wins, we have to provide our driver for interview."

"Then provide him," Chance told her.

"Huh?"

"Your driver, Lyle Danford," Chance said. "He's the winner of record for yesterday's race. He started the race, his car won, so he gets the points and the win. That was the whole object yesterday. All I get is a footnote. And that's the way I want it, Viv. Put Lyle on. Or if he's too banged up, put Robert on. They've interviewed owners before when the driver's injured. Just have whoever it is explain that I'm busy with my ministry."

"With your ministry? You mean you still . . ."

Perky caught herself and stopped talking.

"Still what?" Chance asked her, bristling, and disappointed with himself for it.

"Nothing," she said. "All right. I'll tell them it's going to be Lyle. But if you change your mind, you let me know. Okay?"

"Okay, but I won't change my mind. I'm sure of that."

They exchanged good-byes and Chance returned the phone to its holder. He drummed his fingers on the wheel and, just for a moment, debated turning the car around and heading back to Lake Concord.

But he didn't. He couldn't. It would disappoint a lot of people if he didn't show up at the shop and let the guys congratulate him. They needed that.

And much as he didn't want to admit it, he needed it, too.

Chance had been wondering what it would be like to walk back into RVR's dyno building for the Monday morning meeting. What the reaction would be when he walked into the room.

As it happened, he never got the chance to find out.

Everyone in the shop, right down to the receptionist, the guy who ran the kitchen, and the lady who ran the gift shop, was standing there, cheering, in the parking lot when he pulled in. Then, as Chance parked the Mustang and got out, he realized that it was more than everyone in the shop.

LD was there, of course, at the front of the pack on his crutch and walking cast. And Gage was there as well. So was Duane, which alarmed Chance at first until he remembered that school had been out for a couple of weeks. Max Peters was even there, though Chance knew Mondays were usually a clinic day for him. And two sponsors had flown in for the morning.

More than two hundred voices were congratulating him at once. More than four hundred hands were applauding him. It was, Chance decided, what Roman generals must have experienced on their returns to the imperial city . . . albeit on a somewhat smaller scale.

There were claps on his back, hugs around his neck, and his hand went on autopilot, shaking with all and sundry, nonstop. The most amazing part for Chance was that he knew—and everyone else there knew—that, strictly speaking, he didn't even need to be there for the Monday morning meeting. He'd been a substitute driver—no RVR contract and no ongoing RVR obligation. The purpose of these meetings was to sharpen every team member's skills for the next race, only for him, there would be no next race. The only reason for showing up was this—to get congratulated.

Yet it had been reason enough for him to attend, and reason enough for all these people to wait in a parking lot on a chilly spring morning. Chance felt himself choking up because the hands on his neck, the arms around his neck, were not just the hands and arms of former coworkers. They were the loving embraces of family.

The celebration continued into the dyno building, where the pit crew made a ceremony out of presenting LD and Chance with matted and framed sixteen-by-twenty color glossies of the two of them being lifted out of and into the racecar.

There was no escaping the place without saying a few words. So Chance motioned for quiet, and then he said, "Thank you. You can't know how much this means to me. Or maybe you can, which is why you did it."

He stopped for a moment, gathering his thoughts. Then he grinned and continued, "And I take this to mean that you all will be there for the chapel service in Sonoma on Sunday."

That got a round of laughter and quite a few assurances. Then the teams got down to business, sitting down to review stop tapes. After that they split up, with Gage and Hoss and the 53 crew heading off to their shop, and PT, LD, and their crew walking to theirs at a slower pace, checking their cadence to match that of Danford on his crutch.

The sponsors tagged along with their respective teams. And that left Chance and Robert Vintner all alone in the big common room.

"Well, Boomer," Vintner said, "offhand, I'd say these people seem to care for you."

Chance nodded.

"Offhand," he said, "I'd say I know I care for them."

Vintner nodded.

"C'mon into my office," he told Chance, putting a hand on his shoulder. "I'll buy you a cup of coffee."

They stopped at the kitchen and Vintner poured two ceramic mugs of coffee from the big pegboard full of personalized cups. To Chance's surprise, the mug he received was not the generic RVR cup with the organization's logo on the side. It was his cup: the one he'd never taken home and apparently the one that RVR had never thrown out. In script letters on the side it read, "Boomer."

They went into Vintner's office, where Robert ignored his desk and nodded at a pair of leather wingback chairs near the window. Chance sat down and found a coaster for his mug on a table between the chairs. He looked at the magazines on the table; every one had a picture of an RVR driver on the cover. There were several featuring Danford and a few featuring Gage. And not a few, to his surprise, had his own face smiling back.

"You keep old magazines," Chance told Vintner.

"You wait," Vintner said. "Next month, when the new issues come out? I'll bet the shop that your face is on every single one of them."

Chance laughed.

"All I did is win one race," he said.

"You made news," Vintner said. "News gets the spotlight."

The two men sipped their coffee in silence.

"Well," Vintner said, "you know what I'm going to ask."

Chance lowered his cup. "And you know what I'm going to say."

"So," Vintner sipped his coffee again and grinned, "we gonna dance, or we gonna talk?"

"Robert," Chance said, leaning forward, clasping his hands together. "You've already got two good drivers and two good teams."

"And I'd planned all along to add a third," Vintner pointed out. "I was going to do it year after next, but LD's championship sweetened the pot quite a bit. We've got budget to add a third car right now."

Chance scowled.

"What good would that do? It's June. A guy couldn't start now and be anywhere near in contention for the championship."

"True enough," Vintner agreed. "But we could run a limited schedule—tracks where we know you're gonna be spectacular—and really drum up some serious sponsorship money for next season."

Chance took a deep breath.

"Robert," he said. "The question is not whether I want to drive. Of course I do. The question is whether I'm going to quit on God. And I can't understand how a body would ever do that. I mean, Jesus Christ took the nails, the cross, the tomb—all for me. And I'm supposed to do what? Walk away from my ministry because it sounds like more of a kick to go racing?"

"Now, Boomer." Vintner leaned toward him. "You went into that ministry because you couldn't race. Not because you didn't want to."

"But I'm in ministry now," Chance told him. He paused. "If you can't understand why I can't leave, then I can't explain it to you."

Vintner stroked his moustache, nodding. "Well," the team owner said, straightening up, "I guess I may as well 'fess up. I'm not doing nothing for Sonoma—other than trying to convince LD to hop out after a few laps again and let me put some hot SCCA shoe in his car. But for the next weekend, for Daytona, I've got Hoss and PT each putting together an extra car."

"Why would you want to add to their workload like that?"

"Because it was their idea," Vintner said. "They each do a car. That gives us a primary car and a backup for a third team. And settle down, now. If we don't use those cars in Daytona two weeks from now, then they're superspeedway cars, so they'll be ready and waiting for Talladega, come October. Hoss says he'll get the car ready for qualifying, and he and PT will work together to get it ready to race. Come Sunday, I'll hold the Busch Series crew over to service the car."

Chance shook his head.

"Sounds pretty convoluted."

"It's convoluted so you have time to think," Vintner told him. "If you're ready to sign a contract this morning, I'll have you your own hauler and crew chief within seventy-two hours."

Chance shook his head again, not looking his old boss in the eye.

"I'm not asking for a 'yes' this morning," Vintner told him. "All I ask is that you don't say 'no,' either. Think it over. I can sell the secondary sponsorships on contingency—if you race, they pay, and if you don't, I'm out nothing but paint. As for the hood, I don't care. Leave it blank, put a picture of Nate on it. Whatever you want."

"Robert," Chance said, standing. "You're being very generous and very accommodating. It's tempting. I'll admit that. But I just can't—"

"Think about it," Vintner interrupted. "You've got time. I've already got you on the entry list for the race."

Chance looked at him, brow furrowed.

"I put you on," Vintner confessed, "the day the patch came off your eye."

Chance swallowed.

"I'd better run," he told his old boss. "Thanks for the coffee, RV."

"Pot's always on."

Chance started for home. But then, as he neared the turnoff for Lake Concord, he drove past it and turned east on State Route 49. He stayed on it until Asheboro, and then he caught U.S. 64, following that until Pittsboro, where he turned north onto U.S. 15. And then finally, after a quick call for directions and more than two hours of nonstop driving, he pulled into the parking lot of Foothills Community Church, in Chapel Hill.

Chance walked into the handsome stone building, stopping for a moment in the lobby until he saw the brass plaque with the arrow that said "Church Offices." Following that, he got to an anteroom, but the secretary he'd talked with on the phone was not at her desk—lunchtime, he decided. So he walked to the doorway, where he saw a familiar profile bent over a well-worn copy of *Matthew Henry's Commentary on the Bible*. Smiling, Chance knocked on the doorjamb.

"Stealing sermons, Preacher?"

Brett Winslow jumped about half an inch. Then he saw who was in his doorway and his face split into a grin.

"Chance!"

Brett leaped up and nearly lifted Chance off his feet in a bear hug.

"Man!" Brett said. "I saw you yesterday on TV!"

"Don't you have anything better to do on a Sunday afternoon?"

"Nothing at all. You were awesome, man. So . . . you going back?"

Chance just lifted his head a bit, and Brett pursed his lips.

"I see," Brett said. "You're wrestling with that, aren't you?"

"I am," Chance agreed. "And . . . well, I've got to admit it. I'm surprised to hear you ask about it in that fashion."

Brett nodded, silent. Then he grinned again and said, "Hey, our house is right across the parking lot. You've got to come say hi to Danielle and Kyle."

"Sure," Chance said, following Brett out. "And how is Kyle?"

"He's doing really well," Brett said, nodding. "We did one complete course of chemo with him, and that shrank the tumor quite a bit, but his doctors thought they could do more. So they rested him for a couple of months, and then they did another course, which he just finished last week, and that seems to have gotten the tumor down to the size they want. We'll rest him for another month, now, and then they'll start him on radiation back at Duke."

"Hang on," Chance said as they crossed the parking lot. He opened the trunk of the Mustang and got out an RVR pit cap.

"Kyle'll appreciate that," Brett said with a smile. "He flat out refuses to consider a wig, but he's not too crazy about the cue ball look, either."

The small brick house was pastor-modest and neat as a pin. Music—"Point of Grace," by the sound of it—issued softly from the kitchen radio, and chicken soup simmered in a pot on the stove.

"Honey?" a familiar voice called. "Time for lunch already?"

"Yes," Chance called back. "And who are you calling 'honey'?"

"Boomer!"

Danielle Winslow practically knocked him over with her hug.

"We were so proud! Did Brett tell you? Half the church stayed after the service to watch the race on the projector TV in the auditorium. We all told everybody that this was the guy who took Brett's old job."

Brett grinned.

"The board of deacons decided that they're probably paying me too much, seeing as they took me away from a situation like that," he said. "I didn't have the heart to tell them that driving is not part of the job description!"

"No joke," Chance agreed. "Where's Kyle?"

"He's lying down on the couch, taking a nap," Danielle told him. "The chemo leaves him pretty wiped out the week after he gets it. He usually falls out about halfway through the day. Let me get him."

"No!" Chance said. "Let him sleep."

"And miss the opportunity to see his hero? Are you kidding?"

Chance had steeled himself for the fact that the Winslows' son would be bald. He'd done ride-alongs with cancer patients for Make A Wish. But little Kyle, just a week out of treatment, was beyond bald. He was absolutely hairless—no eyebrows, shiny arms, thin blue veins showing through the white skin over his skull. It was almost like meeting an alien facsimile of a human being.

That went away when he saw Chance, though.

"Boomer!" The little boy ran across the kitchen, sick or not, and hugged Chance's leg.

"Hey, partner." Chance peeled Kyle off long enough to set the pit cap on his head.

"Cool!" Kyle turned to the oven and squatted down, looking at his reflection in the glass of the door.

He turned and grinned at Chance, who shook his head and said, "You've grown, boy. How old are you now? Twelve? Fifteen?"

"Six," Kyle told him, giggling. Then his mother ushered him back to his nap, leaving Chance and Brett alone in the kitchen.

"Can you stay for lunch?" Brett asked.

"I shouldn't," Chance said. "I didn't even tell Cindy I was running over here. I should get back and give her some breathing room; Nate's getting pretty mobile. To tell you the truth, I'm not even sure why I came here—not that it's not great to see you."

"Well, Chance," Brett said, "it's great to see you and, despite the fact that I about jumped out of my skin at the church, I half expected you."

"You did?"

"Sure. I was the one who got you into this, and if you're considering getting out, it's only natural that you touch base with me."

Chance pushed his hair back, shaking his head.

"God's truth, Brett," he finally said. "When I had this done . . ."

He pointed to his eye.

"The main thing on my mind was that, if I got it, maybe I wouldn't get as much of a headache when I studied my Hebrew. But now I've gone and opened a can of worms. And wouldn't you know it? Hebrew still gives me a headache."

"Heck," Brett said, "I could have told you that."

Both men laughed.

"Boomer," Brett said quietly, "do you think I would have suggested that you go into this ministry if I hadn't been convinced—100 percent convinced—from what I'd heard from your doctors that you would never, ever be able to go out on that track again? Because that was the picture we got in Sonoma."

Chance nodded.

"Getting your eyesight back completely changes things," Brett told him. "I heard what you said to the reporters on TV about not quitting on God, and it gave me a shiver. Heck, you could hear the 'amens' in our church all the way over to Raleigh. But that was before you went out and blew everybody else away. Chance, you're not only as good as you ever were. You're better. That puts a very different bloom on the rose, man. No way would I tell you that you are married to this."

"So what should I do?" Chance barely whispered the question.

"You're a pastor," Brett said. "One of your flock, a married man, comes to you with a great big, honking life-change question like this. He can see advantages—and disadvantages—to each side. What do you tell him?"

"Pray," Chance said. "Pray and talk with your wife."

"Bingo," Brett told him. "Here. Let me put some of this soup in a cup for you to sip along the way."

Cindy Reynolds sat next to the window in her sewing room, the stiff gray fabric covers still draped over her sewing machine and serger, her quilting rack folded and stored against the wall.

She'd chosen this room for her hobby because she got focused when she sewed and rarely glanced outside. And since this room looked out over the driveway and didn't have the lake view enjoyed by so much of the house, it made sense to use it for her sewing.

But right now she needed the view of the driveway.

She checked the little Phillippe Charriol wristwatch that Chance had gotten her for their anniversary two years earlier. Chance had left the house at seven, and now it was half past three. Eight hours. More than eight hours. She turned the volume up a notch on the baby monitor, and then she moved the blinds and checked the driveway again.

This was something she'd never learned earlier in their marriage—how to miss her husband and count the minutes until he returned. For five years of marriage, she'd gotten used to the fact that she'd only have him to herself one, or at most, two days a week during race season. But now that little Nate was big enough to travel, she'd gotten accustomed to having Chance with them all day on Mondays, either here at home or traveling with him on the road, and three or four more days every week as well. This sudden return to racing had reintroduced her to something she'd forgotten entirely—the solitude.

She checked the monitor again, then she went into the nursery to make sure little Nate was okay and was still sleeping on his back, which he was. Then she heard the distant whir of the garage door opening. She got to the sewing room just in time see the red tail of the Mustang disappearing into the garage.

Grabbing the baby monitor, Cindy trotted down the stairs and almost ran down the hall into the kitchen. She paused there, setting the monitor on the counter and brushing some hair back from her eyes, not wanting at first to look as if she'd just run down from upstairs, and then not caring, and swiftly crossing the kitchen so she was there to wrap her arms around Chance as he came through the door.

"Hey," he said, hugging her back. "Hi, there. You miss me?"

Cheek against his chest, Cindy nodded. His shirt smelled like outside and him, two scents that she loved. She held him more tightly for a moment, and then lifted her face for one kiss, then two.

"Your phone's been ringing off the hook in your study all day," she finally murmured, rubbing her cheek against his chest again. She felt the good, familiar feel of Chance rubbing the small of her back.

"Have you looked at the Caller ID?"

"Uh-huh," she told him. "*Charlotte Observer, Circle Track, Nextel Cup Scene, Sports Illustrated, New Man,* Perky—about twenty times all by herself."

"She got me on the cell. Anybody else?"

"Yeah," she said, nodding against his shirt. "Six different Cup teams. And that's not counting RVR."

The rubbing on her back stopped.

"No kidding," Cindy said, looking up at Chance's face. "I thought I was the only one who got to court you."

She felt the brush of his lips on the crown of her blonde head.

"You are," he murmured through her hair. "So court me."

She glanced up.

"Court you?"

Chance nodded, kissing her forehead lightly.

"Tell me what's on your mind," he told her.

"As in?"

He rubbed her back again.

"Tell me how you would feel," Chance asked her, "if, a year from now, you were still the wife of a preacher?"

Cindy thought about how alone she'd felt all afternoon.

"Happy." She kissed the front of his shirt.

"And how about if you were the wife of a driver?"

She was still for a moment. A flurry of images flashed through her mind: the Caymans house, the trips, the thought of little Nate going to nice schools. Then she thought of the important one: the smile on Chance's face as he'd climbed out of LD's car in Victory Lane.

"Happy," she finally said again. "Happy either way, so long as that preacher or that driver is you."

Now it was Chance who was quiet for a while.

"And which way," he asked, his voice barely a whisper, "would you be happiest?"

Cindy leaned back, looking deeply into Chance's hazel eyes.

"You know, Preacher-man," she told him, "I read some of your counseling textbooks when you were studying them."

He smiled.

"Did you?"

"I did." She nodded once. "And now, let's see how much you remember from what you read in them. . . . When a woman asks for advice, what is she generally looking for?"

"'Points of view that she may not have yet considered, or may have overlooked in her assessment of a situation,'" Chance quoted, looking up at the ceiling.

"Very good," Cindy said, kissing the front of his shirt. "And when a man asks for advice, what is he generally looking for?"

Chance laughed.

"Say it," Cindy told him, feigning sternness.

"'Validation of his own point of view,'" Chance finally answered.

"Ah-hah!" She tugged the back of his shirt. "Which is what?"

The rubbing on her back stopped again.

"That's just the thing," her husband told her, his voice gentle, small. "I don't know. It flips from A to B and back to A again."

"Then I think . . .," Cindy said, gently unwrapping his hands from her waist, lifting them to her lips and kissing them, "that it's time for us to pray."

CHAPTER 47

Napa County Airport—Napa, California

"Welcome aboard, gentlemen."

"Hey, Pete." Leaning on his crutch, his foot once again in a walking cast, Lyle Danford gave his senior pilot a pair of Dodge/Save Mart 350 pit caps. "For your grandsons."

"Thank you, sir. Did you sign them?"

"Yep. Under the bill. Top was too dark."

Danford turned and looked back at Chance Reynolds.

"You get anything for your boy?"

"This." Chance showed Danford the teddy bear. "Pit caps'll come later. Right now, if he can't eat it, chew on it, throw it, or cuddle it when he sleeps, Nathaniel's not interested. I figure this is good for three out of the four."

"There you go."

The pilot took their carry-on bags and Danford's crutch and stowed them. Then he turned back.

"Oh, Mr. Danford? Milly called from Charlotte to ask if you knew how many folks would be flying down with us to Daytona next week. So she can plan the catering."

"Lessee," Danford mused. "Dottie and me. That's two."

He turned to the back of the plane.

"Hey, Danny," he called. "You flying down with us next week?"

"No, Daddy," Danford's eldest responded. "I'm trailering the GT40 down. Remember?"

"Oh. Right."

Chance looked at Danford.

"You're taking the GT40 to Daytona?"

"To a shopping mall," Danford told him. "Danny, there, found out they've got this charity classic car show going over the weekend. They set the cars up in the mall, and folks vote for their favorites by dropping money into these lockboxes next to each car. Money's going to a children's hospital."

"Well, that's cool."

"It is," Danford agreed. "And I figure that if I run over there Saturday afternoon and drop a couple grand in the box next to our Ford, then we'll be a shoo-in for first prize."

Chance stared at him.

"Just kidding, man!" Danford laughed. "I'm just kidding."

Chance shook his head and opened a newspaper.

"Hey, Dad," Duane said, walking up from the rear of the plane, "okay if I go down with Danny? Help spell him on the driving?"

Danford scowled. Then he put an arm around Duane's shoulder.

"Listen," he said. "I know that you've changed. And I trust you; I truly do. And I know how you love your brother and like to be with him. But that court order is still active, you know? And if your momma and I were to go try to get it reversed now, not even a month after we got it . . . well, that would raise more questions than it would answer, wouldn't it? So I think you'd better fly down with your momma and me. I don't think Danny needs nobody to help him on a one-day drive down to Daytona. But if he does, we can always break someone loose from the crew."

Duane's face clouded for a moment. Then he squeezed his father's hand.

"Sure, Dad," he said. "If that's what you want, I'll go with you."

Duane returned to the back of the plane.

"Skillfully done," Chance told Danford.

"Every now and then I can keep this fatherhood thing on the road," Danford agreed. "What about you? Why don't you and Cindy and the baby fly down to Daytona with Dottie and Duane and me?"

"Thanks," Chance said. "We'd like to. But I've got to drive the motorhome down to Florida."

"What? Your RVR motorhome?"

"No. My SCM motorhome."

Danford scowled. Then he opened the door to the flight deck and said, "Looks like just three of us for next week, Pete. But tell Milly to plan for at least five, anyhow, okay? You never can tell."

Chance and Danford took a pair of recliners facing one another as the engines spooled up. The copilot came back and walked the plane, checking doors and making sure everything was stowed. The seat belt light came on, but he didn't announce anything.

"We're belted in, here, if the boys are, Bill," Danford told the man.

"Thank you, sir. We'll get right under way."

Danford waited until the flight-deck door had closed. Then he grimaced, leaning back in his seat.

"Ribs hurt?" Chance asked him.

Danford squeezed his eyes shut, blinked, and opened them again.

"Everything hurts," he said. "Can't believe I put up with all that to finish fifteenth."

Chance shook his head and set the newspaper aside.

"Robert had last year's SCCA champion sitting on the wall the whole race, waiting for you to let him jump in," he pointed out. "You're a stubborn man, Lyle."

Danford leaned his head back for a moment as the plane taxied out to the runway. The he sat up and looked at Chance.

"You're calling me stubborn?" He raised an eyebrow. "Ain't that the pot calling the kettle black?"

Chance groaned. "Oh, man," he told Danford, "don't go there."

Danford took a little brown prescription bottle out of his pocket, squinted at the label, and put it back. "We're friends, Boomer, ain't we?"

Chance nodded.

"Well, then. I gotta go there."

Chance closed his eyes and shook his head.

"You know," Danford continued, "you got PT and Hoss bustin' their backsides building racecars for you."

"I told Robert they didn't have to do that."

Danford laughed. "Have to? Course they don't have to. They're doin' it because they love you, man."

Chance felt his throat start to close up. He swallowed.

"I know that," he said, his voice barely audible above the jet engines as the plane tore down the runway. "But I . . . I've got to do what God tells me."

The airplane tilted and the rumble of the runway stopped as they broke free of the earth. Outside the windows, the lights of Napa tilted and grew smaller. Danford gazed out the window for a moment. Then he turned back to Chance.

"Fact number one," he said. "You have this thing go wrong and within nine months—I mean, not even a year later—it's fixed by a procedure that has never before existed in the history of medicine."

Chance nodded.

"Fact number two," Danford continued. "Most drivers, they spend time out of the car, and they lose something. But not you. Your first time back in the seat, you set the unofficial record at Kentucky. And your second time back, you win in a car you never even got to practice. Not only did you not lose something, Boomer. You got faster."

Chance listened, glancing away from Danford's piercing blue gaze.

"So if you want to talk about what God's tellin' you," Danford said, "it sound to me like God's telling you to strap in and drive, boy. It really does."

The airplane's engines dropped an octave, and a chime sounded as the seat belt sign winked out.

"I can see how you'd think that," Chance told him. "But I don't."

"Why not?"

Chance tapped the Bible on his knee.

"The last time Jesus entered Jerusalem, he was greeted as a king," Chance said. "The people knew he was the Messiah, but they didn't really understand what that meant. They thought he was going to do something earthly, and save them from Rome. It looked like everything was set up for him to do that. But Jesus wasn't operating by an earthly plan. His agenda was set in heaven. And the heavenly plan was for him to go to the cross and save them from sin."

Brow furrowed, Danford cleared his throat to speak, but Chance held his hand up to stop him.

"There's more," he said. "Before he went to Jerusalem, Jesus told his disciples what was up—that he was going there to be tortured, killed, and resurrected. And when he said that, Peter, his best friend . . ."

Chance took a deep breath. "His best friend basically said, 'No way does that happen to you.' But Jesus told him to let it be. He said . . ."

Chance turned his Bible, to the sixteenth chapter of Matthew.

"'For thou savorest not the things that be of God, but the things that be of men,'" he read.

He took another breath.

"Lyle, I loved being in that racecar up in Michigan. When I made my first pass, it was the first time I've felt fully alive since . . . well . . . I guess since a year ago this weekend. But in the throne room of heaven, Cup points don't mean a thing.

"I'm not saying that to belittle what anyone does, but that's just the way it is. And when the choice is between advancing a heavenly cause that I know I can advance, and pursuing something that just plain doesn't mean anything to God . . . well, that's savoring the things of men, and not the things of God."

Danford rubbed his chin.

"You've talked this over with Cindy?"

"Cindy's good either way."

"She tell you that?"

Chance nodded.

"Well, Boomer," Danford said with a sigh, "then you've got yourself a good woman. A great woman."

The pitch of the jet's engines increased a bit, and Chance felt the change in attitude in his seat back as they climbed.

"You go to see Brett last Monday?" Danford asked.

Chance nodded.

"You see his boy?"

"Yes." Chance nodded, glad for a change of subject. "Yes, I did."

"Poor kid. Didn't that just about break your heart?"

Chance nodded again.

"So tell me this, Boomer," Danford asked, eyes glinting, "did you give that boy anything?"

"Yeah," Chance looked up. "I did. I gave him a pit cap."

Danford smirked.

"A pit cap. That's nice."

"Why bring that up?" Chance asked, perturbed.

"Because," Danford said, "last week, before we left on this trip, I sent that boy and his family $50,000."

Chance couldn't stop his mouth. It just dropped open.

"Now don't you go sayin' nothin' to nobody," Danford warned him. "I gave that money to Sylvester Trapp and told him to just tell Brett that it come from the Cup community. I don't want no credit. I just wanted to help with whatever the insurance didn't cover, and maybe get the family a little vacation to boot. I wouldn't have told you, except to make the point."

"Which is?"

"That I could do it, Boomer. Not that I didn't have other uses for fifty grand, but man, I could do it and not worry about it, you know? I mean, for Pete's sake . . . In what you're doing right now, do you even clear fifty grand a year?"

Chance was speechless.

"Chance," Danford said after a moment, "I'm sorry. I don't want you to think I don't appreciate what you do as a preacher. What you did with Duane? My family owes you a lot. I owe you a lot."

Chance waved the sentiment away.

"No," Danford insisted. "I mean it. But you're what now . . . twenty-nine years old?"

"Yeah. Twenty-nine."

Danford shook his head, eyes heavenward.

"Pete's sake, Boomer. I got boots that are twenty-nine years old. You're young. If you're so all-fired convinced that God wants you to be a preacher, then be a preacher, but for cryin' out loud, get some serious money set aside first. You could race the rest of this season, then race ten seasons more, get yourself a championship—or two, or three—do the right endorsements and licensing deals, and when you turn forty, then you could call it quits and do your preaching. You'd still be ten years younger than Jack Nobles was when he got SCM goin'—and you and yours would be set for life. Now you tell me that don't make sense."

Chance sat quietly, rubbing his chin.

"Well, all this talkin' has made my ribs hurt," Danford said. "I'm gonna take a Darvocet and grab some sleep. You think about what I said."

CHAPTER 48

Charlotte, North Carolina

Speedway Christian Ministries' headquarters didn't look like a headquarters. It didn't look like a church. It looked a lot like the Culligan Water Conditioning place that sat next door to it, and the Tarheel Short-Haul Shipping depot that sat across the street: a brick, one-story office block tacked onto the front of a squat, rectangular, corrugated-metal building.

That was how Jack Nobles wanted it. "A ministry that's on the road," he was fond of telling visitors, "doesn't have a lot of need for window-dressing. This ain't the Crystal Cathedral."

And it wasn't. It had offices for Nobles, an assistant, a director of publications, a five-person chaplains' logistics staff, a temporary office for a comptroller who came in four times a month, and a cluttered cubicle for a part-time director of public affairs who put out the ministry's newsletter and kept the donations fires burning. The big building attached to the offices served as a repository for the Bibles, devotionals, pamphlets, tracts, and testimonial videos that SCM distributed free at every racetrack. And the fenced area behind that was where a chaplain like Chance could put his motorhome during the off-season.

It was asking a lot, thinking that there would be someone working in the building as Chance came driving up in his Mustang at seven in the morning. But the lights were burning in the offices, so he got out. The front door opened at his touch.

"Mary?" Chance called, but not too loud. There was no answer. Not that he expected any. Jack Nobles' assistant had three children, and even during the summer, that meant three mouths to feed, three faces to scrub, and three heads to comb before she came into the office. Chance walked through the small anteroom and looked through the open door of Nobles' office. SCM's founder was there, hair impeccably combed, in his habitual white shirt and tie. His suit coat was on a coat tree within arm's length, and a newspaper lay open on his desk. Chance knocked on the doorjamb.

"Chance Reynolds!" Nobles boomed cordially. "Come on in, boy."

"Sorry to stop by so early," Chance told him.

"Not at all," Nobles said, pulling on his suit coat and shaking Chance's hand. "I've been up for hours. When you get to be my age, you don't need near as much sleep. I think it's the Lord's plan: he gives old coots more time to get where they're going."

Chance smiled.

"Well, son," Nobles said as the two of them sat in a pair of leather guest chairs, "SCM owes you a big note of thanks."

"How's that?"

"I'll tell you how that is. Our biggest time for donations is normally the week after the banquet in New York. Teams get home, they do their budgets, and they send us a check. We've learned to keep a treasurer on full time during that week."

Chance nodded.

"But two weeks ago? The Monday after you drove and won in Michigan? After that profile they did of you on Fox Sports, folks about melted down the lines to our 800 service, calling in with donations. Our website provider said that we got so many credit card donations that they had to add another server, whatever that is. And the P.O. box was stuffed for a week. You know, we've finished the year in the black every December since this ministry was founded, but this year . . . well, let's just say it's gonna be a deeper shade of black. You want coffee, son?"

"I'm good," Chance said. "Cindy fixed me a traveler before I left the house."

"How is Cindy?"

"She's great. She's back to the same size she was before she got pregnant, so she's happy about that. And I think she's really enjoying being a mom."

"That's good." Nobles' white head nodded. "And I imagine she's very happy that your eye surgery worked and you're able to do all the things you were able to do before."

"Uhm . . . yes, sir. She is."

"Which is," Nobles said, smiling warmly, "I imagine, why you're here."

Chance shifted in his chair. He'd wanted to ease into this.

"Yes, sir. You're right."

"Well," Nobles said, giving the coffee cup on his desk a quarter turn. "I guess this is the part where I'm supposed to talk you out of the pursuit of filthy lucre. But it sure seems like God reordered a whole bunch of things to get you back into that racecar."

Chance laughed, despite himself.

"I'm sorry," he told Nobles. "It's just that Lyle Danford told me exactly the same thing."

"Lyle Danford ..." Nobles rubbed his chin. "Lyle Danford's a good man."

"Yes, sir," Chance agreed. "He sure is."

Nobles looked at Chance for a moment, nodding.

"So," the older man asked, "have you made a decision yet?"

Chance shook his head.

"And I'll bet it's tearing you up pretty good," Nobles said.

Chance nodded slowly.

"Well, God bless you," Nobles said gently.

He tapped the desk for a moment and then asked, "Want some advice?"

"Yes," Chance told him sincerely.

Nobles touched his Bible.

"Second Corinthians 9:7," he said. "What's that say?"

Chance closed his eyes.

"'Every man according as he purposeth in his heart, so let him give,'" Chance quoted from memory, "'not grudgingly, or of necessity: for God loveth a cheerful giver.'"

Nobles nodded, smiling.

"Nicely done," he said. "And from the King James, no less."

He leaned back in his chair.

"You know," Nobles said, "it's customary for pastors to employ that verse while beating the tithe out of the congregation. But I think it's also applicable to all the things we give to God. And that includes our lives—our service to heaven."

Chance nodded slowly.

"Chance, God loves you and is pleased beyond tears at the honor that you do him," Nobles assured his young protégé. "I am sure that he is touched at the manner in which this decision is tearing you, because if it didn't have that cost, then it wouldn't have worth, would it? But

Chance, God tells us in his Word, in that verse, how he wants us to give. Cheerfully. Confidently. Not plagued for the rest of our days by 'would have . . .' 'should have . . .' 'could have . . . .'"

Chance nodded again.

"Jesus promises us an easy yoke, Chance," Nobles told him. "And if yours isn't, then you're right to be concerned. I'm not saying every day should be milk and honey. But a ministry plagued by doubt cannot be effective. God has used you greatly in this ministry, but he has also used you greatly in that driver's seat. And how he wants to use you now is between your spirit and his. Want to pray on this?"

"Yes," Chance told him. "I would, very much."

The two men bowed their heads and softly, in the voice of a man speaking to an old and familiar friend, Nobles began to pray.

After they'd finished, Chance felt a calm settling over him.

"Well," he said, "I thank you for your time, Dr. Nobles."

"I thank you for your tender heart," Nobles replied. "And if it would be of any help to you, I should let you know that I always go to the Daytona races, seeing as I can use that time to meet with NASCAR. So if I'm needed . . . for a message, for care-center duty, for an ear, for whatever . . . I'll be there."

"I appreciate that," Chance told him.

Chance walked back through the anteroom and out into the SCM lobby, where he paused. A literature rack was there, full of pamphlets and brochures. Chance selected a couple that showed the SCM logo really well. Then he went out to his car.

"Boomer," Robert Vintner said as Chance knocked at his office doorjamb forty minutes later. "Boy, you look glum. Don't tell me you're here to say 'no' to me."

"I'm not," Chance told him. "Not today at least. Tell me something, Robert. You know the Bible story of Gideon and the fleece?"

"It's ringing a bell," Vintner told him. "But an old one. My Sunday school days were quite a while ago."

"It's in the sixth chapter of the book of Judges," Chance told him. "Gideon is considering going into battle against the Midianites. God's already told him that he will prevail, but Gideon wants a sign. So he sets a fleece on the ground and says, 'All right, in the morning, if the ground is dry but this fleece is wet with dew, I'll know that you're going to see to it that we win.' And in the morning, that fleece is so wet that Gideon has to wring the water out of it. But he's still not convinced, so he asks for another sign, the other way around—that the ground will be wet, but the fleece will be dry. And the next morning, that fleece is just dry as a bone. That assures Gideon that he's in God's will."

"Okay," Vintner said tentatively.

"That's my roundabout way of telling you to get the car ready for this weekend," Chance explained. "But it's also my way of telling you that, like Gideon, I'm looking for a sign. A way to make sure I'm doing what God wants."

"Like what?" Vintner asked him. "Like if you qualify well, then you'll know that God's in the deal?"

"Maybe," Chance told him. "Or maybe it will be something else. I won't know it until I see it."

Vintner scratched his head.

"What the heck," the team owner finally chuckled. "If I'm looking for sure things, I'm in the wrong line of work. You're on, Chance Reynolds. We'll have your car in Daytona, prepped, tuned, and ready for the first practice."

"Good deal," Chance said. "And Robert . . . on the hood? Could you put this?"

He took out the brochures and showed the team owner the SCM logo and the script that read "Speedway Christian Ministries."

"And maybe put SCM's website address on the back of the car," Chance added. "Can you do that?"

Vintner took the brochures.

"I'll give this to the graphics people and they'll have it digitized and applied by morning," Vintner told him. "Uniform, too. We may have to have Sparco FedEx it down to Florida so you can have something to wear for practice, but we'll get it there."

"Thanks, Robert," Chance told him.

"No, Boomer," Vintner corrected him. "Thank you. Welcome back, son. Welcome back."

CHAPTER 49

Daytona International Speedway—Daytona Beach, Florida

The car was absolutely beautiful—robin's-egg blue with red accents and yellow numbers, the SCM logo applied with contrasting orange lines around it so it would show up crystal-clear on television. It looked brand-new, but then again, all Nextel Cup cars looked brand-new as they were unloaded from the truck. Teams took it as a point of honor that, even though their cars might leave a track a mangled mess of scrap metal, they would arrive white-glove clean, with nothing worn, scuffed, or faded, not a scratch on the paint or a wrinkle in the decals.

But when Chance checked the chassis number on the setup checklist, it wasn't one he recognized, meaning that either it was a brand-new car built just for this event or it was one that had only been run in the current season. And since neither LD nor Gage had wrecked a superspeedway car this year, it would be straight and true and good as new, even if the only things fresh on it were the Taurus body panels with the new paint scheme and the V-8 under the hood.

Practice had proven that, with Chance posting top-ten times. He could have posted top-fives, except the car had been running just a bit tight. Both Hoss and PT—who were partnering on the crew chief duties until RVR's Busch team chief became available—had agreed that, as the weather was a little cool for practice, with warmer temperatures predicted for the qualifying session, they would do best to leave the suspension setup alone.

Then Robert, who had gone to the qualifying draw for Chance's team, had pulled the thirty-sixth qualifying slot out of forty-seven teams attempting to make the grid for Sunday's race. And that had turned out to be great news, as the session had begun with the skies sunny and the track temperature warm. But as the session had gone on, clouds had come in, and the track temperature had steadily dropped, even as car after car laid its own film of rubber on the racing groove.

As Chance stood in his new firesuit next to the racecar and helped the crewmen roll it down the line, he noticed that even mediocre drivers were posting lap times within a tenth of a second of those of the early leaders, and the better drivers were improving on them by only a few thousandths.

Finally, as the thirty-first qualifier rolled onto the track, Chance finished up a pit lane interview with NBC's roving reporter, put on his HANS straps and heel cups, and got into the car.

Just like in the old days, Andy Hofert leaned in and helped him get strapped in. But as they got to their radio check, it was Lyle Danford who answered from the spotter's stand with a cheery, "Hey, Boomer, you ready to bust one?"

"Jeesh," Chance deadpanned. "What are they doing? Letting anybody up in spotter's country these days?"

"I had to buy the little gal standing security a hot dog, and Pooch is standing by, just in case I tell you to do anything suicidal," Danford said. "But basically, the answer to your question is 'yes.'"

"Good. Then if I post a DNQ, it's partly your fault."

"Oh, shoot," Danford told him, "make it all my fault. I got three years left on my contract—I can afford it."

"We're third back," Andy warned everyone.

Chance reached to the center of the dash to make sure that the master electrical switch was on. He gave his shoulder straps each a tug and rocked himself more tightly into the seat, then he twisted and pulled on the steering wheel, testing the latch.

"What's the track temp?" Chance asked.

Andy aimed a pistol-gripped gauge at the ground.

"One-oh-five," he said. "That's down fifteen degrees since they opened for qualifying."

"Speeds still going up?" Chance asked.

"Oh, yeah," LD told him over his earpieces. "The better teams seem to be dropping about a hundredth per slot."

The car was rolled forward again, and everything was quiet for a minute. Then Andy called, "Okay. We're on deck. Stand by."

A seeming eternity passed. Then Andy called, "Fire her up."

Chance closed the ignition, lifted the starter toggle, and both felt and heard the car shake itself awake. He tried one ignition box and then the other, noting with satisfaction that the RPMs did not drop on either one. A flick of another switch brought a stream of cool air into his helmet.

"Buttoning her up."

He helped with the net as Andy closed and taped the top releases. Then he dropped his visor. A second later, he felt the double-thump on the roof as Andy called, "Clear!" Five seconds after that, he was sweeping along the entry lane, in fourth gear already with the RPMs rising.

"Looking good," Chance called as he ran down the backstretch at full throttle. "Feels good, too."

"Okay, then," LD answered. "Just follow that racing line, smooth as a baby's bottom."

Chance roared under the flag stand and the clock started running. He kept his foot on the throttle and followed the groove, alert for any twitch, any bump, any nascent wheel hop that would tell him he was trying to overcontrol the racecar. But he didn't feel any.

"Okay," LD called as Chance exited the fourth turn. "Make your apex later on One by about thirty, forty feet. See if we can't use the hill to pick us up a bit."

"Will do," Chance said, and this time the centrifugal force held his helmet against the bolster as if it had been bolted there.

"Same thing in Three," LD said.

"All right," Chance answered on the backstretch. Then he added, "How far down are we?"

"We ain't," LD told him. "We're tied. This is for the pole."

Chance took the next two turns expertly and waited until he was well past the flag stand before he hit the kill switch. On the tall marker tower past the end of pit lane, he saw his car number wink on in the number one spot.

"Yowza! That feels good. Thanks, LD . . . LD?"

"He's gone," Pooch replied. "Just hightailed it down the steps. He's got to get back to his car. He's qualifying in the forty-sixth slot."

"Ken, we're here with Chance Reynolds, who seems bent on spelling comeback with a capital 'C' this season, with a win two weeks ago in Michigan, subbing for the injured Lyle Danford, and now a pole today, at least for the moment, on his first qualifying attempt of the season.

And Chance, what is with this car here? Your car sponsor is your current employer—is that the case?"

"I'd better set the record straight on that one, Marty," Chance said, laughing, looking straight at the TV camera. "Don't worry, folks. Your SCM donations are not being used to send me racing! Actually, Robert Vintner and I didn't want to ask a primary sponsor to commit to this car until we have a regular deal going forward. So we had the space on the hood open, and I asked Robert if he would be kind enough to put the SCM logo on there, and he did."

"SCM being, of course, Speedway Christian Ministries, with which Chance Reynolds has been serving as Nextel Cup chaplain since his unfortunate accident more than one year ago," the commentator added. "But Chance, you mentioned a regular deal going forward. Two weeks ago, you said you had no plans to return to regular racing. Does this mean that we can be looking for you to hang up your collar and take up your helmet on a regular basis in the weeks ahead?"

"Uhm, actually, I don't own a collar," Chance said, obviously making an effort to grin. "And we haven't really signed anything yet. This is all on handshakes. But if the right prospects are there . . . I mean for my family, for me, for Robert Vintner and the other folks who have invested their time for me, and for my ministry and my work for Jesus Christ . . . then I feel I've got to keep the doors open."

The image changed to that of a red Dodge roaring around the track on its qualifying attempt, and Sylvester Trapp tapped the remote and shut off the television set.

"Well, that's it," he said, walking resolutely across the hospitality suite. "He's out the door."

"Yes," Jack Nobles agreed. "In fact, I called him on his cell phone as he finished that first lap, and left him a message that I'd be happy to take the chapel service tomorrow."

"At least he mentioned Jesus in his airtime," Trapp said, shrugging. "But I'd expected better of him."

"What?" Nobles asked. "You expected him to take a vow of poverty—not only for himself, but for his family—when he has an ability like this?" Nobles sighed and picked up the Bible on the table. "You know, the worst part is that most folks just assume that's the way God intended it," he told Trapp. "Yet if you read this book, it says that God had the rest of the tribes of Israel tithe their income to the tribe of Levi, to support them."

"And?"

"And," Nobles continued, "there were twelve tribes, Sylvester—eleven tribes tithing to support one. Do the math. Even if you figure that the Old Testament tithe was just 10 percent—and there's good evidence that it was more—that means all these other tribes survived on just 90 percent of their income. But eleven tenths is a lot more than just 90 percent. It's 110. In God's own plan, the people who served him directly had the best lifestyles in their nation—because they had the most disposable income."

Trapp said nothing.

"So," Nobles continued, "you tell me. Who's deserting who?"

It felt weird for Chance, coming into the drivers' meeting on Saturday afternoon. People were clapping him on the shoulder, offering congratulations, and he hadn't even kept the pole.

He hadn't figured that he would. With twelve cars qualifying after him, and the temperature still rising on the track, the luck of the draw had taken over. All other things being equal, the later you went, the faster you ran. It had been almost inevitable that someone would go faster, and in the end, five other cars, including Lyle Danford's, had. Yet Chance and LD had ended up in the same row on the starting grid—the third—and the television people were spinning that for all it was worth.

Nor did RVR have to worry about that footage not being shown. Mother Nature had virtually guaranteed it. Next to the sounds of conversation, the most prevalent sound in the meeting area, an open section of garage, was the sound of rain striking the asphalt outside.

"Okay, have a seat and let's get started," Jake Crockett said over the public-address system in the garage. "First things first. If you've been over to the Nextel Cup hauler and taken a look at the weather radar, you've probably seen that it's solid green all the way out to Ocala. So we're delaying the official start of the race until eight this evening, and if the weather is still an issue then, then we'll make a decision as to whether we have to postpone the race until one o'clock tomorrow."

Groans went up all around and Crockett said, "I know. I know. If we can make this happen today, we will. I was hoping to be home on Sunday, too. But I don't arrange the weather, boys, I just report it. If you don't like the way the sky looks, just take it up with the man in charge—chapel service is right after this meeting."

That got a brief round of laughter. Then Crockett ran briefly through the local venue standards—the pit road speed limit, the apron rules, how to find the marker where the leaders were to go to speed upon receiving a green flag. The whole thing took about twenty minutes, and then about half of the crowd left while the rest stayed on for the chapel service.

Chance made an effort to cross the sea of folding chairs to get over to where Lyle Danford and his two sons were sitting, but too many people wanted to shake his hand. He hadn't even gotten halfway across when Dr. Jack Nobles was asking everyone to be seated, so he found a chair where he was.

"For those of you who don't know me," Nobles began, pointing to his own white hair, "this is not what a good qualifying run does to Chance Reynolds—I'm somebody else."

That got a rise out of the group, and Nobles used it, speaking conversationally, but steadily pulling the group into an examination of the gospel of Mark and the numerous references it contains to Jesus seeking solitude to reflect and recharge, and its obvious application in a modern life full of cell phones and email and text-paging. It was a good message that got a lot of nods, and when Chance looked over to see how the Danford clan was taking it, he was struck by the spectrum of reactions.

At the one extreme was Danny, Danford's eldest, who was obviously there solely to please his father. He was sitting up, and not making a show of not listening, but his eyes kept getting drawn to the side. That was where a couple of cute twenty-something women—probably the daughters of sponsors, since they had garage passes—were standing, hoping to recognize someone famous, a more difficult prospect than one might think, as all of the drivers were wearing street clothes.

In the middle was LD, who showed that he was listening by nodding in the right places, but displayed little emotion beyond that.

And at the other extreme was Duane, who was leaning forward and following Nobles' every word. In his hands was the New Testament and Psalms that Chance had given him back in Charlotte, and Chance was happy to see that the paperback looked decidedly tattered.

Unless they wanted a word with the speaker, drivers usually didn't stick around after the chapel service—lingering invited autograph requests from fans with garage passes. So Chance was on his feet and moving toward the Danfords just as soon as Nobles had completed his message.

"Hey, Boomer." LD grinned. "You order this weather?"

"Hey. Something's got to make all those oranges grow."

Both boys said hello, and then Chance handed Duane a box.

"What's this?"

"It's a Bible," Chance said. "The whole thing. What I gave you before was just the New Testament and Psalms, but that's just twenty-eight books. The whole Bible is actually sixty-six. This gives you all of the Old Testament, as well as the New. Have you hit any places in the Gospels where they're talking about the Scriptures being fulfilled?"

"Yeah," Duane said, recognition on his face.

"Well, this has those Scriptures in it."

"Outstanding."

Chance turned to Danny.

"I've only got the one with me, but I've got a couple more of those back at my motorhome. Would you like one?"

"Gee, thanks, sir," Danny said, looking in Chance's direction, but not really at him. "But I'm not really much of a reader."

"How about you, LD?" Chance asked. "Fix you up with a Bible?"

"You know," Danford nodded, "looking at something like that just might be the way to pass a rainy day. Yes, sir, Boomer. I'd appreciate that."

"Then I'll bring one by."

Chance did just that as soon as he got back to the motorhome that RVR had rented for him and Cindy for the race weekend. He took a gift-boxed Bible out of the modest supply that he had flown down with from North Carolina, tucked it under his jacket, and trotted through the late afternoon drizzle over to Danford's richly appointed Prevost. He was still fifty feet away when he heard a motorcycle starting up, and seconds later, a yellow Kawasaki Ninja went zipping by him, its headlamp on, its helmeted rider raising a gloved hand in greeting.

Chance ducked under the Prevost's awning and knocked on the door. It opened and a pair of steps came whirring out of the motorhome's underbelly.

"C'mon in, Boomer," LD said.

"Just for a minute," Chance said, stepping into the scent of polished leather and finished wood. "I just wanted to drop this off."

"Well, I appreciate that," Danford told him, opening the box. "Well, would you look at that. Leather cover and all. That is one handsome book, Chance. Thank you very much."

"You're welcome," Chance said. "Hey . . . was that Duane's motorcycle I saw pulling away when I came over here?"

Danford nodded.

"Danny had room in the trailer when he brought the GT40 down," he explained, "so he hauled it down for him."

"You're letting him take off and go riding?"

"I let him go to work," Danford said, looking up. "And the team is staying at a hotel not far from here. So I figure running back to his room is work."

Chance put his hands in his jeans pockets and looked out the window for a moment.

"Why's he running back there in this drizzle?"

"He said he needed to pick up his mechanic's gloves and some other gear he needed for the race, just in case we start today," Danford said.

Then, seeing the scowl on Chance's face, he asked, "What?"

"Well," Chance said, feeling his way gingerly, "gloves and gear like that are usually carried on the hauler, right? And even if they weren't, why wouldn't he have them with him already? I mean they didn't announce a delayed start until the drivers' meeting, just before chapel. That being the case, he should have brought everything with him when he came over this morning. He shouldn't have any need to go back."

"Oh, man," Danford said, recognition dawning on his weathered face. "Oh . . . man."

Duane walked into the Daytona Beach Crowne Royale, ignored the bank of elevators that would take him up to his room level and, glancing around, walked over to the pay phones in the alcove just beyond. Pulling out the worn piece of paper with the pager number on it, he dropped thirty-five cents in the pay phone, dialed the number, keyed in the number of the pay phone, followed by a pound sign, and waited for the confirmation beep before hanging up. Then he turned and watched the lobby.

Two minutes later, the pay phone rang and Duane picked it up.

"Yeah," he said simply. "It's me."

Hunched close to the phone, he listened to what the caller had to say, then said, "Yeah. I got it. . . . No, really. I do. . . . Okay, fine. You want me to repeat it? I'll repeat it. The drop's at eight-thirty tomorrow morning, in an old garage that sits back behind a Denny's at Dade and Everglade. There. Satisfied?"

He hung up.

"No," said the familiar voice behind him. "I ain't satisfied. Not by a long shot."

Duane's shoulders sank. He didn't even need to turn around.

"Dad," he said weakly. "It's not what you think."

Chance had been right. You could crowd a fair number of people into a motorhome like Lyle Danford's and still have plenty of room left over. Right now, besides himself, there were Danford, Danford's wife, both of his sons, and Max Peters, and there was still room enough in the sitting area for half again as many people.

"Dad," Duane pleaded. "It's like I told you. Nothing's going on."

"Stop it," Danford boomed. "Stop . . . lying. You've lied enough. Standing up in front of everybody I know, tellin' them how you've come to Jesus. I hope you're proud of yourself, boy. You sure pulled the wool over my eyes. Here I was, fat and stupid. If it hadn't been for Boomer, here, I'd still be that way."

"I'm not lying," Duane protested.

"Stop it!" Danford was yelling now. "Don't try to cover lies with more lies! I heard you with my own ears. Eight-thirty tomorrow, in the garage behind the Denny's at Dade and Everglade. What's going on there, Duane? Church social? I don't think so."

"Max," Chance asked the doctor, trying to calm the situation a bit, "what can you tell us about Duane right now? Is he using anything?"

"He doesn't appear to be," Max Peters said. "I'd need to take a blood sample to be sure. Would you mind if I did that?"

Rolling his eyes, Duane bared his arm and held it out as Max got a sample kit out of his medical bag.

"We won't have results on this until later in the week," Max said as dark, red blood filled a short, stubby vial.

"Don't matter," Danford said.

"You," he pointed at his younger son, "are not going back to the hotel tonight. You are staying in this motorhome. If you leave, it is with your mother or with me. If we race tomorrow, your mother is going to be sitting in your pit box, and if you leave it, she leaves with you. You gotta go to the john, you come back here and go to the john. You do not leave her sight. Am I clear?"

"Yes, sir," Duane said.

"Well, that's that," Danford said as Peters sealed and signed the sample and put it back in his bag. "I guess we've done what we can do now. But Duane, I've got to tell you. If that sample comes back and Max tells me there's anything in there but whole milk and Cheerios, I don't care if we're already back in Carolina. I will fly your backside down here and turn it over to the authorities, together with that test result and an affidavit from Max. I am plain done messing with you, boy. You understand?"

"Yes, sir," Duane said.

"Good," Danford told him. Then, turning to Chance he grumbled, "So much for the new man . . ."

CHAPTER 50

"Looks pretty dark," Cindy said as she peeked out the motorhome window at a second day of overcast skies and drizzle. "Do you think they'll get the race in today?"

"They'll do what they can," Chance said. "We only need eighty-one laps to make it official so, seeing as we were rained out yesterday, I imagine NASCAR will push to get something in whatever window we can find, even if it means running under the lights. If that doesn't work, they move it to Monday. After that, I guess they'll just have to do a new date at the end of the season. Everything here needs to be in Illinois by Thursday."

"Speaking of which," Cindy said as she got Nathaniel dressed, "your mom called. She and your dad said they can meet us for coffee at the Ford tent around eleven-thirty."

"Okay."

"And your father was wondering if the two of you could look at motorhomes tomorrow, so he can get one in shape for Chicago," she continued. "He's still beside himself that RVR had to rent one locally for this weekend. If we race today, can you go with him on Monday afternoon to look at something?"

"I'll . . . I'll see."

Cindy looked up from what she was doing.

"You're still not sure about this, are you?"

"I'm not," Chance admitted. "I've asked God for a sign, but I've not seen anything clearly yet."

"Just wait," Cindy assured him. "God will make himself clear in his own time."

And that's when the knock came.

"Lyle!" Chance said, opening the motorhome door. "Come on in! What's up?"

"Man," Danford said. "I feel stupid even asking you, Chance."

"Come on," Chance told him. "It's me, man. What do you need?"

"Well, the Perkins Tools PR guy has thrown together a breakfast at nine for his distributors—the ones what stuck around after we scrubbed the race last night. He wants Dottie and me to stop by, and I still owe him a couple of appearances on this year's contract. We really need to at least stop in and meet-and-greet, and it just won't work to drag my juvenile-delinquent kid along. And Danny's already took off—that show ended last night, so he had to go pack up the GT40 before the shopping mall opens this morning. Would you mind keeping an eye on Duane while Dottie and me run off?"

"Sure." Chance blew a kiss at Cindy, grabbed a jacket and cap, and he and Danford set off into the drizzle.

"This is one stinkin' shame," Danford said. "Me having to roust you out of your motorhome because my seventeen-year-old son needs a babysitter."

"Well, it's for the best," Chance told him. "It'll give Duane and me an opportunity to talk."

"Don't waste your breath," Danford said. "It sure didn't take, none, the last time."

They walked on through the drizzle, Chance saying nothing.

"Not that I'm blaming you," Danford added. "He's just a bad kid. That's all there is to it."

The two men skirted a puddle.

"I don't think so, Lyle."

"Sure be nice if you was right."

They got to Danford's motorhome, where Duane's motorcycle was parked under the awning.

"Stinkin' rice-burner," Danford grumbled as they passed the bike.

Dottie Danford was straightening things in the motorhome's sitting area as they came in.

"Where's Duane?" Danford asked.

"In the bedroom," his wife told him. "He went back there right after you left.

"He took his Bible," she added hopefully.

"Well hoo-ray," Danford grumbled disgustedly. Then, before he could say more, there was the sound of a motorcycle starting up outside.

"What the—?" Danford covered the distance to the bedroom door in three strides, yanked it open, and smacked the wall beside it.

Chance looked in as well. The screen had been taken off the bedroom window, and the curtains were blowing where the window had been popped out of its channel. Duane's Bible was lying open on the bed, and a verse had been underlined in Proverbs. Chance looked closer and saw that it was Proverbs 18:24.

"'Closer than a brother,'" he whispered to himself.

"'. . . a brother . . . ,'" he repeated.

Then the color drained from his face.

"Come on," he told Danford, his voice shaking as he headed for the door. "We've got to hurry."

Danford's Ford Motor Company loaner car for the weekend was a gunmetal gray Ford GT that the two men just barely squeezed into with the convertible top up. The older driver pawed at the dash as he broad-slid out the tunnel-road entrance onto Speedway Boulevard, past the startled, rain-slickered Florida state trooper directing traffic.

"Man!" Danford bellowed, slapping the dash. "No phone! You got your cell phone with you, Boomer?"

Chance felt at his belt. The slim plastic horseshoe of the phone's empty belt clip was all he found.

"No, I left it with Cindy."

"Wonderful," Danford grumbled as he passed taxicabs and shuttle buses at better than a hundred miles an hour. "I don't even know where Dade and Everglade is, do you?"

"I don't," Chance said. "But give me ten seconds and I will."

He punched up Microsoft Pocket Streets on his PDA, entered the name of the intersection in the search field, and touched "Find" with his stylus. A map with a tiny red circle appeared.

"Keep going the way we're going," he yelled to Danford over the sound of the engine. "We're going to take a left at the next light."

They tore down street after rain-slick street in that fashion for the next two minutes, Chance calling the directions and Danford power-sliding the little sports car into turns. Then Danford looked up at his rearview mirror and said, "Great!"

Chance turned around. No fewer than three police cars were bearing down on them, lights flashing and sirens wailing.

"What do you think?" Danford said. "No way can they keep up with me."

"No," Chance said. "Pull over. It's better. They've got radios. We can get help to them faster."

Nodding glumly, Danford got into the right-hand lane. But then, even though he was still doing better than 90 miles per hour, all three police cars went screaming right on past him.

"What the—?" Danford muttered. "Okay. Fine. Which way next, Boomer?"

"Straight ahead," Chance said, his voice weakening. "Just follow the . . . follow the cops. . . ."

They stopped half a block short of the Denny's. Police cars and emergency vehicles had blocked off the intersection, and uniformed police officers were turning back traffic. It took them five minutes to cover the last quarter-mile. As they got closer, they could get a glimpse of the concrete-block garage. Smoke was pouring from its windows and firemen were pulling hoses toward it. Just beyond the police barricade, a red Ford pickup truck was off to the side, hitched to a long, black, unmarked trailer.

"Good Lord," Danford said softly, "that's my truck and trailer."

He pulled to the side and the two men jumped out. But before they'd even reached the line, a uniformed cop was walking toward them, palms out, saying, "Sorry, gentlemen. Police officers only."

"I gotta get through," Danford told him. "My boys . . . my sons are in there."

A siren squawked behind them and they jumped aside as a white Econoline van passed through the barricade. On its back doors were the words: VOLUSIA COUNTY CORONER.

"Oh, no." Danford groaned.

"Please, Officer," Chance asked the cop. He showed him his chaplain's ID. "Is there anything you can do? He's worried about his kids."

The cop scowled.

"Stay here," he ordered. He stepped back and said something into the radio microphone on his shoulder strap. Two minutes later, a middle-aged man wearing a bulletproof vest and a pistol holster came jogging toward them through the barricade. When he slowed to a walk, Chance noticed that he walked with a limp.

"Mr. Danford?"

LD nodded.

"I'm Ernest Donlevey, with the Drug Enforcement Administration," the middle-aged man said, shaking LD's hand. "You can rest easy, Mr. Danford. Your son's not in there."

"He's not? But . . ."

"Not ten minutes ago, we saw Duane coming this way on his motorcycle," Donlevey said. "I recognized him right away. I tailed him back in Charlotte, sir. But he didn't go to the drop. He pulled next to this truck over here, waved at the driver, and finally pulled his motorcycle right in front of him and forced him to stop. The driver got out, Duane got off his motorcycle, and the two exchanged words. They even shoved each other. They talked some more, the driver got on the back of Duane's motorcycle, and the two of them took off. Whole thing couldn't have taken more than a minute."

Danford looked both perplexed and grateful.

"And then," Donlevey said, "as they were driving away, the people in the garage, there, must have seen them leaving. One of them came out with a hunting rifle and took aim at them, so our sniper took him out from across the street. Then we moved in."

"Sniper?" Chance repeated.

"Oh, yes, sir," the DEA man affirmed. "We've had this place staked out since six-thirty this morning."

The Ninja was parked outside Danford's motorhome when Chance and Lyle got back. As they walked to the door, they could hear Jack Nobles' familiar baritone voice, and it became clearer as Danford opened the door.

"Thank you, dear Lord, for hearing this repentant young man confess your Son as his Savior," Nobles prayed. "We know you change lives, Father, and we beg you to change his. Danny Danford's sins are cast, your book tells us, as far away as the east is from the west. We ask you now to remove him from their roots and to set his feet on a path that glorifies heaven."

And three other voices replied, "Amen."

Chance craned his neck to see past LD. Dottie Danford was standing at the kitchen counter, weeping. Jack Nobles, Duane, and Danny were kneeling together in the sitting area of the motorhome, an open Bible on the floor in front of them. Danny, Chance saw, was weeping even more vigorously than his mother.

Jack Nobles looked at the doorway.

"Well, get on in here," he told the two men, "and give me a hand, will you? I can't get up!"

CHAPTER 51

"It wasn't Duane's fault," Danny said, his voice thick with emotion. "It was mine. I was doing this stuff long before Duane ever thought about it. I just hid it better, that's all."

"But why?" Danford asked.

"Because I . . ."

Danny swallowed and shook his head.

"Because he didn't think he was ever going to be good at anything that meant something to you," Duane told his father. "So he wanted to start his own race team."

"And that's why you did it?" Danford asked Danny. "Racing?"

"At first." Danny nodded. "Later on it was just so . . . so I could really be successful at . . . something."

Danford looked back and forth at the two boys.

"But I heard you," he told Duane. "I heard you set things up."

Duane nodded.

"That deal got put in motion months ago," he said. "Back before all of this"—he nodded at the Bible in his hand—"happened. And even back then, we knew the cops were onto me. But it didn't look like they knew about Danny. So we set it up that Danny would trailer your GT40 down here. We needed someplace that we could hide the . . . the stuff . . . so we could take it back to Charlotte, and the trailer seemed like the perfect way to do it. Then I found Christ, and I tried to talk Danny out of it, but he wanted to go through on it."

Danny looked up and nodded his agreement.

"So I came up with a new plan," Duane continued. "I figured that I could go ahead and call the contacts down here and get the details, but I could just tell Danny the wrong location, send him off to wait around in New Smyrna or something. That way the guys with the dope and he would never hook up. Except you heard me, Dad, and then yesterday you blurted out where the drop was, right in front of Danny. So I didn't have a choice. I just had to go stop him."

"How'd you stop him?" Danford asked.

Danford's two sons exchanged a look, and Danny cracked a grin.

"At first he said he'd kick my backside," Danny said. "But what got to me was when he said that my father loved me, and I shouldn't screw that up. And what really did the deal was when he said that, actually, he was certain that I had two fathers who loved me."

The grin had vanished. Danny lowered his head again and Lyle Danford lifted his eldest son to his feet and wrapped his arms around him.

"Well, Boomer," Danford said as they stood under his motorhome awning, "you definitely seem to have unscrewed up my life."

"Wasn't me," Chance said.

"You was involved."

"Like a chicken's involved with bacon and eggs," Chance said, and the two men chuckled at the worn old joke.

"And I seem to be odd man out," Danford said.

"How's that?" Chance asked.

"It's this," Danford said. He stepped back into his motorhome and came back out with the Bible Chance had given him that morning. "My boys seem to have grasped the point of this book, but I haven't. . . . Do you reckon you can give me a hand with that, Preacher?"

Chance stepped out from under the awning and gazed upward.

"The sky's clearing up," he told his old friend. "Why don't we take a walk and talk about it?"

EPILOGUE

Even in the confines of Ford Motor Company's infield hospitality tent, the sound of the jet dryers being pulled around the track was unmistakable. Sunlight dappled the grandstands, and slices of blue sky showed between the clouds.

"Well, Son," Nate Reynolds said, "it looks like you're going to get your race in today after all."

Nate Reynold's weathered face was split by a smile. He looked satisfied, complacent. It almost made Chance want to bite his tongue. But he couldn't.

"Dad," Chance told him softly, "I'm not running."

"What?" Nate Reynolds turned his way, perplexed. "Not running today?"

"Not running," Chance said, "at all."

Chance's wife looked up from their sleeping baby, a smile growing on her face.

"You got it, didn't you?" Cindy asked him, the excitement obvious in her voice. She handed little Nate to her mother-in-law.

"You got your sign."

"Like a billboard falling on my head," Chance told her. "I'm sorry, sweetheart."

"Never be sorry for good news."

And the two of them kissed as Nate Reynolds whispered to his wife, "What's going on? He's not driving?"

Chance kissed his wife again, this time on the top of her head. Then he looked over at his father.

"Will you still be proud of me, Dad, even if I'm not driving?"

Nate swallowed.

"Son, I'd be proud if you was pumpin' gas, so long as it wasn't something you was forced into. But is this really what you want? You've thought it through?"

"I've not only thought it," Chance told his father, "I've heard it in my heart. And now, if the three . . . uhm . . . if the four of you will excuse me, I've got to go talk to Robert. If I let him know early enough, he can have that car parked somewhere where the TV guys can get a shot of that logo on the hood."

As Chance walked off, Nate Reynolds looked at his daughter-in-law—at the smile on her face and the tears in her eyes. He put his gnarled hand on her slender shoulder.

"How about you, Cindy?" Nate asked her. "Are you sure this is all right with you? A family don't get all that wealthy from preaching, you know."

Cindy looked at her baby in Marilyn Reynolds' arms, and then she looked at her Chance—strong, tall, walking confidently across the paddock, the jet dryers still screaming in the background.

"Yes, they do," she told Nate, never once taking her eyes off her husband. "Absolutely, they do."

AUTHOR'S NOTE

Richard Petty is one of the bravest men I know; he strapped into the passenger's side at a test track several years ago and let *me* drive. Then, after a few laps, we swapped places and he showed me how to do it right.

Two decades of knocking around the fringes of motorsport, writing features and profiles for magazines such as *Inside NASCAR*, have afforded me the rare opportunity to speak one-on-one with giants of the sport, "King Richard" included. The complete list would take another book, but I'd be remiss were I not to acknowledge magazine interviews and garage-area conversations enjoyed with Buddy Baker, Neil Bonnett, Ward Burton, Dale and Kerry Earnhardt and Dale Earnhardt Jr., Bill Elliott, Ray Evernham, A. J. Foyt, Jeff Gordon, NASCAR President Mike Helton, Dale Jarrett, Junior Johnson, Bobby Labonte, Dave Marcis, Roger Penske, Andy Petree, Kyle and Adam Petty, Ricky Rudd, Ken Schrader, Mike Skinner, Rusty Wallace, Darrell Waltrip, and Cale Yarborough.

Mark Martin spoke at length with me on what it feels like to crash a Cup car—one element of driving with which I have no desire to gain personal experience.

I have not yet had the privilege of speaking with Jamie McMurray, but need to cite him, nonetheless. In this book, I needed a phenomenal and almost unbelievable accomplishment for a rookie driver, so I had Gage Grissom win his second Cup race. After my manuscript was finished, Jamie actually accomplished that feat. I debated changing the book but did not on the basis that, whatever I tried, some young "hot shoe" would eventually go out and do it. So I leave the story as is, but note that the record is Jamie's and *Turn Four* is a work of fiction.

Technically oriented readers will observe that, for the purposes of this story, I have compressed the rule changes of several seasons into the space of two. I've also changed some procedures for the purpose of dramatic effect. Any other departures from reality are the result of my being a features writer and a novelist, rather than a technician. Flaws herein are the products of the author.

I thank Dave Lambert, Bob Hudson, Sue Brower, and all the other folks at Zondervan for the masterful cat-herding required to turn my writing into a readable and marketable book.

I thank my wife, Linda, and my daughter, Carly, for their tolerance of the prolonged absentmindedness I fall into when writing a novel.

And I thank Jesus Christ for not only rescuing me from a well-deserved fate but for giving me the great gift of this ministry.

Before I go, two special notes:

My spiritual, theological, and fraternal touchstone through this book was Dale Beaver, Nextel Cup chaplain with Motor Racing Outreach, the model for SCM in this book. Dale and his wife, Andree, shared with me the essence of a chaplain's life, all the while scrupulously preserving the confidentiality and privacy of their flock. Dale, Andree, and MRO are a powerful illustration of just how effective a "ministry of hanging out" can be, and literally thousands and thousands of racing participants and fans are now heaven-bound because of MRO's call to Christ. They deserve your support, and information on contributing to this worthy ministry can be found at http://www.go2mro.com.

Finally, much of this book centers around a father struggling to regain touch with his family. That's the stuff of good stories, but I cannot stress how often in NASCAR I have encountered the opposite: fathers who devote great energy to relating with and encouraging their children. Certainly, that's the case with Kyle Petty, and this book is dedicated to Adam Petty—Kyle and Pattie's son, and a faithful picture of Jesus in whom any parent would be bust-your-buttons proud.

Adam went home to heaven in May of 2000. He is remembered in perpetuity through the Victory Junction Gang Camp, an amazing facility for chronically ill children. It, too, is richly deserving of your support. Details for donations can be found at http://www.victoryjunction.org. And if you are unsure what amount to donate, let me be so bold as to suggest the amount of $45. Forty-five was the number of Adam's racecar.

Thanks for giving, thanks for praying, and thanks for reading.

Tom Morrisey

A GLOSSARY OF RACING TERMS

aero—Aerodynamics. Aero technology is used to make a racecar more "slippery," so it moves through the air more easily and to generate downforce to make the car "stick" to the track under speed.

aero push—Understeer (the front end drifts to the outside of a turn). Caused by a lack of downforce on the front of the car when airflow is blocked by a competitor.

apron—Pavement adjacent to, but not part of, the racing surface.

ARCA—Automobile Racing Club of America. ARCA's ReMax Series is used by many NASCAR organizations as a cost-effective "bush league" for training promising drivers.

behind the wall—The garage area. When a car is damaged too severely to fix on pit road, it is taken through an opening in the pit wall for further assessment and, if feasible, repairs.

black box—A NASCAR-mandated recording device carried by all Nextel Cup Series cars to measure the deceleration forces sustained during a crash.

black flag—An official order to return to the pits. This is usually done when a racecar is unsafe or in violation of the rules, although a team may request to have their own car black-flagged if a pit stop is necessary and radio communication with the driver is impossible.

brake bias—Proportional amount of braking force directed to the front and rear brakes. On a Nextel Cup car, this can be adjusted by the driver with a dash-mounted knob to help control how the car corners under braking.

bump-and-run—To overtake a competitor by bumping him from the rear and causing him to momentarily loosen—i.e., to lose a portion of his rear-wheel traction.

camber—The degree to which a wheel and tire are tilted from the perpendicular, relative to the track's surface. At many Nextel Cup events, it is common to use a significant amount of camber on the right front wheel so only a thin strip of rubber on the inside edge of the tire bears the weight of the car at rest. This allows the entire width of the car to grip while cornering, when centrifugal force presses the tire to the track.

catch can—Watering-can-like device slipped onto the fuel overflow tube and used to keep overflowing fuel from spilling onto the ground during refueling.

check up—To hit the brakes.

chrome horn—Front bumper (or valance). To "use the chrome horn" is to strike another car, even though, technically, NASCAR Nextel Cup racecars no longer have bumpers, chrome or otherwise.

cool cap—Water-cooled skull cap worn under a helmet. An alternative is to blow chilled air through a special outlet built into the helmet.

cool suit—Undergarment through which chilled water is circulated to alleviate some of the heat that builds up in a racecar. Some NASCAR over-the-wall crew members also wear cool suits to help control the heat that builds up while wearing firesuits and other safety gear. Crew members disconnect themselves from the coolant source for the brief period it takes to service a car during a pit stop.

cut down a tire—To lose tire pressure due to physical damage to the tire.

DNF—Scoring abbreviation for "Did Not Finish."

DNQ—Scoring abbreviation for "Did Not Qualify."

draft—To follow closely behind another competitor and receive assistance from the forward-moving air in its wake. Because the drag on the lead car is also reduced, drafting tends to make both cars—or all of the cars in a line—travel faster.

drop the hammer—Open the throttle completely.

Earnhardt bar—A vertical safety chassis member located behind the center of the windshield. Its purpose is to prevent another vehicle from intruding into the cockpit through the windshield in a collision.

endo—To flip a car end over end.

fab shop—Fabrication shop. That part of a race shop where the chassis is fabricated and repaired.

free—Same as "loose."

freight-trained—To be passed by a number of cars in succession.

front stretch—Technically, that section of track between the start-finish line and Turn One. Now commonly used to refer to the track section between Turn Four and Turn One.

fuel cart—The hand-drawn wagon used by a team to ferry eleven-gallon cans of gasoline between the fueling station and the pits.

fuel cell—Impact-resistant on-board fuel reservoir that replaces the gas tank in a Nextel Cup racecar.

gentlemen's agreement—An agreement between two competitors to cooperate with one another to their mutual benefit (i.e., "if you'll pass on the outside, I'll go with you"), generally arranged through the respective drivers' spotters.

golf cart—Vehicles used by race teams and other organizations to shuttle personnel around a racetrack. Actually a motorized utility cart with either a small flatbed or a bench seat where the clubs would be if the vehicle really were a golf cart. The small vehicles so resemble what is used to go from tee to green that they are referred to as "golf carts."

green—1. A track open for racing competition, signaled by a green flag from the starter's box; 2. Refers to a track on which insufficient rubber has been deposited by traffic to create optimum grip.

groove—The optimal racing line around a track. Some tracks will have more than one, depending on how a car is set up, in which case drivers will refer to the "upper groove," the "lower groove," etc.

HANS device—"Head And Neck Support device." A restraining system designed to keep a driver's neck from hyperextending during collisions.

Happy Hour—The final on-track practice session before race day.

heel cups—Heat-resistant shields worn over a driver's shoes to help shield the driver from exhaust-system heat rising through the floorboard.

hooked up—A car that is optimally suited to track conditions. A car that is handling perfectly is "hooked up."

Hutchens device—An alternative to the HANS device that utilizes straps connected to the vehicle's seat belts. Named for its inventor, Bobby Hutchens, an engineer with Richard Childress Racing.

infield care center—On-track emergency medical facility maintained at every NASCAR Nextel Cup venue.

kill switch—A steering-wheel-mounted switch that allows the driver to disable the ignition system, cutting power to the car.

loose—Oversteer. A condition in which the nose of the car tends to steer inside of the intended path of travel, and the rear end of the vehicle drifts to the outside.

marbles—Bits of tire rubber and abraded pavement that accumulate in the upper portion of a racetrack and rob a vehicle of its traction.

midget car—A popular form of open-wheel racecar, so called because it appears to be a smaller version of the old style Champ cars.

NASCAR—National Association for Stock Car Auto Racing.

NBGNS—NASCAR Busch Grand National Series. The NASCAR touring series that is just below Nextel Cup in prestige. Also known simply as "BGN," "Busch," or "Busch Series."

nerfed—Pushed out of the way.

NNCS—NASCAR Nextel Cup Series. The most prestigious stock car racing series. Also known as "Nextel Cup" or "Cup" racing.

Nomex—Brand name for a popular type of fire-resistant fabric.

on the bubble—In immediate peril of being knocked out of a qualifying position by others who have yet to make their qualifying attempts.

oversteer—The tendency of a car to turn inside the arc that the driver intends, usually because the rear end is tracking outside of the front end. Also known as "loose."

pace car—A high-performance street car that leads the field as it forms up for starts and restarts. Also used to keep the field at a safe speed during yellow-flag laps. In recent years, it has become NASCAR's practice in Nextel Cup to use two pace cars in the warm-up laps before the beginning of a race—one at the front of the field, and one halfway back in the pack. The two cars run a lap at the same speed as the pit road speed limit to help teams determine the tachometer reading for that speed, since Cup cars do not have speedometers.

panhard bar—Same as "track bar."

partner—A driver who cooperates with another (by drafting together or, in the case of cars pitted next to each other, pitting together) to help advance both cars. Partnerships can and often do cross team and manufacturer boundaries, but are subject to immediate dissolution if either partner is presented with an opportunity to make a significant gain in position.

pit box—That portion of pit lane assigned to a particular car for its service. All four tires of a car must be completely in its box during servicing or the competitor will be black-flagged and brought back into the pits for a fifteen-second "stop-and-go" penalty.

pit cart—Large carts that are a combination toolbox and scoring stand, positioned behind every Nextel Cup, Busch Series, or Craftsman Truck Series pit box. Also known as a "toolbox" or a "war wagon."

pits—Track-adjacent workstations used for refueling, tire changes, chassis adjustment, and other minor repairs during a race. Major repairs are done in the garage area.

provisional—A starting position granted to a car that failed to gain one during conventional qualifying. Provisionals are granted based on a combination of availability and owners' points.

push or pushing—See "tight."

qualifying—Time trials held prior to race day for most races. Lap times are used to determine each car's positions on the starting grid, with the cars with the lowest lap times starting at the head of the grid.

racing deal—an unfortunate but unavoidable situation that leads to an accident. Typically used thusly: "It wasn't anybody's fault; it was just one of those racing deals."

roof flaps—Hinged roof panels that open when a Nextel Cup car spins out. The panels disrupt the lifting effect of air moving across the roof of the car and help prevent the racecar from becoming airborne.

rookie stripes—Yellow bars painted on the rear of a car to indicate that the car is being piloted by a driver new to that series.

RPM—Revolutions per minute. Generally a measure of engine speed.

rub—To bump or strike another car, usually from the side.

SCCA—Sports Car Club of America. A racing organization that generally competes on street and road courses, as opposed to ovals.

scuffs—Tires that have been partially worn by being run on a car during practice laps or the earlier laps of a race.

shoe—A driver. A driver who is enjoying considerable current success is known as a "hot shoe."

side-bite—Traction during aggressive cornering.

Sparco—Brand name for a popular line of safety equipment.

spoiler—An adjustable airfoil mounted at the back of a racecar's rear deck. Steepening the angle of the spoiler increases rear-wheel downforce, but also tends to slow the car. Minimum spoiler angles, sizes, and thicknesses are mandated by NASCAR.

spotter—Crew member who advises a driver of track conditions that may not be observable from the driver's seat. In Nextel Cup, at least one spotter is now required by NASCAR for all races and practices. At most tracks, spotters watch races from an observation platform atop the grandstand, and at some tracks, multiple spotters are used to eliminate blind spots.

sprint car—Open-wheeled racecar designed for racing short distances.

stickers—New tires that have never been on a car, so called because they still have the manufacturer's shipping label applied to the running surface.

team orders—Instructions from a team owner or general manager to drive in an uncompetitive manner (blocking other competitors, or holding back) in order to allow a teammate to advance. While sometimes obeyed with great resulting controversy in other forms of motorsport (such as Formula One in years past), team orders have always been rare (and, when given, typically ignored) in NASCAR.

tear-off—In Nextel Cup, a removable plastic film that is applied in several layers on a racecar's windshield (in other series, a "tear-off" may refer to a similarly removable film applied to a racer's helmet visor). Should the windshield become fouled with tire rubber or oil, a pit crew member can quickly tear a layer off to provide a clean surface.

tight—Understeer. A condition in which the nose of the car tends to steer outside of the intended path of travel.

track bar—An adjustable anti-sway bar joining one side of the rear suspension to the other. Steering characteristics can be changed by raising or lowering the outer end of the track bar, and this is done with a jacking bolt accessed through a hole in the rear window. Also referred to as a "panhard bar."

trailing arms—Metal structural arms that run from the midline of the chassis to the axle housing ends and help locate and align the rear wheels. A broken trailing arm—which is sometimes the result of a lateral collision with the wall—will move the rear wheels out of position, causing the car to handle erratically. At the time of this writing, NASCAR rules mandate that all trailing arms used in NASCAR Nextel Cup be based on a design used on the General Motors 1962 Chevrolet pickup truck.

trailer—The towed portion of a transporter. NASCAR Nextel Cup trailers are fifty-three feet long and most are manufactured by a company called FeatherLite.

transporter—Custom eighteen-wheel tractor-trailer rig used to carry a racecar and all of the materials necessary to maintain it. Most transporters also have a lounge area used for conferences and an observation deck from which to observe racing and practice runs. Also known as a "truck," a "trailer," a "hauler," or a "rig."

understeer—The tendency of a car to turn outside the arc that the driver intends. Also known as "push," "pushing," or "tight."

valance—The air dam that extends down from the front or rear of a stock car.

wedge—The amount of tension placed on the individual coil springs at the rear axle of a stock car. Wedge is adjusted with an extended ratcheting wrench through holes in the rear window. By changing tension, a race team can change the way in which weight is distributed among the four wheels of the racecar.

yellow—Caution lap during which passing is not allowed, signaled by a yellow flag at the starter's box and flashing yellow lights around the track. Until mid-season in 2003, competitors were allowed to continue to pass until they had completed the lap (i.e., passed the flagman's stand) on which the yellow flag was thrown.